# RUN THIS WAY

# RUN THIS WAY

SURFSIDE BEACH SERIES
BOOK 2

## KELLY CAPRIOTTI BURTON

First Printing, 2022

This is a work of fiction. Names, characters, organizations, places, events, and incidents are either products of the author's imagination or are used fictitiously.

Published by Kelly Capriotti Burton
Cover photo and design by Kelly Capriotti Burton
Author photo by Alicia Ortman Photography

ISBN: 9781736117460

kellofastory.com
Surfside Beach, South Carolina

To *Mom* & *Dad*,
I KNOW EXACTLY HOW BLESSED
I AM TO HAVE YOU.

& TO *The Runners*,
FOR THE SAME REASON.

# Part 1

# ♡PROLOGUE
## *Julie*

"Daddy, I'm−"

"Don't say you're sorry, Julie. You're not. I love you, but I don't want to talk about it any more."

Her dad hung up. She let the phone drop to her side like it was a bag of bricks. The conversation wasn't a surprise. That fact didn't make it hurt any less.

But Chad had walked into the room. He was fresh from his shower, all damp hair and glowy complexion and generous smile.

"Who was on the phone?" he asked casually.

"Oh, well..." She might as well tell him. "My dad."

"Aw, how is he?" Chad had never met her dad, but he seemed, well, *fascinated* was too strong a word, maybe, but invested. He was *invested* in everything about Julie.

"*He* seems fine," she said, more curtly than she wanted to sound. Chad should not see how churned up she was at the moment. It was too much for her, and so it was too much to share. "He just wanted me to know that he and Jessie are getting married. Next month. Getting *married*."

"Aw, Julie…" He took a few steps closer to her. Her arms were crossed, though, and she didn't uncross them.

"It's not a surprise," she said, her voice still dripping with vitriol despite her efforts. "I mean, I didn't expect to hear it twelve months and eight days after Mama died. It's like he mapped out the exact, appropriate number of days to wait before breaking the news. Except, my sisters probably knew before me. I'm sure they're helping choose flowers and testing the catering."

"Are they having a big wedding?" he said, lightly as seemingly possible.

"Well, I didn't ask for a lot of details!" Yeah. She was definitely snapping. She tried to cover it with a scoff. "On the beach, of course. Such a cliché. She just renewed her vows with her husband there." None of that seemed to matter to Daddy or Jessie. They were just moving the hell on.

"I'm sorry, Julie."

Chad looked crestfallen. She felt bad. She really did. But she could not come down from where she was. She could not meet him in his empathy and hope for a happy family vibe with her dad and his… new wife. New. Wife. Mrs. Jessie, whom they had all known for years. Or "Aunt Jessie," as her twin sister Katy insisted on calling her.

She forced a smile. "I know you are. Thank you." She exhaled then. "I'm gonna go for a walk. I'm fine, okay?"

He took her hand and kissed it. Pure chivalry. He was too much for her, really. Sunny. Open. Warm. Hospitable.

Kinda like Jessie.

And with that, she put thoughts of her father and his future new bride from her head. Not bothering to re-tie her running shoes, she smiled wanly at Chad and rushed out the door.

And without thinking twice, she ran toward High Street, where she hoped, just maybe, Ian would be waiting for her.

# CHAPTER♡ONE

## *Julie*
### *Five Months Later*

AFTER WEEKS OF SILENT CONVERSATIONS ACROSS PA-
TIENT ROOMS AND THE COFFEE CORNER, after a few clandestine lunch getaways, after one incredible whole night with
him, Julie had expected more. She knew he couldn't exactly pull
her into his arms and comfort her. And typically, she was not in
need of reassurance. But this was...

*This is trauma*, her inner voice told her. It sounded like her
mother, whom she wished more than ever she could call right
now. She would be smooth and unrelenting as steel and still as
inviting and warm as a cup of tea on a rainy afternoon. *Stop waiting for someone to see it in you and get yourself some help.*

Julie shrugged. *You can't tell me what to do.* You *left!*

Even so, it would be easier if *someone* could tell her what to do.

"Julie, Dr. Bramer and I would like to speak to you at nine, please, in his office."

Julie looked up at her direct supervisor, Rhonda, and smiled wanly.

"Of course."

Her resignation letter was typed, signed, and in her bag. She couldn't just walk out; questions had to be answered. There would, of course, be an investigation. She'd already accepted that the only closure she was likely to receive was the professional kind; she already knew what she needed to do immediately after this meeting. She was relieved it was happening in twenty minutes and not in two weeks. Her entire being was twitching. It was time to move.

♡

"It's not that simple, Katy!"

The next morning, Julie was trying to keep her voice even, grateful they were regular-talking and not Facetime-talking. She was having a hard time maintaining her usual calm, and her twin sister was typically the first to see right through her (along with her dad, who was a former principal and had an eerie knack for seeing through pretty much anybody).

Katy was suggesting that she move *home*. Julie wasn't sure what "home" even meant. There were layers and layers of complication to the whole sordid mess, but in Katy's eyes, it was always just a straightforward matter of moving onto the next thing.

Julie recalled her first weeks of freshman year of high school, when she would walk the halls every morning before the bell with her best friends Shelly and Stacy. Of course, they had no idea where we were going, but they always had a vague idea whom they wanted to see. If they found themselves kind of lost, Shelly would call out, "Nonchalantly turn around!" And they would giggle at the irony as they rotated, ostentatiously Rockettes-style, and started walking the other way.

Julie had been using the phrase ever since, though she rarely really practiced it. Now it seemed she might now have a choice. At age twenty-nine, she was quitting the pursuit of her Master's degree in Midwifery and no longer wanted to use the nursing degree she actually held. *Something* had to turn.

But she couldn't just Rockette-around. She needed a pivot strategy. She needed to secure a job somewhere, preferably out of the field of Obstetrics, and she needed to figure out where she was going to live.

She was loathe to admit that Phoenix had never felt like home. But Surfside Beach, the little South Carolina town she'd grown up in, didn't seem like the default Katy was making it out to be. Katy didn't even live there; she lived an hour away in Wilmington. Their older sister Danielle and her husband did live there, with an ever-growing load of kids. And their widowed father lived there, now with his second wife. The ground was more than shaky, and it didn't help that his wife's son, David, had initially moved out to Arizona with Julie... like *with her*. That hadn't lasted two months, and Julie had somehow managed to avoid seeing him (dear Lord, he was now officially her *stepbrother*) in all the months since then.

"Then make it that simple," Katy was continuing. "Get over your weird thing with Daddy and Jessie. Their place is great, and they have plenty of room. Crash there until you find a place. I'm sure you'll have a job in no time..."

"I'm not *living with them*!" she hissed. "Don't be ridiculous."

"Fine. *I'm* being ridiculous. Then crash with Danielle. God knows she needs a nanny."

That almost sounded as uncomfortable as staying with Daddy. Julie loved her niece and nephew, and she was definitely excited about the new one coming, but babysitting...

"Not happening," she sighed. "Look, I just wanted to tell you what happened. So don't say anything, and really, don't try to fix it for me. I will figure something out."

"Oh, I know you will." Katy sighed right back at her. It was like they were reading cue cards. "Just... listen, Jules, I know you aren't used to being in limbo, but I promise you, it's not so bad. It's where you figure out what you're made of and what you really want."

"Okay. Thanks. Let me know when your next TED talk is. Now let me go. I need to get some stuff done before Chad gets home."

"Does he even know?"

"*Bye Katy!*"

Julie flung the phone onto the couch. It bounced off and landed on the plush, sage rug she had just bought the week before. She looked around the living room, decked out in tones of wood and green so precisely that it could double as a health spa lobby. It smelled like juniper and spearmint and was her favorite room in the world.

And she was leaving.

Chad did *not* know. And Julie didn't want to tell him, because she was certain he would not understand and would disagree with her decision, but she couldn't think of any reason to lie to him. She couldn't even think of a lie.

She had failed miserably - epically - in her choice to be a mid-wife.

She just needed to go home, wherever that was going to be.

# CHAPTER♡TWO

## *Paul*

"Julie is moving home."

Jessie looked up at Paul from whatever Jessie-project she'd been squinting at for the last hour. Neither of them was wildly successful at being retired. She was writing all the time, he was teaching one European history class at Coastal Carolina University, so far. Jessie stayed much busier though, and he rarely had any idea what she was working on, but it always involved words, pictures, and a modicum of obsession. She took a deep breath before she answered him, and he suppressed a smile, because though his daughter's predicament was both uncharacteristic and unfortunate, watching his sixty-year-old second wife try so hard to fight her sassy instincts and be supportive to Julie was, at the very simplest, amusing.

She snapped down the lid of her laptop, blinked a few times as if focusing, and leaned into the table, as though to demonstrate that she was, in fact, hanging on his every word.

"Okay." Pause. "Cool." Pause. Slow nods. "Um... how is *home* being defined these days?"

He went ahead and exhaled the laugh right out. He and Jessie had only been married three months, but they'd been in each other's heads for over sixteen years. That was nearly how long they'd developed curriculum together, all while they and their families became friends. A fraction of it had been the very surreal aftermath of a car accident that killed both of their spouses and found them picking up their pieces together.

Looking at her now, across the table, *their* kitchen table, a centerpiece in the whole new home and life and reality established in Paul's mid-sixties, he had to shake his head. Some days, it seemed too good to be true, and almost every day, he was baffled with the complication of it, and the lightness he felt in spite of that.

Julie was the only one of their combined large brood who wasn't on board. She was the only one who didn't come to the wedding, who hadn't even been back since moving away a few months after her mama died. And though admittedly, Paul was relieved any time some proverbial or literal noise was muted in his surroundings, Julie was the one of his three daughters that Paul considered, well, a confidant. And he missed her.

Jess, on the other hand, was *it*; the *only* one who saw all of him, mostly all of him, mostly all the time. That phenomenon was new, too. Typically, people saw exactly what Paul allowed them to see, and very few could get beyond that. Leah, his late wife, the mother of his three daughters, did sometimes. Jessie's original husband Randall (*Paul could never think of him as Jessie's first husband, as Jessie and Randall would have never divorced, and counting them off that way sounded like they were exes*) did on occasion, and so did their pastor and friend, Carter. Sometimes, some of the kids did, depending on the circumstance. It wasn't that Paul didn't want to let people in or that he didn't love them.

It was just easier this way.

Nothing about starting his life with Jessie was easy, but she was. She broke through his barriers so seamlessly that he didn't notice until she was absent-mindedly caressing his neck halfway through a movie and he was so relaxed into her touch that he felt high, as happy as he'd ever imagined, or fell asleep, as safe and secure as he'd ever been.

"I have no idea," he answered her, with complete honesty.

"Did she... offer any ideas?" Jessie's eyes flickered around the kitchen nervously. A pocket door next to the pantry led to a pow-der room, a small hallway, and finally, a tiny, private, livable suite. Katy, Julie's twin sister, spent the night there sometimes when she came down from Wilmington, and Jessie's youngest son Da-vid when he came from Knoxville. Mostly, it sat empty, a fun se-cret hideaway in their gem of an off-beach home.

"Not one," he said, pointedly. "I can't imagine she'd want to come here, not when I... we... haven't even seen her since..."

"You don't have to say 'we' for this one, love," Jessie answered, pushing her chair away with a swift burst of energy. He knew she was either going to wipe the clean counter down or make her sev-enteenth cup of coffee for the day. It was the latter.

The dance of "hers, mine, ours" and "Life with Leah," "Life with Randall," and the always-laughable "New Normal" still took precedence in their everyday banter. Jessie had come a long way, but she still worried a lot more about everyone else's feelings on their life together than he ever would.

"'We' own this house, Jess," he said, working on his tonal bal-ance so that he sounded more cohort and less Captain, which sometimes came naturally to him, especially when someone was being indecisive or meek. "I would never make a decision about who stays here without your agreeing."

She turned around with her mug in hand. (This one said, "I'm Alexander HamilDONE with you," and Paul both rolled his eyes and stifled a giggle every time she used it.) "Thank you. And I would never say one of our offspring couldn't stay here, unless he or she was holding a murder weapon or accompanied by a Kardashian."

"You would probably just have them toss the weapon in the neighbor's yard first," he answered, a nod to the west, where the dog-hating, grass-loving, HOA-president-wanting-to-be Katherine Perkins lived, waiting for one of their grandkids to accidentally look at one of her flowers.

"True. Ooh!" She turned to the half-full coffee pot. "Want some?"

He shook his head and watched her little creamer first, coffee second, sip third, sigh fourth routine. She returned to the table, but to a seat next to him rather than across. One hand firmly clasped around her prize, she reached for him with the other. He gratefully took it and squeezed it reassuringly.

"She's not coming to stay with us. It wasn't even an implied question." His brow furrowed as another thought crossed his mind. "Come to think of it, she didn't ask about any of the rentals either, which is good, since I didn't tell her I'm 90 percent clear of that headache. She is probably going to work something out with Danielle for a week or two and then figure it out from there."

"Hmm. That doesn't sound like her, not to have a detailed plan."

"I know." He liked that Jessie knew his daughters, though Julie had become quite unknowable in the last year. The call had been informative but polite, with an undertone of humility that was more than unnatural for her. "She played her cards very closely. I'm not sure what all is going on, but she's suddenly disgruntled with midwifery and Arizona and was adamant that we would talk more when she gets here."

"Okay." The cup was already empty. "And when is that?"

"She's driving, of course. Leaving tomorrow, so..." He paused. "I guess three days or so, depending what kind of time she makes."

Jessie smiled at him, not her full-on smile of excitement, giddiness, or play, but her attempt to be reassuring though she felt anything but. Holding onto her hand, he stood.

"Listen, I made it clear to her that we can talk, and we will help her how we can. There is nothing to worry about right now." That was laughable, too. He might as well tell his wife not to breathe or to skip making tacos on Tuesdays.

"I believe you," she said, and Paul remembered her telling him that her translation of that phrase was *I believe you believe that.*

"Then come on," he told her, nudging her to stand. "Second to last Friday treatment coming right up."

# CHAPTER♡THREE

## *Julie*

JULIE SPENT MOST OF NEW MEXICO LISTENING TO '90S COUNTRY AND TRYING TO IGNORE CHAD'S CALLS. She texted him during every stop and asked him just to quit, just to give her a little time.

She didn't text Ian until Oklahoma, when "How Do I Help You Say Goodbye" made her pull over to ugly cry. All she sent was, I already miss you so much, and all he answered was, Same. And all she thought of for the next seven hours before she stopped again was how much more she wished he would say and how much more she wanted to say.

After another thirteen hours of driving and negotiating with herself, listening to a manic mixture of songs, mentally composing messages to Ian that she would never send, and imagining all the scenarios that would likely never happen, she was in Wilmington, at her twin sister's little ground floor condo.

Often, Katy's very presence got on Julie's nerves. She didn't usually let it get the better of her, but stepping out of her some-what-battered Kia Soul and seeing her twin's wide-open smile and shiny red Mustang in her parking spot (how it grated their father that Katy bought her own after she stole and subsequently trashed his not so many years ago), Julie wanted to get right back in her much more subdued ride and take herself anywhere else.

"Sis! What up?!"

Before she could get her hair out from under her purse strap, Katy had enveloped her, arms around her neck, one leg around hers, swaying back and forth from the waist up.

Sigh. Katy was a lot. Sometimes Julie found it hard to believe they were related, much less twins. Julie was the tallest of the girls, standing five feet nine like Paul, with their mother Leah's sharp angles, straight posture, and long, lean, limbs. She'd let her light brown hair grow out in Arizona, so it went down her back, usually in an elaborate braid or a bubble ponytail or some other work-friendly style, pulled away from her face, which she was often told stayed in the *RBF* position.

Katy, on the other hand, was a sun-bleached blonde, her hair in beach-waves that reached her forever-tan, beach-loving shoulders. She had green eyes like their dad, but was slender like their mom, with apple cheeks all her own, her smile as generous as Julie's was reserved.

But Katy was safe. So Julie squeezed her back before detangling herself. Then she detangled her hair from her purse strap, gathered a few of her bags from the Kia's backseat, and, with her arms overloaded, kicked the door shut.

"You sure it's okay for me to stay here for a few days?" She already knew the answer.

"I'll share my bed!" Katy brushed by Julie, reached into the

Kia, grabbed a trunk from the passenger back seat, and kicked that door shut. She was halfway to the front door of the condo before Julie could take more than two steps. She didn't see Julie roll her eyes. There was no way they were going to share a bed. No way...

"What happened to your couch?" she asked, juggling her bags and following Katy inside.

"What? Oh. Well. I sold it last month. Had the chance to play a gig in Atlanta, but I was a little strapped on the extra cash to get there, and I never sat on it anyway, so... I mean, the recliner reclines. You just have to kick the hell out of it to get it back upright. Didn't you bring any of your fancy crap back with you? I figured you had a Pod being delivered or something."

Julie tried to keep the frown from crossing her face. She had, in fact, left a 2000-square-foot house full of furniture behind in Arizona. Nice furniture. Bamboo and linen and nothing that required a kick to function properly. She didn't want to negotiate with Chad, and she definitely didn't want to waste more time with a moving truck. So here she was, exhausted and sweaty from the drive, sans any furniture of her own, contemplating a restless night huddled in her sister's double bed like they were six years old again.

Katy read her face anyway and might as well have read her mind. "Did I mention Dad and Jessie have an entire guest suite? Like a separate apartment? I've thought about just living there, but it's too far, and I don't want to have to build my clientele up from scratch. Well, I mean, once Jessie feels good and starts cooking again, I could be swayed."

Julie braced herself. *They're married. They're* married. *You have to get used to this. Jessie is not your enemy. How many times a day will I have to hear her name? Why is she such a damn good cook and can we get our hands on her hummus without there having to be an actual conversation?*

She couldn't force a smile. Katy would see right through it, anyway. She just honed in on the one non-sensical thing her sister said. "What do you mean, when she 'feels good?'"

"Daddy didn't tell you?" Katy had flopped right on top of the trunk and was about to open Julie's very conspicuous Kate Spade hat box on the floor next to it. Julie reached over to smack her hand.

"Leave it alone! Tell me what?"

Katy looked at her like she'd grown another head. "Jessie has cancer."

Julie's bags fell out of her hands. Before she knew it, she was sitting on the floor, and the rest of the tears she'd been holding since Oklahoma were quietly, unceremoniously unleashed.

And there was Katy, sitting right next to her, awkwardly patting her back with a silent "There, there," and a silent, "What the hell?" Julie was thinking the latter, too. Of all triggers to break her, why that one? She didn't care about *Jessie.*

"I didn't think you liked her, Jules. You ready for wine?"

Julie sniffed and giggled. "It's 9:30 in the morning. I think. So practically sunrise time for me."

"Who cares? Come sit at the table. Tell me when you started caring about Jessie so much."

Katy bounded up from the floor while Julie dragged herself. It was possible the toll of the last week had settled into her muscles. She was stiff and slow and a little groggy, but also intensely craving a run back in her blessedly flat homeland. She'd have one glass of wine, a shower, a nap, a workout, and feel better.

"I *want* to dislike her," Julie muttered while Katy poured. "There's a difference."

"Okay. I get that. But I still didn't expect this reaction, or I might have put it a little more gently. Anyway, she's gonna be fine."

Julie rolled her eyes. People outside of health care used terms like "fine" so casually. Even the "easiest" kind of cancer was life-disturbing at best. And that was the other stab for Julie, contemplating how to make Katy see that without sounding like an insufferable know-it-all.

"He's already been through so much," she said, at last.

"So you're worried about Daddy?"

*Whyyyyyy did she have to make Julie explain every tiny nuance? Okay. Take a breath, Julie. Your sister is rescuing you this time. Patience. Start at the start.*

"What kind of cancer?" she asked.

As Katy explained, Julie began to feel calmer. Maybe Katy didn't understand all the potential complications, but it certainly sounded like Jessie had a form of the disease that was not only easily treatable but highly *curable*. Uterine cancer was also typically less traumatic for a woman past her child-bearing years, so there was that.

"Okay. Okay...so how is Daddy handling it?"

"Probably better than you are."

Julie rolled her eyes again. "Possibly. Katy, consider my... *initial* reaction...had less to do with Jessie and more to do with the state of my whole damn life."

"Yikes." Katy took a long swallow from her own glass and seemed to be ponder her sister's words, which was a true effort against her own instincts. "What the hell happened, Jules? Did

Chad play dirty? Because if it was just a break-up, then I know you would have fought to keep your luxury desert casa and not be out here with your designer hatbox in my flea market of a living room."

"Chad didn't do anything," Julie muttered. She looked straight into Katy's eyes and left no room for negotiation in her voice. "I'm not ready to talk about it yet. I'm fine. I just needed to leave there. Now how is Daddy? He didn't say anything at all about Jessie's..."

Julie didn't finish. Why should her father have said anything? She had barely shown his new marriage a modicum of regard and certainly no respect. She knew he loved her, but she also knew he wasn't going to enable behavior he found unwanting or juvenile. She had tried before leaving for Arizona, tried to convince him that moving on from their mother so soon was a mistake, that everyone was going to end up hurt, most of all, him. Well, if she was honest, she meant them, his daughters, and even more precisely, *herself*.

And it happened. Julie and David broke up. Daddy and Jessie broke up. He'd ended up alone and all but homeless, holed up in one of his rental properties recovering from surgery and having Katy take care of him, which, it went without saying, was the height of humiliation for him.

Instead of finishing her thought, she simply muttered, "I never wanted him to be lonely."

"Well, he's not," Katy said, her simple brevity welcome in the moment. "So let's talk about you. You don't have to tell me all your deep, dark secrets – yet – but I know you don't want to sleep on my recliner forever, so what are you going to do?"

Julie finished the last swallow of wine and looked at her sister, those blunt blonde ends grazing her tanned shoulders, the wide green eyes that were their dad's without the solemn mask, the expectant air about her, as if something huge or amazing was going to happen at any second, and she was *here for it.*

Julie found herself grateful that Katy's life force was filling the room on behalf of both of them. Because sometimes, that same air made Julie shrink into herself, wanting neither to participate or disappoint. She didn't feel energy crackling in her soul. She wasn't motivated to chase a crazy dream or cease the day in any way other than by being disciplined and, well, excellent. And now, even her ambition felt drained from her. She was not the twin who hijacked their father's car and drove across the country like a country song.

No. She had driven her own car and failed just as miserably.

# CHAPTER♡FOUR

## *Paul*

THE WIND ON OCEAN BOULEVARD WAS STIRRING UP A LITTLE BIT OF TRASH THAT MORNING. Paul sighed and scooped up a crushed Bang! can, a Bojangles bag, and a Snickers wrapper and shoved it all in the nearest dumpster, inwardly chastising the tourists for their variety of poor choices.

Wiping his hands on his shorts, he walked briskly for a few seconds and then broke into an easy run. The sun had long since risen; sleeping next to Jessie still made it hard for him to get up early. She was nocturnal for sure, and it hadn't taken him long to fall into her rhythm. Some mornings it was past eight when he woke, which still felt like the equivalent of playing hooky for a former principal. The peace they'd attained during waking hours was still hard-fought and tenuous a lot of the time. The peace with which they slept, usually touching, burrowed under covers with the ocean breeze typically whirling into the east facing window, was too pleasant a gift to sacrifice, even for pre-dawn, pre-ridiculously-high-heat-index exercise.

He had all day, after all. Running was a newfound love for him, one he picked up after his short-lived job as executive director for a local charity. It had turned out he just wasn't suited to sit behind a desk or to beg people for money (laughable, as being a private school principal had entailed a lot of both). He'd stayed on as a volunteer, actually spending time with some kids who needed "big brothers" (also laughable, as he was more like a great-uncle), and he and Jess happily worked at a few fundraisers. He just didn't want to be in charge of it anymore. Honestly, he didn't want to be in charge of anything anymore. One lecture a week to young adults who equated European history to what they watched on *Reign, Poldark, The Crown*, or bless their hearts, *Game of Thrones*, was absolutely enough.

After the third time he'd had to hop onto the sidewalk to avoid a car whose driver was not paying attention, he decided to turn and made his way up First Ave North, somewhat regrettably leaving the oceanside, but finding solace in the old trees that seemed to whisper bits of wisdom as well as provide occasional shade. It was only 8:06 now, but summer had crept right into the end of September, and he was already baking and drenched within his first mile. He wouldn't go very far today; he wanted to check in on Jess in case she was having a rough morning.

*Laughable.* Jessie often chastised him for being a terrible patient (he certainly was), but now he could see that she was the absolute *worst*. When it was the aftermath of her surgery, she did okay. Dealing with six weeks of radiation, after which she mostly felt okay but sometimes did not, was the worst.

She'd gone upstairs to their room when they got home the previous afternoon, and fifteen minutes later, he followed. He hoped to see her in bed, fans blasting, maybe in her bra and smiling up sleepily at him. What he found was her rummaging purposefully through the overstuffed bottom drawer of her dresser, the background playing some dimly-lit Netflix show set in the woods and featuring beautiful women in flannel shirts delivering babies and giving first aid to fishermen to the backdrop of moody covers of ironic '80s songs, the shades drawn but all the lights on, nothing suggesting rest.

He'd stood in the doorway, leaning against the frame, a bit annoyed with her, completely amused by her, drinking her in like some sixteen-year-old fool. When she finally noticed him there, she looked away sheepishly, teenagerish in her own right, shrugging at her compulsive need to find whatever scrap of something she'd been looking for and, he could see, basking in his adoration.

Katy sometimes called them "cute." She even gave a toast at their wedding reception, just shy of fifteen months after the death of her mother, and employed "*adorable.*"

"Daddy and Jessie look at each other like one of those adorable couples featured on Hallmark's 'Christmas in July.' Not the main couple, who has to overcome country mouse/city mouse, Scrooge versus The Ghosts, or any other form of trumped-up conflict that stands in the way of happily-ever-after. No. Daddy and Jessie are the owners of the bed-and-breakfast, the ones whose coffee tastes magical and centerpieces are always fresh flowers and who look at each other like they know they're in a cheesy movie, but they don't care. They're making beds with hospital corners and serving homemade scones seven days a week, matchmaking out-of-town loan officers with local reporters, and having the unexpected time of their lives."

Most people had laughed, a few nervously. Paul had to blink a lot so as not to show the moisture collecting in his eyes. Katy was anything but subtle or shy, and her over-the-top narrative might have been a little much for two widowed people having a quiet wedding off the beach, but she'd nailed it. She'd totally grasped what it felt like for him to be with Jessie, too good to be true, and yet, true.

All of it was, really. Well, most of it. Ideally, Julie would never have left, or would have come to their wedding and been reconciled. But nothing was perfect, even if you subtracted the *spouses died in tragic accident* factor of his and Jessie's equation. They had a total of seven grown kids and all the extensions from there, not to mention the nieces and strays they'd collected. Something was always going to be wrong. Someone was always going to be missing. It was easier for him to accept that than it was for Jessie, but it wasn't *easy*. He missed Julie.

The sweat was pouring off of him and Surfside Drive beckoned him. He picked up his pace for the half mile or so it took him to get to Benjamin's Bakery, pushing all thoughts aside to concentrate on the goal of sipping the world's best cold brew.

He deftly ordered the daily special from Regina and let her know he'd wait outside, where his stench wouldn't be quite so off-putting. Life was too short to go home and shower first. He'd just finished stretching and settled himself at a table when he looked up to see a familiar, non-bakery-staff face carrying his bagel and coffee, along with a second, steaming cup and a huge breakfast burrito, toward him.

"Hey man!" Paul greeted, "I didn't even see you in there. What's up?"

"I was in the bathroom. They called 'Paul' and I knew there

would be a sweaty old redneck outside in short shorts, waiting on his girlie drink."

Paul laughed and kicked out a chair for his friend. "You can insult me all you want but leave my coffee alone. Look how dark it is. That is *not* a girlie drink."

Johnny raised his eyebrows as Paul began the meticulous process of stirring in four packets of sugar. "You're right. It's practically petroleum the way you drink it. What are you doing running in this inferno?"

Paul shrugged. "Just getting it in. I'm at the point where I get a little crazy without it."

Johnny nodded. A retired journalist, he'd met Paul while they each waited in the typically-lengthy bakery line a few months before. Johnny was tall, large, and while strong and agile enough for a guy in his sixties, definitely held no interest in running or other athletic pursuits. He'd attempted nine holes with Paul one day and cursed the entire time. He preferred bookstores, movie theaters, and restaurants.

"How is Jessie?"

"Stubborn. And fine."

"Treatments done?"

Paul took a long swallow. "One more week. Three more sessions."

"Damn," Johnny said. He relished a bite before continuing. "Radiation is like a second job."

"Nah," Paul said, sitting up straighter, more fervor in his voice. "It's her only job. A second job, for me, is convincing her of that. She keeps finding 'little projects' that she swears won't take much effort, like 'refreshing the patio,' which really means new-old furniture that needs refurbishing and a new ceiling fan and painting the floor. The floor. A little project. Just a little one."

Johnny raised an eyebrow. "Why you mad, bro? Sounds harmless enough."

"I just wish she would take it easy. She has no chill, not one ounce of it. She always has to be doing something, like life is about earning all her Girl Scout badges or something."

"Dude. She's not branding cattle. Ambitious women do not like being told to chill out. Trust me." Johnny glanced appraisingly at Paul's face before returning his attention back to his burrito.

Paul contemplated the words of his twice-divorced friend. Perhaps he knew some things Paul hadn't grasped yet. Leah had been ambitious, but she never paused to notice whether Paul had any objections or not. And he almost never did, so it worked out between them, in their way. But his and Jessie's way was different, and right now, he wanted to object often.

"You look like the weight of the world is on you, man," Johnny continued. "She's okay, right?"

Paul exhaled. He didn't want to look that way, certainly not so obviously burdened that a fairly new friend could read his typically guarded emotions. He took a long drink of coffee before he answered.

"You know," he started, "it's different the second time. Everyone's personalities are already very well established. So I tend to just... hold my peace."

"If it ain't peaceful, what are you holding?"

Now Paul raised an eyebrow. "I didn't say it wasn't peaceful."

"You are afraid to talk to your wife about her stress level. And about your worry level. That's not peace. That's bullshit. Trust me."

Paul laughed curtly. "You keep saying that. Tell me again how well you communicated in your marriages?"

Johnny nodded, unoffended. "Point taken. You don't think I learned anything? I ran around on my first wife. Multiple times. Mindlessly. I was a stupid kid and had no business being married in the first place. But the second time? I loved Janine too much, and I pushed her away. I was afraid of losing her, so I *kept the peace*, I thought. Never argued. Never made a decision or questioned one of hers. Never even disagreed over what to eat for dinner. And I bored her to tears until she cheated on me."

"I'm not even sure I believe you," Paul said. "Those are two extremely different scenarios."

"Believe what you want," Johnny said. "But if you only believe one thing, let it be that guarding the truth from Jessie will get you nowhere. She probably already knows, and from what you've told me about her, she's dying to hash it out with you."

*Spoken like a man who has never* hashed *with Jessie Romano Oakley.*

But then he reminded himself: Jameson. She's a Jameson now.

# CHAPTER♡FIVE

## *Julie*

To: JULIEJAMESON.BSN@GMAIL.COM
From: ibforfun@rocketmail.com
I was just thinking about you. A song came on the radio while I was getting coffee. You left your mug here. I used it. I figured if anyone thought it was weird, they wouldn't ask, but I could say mine was dirty. That's mundane. I just don't know what else to say.

To: 'Ian's Ridiculous Email Account.'
From: 'Julie Jameson'
I guess I need to get a new email address. That's always a pain. The first one I ever had was 'juliesnew1@yahoo.com.' I miss those Yahoo commercials. And I miss you, too, but... I also don't know what else to say. *IBforfun*. That's all. And the fun is over, isn't it?

Thirty-six hours after her arrival, after they'd had a nostalgic dinner of ramen (the thirty-seven-cents-a-package kind, not the macro-balanced, egg-on-top kind), Diet Dr. Pepper, and chips with Frito Lay canned bean dip while watching *Mean Girls*, on the *floor*, Julie was officially done with her bunking arrangement at Camp Katy. And she knew it wasn't the time, but she was going to talk to her sister about her lifestyle. She might have a surfer body now, but all the processed crap and drinking was going to catch up with her. And she needed a damn couch. And a savings plan. She wasn't a kid anymore.

Julie had formulated a plan. *She* had plenty of savings because their Daddy wasn't holding her inheritance like he was Katy's (per their nebulous mutual agreement). Even though she had some student loan balances and a small car payment as well, her bills didn't equal much at the moment. She also had no job, but that was a matter of hitting the skids and finding one.

There was just one pretty major swallowing of pride she would have to do first.

"What time do you work tomorrow?" Julie asked her sister.

"Hmm. Store from ten until two. Lessons at four until... 6:30, I think. What's up?"

"Eh. That won't work." Katy worked at a music store in the mall and taught guitar. It might as well have paid her in bean dip, but she loved it. "Please keep calm about this. I'm going to go down and see Daddy tomorrow." Surfside Beach was just over an hour away, but it would be too late for her to wait for Katy.

"Keep calm? What do you think I'm going to do? An interpretive dance? Sing a little ditty? I can't believe you haven't even called him since you've been here. I thought you were his great protector since–"

She shut her mouth, receiving Julie's icy glare in the nick of time. Julie had, in fact, gone a little overboard trying to care for

Paul since Leah died, as though their independent and kind of stoic dad had become needy and clingy overnight. His roughest time, trying to take over all their managed properties, injuring his ankle to the extent he needed surgery, and ending up broken-hearted and homeless after his first stint with Jessie, all happened *after* Julie moved away. He'd made it clear in the middle of his mess that he didn't need her and maybe didn't even particularly *want* her around.

"I told him I would be here this week. I didn't give him an appointed time. And this is what I mean by 'calm down.' I know you want there to be fireworks and hugging it out and whatever, but Daddy and I have a lot of shit to talk through before we can start... whatever."

"Whatever?" It was Katy's turn to glare. "You mean acting like a family again? C'mon, Julie. You were supposedly so concerned that Jessie was going to hurt him and *you're* the one who's broken his heart. You haven't even seen him in over a year. Christmas. Mom's birthday. The—the *anniversary*. None of it."

*Doesn't she think I know?*

"I *KNOW*!" she snapped. "I get it. All of it. I'm the one who did it. I'm the one who lives with it. All I'm saying is, don't push. I might be on the outs, but Daddy and I understand each other. We'll figure it out, and we don't need meddling. I don't need help with this."

Katy nodded, a cynical expression that would have enraged Julie if she didn't happen to be in the right for a change. "Then why did you ask if I was working? To make sure I *couldn't* go with you?"

They both knew that wasn't true.

"Something like that," Julie muttered.

"I'm going to bed," was Katy's answer. "You coming?"

"We are one cheesecake away from turning into the Golden Girls."

"Maybe thirty is the new sixty." Katy bounced into the next room, leaving Julie alone with her sense of dread.

Julie pulled up to *the* house, her dad's new home with his new wife. "Of course," she muttered aloud. It was not overtly beachy from the outside. Jessie's old house had been right across the street from the beach, and one couldn't help, she supposed, acquiring shells and starfish décor and beach rope baskets and white-washed things when that close to the ocean.

Meanwhile, Mama and Daddy's old house had been overtly modern-suburban. Julie and her sisters had grown up a few miles west of the coast, enough to make a difference, to feel like they were not at the beach all the time. Leah had loved flowers, Paul loved tending to them, so their yard and garden were always expansive and lush. The lines in their house were clean, their textiles solid, their accents weren't bold but whimsical, like the elephant coffee table in the formal living room or the enormous sad clown painting in the tiny powder room. (It was in storage now, waiting for Katy to have a real place to hang it. The rest of them actually hated it.) They'd had a state-of-the-art chef's kitchen, especially humorous because they ate out seventy-five percent of the time.

Daddy's house with Jessie had curb appeal somewhere in the middle. It was white-washed siding except for what appeared to be the original face, made of gray and white brick. He'd said that the cottage was "Harry Potter-esque," looking small as a camping tent from the outside and opening up to a house that could hold the whole extended family for the duration of the Quidditch tournament on the inside.

There were teal blue shutters, while the front door, the mailbox, and the side-facing porch swing were painted a bolder turquoise. The magnolia in the front yard still held blooms and was encircled by a bed of dark red mums. Paul was probably one of the only people in town who didn't buy random pots of them at the grocery store that would be dead next to the Jack-o-lanterns a week later.

It all looked sweet and beautiful, and Julie wiped impatiently at the tears filling her eyes. *He deserves to be happy, just like you do. Jessie is not your enemy.* It was the pep-talk she'd given herself all the way from Wilmington, and before that, much of the way from Arizona. She checked herself in the mirror and then made her way up the driveway.

*I have to knock*, she told herself. It might be her father's house, but it wasn't her *family* house, and she'd never been there before. She took a deep breath at the front door, and—

It opened.

*Was it an actual Harry Potter house?*

"Julie!"

Well. That was a magical little way to soften the blow. Abby, Jessie's daughter-in-law, had opened the door. It was impossible not to like Abby. She was a total supermom of three, but a mellow version, not a perfect Pinterest version. She worked in advertising *and* made stuff for the bake sales. She'd been around as long as Julie remembered knowing the Oakleys. Ideal neutral territory, she hoped.

Abby gave her a light hug, not too intrusive, and gave away the magic trick. "Jessie saw you coming up the driveway. She has a thing about none of us kids knocking on the door. You know—"

*You know how she is*, is what Abby was probably going to say. And Julie could admit to herself that she probably did, at least a little. Jessie had been her dad's co-worker and her mama's friend for years and years. They all went to church together and did some holidays together and were beach-family, *chosen* family, because so few people had roots there. Julie never thought much about her one way or another. She was a great cook and could endlessly quote movies and songs. She had a somewhat interesting job writing curriculum. She seemed to know everyone in town and could juggle a whole bunch of roles. She was a nice person.

And she stole Julie's dad before her mama was cold in the ground.

*Oh jeez.* Not helpful thinking at all.

Julie offered Abby a tight smile. "That's... nice. Is... is my dad home?" She saw his Jeep beyond the house; the driveway extended past it to a rare detached garage, but who knew what he was up to these days? Apparently, shockingly, he had taken up running, which he'd always hated when his wife (*God help me. His first wife. My MOTHER*) was into it.

"Yes, yes. Mom... Jessie and I are just heading out. Listen, Julie." Abby closed the front door behind her. "Can I just be transparent for a minute?"

Julie stared at her, amazed that anyone in this family asked that question first. It always seemed like someone was ranting, confessing, emoting, or speechifying all the time anyway.

"Sure."

"I know... I mean. Whatever. We're grown-ups, and you can handle straight talk. I know this is hard. I know you haven't seen your dad since you moved away. And this is weird. He's remarried. All the context of everything is different. Just..."

Okay. She liked Abby enough, but if she was about to tell her how to handle her own father, this wasn't going to go well.

"Just know that this is still home. Some version of home. Nothing is perfect. None of us has it all figured out. Every Oakley misses Randall, and your dad and sisters and family miss your mama. It's weird and hard, but... it's... safe? I think that's the best word. I don't know what you've been through, but I know you have a good support system here, and it will be okay. And um, well, I don't know if you heard somehow, but my mom died just a few months ago." Abby paused for the smallest moment, but Julie could see it then, the look of a girl who didn't have a mama anymore. She ached. "So anyway, if you need a friend who's not quite so much in the thick of *this*," she gestured vaguely toward the house, "all the time, well, I'm here. Facebook me if you don't have my number. Okay?"

Julie exhaled.

"I'm so sorry about your mother. I didn't know. And I... I just don't know what to expect. Not just from him, but from myself." Damn these Oakleys and how easy they were to talk to. "So thank you, Abby. I really will keep that in mind."

"Jessie will probably avoid you if that's what you need today. Do you want me to...? I mean, there are a few other doors." Abby was being serious, but her eyes were amused. Julie got it. Her own older sister was a mother to almost three and they just had less time for B.S.

"Thanks. No. It's fine. I know Daddy probably makes me sound like a ticking time bomb, but this is their home. I'm not going to dictate where she walks."

"Gotcha," Abby said. "Well, come on in."

All right then. There was an entryway, but it was completely open on one side, basically part of the living room. There was no place to hide, to take a breath, to steel herself. She side-eyed the space but couldn't see anyone there. She heard music playing from the TV; it sounded like typical '80s soft-classic-adult-whatever. She smelled coffee, and also vanilla and cinnamon, either candles or homemade muffins Jessie had probably whipped up in the off-chance one of their hundred relatives or besties stopped by...

*Stop. It.* She willed herself to soften. She willed herself to make this reunion –

"Jules."

Her father's voice was raised in volume, but his tone was steady, familiar. He must have descended from the stairs she could now see just off the kitchen. The house had a weird layout, and she suddenly got the whole Harry-Potter thing. It kinda looked cobbled together, nothing like where Paul and Leah had raised them, nothing like Jessie's beach house. It would almost be shabby if it wasn't so dang... perfect.

She looked away from the décor and met his eyes. Just his eyes because she knew they would be the same.

"Hi, Daddy."

And suddenly, she was frozen. Her legs wouldn't work. It reminded her of the day she and Mama had run a 10K at Disney World, and then did two parks with everyone else, and by ten that night, her knees just wouldn't bend anymore. But this time, the aching lack of energy was not in her legs, just in her. She'd missed him so much, but she wasn't even sure he was the same person she'd left here over a year ago.

If her standing still seemed strange, Paul didn't show it. He walked all the way to her, waiting for her to put down her bag.

When she didn't, he gently pried her fingers from it and dropped it on the floor. She watched it fall, and he lifted her chin so that she had to look at him again.

"Welcome home, baby," he said.

That was all it was going to take, at least for now. She crumbled, just melted, into a mess of tears and unintelligible words the likes of which she hadn't done since middle school, or the week Leah died. Her mama had been her hero, but Daddy had been her best friend. She thought... until...

"I'm sorry!" was the only phrase she could muster clearly.

Paul's arms were around her, his hand stroking her hair, his voice whispering nonsense comfort like she was four years old again. His implied forgiveness made it worse. She'd moved through the last fifteen months and a cross-country drive ready for a fight, and he wasn't going to give her one at this moment. There was no anger to match hers and no place for hers to go.

In lieu of a fight, the fighter in her turned to the fixer. She had questions to ask him, tasks to relay, steps to identify, and a big favor in mind. She pep-talked herself through this, too. *Just be. Let him love you. Let him comfort you. Don't worry yet. Shut up, Julie.* She swore if people could hear her internal monologue, they'd never think she had it all together all the time.

When his shoulder was so soaked from her tears that it was making her face slide off, she let go. Her dad had always had an uncanny ability to hug until the other person was finished. Honestly, she wasn't sure she'd really been hugged since she left for Arizona.

(Save for Katy's weird half-tackle, of course).

"Well. You look great," he said, dabbing one of her puffy eyes. They both laughed a bit.

Julie took that moment to look at him. He was lean like always. Wearing jeans that were a little baggy, a black mechanic-style shirt with some business logo on it, a Surfside Beach Co. hat covering his shortly cropped hair. Mostly the same. Still her dad.

"You want to see the house? You want to see the beach? You hungry? Tell me what you want."

She giggled again to keep from crying again. Did he know how loaded that question was? Probably.

"Oh, Daddy," she sighed, trying to sound as steady as he did and speaking the words before she chickened out. "Just... for a little bit, a few weeks maybe, until I have a job, which shouldn't take long, I could really, really use a place to stay."

An hour later, Julie could hear them, not the words, just their voices, over Dad's speakerphone. She couldn't even really make out the tones, so she imagined what they were. Her dad, probably calm, firm. Jessie, probably impassioned, maybe a little defensive. She sighed out loud from her seat on the porch swing, certain no one could hear her.

*This is the worst.*

Katy had actually left stuff in the guest suite, not just random toiletries but some clothes. Casual stuff. Things that could be used at the beach or outside, for doing nothing or going to bed. Julie had changed into acceptable shorts and a tank top; she was already wearing running shoes. There was no reason to dress up. She borrowed Paul's earbuds and was set to go for a jaunt in the mostly-unexplored Surfside Beach neighborhoods. But as soon as she stepped outside, she felt deflated of energy, of motivation, of desire.

*You won't always feel motivated. So you have to be disciplined.* This was one of the rare nuggets that *both* Leah and Paul had instilled in their daughters. Have routines. Pray. Exercise. Don't eat crap all the time (She refrained from commenting on her dad's addiction to sweet tea and from the looks of his little, mostly-camouflaged pouch, Jessie's baking).

Julie hadn't run regularly in a few months. She didn't want to think about how much endurance she'd lost. So she picked the most depressing playlist in her arsenal and started walking.

After two of Pink's greatest hits, she felt loosened up enough to pick up her pace. She didn't know the streets well but knew exactly where Ocean Boulevard was. She headed there, already sweating in the southern sun. She made it to the Surfside Pier before she decided her shoes, which, if she thought about it, she'd bought before she moved to Arizona over a year ago, were shot. Imagining shin splints, a constant of her high school years, she started walking again, back toward her dad's house.

Toward home? Was she really going to do this, after all the fighting and distance and how she still felt her mother was being betrayed, was she really going to move into *their* house? It made her want to run the other way, as far away as she could. But not with Katy, God bless her. And not back to Arizona, because those bridges were charred and still smoking. Where? Where else could she go?

Her phone dinged. She took it out of where it was stuffed down her bra (Katy's shorts really were inadequate for a real run) and gave a quick look. It was her older sister, Danielle.

I'm so excited. You'll only be seven-and-a-half- minutes from us. Not that I'm counting on you to babysit or anything. At least not right away... :wink emoji:

She sighed again, picturing her sweet, towheaded nephew Christian, perfectly five-years-old and an amazement to their family who'd only been comprised of girl-children until he was born, and curly-headed Vivi, now fully a toddler, fully royalty, likely exhausting. If Julie felt worse about anything other than the lengthy hostility with her dad, she felt awful about missing an entire year of their little lives.

> I'll come over tomorrow. Grabbing my stuff tonight, I guess. Can't wait to see you and the babies. This is all a little weird...

She wanted to add a million dots to that ellipses. *Weird* didn't describe it. Sighs didn't express it. If she had the stamina she'd had a year ago, she'd run all the way to the cemetery and ask her mama to forgive her for what she was doing.

# CHAPTER ♡ SIX

## *Jessie*

"WELL," I SAID, DROPPING MY PHONE ON THE TABLE. "THAT WAS PAUL."

Abby understood my tone and came pretty close to rolling her eyes at me. Though she was my daughter-in-law, her first-born and my last-born had been raised together, so I wasn't overly mom-ish to her. We were basically ride-or-die. And she'd been doing a lot of riding with me since Maggie, my best friend since actual forever, had moved away to Charlotte, and more somberly, Abby's own mother, Whitney, had passed away about six months later.

"I figured," she deadpanned. "How's it going?"

"She's going to stay with us for a while."

Abby feigned a shocked expression. "You don't say? I am *floored* at this turn of events!"

I would have uttered what seemed to be our family motto, but we were at the tea room, and f-bombs felt particularly out of place there. So I muttered "FFS" instead.

Abby did roll her eyes then, and I was grateful that Carla, the owner, chose that moment to set our quiche and soup orders down on the table before us.

"I wanted to let you ladies know something right quick," Carla said, providing an even more welcome distraction.

Carla was the sweetest mashup of southern and British. Everything about her reminded me of Lady Cora on *Downton Abbey*, except that instead of elegant frocks, she wore elaborately patterned overalls over pastel-colored t-shirts, her long gray hair typically in two braids that looped back into a bun. She was the definition of adorable and of a seventy-something-year-old that didn't mind being referred to as such.

"Sure, Carla," I said. "What's going on?"

"Well." She put a hand on her slender hip and searched for the words. "I am trying to find someone to buy this place from me. Well, you know, buy the lease and the business."

"What? Carla, nooooo!" I exclaimed.

"Yes, honey, I know," she said, patting my hand. "But I talked to my sons up in Mass and we agree it's time I'm not on my own anymore. And if I'm going to move, I'd like to do it while I still have life left in me..."

"God bless you," Abby muttered. "Moving *takes* the life out of you."

"It sure does, sweetheart." I narrowed my eyes at Abby. *Way to be encouraging.* She shrugged back at me.

"Anyway," Carla continued, "I thought I'd let y'all know before I go public. I know you know a lot of people and maybe you'll know someone who's interested in the business. Now, I have all the documentation ready. It took me three years to start turning a real profit, but here we are six years in, and it would be a nice little turnkey business for someone. Hopefully, someone who wants to keep it a tea room and not turn it into another version of a sports bar."

"Amen to that," I said. "Oh Carla, I hate to see you go, and I hope it doesn't close altogether, but I will ask around. And we will think of someone!"

"I knew you would have some ideas," she said. "I'll be back to check on y'all soon."

As soon as she was out of earshot, I widened my eyes at Abby. "Are you thinking what I'm thinking?"

"She should post in *Surfsidians*? I don't know, Mom. Those people get awfully crazy in there."

"Nooo, Abby! What if *we* were the new owners?"

"What? Wait..." Her face went through several changes in the next ten seconds, from immediate protest to puzzlement to curiosity. "Well, actually, maybe. Maybe we should talk about it. I'm going to have to do something again soon, and it might as well be fun, if at all possible."

Abby had resigned her marketing job when her mom got sick the year before. I was certain she could have asked for it back, but like most of us, she came out on the other side of losing a parent so different. And she and Sam, my darling Sam, each losing a parent within the span of a year had taken its toll. I was proud of them for making space for her to stay home and truly circle the wagons of their family. So proud.

"Let's mull it over," I said coyly. In my head, I was already brainstorming a new name, menu changes, and itching to throw Carla's hideous decorative teapot shaped like Charlie Chaplin's head from its shelf into the nearest bonfire. "Just keep it between us for now."

"I'll probably forget the second Summer starts telling me about her day," Abby quipped. "Now, getting back to Julie..."

"I feel bad for her..." I said, knowing I didn't sound convincing.

Abby took the mantle from me. "I feel bad for her, too. But she at the very least owes you an apology, and I don't mean some half-assed email after your engagement or a generic FTD arrangement instead of her presence at your wedding. And whether she gives you one or not, this is not the time for you to start cooking all her favorite foods."

"Ha!" I choked a little on a swallow of heavenly chai. "I don't even know her favorite food. I don't know *her*. And she's moving *in*. Am I crazy? Is Paul?"

"Yes." Abby lifted a spoonful of tomato cream and inhaled before tasting it. "Bless. This is perfection. Yes, Mom. Paul is crazy. He's probably crazy with his own guilt about not having a family home for his grown daughters to move back into if they need to. And he's a little crazy for asking this of you with everything that has happened and is happening–"

"Abby–"

"I know, Mom. I know you're fine. But it's hard enough for you to admit you're not in full fighting form. Now, you will have the pressure of wearing a poker face 24/7 for a person living in your house. A person who makes you uncomfortable and certainly isn't familiar. A person who has mostly only expressed resentment toward you. Yeah. It's a crazy lot to ask, and I am a little surprised at him because he knows you are crazy, too, and you cannot say no."

By the time she was done, I had eaten half of the world's most delicious (and ridiculously tiny) quiche Lorraine in a mostly-conquered coping mechanism of drowning my stress in really good food.

"*He* can't say no, and neither can I. You're right. It's all crazy.

This situation is unnaturally crazy. But I don't see any options. And she's very... resourceful. Smart. She probably won't be there long."

"Famous last words," Abby said. "What happens when your wayward child finds his way back home? You gonna stick David in the cousin bunks? Because he is not moving in with us!"

The thought of that possibility, of my youngest finally moving home from Tennessee where he'd escaped *post-Julie* and having to finagle every damn thing because that vixen (*Stop it, Jessie!*) was staying in the guest room, gave me a hot flash. It wasn't menopause; it was the radiation.

"If I ever owned this place, I would serve alcohol. Nothing fancy. Maybe some Bellinis. Definitely mimosas. Mexican coffee. Irish coffee."

"Mom!"

"Off-track. Yes. Anyway... I guess I just have to talk to him when I get home. Hopefully in private. Hopefully that will still be a thing."

Abby shook her head. "It's *your* house. Make it a thing. Make *him* make it a thing. And Mom? I'll have Sam tell David, okay? You really... I know *you're fine, it's fine, everything is fine*, but you really don't need the extra stress right now. Just go about *your* business, *your* routine, the best you can. Let Paul handle Julie. And let Paul keep taking care of *you*. He can manage."

I knew he could. Of course, he could. But everything was complicated. And I didn't want to ask any more of a man who married me fifteen months after our spouses died and then started taking care of a cancer patient wife three weeks later.

"I'm sick of all of it," was all I could say.

Abby set down her fork and grew very serious. It was one of my favorite qualities about her. It would not have mattered if all three of her kids had been surrounding her, causing their specific kinds of chaos, dinner cooking, dishes piling, proverbial dog barking (our family was noticeably absent of canine pals lately). She could drown out everything and focus in on someone on a dime when she felt it necessary. As a fellow mother-in-chaos, the ability astounded me; I didn't have the current chaos and still didn't have the ability.

"What is *all of it*? What do you mean? Is something else going on?"

I sighed. I hadn't meant to sound so dramatic. "How did we get here?" I said. "We just summarized it. Tragedy. New marriage. Kids moving away. Estrangement. Cancer. Awkward living situation. How did that not become enough for me to be sick of?"

She laughed. She covered her mouth with her napkin and just… *guffawed*. I smiled and took another sip, another bite, let her experience the absurdity. We were used to that by then, too.

"You're right," she said, trying to breathe normally. "It's enough. I'm sorry for asking."

"But," I said, pushing my plate away. "I am afraid to ask him. I'm afraid if I ask him for anything else right now, when it comes to Julie, it's going to cause a fight. And I don't feel ready for that at all."

"I mean… everyone *fights*."

"We don't," I said.

If she leaned in any closer, she was going to be in my lap. "Abby. It's fine. I'm not naive. I know couples are supposed to fight. That's why I'm… bothered. Because we don't. And I even know why. After our break-up, we are both afraid to rock the boat."

"And that doesn't work long term."

"No. It does not."

We allowed silence to commence. She finished her soup. I poured more chai. The scones were gone. That made me sad. I peeked quickly at my phone and saw three text messages from Morgan, my pastor's wife and another longtime bestie, who'd taken to sending me encouraging scriptures and ridiculous reels on the daily.

"I will talk to him," I said quietly.

"I know you will," she answered. "And I know it will be fine."

I thought so, too. But I did not feel the *know*. I felt instead like I was walking into a bit of a minefield in the home I had painstakingly established, and no matter where I stepped, something was going to explode.

# CHAPTER♡SEVEN

## *Julie*

JULIE SAT SULLENLY IN THE PASSENGER SEAT. Dad had the top down off the Jeep, which she guessed was typically fine for fall, but it was three in the afternoon and the coastal sun was baking her, and she didn't know why she couldn't just go by herself to buy a pair of damn shoes.

He wanted some more of the good socks, he said. "He jumps at any reason to go to that place," Jessie said, too cheerfully, so incredibly awkwardly, with way more familiarity toward Dad than Julie could ever, ever imagine being comfortable with. At least she wasn't coming, too. This was bad enough.

But Dad seemed oblivious to it. He had some kind of Yacht Rock station on and he was smiling all the way. She kept herself distracted with math. *I have this much in savings. I can get an apartment not potentially featured on Myrtle Manor for this much. I have enough for a deposit and two months without touching the security account. I can sell my car and get a smaller one. Wi-fi is probably included. I can sponge off Danielle's Netflix and Prime like Katy has been doing to me for years. I need this much income. I can do some telehealth and save enough in a month or two and not be pinching every penny. But then I will be at their house all the time. Maybe I should just ask Dad for a loan. Surely, he doesn't want me there. Maybe I should just cut my losses and dip into the safety savings. I will pay it right back. I am disciplined AF.*

Before Michael McDonald could start belting another one, they were there.

"We're here."

"Yes, Dad." *I see that. With my eyeballs.* His sunniness felt a little insane, and she struggled not to answer with saltiness.

She stared at the sign over the end unit of the plaza. "Run This Way." Punny. She wasn't sure if it was clever or cheesy, and she hadn't even known it was here.

"Was this store here before... I moved?"

"Maybe? I never paid attention. I think this space was something else, though. Stationary? Gelato? Wine and Design? I don't know."

"Pins it down, Daddy," she murmured as they stepped inside.

The door ding-donged and Julie felt a warm rush as she took the place in. Her mom would have loved it. The rustic fixtures of wood and brick hinted at the outdoors, with simple display shelves highlighted in army green and stone gray. Her dad immediately started picking up shoes and glancing through socks. Her own attention was secondarily captured by the Viszla curled up next to the window, its brown head pillowed on a hideous, torn-up stuffed troll. She bent down to pet the soft head. The pup opened one eye, sized her up, and decided better of it.

"Can I help you, since he obviously isn't?"

"Oh. Hi," Julie answered the male voice, without turning around to regard the source. "What's this sleepy guy's name?"

"Mr. Pickle. Just Pickle for short."

*Mr. Pickle?* That was absolutely the most stupid name she'd ever heard. She relaxed her wince before turning around.

"Well. Nice to meet... him." She couldn't bring herself to say it.

"I thought his name was Tex?" Paul chimed in.

"Ah. Yes. Hey there. My... stepdaughter nicknamed him Tex. It kinda stuck."

*Fix your face, Julie.* It was Mama's voice again. Julie stood and gave her formal smile to... whomever he was, who stood about six inches taller than she, had tousled, tawny brown hair that somehow seemed more surfer-ish than runner-ish, an unkempt beard, and a general look of boredom that made her wonder if she had made a mistake. Maybe he was another customer. Maybe someone had forced him and his bizarrely-named dog there under duress.

"Tex is adorable," she said. "Um, I need some new shoes. I guess my dad is a regular here, so..."

"Yeah. Good to see you, man." He crossed the narrow space to Paul and stuck his hand out, suddenly seeming less like a slacker who didn't know his dog's name. He turned back to Julie. "I can help you out with that."

"My daughter has been running a lot longer than I have, so I'm shocked she's never been to your store before. Anyway, she should be an easy sell. Always knows just what she wants."

"That doesn't always make it easier," he said, winking at Paul and definitely not fooling Julie with what she assessed as a condescending smile.

With her dad strolling around the store like a kid in a candy shop, Julie had the sole attention of the proprietor. She winced a little when he told her to pop her shoes off so he could see her

arches in motion. As ridiculous as that sounded, she did as instructed, walking with her shoes off, answering some questions,
and then raising an eyebrow when he said, "I'll grab a few things
for you to try. What's your name?"

"Julie."

"Great, Julie. I'm Robin. Be right back."

She immediately raised her eyebrow again and wondered.

"Dad, didn't you say the owner's name was Nick?"

Paul was completely focused on a rotating rack of sunglasses.
"Mmm-hmm. Yeah."

"And is that guy the owner?"

"Yeah, Jules."

"Well, he just told me his name is—"

She was cut off by the return of What's His Name, holding
three shoeboxes and gesturing to a bench. She sat and dutifully
tried on all three pairs. She knew immediately that the first one
was what she wanted, but she tried out the second two, figuring
Dad needed more time to poke around. She curiously observed
the process this guy used to help her decipher the best fit for her
(she'd only ever ordered running shoes from Amazon, based on
what Mama told her would be good for her). She also noted that
he seemed way too tousled and quirky (*Ugh, like David*) and at
the same time, like a completely polished expert (similar to most
other guys she ever wanted).

"These are going to be perfect," she said, picking up the left
shoe of the first pair, with a light-as-air, contoured upper and just
enough cushion. Kenova? Kivara? She couldn't remember what
he called it.

"What is this one again?" she asked, as he returned them to
the box.

"Saucony Kinvara. Light mid-distance trainer, great racing shoe."

"I don't know how you keep track of all these models," she said, "Seeing as you can't remember your or your dog's name."

By that time, they were at the counter. He paused with the scanner in his hand and cocked his head at her.

"Yeah. I'm a little short-staffed at the moment. I lose track of vital info at times."

Was this guy for real? He went about explaining the customer loyalty program as though what he'd said, or having multiple names for himself and his dog, made any sense in the world.

"Short-staffed, huh?" Paul said, standing at her side and presenting his credit card before she could pretend to protest. She'd chosen the least expensive of the three shoes, but they still weren't cheap.

"Don't," Julie muttered under her breath. If Paul heard her, he didn't acknowledge.

"Yeah," the owner answered. "I just had someone leave a few weeks ago, so I have one full-timer who enjoys a day off or two every week. And it's getting a little too busy to only have one person covering at a time."

"Jules here happens to be looking for some employment."

*Damnit, Daddy.*

"Oh, I'm sure she's overqualified," the guy said.

"Not for changing careers," Paul deadpanned.

Julie wanted to sink into the floor. Reality was, she was kind of in love with the whole idea of this place. There were all kinds of running events listed on a chalkboard wall. The shoe-fitting process appealed to her precise, scientific side and her show-me-all-the-pretty-things side. And it surely would beat any kind of general retail job.

But it was still retail, after eight-and-a-half years in the *medical field*. What was she going to do, make minimum wage helping people tie their shoes? No. She could not.

Then again, she was living with Dad and Jessie.

"What are the hours like?" she said, staring Nick-Robin in his chocolate brown eyes.

"Probably something like twenty-five to start."

That was doable. She could still pick up some telehealth hours on the side. But—

"And what is the dog's name? For real."

"Carnitas."

Her Dad had just dropped over 150 dollars at this guy's store, and probably hundreds more since his running obsession started. And here the fake-named dude was still lying to their faces. She just knew it. He was staring back in a way that communicated it quite clearly. It was ludicrous.

And she really, really liked it.

Julie glanced at a little plastic holder by the register and picked up a business card.

"Robin N. Murray, do I apply online?"

"You're going to work at the running store? I cannot believe it."

"I cannot believe you are spending the night here when you have your own place to live."

"I cannot believe you ate a salad for dinner when Jessie's lasagna was available."

"I cannot believe you don't weigh 100 more pounds with the

way you eat. Can you move so I can put this stuff away?" Julie, arms piled with shorts and tanks, apparently her new work clothes, looked pointedly at the armoire door that Katy was body blocking.

Katy sidestepped. "I cannot believe you get to spend your days with Hot Running Nick."

"I cannot believe you don't understand how much I want to have my own hot running water."

There was a pause before Katy laughed, and then Julie couldn't help joining her, as she struggled to unpack a few books and pictures from her trunk.

"That was terrible," she said.

"I know," Julie agreed. "I am pinching myself, too. I just want to be back on my own. Did you know that Nick isn't even his name?"

Julie had emailed *Robin* the night she'd gotten her new shoes (which helped her cover four smooth-sailing miles in the interim). She had a reply from him before she even went to bed that night, telling her to come by the store any time the next afternoon for an "outdoor" interview. Geez, this guy was odd. She didn't know if there was going to be some sort of running test, so she wore joggers and a tank top, plus her new shoes, and a ponytail that took way too long to perfect. When she got there, he said they were taking *Pote* for a walk.

"It's French for 'mate,'" Robin had said.

"It's nice," she told him. "Why French?"

He shrugged as they walked along. "'Pote is actually after a TV character, but the French word packs a little more meaning. He is my mate. Roommate. Office mate. Mate. Pote. Best dog ever."

"Does he run with you?" The store was partially covered with bibs and medals that she assumed were his.

There was a pause. "Mmm. Yeah. I mean, he did. I haven't been running much lately."

"Injury?" she asked casually.

"Complete lack of motivation," he deadpanned.

"Look." She stopped walking. "Robin? Nick? Whatever? I am going to level with you. I need a job kinda quickly. I have zero retail experience, but I like to run, I have much more-than-average physiological knowledge, and your shop is really, really cool. But I cannot deal with bullshit, okay? I can guarantee you if you hire me, I will be the absolute most efficient little firecracker of an employee your thirteen dollars an hour can buy. But I am going to need you to guarantee me that you're not playing games. And we start with the names."

He almost smiled. "My name is Robin. The card isn't bullshit."

"But...?"

"But nothing. Nichols is my middle name. Nick is a more mainstream name for a male proprietor in Horry County, South Carolina. I never minded Robin until I moved here."

"You shouldn't mind it now. It's a nice name, and the rednecks are mostly harmless. What about the dog?"

"He is for real Pote."

"Then why all the games? Tex, for God's sake? Mr.-fricken-Pickle? Mexican pork?!"

Robin smiled.

"My stepdaughter did call him Tex. The others were me just messing with you."

*Did.* That was for another time, maybe. "Why do you do it?"

"Why do you want to work here?"

Julie looked down at her new shoes, their stark white soles next to the black and purple and blue and orange of the "Future Noir" colored upper. Maybe if the guy worked with products that had names like that, it wasn't too much of a stretch for him to be a... creative namer.

When she looked back at him, she said, "I'm hitting the refresh button on my whole life."

"Fair enough." He started walking again. And not looking at her, he said, "I can't do that right now. So sometimes I make stuff up. But just to the customers. No bullshit with you, okay?

"Fair enough," she'd echoed, and that had been that.

Katy was shaking her head, reading off random facts about Nick-Robin that she found on the store's Facebook page. His personal profile didn't have anything public on it from the past five years, and his profile picture was Pote.

"Well, he's a mystery. That will be fun."

"I don't need a mystery," Julie said. "I just need a simple nine-to-five so I can figure out my next move. And *move*. The hell out of here."

"Hey... girls..."

The guest suite bedroom was really just an offshoot of the living space, with only a curtain to close off the doorway. And there in the kitchen area stood Dad, with Jessie slightly behind him, each of them holding a canvas grocery bag and a version of the same small, forced smile.

"Hey!" Katy echoed, oblivious.

Julie rolled her eyes and inwardly groaned. She'd managed to avoid more than a quick, formal "hello" with Jessie for the past two days, and though she knew it could not be avoided forever – (and that this was Jessie's own damn house) – she had not expected this intrusion into what was supposed to be her, albeit temporary and borrowed – space.

Paul was staring at Julie, a thousand unsaid words in his blazing eyes. Julie stared back. Katy started to yammer about what was in the bags. Jessie set hers down on the table.

"We grabbed some... staples... from the market. Thought you'd like to have your own stash. Enjoy." There was a small quiver in her voice, but she managed to look Julie in the eye, and then smiled graciously at Katy, before she turned and briskly left the room.

Paul, in turn, slammed his bag on the table.

"Really?" he started.

"Oh Daddy, I didn't even *say* anything. And I certainly didn't expect that the two of you would just be *standing* there."

"In our house?"

"In the guest space." Katy snickered at Julie's "pediatric" voice. It was a family joke, often followed up by some mention of a sticker or a lollipop, but that wasn't happening this time.

"I don't need you to explain it to me, Julie. What I do need is the slightest respect in my own home. Just the slightest."

"Dear Lord, Daddy. How did I disrespect you? Or before you get going, any*one* else? All I said was–"

"I heard what you said! You're so ungrateful!"

Katy snapped to attention. "Daddy, she–"

"Stay out of it," Paul snapped just as Julie said, "Shut up, Katy." Then Paul continued, "I don't need you to defend my own daughter to me."

"I just don't think she meant anything by it..." Katy muttered. Then she flopped on the couch and unlocked her phone, pretending to ignore them.

"I'm not ungrateful," Julie said evenly, still sounding like she was preparing an inconsolable child for a needle stick. "I appreciate very much that you and your...Jessie... are giving me a place to sleep, and apparently supplying me with ice cream and..." She peered into one of the sacks, "...organic cookies. But let's not pretend this arrangement is comfortable for anyone. And let's not pretend that I am the only one who is miserable and maybe a little mad that I'm here. Come on, Daddy. We can at least be straight with each other about that."

"I'm happy you're here," Paul said evenly.

"I wasn't referring to you."

"You mean Jessie."

"Of course, I mean Jessie."

"How would you know how she feels when you haven't had a single conversation with her?"

"He has a point," came the voice from the couch.

"Shut *up*, Katy!"

The unison of both their frustrated voices shocked them into silence. Paul looked at Julie. Julie looked at the canvas bags. Katy nearly rocked back and forth in her attempt to keep her opinion to herself.

"I'm not ready," Julie said evenly.

"You're not ready for what?"

"A relationship. Whatever you want this to be between me and her. I get it. Danielle is fine with this. Jessie's daughter is her best friend. The kids need grandparents. And Katy could get along with a serial killer if he fed her homemade pasta. But I am not over Mama, and I am not ready for this."

Paul took a deep breath, a sure sign of careful word choice. "No one is over your mother, Julie, so I am not going to dignify that.

But to summarize, you are ready to live in Jessie's house, but not have a conversation with her. Do I have that correct?"

"I don't see this as living in her house."

"How can you not?"

Katy started muttering, barely under her breath.

"Can I help you, Katy?" Paul shot.

"I just said this is stupid."

"Wish I could argue," Julie said, as Paul answered, "Well, I agree."

There was a moment of stubborn silence. Julie broke it with, "We're at an impasse, Daddy. If there is something specific you want me to say or do, I will. But I am just biding time, trying to be polite and stay out of the way. I don't want to stir up anything, I don't want to upset anyone, I'm glad you're happy, and I just want to be left alone about it."

Julie then exhaled, relaxed her shoulders, and raised her eyebrows at him, waiting for a response, satisfied that her peace offering, such as it was, was good enough.

"It doesn't work that way," Paul said, so quietly she had to strain to hear him.

"I'm sorry. What?"

"That isn't good enough. That isn't how family works."

"We aren't a family, Dad!"

All the energy, even the tension in the room, seemed to be sucked up into the finality of that. Paul looked away from her, over to Katy, and then back in Julie's eyes.

"We're not?"

The sadness is his voice was palpable. She knew he wouldn't get it, would make it about something other than what it really was.

"You can't make this an all or nothing. You can't say we are all family or none of us are. You're mine. You can be Jessie's too. I accept that. But she isn't mine. And you have to accept that. We are all grown-ups here, and you can't just force it like I'm a seven-year-old who needs a mommy. I need my dad, and I'm grateful you're here for me. I'm grateful you have someone looking after you, and I'm glad she's gonna be okay. I'm sorry if you mistook that for more. But that's all, Daddy. That is truly all I have to give right now."

Katy stood up, her look of dejection almost matching Paul's. "Julie—"

"No, Katy. Your sister is allowed to speak the truth."

"*Her* truth. Julie, give him a break!"

Julie glared at her sister. How could she not get it? How could she just mix in with all this blended family bullshit?

*Why are you sleeping in their house then, loser?* It wasn't her mama's voice that time. Was it Ian? Was it just her? Look how far she had fallen. Even her internal monologue was unrecognizable.

"I don't want to hurt anyone, Daddy," Julie concluded, quietly. She hoped that was enough.

"We all hurt nonetheless, Jules."

They did. And that truth, coming with matter-of-fact somber-ness from him, stung her in a brand-new way. Why couldn't she just get on board? Why couldn't she just be happy for him? Why couldn't she just be nice to this woman who had just dropped off her favorite artisan crackers for no apparent reason?

Why couldn't she have been happy with Chad?

Why did she run away the moment her career hit a bump?

*What the hell was wrong with her?*

"Yes," she said to him, barely glancing before she had to look away. "We do. And I am sorry for it."

"Me too, Jules."

"Tell Jessie... please, just tell her... I am grateful... for the hospitality."

Paul cleared his throat and straightened his back. "I won't do that. You need to talk to her yourself."

"I..." She looked past him, picturing her mama there, standing straight and lean, poised and knowing, during so many niggling disagreements Paul and Julie had had through the years. Just like Katy, she would interject, sometimes with humor, sometimes with sarcasm, always with a sassy blend of wisdom. Sometimes she would get frustrated with both of them and snap something before storming away. Most of the time, she just let them argue because they'd work it out. They always did. But this time, Julie didn't see a way how.

If Leah were there, she'd be taking it all in, nodding, not changing her facial expression to smile in encouragement or narrow her eyes in admonishment. She would wait to take Julie's proverbial temperature, and then she would respond in the way she saw best.

Julie wanted her so much in that moment.

"It feels like you don't miss her," she said aloud, barely above a whisper.

Paul exhaled slowly. The room got so quiet that Julie wondered if Katy had left. She usually could not physically hold her tongue that long. But she was still there, on the couch, looking at a magazine page in her lap, her eyes glassy with tears.

"Of *course*, I miss her." Paul accentuated every word.

"But not enough." Julie regretted it the moment she said it.

"No. Not enough, Jules. Not enough to satisfy you, apparently. Not enough to be alone and miserable for the rest of what life I have left. Not enough. If you want to be miserable enough for all of us, I will try my hardest to let you. But it's *not* what your mama would have wanted. It's not. And it won't bring her back."

*Nothing will bring her back.*

*And I do want you to miss her more.*

"Daddy—" She didn't have anything else to say. They both knew it.

"I'll leave you alone," he said, not gently. She heard the hurt in his voice, and her only defense was to recall the callous on her heart that had been there her entire time in Arizona. She had to work more hours. She had to get out from under his disappointment and from under his happiness with Jessie. This would not do.

Katy was now gaping at her from the couch. "I can't believe you're going to end the conversation like that."

"You talk to me like you've always been Daddy's perfect angel or something. Just stop."

"I was a *teenager*, Julie."

"Well, you aren't now. So, unless you want to stand here and tell me what a great success you are and how you've been here for him through thick and thin while I've abandoned everyone and everything, then you can get out, too."

"I *was* there for him, when—"

"When I wasn't. And it was the least you can do."

"You're such a bitch."

Julie wasn't surprised that the venom didn't even phase her. "Just go, Katy. I'm done."

She stormed out but Julie heard every word she muttered. "Yeah, yeah. Run away again. You might as well not even be here."

♡

With Katy finally retreated to the stupid bunk beds, (Julie was not going to share her bed. If that twit was insistent on adolescent slumber parties when she had her own perfectly adequate place, she could sleep where the children did), Julie popped open her laptop and stared at another email she had gotten.

2ND REMINDER: STATE OF ARIZONA RN LICENSE RENEWAL.

She wasn't going back there, couldn't go back there. She thought of the things she'd left behind after more than a year. A really fun, dynamic church. A house full of curated, grown-up furniture. Gorgeous mountains and the memories of a few hikes and even a horseback ride at sunset. Not one friend. The first job at which she'd ever failed. Chad. Ian.

There hadn't been much of anything from Ian since the day after. The day she resigned the clinic, right after they'd told her there was protocol but that unfortunately, in their industry, *these things happened*, she couldn't even look at him before she left the room. That night, he'd tried to call. It was already after six, and she didn't answer the phone, didn't know when Chad would come walking in. A moment later, there'd been a text –

I know you're sitting there holding your phone. Answer please.

No inflection. No emojis. She couldn't tell what he might want to say to her. Ian was always terse, even in moments of passion. He'd given no indication during their discussion that he held anything but professional regard for her. And he was believable.

*I can't talk right now,* she'd answered.

*Don't leave. This is medicine.*

Medicine. Did he think that's all it amounted to for her? This was life and death. This was failure. This was her putting all her eggs in the wrong basket. It was humiliating.

*Why do you want me to stay?* She texted back. And to herself, before he even answered with the inevitable, she declared, *Leaving is the only option.*

The three dots lingered on her phone, long enough for a little hope to rise up. Maybe Ian would make it all go away. Maybe he would propose a magical solution she couldn't see. Maybe he would give up his practice, give up his life, and they would leave town and start over.

*You can't run away from this.* It was her mama's voice. *That's what you did coming out here. And it didn't work.*

His answer finally came.

*Julie... I have a small window. Why don't you meet me at the corner and we can talk for a few minutes at least. Okay?*

Sigh. A small window didn't sound like a rescue, but she was going to take it. Of course, she was. And he knew it.

*I'll see you there.*

She would leave before Chad got home, and with any small amount of luck, provided by Ian, she would know her next move by the time she got back.

And she did. And here she was.

# CHAPTER♡EIGHT

## *Paul*

JESSIE LIFTED HER HEAD FROM PAUL'S SHOULDER APPROXIMATELY THREE-AND-A-HALF SECONDS AFTER SHE'D RESTED IT THERE.

"I forgot to text Morgan back. Let me—"

"Jess. Watch the movie. Morgan will still be there in ninety minutes."

"I just..." She paused. Paul could feel the adrenaline coursing through her. She always did this. There was an inner circle of approximately thirty people and an innermost inner circle of around ten and the communication was constant and she never turned it off. He used to think she had boundary issues. Now he believed it was an addiction.

He didn't press. She didn't get up to fetch her phone. After a beat, she settled back in next to him.

Before the opening credits were over, she murmured, "I'm sorry I get so distracted."

He squeezed her, appreciating that she didn't notice how distracted he was. There was no way he was going to tell her about the confrontation with Julie. Instead, he said, "You never have to apologize to me for being who you are."

That escalated quickly, he thought, but if she thought so, she didn't let on. A moment later, her presence stilled (she stopped "vibrating," Katy would say), and her head resumed its welcome position, resting on him.

*Twelve Years Ago*

"Well. It's quiet again."

Leah had sat next to him on the couch, where Paul was not really watching a MASH marathon on TV Land. He cocked his head and pretended to listen, as much as one could hear silence from down the hall. "For now, I suppose," he conceded. "I'm sure more yelling will commence at any given moment."

"I don't think Julie is speaking to her," Leah said.

"I don't think *I* am speaking to her," he answered.

"Then there probably won't be yelling."

*Simple as that*, he thought. He preferred yelling to silence. He preferred conflict to acquiescence. He had just spent six exhausting days, and he didn't want to count how many hundreds of dollars flying to California (for the second time in four months) to retrieve their eighteen-year-old and drive her home, in *his* Mustang that she had taken off with and immensely devalued by practically living in it, and God knows what else. During his first attempt at bringing her home, he'd been accompanied by Randall Oakley, who got to witness Paul and Katy at their absolute worst. She was "modeling" for a very questionable women's clothing line, drinking away most of her wages, and had shaved off most of her hair.

Lack of money and opportunity and a surplus of fear and shame had changed her mind about coming back with him on the second try. Paul had driven thirty-six hours over the past three days, with Katy and her guitar case smushed into the backseat, and mostly in utter silence. Every time he attempted to engage her, they both ended up yelling until they were hoarse. She had cried and cursed. He just cursed. It was the first time in his eleven years of sobriety that he wanted a drink almost more than he could stand.

When they finally arrived home, Leah was standing in the driveway, arms crossed, hip slung, waiting stoically. Based on their phone calls along the way, and the emotional turmoil of the preceding months, Paul expected her to yell, too. But as soon as Katy emerged from the back seat, puffy-eyed and limping from the cramped quarters, Leah ran to her and held her.

It was a real prodigal daughter moment, including the part in which that guitar case fell open in the driveway and revealed *nothing*. Their child, who'd been provided everything, had not only stolen from them, but squandered every possession she'd brought with her, and all Leah had was a hug.

It had pissed Paul off beyond reason. He'd stormed into the house and took a long shower, fuming. Empathetic to her father's mood, Julie had picked up on his need to see admonition over forgiveness, and she scolded Katy until a huge argument ensued. Leah got involved in that, admonishing both of them, Paul, and herself throughout. They'd all had a hand in this, she said. Katy never should have left the way she did (*grand theft auto*, Paul wanted to interject). She should have come home with Paul three months before. Leah and Paul should have been more understanding of her choices before she ran away. And Julie should quit judging her for not being... like Julie.

Paul had stayed silent for most of it, until this moment.

"I could probably yell some more, Leah," he said, in an ironically quiet tone. "I'm not actually sure I've ever been this angry in my life. My *entire* life."

The declaration held weight with Leah. She was the only one who knew the details of Paul's upbringing, the physical abuse inflicted by an out-of-control father, the emotional neglect of a mother who wouldn't protect him or his brother. It had taken Paul years, which included a frightening period of alcoholism that nearly destroyed their marriage, to work through the residual anger and pain of it. He'd given his kids every good thing he had and every good thing he could muster. And Katy had spit it back in his face.

"She doesn't understand, Paul. She isn't like you. Lord, she isn't like either one of us. These kids do not have the life experience we had as emerging adults, save for Julie, and I wish she had less of it. You cannot expect her to see things like you do."

"I wish she could see anything, anything at all, like a somewhat reasonable, semi-compassionate human being."

"So do I, " Leah murmured. "But she is who she is right now. We just keep... trying to steer."

Paul leaned his head back against the couch, whatever he had left since returning home draining from him in a final, deep exhale. He closed his eyes.

"Maybe you should go to bed."

Leah's hand rested on his knee, caressing him. It was a rare moment of intimacy between them, and it almost jolted him to action.

She didn't touch him often, and usually not unless he touched her first. In fact, they seldom communicated as much as they had in that moment.

He let out another, smaller sigh.

"I know this has been hard on you," she continued.

"It's been hard for you, too."

"Yes, but..." She moved a little closer and leaned her head on his shoulder. "Paul. You're such a good daddy. Don't let this... derail... you..."

He put his arm around her, pulling her closer. "I'm not derailed. I promise. I am bloody exhausted, and I don't know what we're gonna do with her. But I'm fine."

"Fine. Just fine," Leah answered, and he could hear the smirk in her voice.

"Never been better," he declared, and with that, they both dissolved into laughter.

That had been nine years before Leah died, and he could count on one hand the number of times they had sat like that, close on the couch, leaning together, feeling similar feelings.

With Jessie –

(Unlike Jessie, he didn't even try not to compare his two marriages. It was inevitable, and he didn't feel one damn ounce of guilt about his humanity.)

– it was part of every day.

They made it to the second half of the movie, around the time the sad woman threw her hiking boot over the edge of the mountain, before Jessie, not looking away from the screen, asked him, "Do you think she'll ever eat dinner with us?"

"Reese Witherspoon?"

He suppressed a laugh, but just barely.

"Oh God, I wish," Jessie answered, not missing a beat. "But also... Julie."

Now Paul suppressed a sigh. The balance of peace in his home teetered on a fragile precipice of its own, and he believed the best way to protect it was to let Julie keep to herself and carry on like she wasn't *really* there, unless... well, unless she chose to make her presence known. Or felt.

If that happened, the peace would almost certainly suffer a crash landing more destructive than what befell Reese's hiking boots.

"Jess..."

He would choose his words carefully. She wore her heart so openly that it might as well have a target on it. It was a terrible foil for Julie's cool resignation.

"Paul, I know. We aren't going to hug and cry and learn and grow together." Surely, she was quoting another TV show. Where did she get these quips? "But maybe we can be slightly more than civil. She's your *daughter*."

"She is. And I..."

*She doesn't want to be a part of this. She won't give in. She feels like being nice to you would betray Leah. I know you won't rest until something changes. And I don't know if it will.*

Julie had confirmed all of this that very evening.

"You don't have to protect me."

Jessie had turned to face him. Her eyes blazed with passion, for the subject at hand, for their family, and for him. He reached out to touch her cheek.

"I know I don't have to. And I don't want to feel like I have to protect you from my daughter. But I know you both. And I wish you could just give it time for now. You haven't done anything wrong, but there is nothing you can do *right*, either. She just isn't there, yet."

Paul was also pretty sure that Julie had her own relationship woes going on that had nothing to do with her father's love life. Two weeks ago, he expected to hear any day that she and that Dr. Chad guy she was living with were engaged, and then all of a sudden, she was back and hadn't brought him up once.

Jessie put her hand on top of his, somehow embracing him without putting her arms around him. She was a magician at loving, and he smiled at her.

"I won't push. I promise," she said. "But maybe Sunday dinner? We could invite Danielle and Matt and the kids, and make something Julie really likes..."

"Okay, Jess."

But she wasn't done. "I know how it feels... to be a young woman and miss your mama... I'm just sad for... them."

Paul moved his hand to her lap, rubbing her thigh, feeling what she felt. He hated that his daughters had the particular sadness they did; he mourned for the moments Leah would miss and the grandchildren she'd never know. But unlike Jessie, he accepted sadness. He accepted that he couldn't fix it.

He brushed his wife's lips with his and said, "She likes homemade fried chicken, with mashed potatoes, no lumps, and white gravy. Green bean casserole. It's her favorite meal. You put deviled eggs with that, and she might call you *Mamacita* before you know it."

"That sounds strangely like your favorite meal," she answered, returning the kiss, rolling her eyes at him.

"What can I say?" Paul quipped, trying to convince himself as much as Jessie. "Like father, like daughter."

# CHAPTER♡NINE

## *Julie*

JULIE RETURNED FROM HER LATE MORNING RUN GRATE-FUL THAT JESSIE'S CAR WAS GONE. She hadn't actually seen her more than three or four times in total. But she was starting her new job the next day and would have less command of her schedule.

*You might have to start actually getting over yourself.*

She had to admit, there were a few things that made living there more than tolerable. One was the proximity to the beach. At walking pace, she was less than five minutes away. She often finished her runs there, took off her shoes, and walked in the water, trying to recapture the feeling she had as a kid, when she'd imagine that the waves were magically washing in answers to her wishes. Sometimes they granted her whatever American Girl doll or book she wanted or the featured Blizzard at Dairy Queen. When she got a little older, it was a perfect score on her Spanish test or a great, drama-free night at Homecoming or the perfect guy. *Why was that always a thing?* She didn't make wishes now. She just let the water make her feel cooler and calmer. Okay, and maybe she did wish some things. The waves would not bring her Mama back, or Ian to her, but maybe they would bring her peace.

She also loved the kitchen in Dad and Jessie's house. At first glance, everything looked so clean and rustic, all shades of white and gray. But there were all these eye-catching touches, hints of sparkles and pops of patterns that hinted at "beach" but didn't hit people over the head with it. She couldn't help thinking how much her mom would have loved the antique little red Tonka pickup with a toy surfboard strapped to the top, nestled on the bookshelf amongst a vast array of novels not arranged by color. Had it not been for the family pictures, the books and books and books, and one cinderblock wall that everyone had taken to writing on, for crying out loud, it looked really close to how Leah used to stage some of her vacation rentals.

Daddy was sitting at the little breakfast table, reading an obnoxiously thick book. She planted a kiss on top of his head before sitting across from him at the table. Wordlessly, he passed her his jar of sweet tea with a lemon wedge and a sprig of mint and got up to fetch another.

Suddenly, she was at home, and overwhelmed with gratefulness for him.

"How are you, Daddy?" she asked, feeling shy.

He took a sip from his own tea, peering at the condensation already collected on the oak table. "You really want to know?"

It took her aback. He was talking to her like an adult, being real. They had not communicated like that since *before.* And she wasn't sure she did want to know, but she definitely didn't want him to change his approach.

She nodded.

"It's been rough," he said. He didn't meet her eyes but stared out the window. She tried to ignore that he was looking older, a little more silver in his hair, more lines around his eyes and down his cheeks. She could tell he wasn't going to volunteer any more and decided she'd have to pry.

"I'm sorry," she said, carefully. "I know it's not the best time for me to be here. I promise it won't be for long."

He finally looked at her, a little bewildered. "What? No. It's fine. I just wish... It's fine. And maybe not a bad time for a nurse to be around..."

"Daddy, Jessie... I mean, she's okay, right? Katy said the cancer was all stage I, confined to her uterine lining, no further treatment? The radiation was mainly preventative? Is she having any side effects?"

His eyes widened. She'd just asked him more questions regarding Jessie than she had in two years.

"Yes. Yes. And not really. This is the last week of the radiation. She's, um, very much done with having to bother with it, and she's very tired, which she isn't used to. But she... we... have been really blessed. There's no reason to worry about any of it. It's gone."

Julie let that linger. They were a *we*. One of those couples. She'd known Jessie and Mr. Randall a long time; they were one of those couples, too. Mama and Daddy... were not.

Maybe some women just knew how to make that happen, how to establish a partnership, how to nuzzle in close. She certainly didn't know how to do that, but she couldn't deny her dad was different than before Jessie. She reached across the table to his hand.

"You look so tired today, Daddy. Are you positive everything is fine?"

He squeezed her fingers so hard, it hurt. "Yeah, Jules."

"You scared?"

She used to talk to him like this all the time, when she was teenager, and even right after Mama died. He didn't have a lot of friends; she liked being his friend. But they had lost it.

His tea addiction delayed his answer. For a moment, she thought maybe she hadn't earned his confidence back just yet. But once his jar was drained, he answered simply, "Yeah. Irrationally. Insomnia-inducing. Secretly... so don't tell anyone."

"I'm probably not going to go sit on the edge of the bed for a heart-to-heart," she said, nodding in the vague direction of the master bedroom. He smiled. "But... I bet she probably knows. She seems to... well, she seems to look after you pretty carefully, and Daddy, you have resting worry face right now..."

"It's getting better," he said, giving another squeeze. She couldn't remember the last time they'd held hands. "And I made her promise to pretend she doesn't notice."

Julie giggled. "That's dumb."

Paul shrugged. "It seems to be working."

"You're nuts," she said. "And Daddy, stage I uterine cancer is highly curable. *Curable*. That the radiation was optional, and she's done it... she's going to be fine. Try to relax."

"Why didn't I think of that? You getting more tea?"

"Of course." She rose from the table and returned with the pitcher. Then she fetched the Oreos from the pantry that she assumed would be there. It felt a little weird to be familiar here, but she, too, pretended, it was fine.

"You want to talk about how you actually are?" he asked.

"Not really," she said, pulling apart one lovely little chocolate sandwich and scraping off the creme with her teeth, to savor separately.

"Will Chad be coming to visit any time soon?"

"Doubt it," she answered, concentrating on wafer number one, feeling a bit squeamish. How much did he know about Chad?

"That's all you're going to say?"

"We broke up, Daddy."

"I figured, Jules." He popped an entire cookie into his mouth and waited her out. She sighed.

"I'm not ready to talk about it."

He nodded.

"I know you wish Katy and I were more settled."

He nodded again, with a smirk. No one really expected Katy to be settled, ever.

"Chad was fine. And Arizona was fine. But you... you of all people, maybe, should understand. I want more than fine."

The sigh that came was deeper.

"Can't really blame me, can you?" she added.

"Julie—"

"No. Daddy, it's okay." She pushed the cookies toward him, tempted to get out the milk and start dunking. "I know you and Mama were *fine*. And I accept that it worked for you, for a long time. I just... I just think I want something different."

For a flash, she saw a look in his eyes she had never wanted to see again. It was the one she found on him when she got to the hospital, the day Mama died.

That day, Julie was the last one to get to the hospital, to the conference room that had been opened up to allow all of the Jameson (*us*) and Oakley (*them*) families to process the news, ask and answer the questions, sign the forms. When she walked in, there was the same amount of chatter as there always was when their families were together (like a small mob, really). It was just quieter. She'd scanned the room and saw Daddy sitting in a chair, staring at the table in front of him. Danielle was standing behind him talking to Jessie's older son, Sam. Katy was sitting next to him, holding their baby niece Vivi, talking on the phone. Daddy's face was white. Julie knelt on the other side of him, grabbed for his hands and made him look at her. She cried. And then he did, too. But there was more than shock or sadness on his face. There was guilt and fear she hadn't seen since she was a kid.

And there in his new kitchen, she saw it again.

"Daddy. I know you took care of Mama. And I understand."

"I'm not sure I understand. How could you?" he asked, in a gravelly voice that was covering his emotions. She knew he'd had this talk with Katy, back when he and Jessie had broken up for a while and he was homeless, post-surgical, and basically a total wreck. But Julie had never given him a chance to have it with her. She supposed, even if she wasn't ready, she was (gulp) *needy*.

"Maybe I'm like you," she muttered.

"I hope not," he said, with a gentle push of the Oreos back toward her.

She took another, prepared to ask one question and then listen.

"Did you and Mama love each other?"

# CHAPTER♡TEN

## *Paul*

PAUL CURSED THE SUN, THE BEACH, THE HUMIDITY, AND HIS OWN ADDICTION AS HE SLOWLY JOGGED THROUGH THE SAUNA THAT WAS SURFSIDE BEACH IN WHAT PASSED FOR FALL IN SEPTEMBER. He hated running in the afternoon, but the morning had been busy, and he wanted to sweat out the unexpected – and unexpectedly grueling – conversation he'd had with Julie the day before. Instead, fifteen minutes in, he was stopping at the park and practically bathing in the water fountain. He could feel the sweat soaking into his earbuds, soaking into every part of him and dripping off onto the pavement. He was only a mile from home, but he might have to walk back.

*If she sees me, she'll know,* Paul thought. Jessie's last radiation treatment had been that morning. She insisted they go for a celebratory brunch on the way home, and by the time their food came, she was almost falling asleep in her "virgin mimosa." (God, how he loved her ridiculousness). She tried to recover, but he asked for to-go containers and actually put her to bed once they were home. The fatigue of radiation cramped her style much more than the surgery that removed her actual cancer, and he was thankful Julie had started her new job, knowing her absence would set Jessie at ease enough to sleep.

She should always be at peace in her own home. That she wasn't was his own failure.

As he turned around, his "Rediscover the Eagles" playlist was interrupted by a ring.

Crazy Ass Maggie. That was how Jessie's best friend had edited her own contact information in Paul's phone, when she came to be with Jessie after her surgery and made Paul promise to text her every morning and night until she gave him permission not to.

"What's up, Mags?" he answered with a smile.

"How's my girl, sweet man? Today was it, right?"

He nodded, and then remembered she couldn't see him. "She's done. Thank God. She's home sleeping. Thank God for that, too."

"That's a small miracle," Maggie agreed. "How is everything else going there? No one has fired the first shot yet?"

Paul sighed before he could catch himself. He actually quite liked Maggie, but he still wasn't used to the intimacy she shared with Jessie, and how it implied a level of intimacy with Paul. She seemed to know almost everything that went on in their daily lives and pulled no punches bringing things up.

Leah had three sisters, and Paul could not remember talking to any of them on the phone other than the day she died, as well as a few conversations afterwards that he would rather forget. They had their own language among them – much like Jessie and Maggie did – but Paul was not invited into it. There were the sisters, and then there were the husbands. They did not intersect in a meaningful way.

But as he had to try to explain to Julie, often, he and Leah didn't even intersect in a meaningful way...

"Jess and Julie are being respectful of each other," Paul said. "You should be impressed. I am." He hoped that was enough to end the conversation.

"Hrumph," was her reply. "That will do for now, but hopefully, we can get to a better status than that, my guy."

He found himself nodding again, but Maggie continued on as though she had seen him and knew he didn't really want to say anything else. She mentioned the next time she and her husband Don would be coming to visit from Greenville, she asked about Katy and Danielle, and then she made a kiss sound and said, "Hang in there, Paul. All my love to you and our girl."

And she hung up before he said another word. He smiled. If he'd ever had a sister, he supposed he would wish for one like Maggie. She filled in all the spaces and asked very little beyond Paul's much more mellow presence. They shared a genuine affection, and of course, they shared Jessie.

He walked through the front door just after three, and the house was uncharacteristically quiet, even for their post-cancer-diagnosis era. Though Jessie was always tired after her treatments, she usually fought through the fatigue until what she considered an acceptable bedtime. Once in a while, he convinced her to take a nap *with* him. It was the only way his stubborn, quirky wife could rest during the day and not worry about appearing weak.

But today was different. He wasn't sure if it was the finality of the last treatment or... well, FFS, it could be any number of things from the last year and a half or all of them combined. But when he crept upstairs to check on her, expecting a fake slumber or an all-out cleaning party to greet him, he found her in the deepest sleep he'd ever seen her experience.

He closed the door and decided he would do something special for her. Smiling to himself, he texted Maggie first, and then Julie to check her schedule, and then Danielle, and marveling at how overwrought with females his life was – still and again – he put the thought of a puppy back on his radar and headed out to the store.

Shortly before 8:00 p.m., Julie walked into the kitchen. Paul had his back to her as he worked at the kitchen sink.

"Oh Daddy..." she sighed.

"What? Oh, hey Jules."

"I'm sorry if I interrupted something." She didn't have to walk through the kitchen to get to the guest suite. It felt intrusive to do it, but rude not to, and she constantly overanalyzed it. "I'm just tired, and dinner at Danielle's was..."

"Not relaxing at the end of a workday?" he said with a knowing smirk.

She smiled back. "Nice, but definitely not relaxing."

"It's fine," he said, turning back to a stack of food containers. "I'm just cleaning up."

There was a requisite awkward pause. Julie didn't know that Paul had asked Danielle to occupy her for dinnertime, but it wasn't that hard to guess.

"Was your dinner okay? Did you *cook*?" She tried to sound light and interested and found that she wasn't faking interest. It

actually intrigued her that her dad could and would cook anythi
not out of a can.

Paul shrugged, turning to give her attention. "I did. Nothi
fancy. Um... Maggie talked me through a roast chicken. I didi
destroy it, but Jessie... was not up to a big dinner tonight. I pro
ably should have known, but she's been pretty status quo aft
most of her treatments, so I just took a shot."

"Oh, Daddy."

"Stop saying that," he teased.

"It was so much work, though. Did you eat? Was it good?" SI
caught a glimpse at the table, now cleared except for two accoutr
ments: three bouquets of wildflowers, arranged in a row in mate
ing Mason jars, and a glass display with a small, chocolate-ic
cake in the middle. It screamed Jessie, but the atmosphere and h
mood guaranteed that it was Paul's doing, not Jessie's.

He answered with another shrug. "Not bad for a first timer. Ju
not–"

Not what he expected. Not what he wanted. I get it, Daddy
so do.

"It's probably still warm, if you're still hungry?"

"Oh my gosh, no. Thank you. We had English muffin pizz
and sugar cookies... with icing! I am stuffed," she giggled. "B
maybe I will take some for lunch tomorrow if there's enough?"

"Of course," he said, opening the refrigerator to store the le
overs. "I guess it was a good first day if you're going back again'

She sighed, deeply, and looked longingly for a moment at t
cake.

"Ooh," he continued. "That could mean a lot of things."

She described it with what seemed to be her new favorite wor
"It was fine."

♡

In fact, it had been a pleasant day. She walked into the store ten minutes before it opened and was greeted by a ball of energy packaged in a sub-five-foot frame, slender as, well, a prototypical marathoner, complete with compression shorts, a "Run This Way" tank top, neon yellow shoes, several runner-y tattoos, and a bobbing ponytail accentuated by a headband that read "I Run for Donuts." Her energy crackled about as high as Katy's usually did. Julie braced herself.

"I'm Darcy! I'm so happy you're here!" For a second, Julie thought the little sprite was going to hug her, but she instead offered a surprisingly hearty handshake, which is when Julie noticed her absolutely sinewy forearms. Impressive.

Within the first fifteen minutes, Julie learned that Darcy was, in fact, a distance runner and an *ultra*marathoner, who loved donuts, and iced coffee, and boot camp-style workouts, hence her ripped-ness. She was twenty-four, almost finished with her personal training certification, and was, of course, dating a gym owner, with whom she'd moved from Columbus, so he could start his business.

Julie felt her cynicism dangerously wavering. This woman was impressive and kind of precious.

At mid-morning, Darcy told her, the store would not be terribly busy, although foot traffic ("LOLz! Pun intended!") was picking up. So, Darcy quizzed Julie on her running history (super-casual in comparison to hers) and then started teaching her The Shoes.

Julie had graduated Magna Cum Laude and been a Sigma nurse ever since. She had been focusing on the same information for years, and even though the inner workings of the female reproductive system and labor and delivery were more complex than fitting someone for the perfect pair of kicks, her head was spinning by lunchtime, which was when Nick-Robin walked in.

Julie paused with a forkful of apple pecan salad halfway to her mouth. Darcy had sent her to have lunch at the tiny bistro table by the back door and eating in front of her new boss felt like it put her at a severe disadvantage.

Thankfully, Pote broke through the potential awkwardness, jumping up to put his head right on the table next to Julie's bowl.

"Well, 'ello there, mate!" she exclaimed in a horrible, fake-pirate accent.

Pote approved, giving her wrist a lick before getting down.

"Hey there," came Robin's (Nick's?) voice, but she barely saw him as he breezed past her toward the storage room, where he kept a makeshift office space.

Julie gave a silent thanks that she was not Katy and didn't need the room to be at a full swing conversation at all times. She finished her salad inside five minutes while scrolling Instagram, deciding to unfollow her church and a few favorite restaurants in Arizona.

And then she stared at the photo that topped her screen after it reloaded. It was Ian and his wife, backdropped by a breathtaking Arizona sunset, complete with a purple and orange painted sky and the silhouette of towering cactus plants. Ian was holding a sparkler and kissing her cheek... Fawn; her name was Fawn. And Fawn had two hands clasped over her tiny belly and a huge smile on her face. The caption read, "Our little firecracker, coming in July."

*Take a breath. Fix your face. This isn't your story.* She welcomed her mama's voice and obeyed. Work. Focus on learning the names and prices and biomechanical effects of all these shoes. Move forward. And with Ian's beaming face stuck firmly in her head, she walked back to the showroom to embrace her so-called new career.

"Well, hello, Miss Julie. Welcome aboard!"

Julie took in the woman whom she'd assumed was a customer. She was wearing what appeared to be Alice in Wonderland-print running tights with a tank and shoes that were the exact same shade of royal blue. She had long and wavy gray hair which cascaded down to the small of her back, tamed only with a pair of matching blue sunglasses atop her head.

And her eyes were twinkly.

"I'm Hazel," she said. "I don't work here, but I should."

Julie blinked, not sure what to say.

"Hazel is one of our regulars," Darcy explained. "And she's a store ambassador, and she probably knows more about shoes and running than even Robin does." Julie could hear a snicker from the back. "So she's around a lot, and she volunteered to help train you!"

"Well, awesome. It's nice to meet you. I'm Julie."

Of course, Hazel had already said her name, but the conflicting energy in the room had thrown her, Darcy and Hazel being light as feathers and twinkly as stars; Nick-Robin and Julie being more serious and much, much more awkward.

If Hazel noticed, she didn't show it, and promptly launched Julie into full play-acting, telling her a backstory that may or may not have been fictitious about her sub-four-hour marathons, a years-old metatarsal fusion, a nagging lower back problem, and her abhorrence for the color purple and two of the brands they sold. Darcy was giggling through most of it; Julie's head was spinning.

Were they salespeople or therapists? Should she expect this from every customer?

Around the time Hazel was being Customer #3 (a warehouse employee with low arches who "only runs if something is chasing her, hahahahahaha"), Nick-Robin came out with a bundle of papers and a rueful smile.

"How's it going so far?"

"I thought obstetrics was complicated. I had no idea."

As soon as she said it, she thought she probably sounded like a pompous ass, but again, if anyone noticed, they didn't let on. Darcy and Hazel had opened a shipping box and were oohing and aaahing over something called a CloudMonster (*A shoe? A horror novel?*), but Nick-Robin was looking at Julie with the same small, knowing smirk on his face.

"You seem smart enough. You'll probably get the hang of it."

Julie felt her face redden. Damnit. She used to be so confident.

They stood at the counter and went over employee things, pay schedule and W-2 and discounts. When the next customer came in, he asked Julie to shadow him as he went through introduction, analysis, fitting, and after about twenty minutes and four pairs of shoes, a sale.

She watched in slight amazement as Nick-Robin shook hands with the white-haired lady using a cane he'd been waiting on and walked her to the door, then opened and held it for her.

This went on repeat three more times before her first shift was over. By the time she was done, she knew the names of eight brands of shoes and, not any less important, what to call her new boss.

♡

"Well, I feel less like a dunce for calling him Nick all this time," Paul said. They'd continued their conversation on the porch, a full moon providing extra light and a very welcome autumn breeze blowing. "What a strange little game for him to play. And it sounds like you'll meet a lot of colorful people," he added. "And you like it?"

What a loaded question. "I think I do," Julie finally said.

"You're afraid to like it. Because it feels like such a step down from what you were doing, and what you thought you'd be doing."

"Daddy—"

"Sorry."

They both shrugged. "You always know what I'm thinking," Julie said, "But maybe you can just hide it for a while because I don't even know."

"Jules." Paul heard his own tone change into the proverbial Dad Voice, which typically lowered the chances tenfold that his next words would be accepted by his daughter. He went with it anyway, because things with Julie had already gotten worse than he ever dreamed possible, and she'd still returned home. Well, she'd returned to him.

"What happened out there?" he asked softly. "You went to Arizona like a launched rocket. Every phone call, you were a ball of fire, school, the center, the church, first David, then Chad. You had it all under control. Everything was great. What happened?"

There was no way she was going to tell him. As well as he knew her, why didn't he know that?

"I happened," she answered, blinking away the tears. "What I always do. Nothing is ever good enough. No one is ever good enough. No achievement is ever good enough. I am never good enough. So, my relationships failed, and to top it off, my job choice was a failure, too. I'm sure you will know all about it at some point, but today is not that day."

Paul smiled at the age-old *Return of the King* reference. Julie was the only one of his girls who would ever watch it with him. "Today, we fight?" he answered wryly, raising his eyebrows.

"I don't want to fight with you again."

"I don't want to fight with you. Why would we be fighting now?"

She sighed loudly. "Daddy..."

"I know." Now he exhaled all the false hope he'd been holding on to. "You're not ready."

"It's not about being ready. I'm not waiting until I am ready. I am telling you, I don't–*I can't* –accept it. It's not about Jessie. And it's not even about you. I just can't accept someone, anyone, taking Mama's place. I want you to be happy, but I just can't be a part of it like there's nothing wrong."

Paul gaped at her. Every time he thought there was some progress, she stopped making any kind of sense to him. "How can you reconcile that? How can you say you want me to be happy and then reject my... my *life*, Julie? It doesn't work that way!"

"What did you think would happen, Daddy? That I would move in, sulk for a few days, and then we would start cooking dinner together? I thought you knew me."

"I thought you..." He couldn't finish.

She reached across to his chair, next to hers on the idyllic front porch. She took his hand, and he let her, but he didn't squeeze back. "Right. Don't finish that. Because I *do* love you."

Her words hung in the air for an uncomfortably long moment.
*He doesn't believe me.*
Paul let go and stood.

"I know that's what you think, Jules. But those are words. And relationships... real, adult, meaningful relationships, don't exist on nostalgia and warm feelings. There has to be work. And I know my getting married again is not easy for you. It's actually not even easy for me all the time, but real, adult, meaningful relationships, and building a life when it's fallen apart, is worth the work. It's worth some sacrifice. And as your dad, I hate that you are hurting, but you're being selfish, and I'm not going to tell you that's okay. You're refusing to do *this* work with me, and so you're not going to get the meaningful relationship. I can't compartmentalize my life like that, even if I am a guy."

Julie watched him walk away. Her first instinct was to let herself fall apart, but she refused. Not here. Not on *their* porch, in *their* chairs, at *their* house. She steeled herself instead. How could he talk to her like she didn't work hard, for herself, for her family? Who was there when he was depressed and despondent over his mother dying? When Katy ran away? *When Mama died?*

She would not be manipulated into accepting things that she didn't agree with. There was a line, and that was it.

"Sorry, Daddy," she murmured. And then she did what she'd come outside intending to do. She took off running.

# CHAPTER♡ELEVEN

## *Jessie*

"Sleepy head," a voice called. "I have elixir of the gods in my hands at this very moment."

How long had I been in bed? I vaguely recalled going to the bathroom a few times, but it was closer to sleepwalking. I surely hadn't slept this long in my life… except maybe when I was a teenager, but that wasn't really this same life anyway.

"What time is it? Mmmm… what day is it?" I asked.

"The radiation finale was just over twenty-four hours ago," Paul said softly.

My eyelids felt like lead and my head felt heavier, but I could smell the promise he'd made and almost swooned. Sitting up, only barely peering at him, I reached for the mug, pausing in the pass to caress his thumb.

"Hmmm. Have I ever told you how much I love that?"

I was having my own love affair with my coffee, but after my second swallow, I answered, "What?"

"How you always touch me," he said.

Shockingly void of reluctance, I set my mug at the bedside table and held my arms out to him. Had we been on a Netflix show, the camera would have cut away until we were seamlessly holding each other. In real life, there was scooting and grunting, finagling and finally giggling, until he was next to me in the bed, fully clothed and fully resting on my chest, for a change. He'd been holding me for the last few months. I wanted a turn.

"I love touching you," I said.

I felt his smile break out right against my chest. "But this can't be too pleasant for you. I need a shower…"

"It's fine, Jess."

In our new world order, "fine" had many meanings. In fact, at my version of a bachelorette party, which was actually just a really bougee dinner with all my girls and closest girlfriends, Morgan had given me a shirt that reads, "It's fine. I'm fine. Everything is fine." I wore it the day of the wedding until it was time to change. I wore it before and after my surgery. I'd probably wear it again after I showered. And I really hoped that his "fine" was a real, permeating *fine*.

"Have I missed anything?" I said, lightly.

He raised his head a bit and laughed. "Well, Maggie helped me cook a nice dinner for you."

"Maggie was *here*?!" I must have been in a coma to miss that.

"No, no. You'd have definitely known that!" Now I giggled. "Over Facetime."

He could not possibly know how sweet that sounded, how venturing that far out of his comfort zone for me made me feel better than anything had since that stupid diagnosis. "That's… amazing." I tried to keep too much emotion out of my voice. "I'm so sorry I missed it."

"Who could have predicted you actually resting?"

"Haha." But he was right. "What did you make?"

He told me about a roast chicken and the leftovers downstairs. I had woken up feeling a little queasy, and now I decided it was low blood sugar and I needed chicken, now.

"I can bring it to you," he insisted.

"Please let me get up," I insisted back. "I'll whore-bath real quick and be right down."

He shook his head at my tasteless, though oft-used expression, and nodded. "I'll get it ready."

"Meet you on the patio," I said cheerfully and watched that lovely man who'd cooked for me head downstairs to wait on me some more.

After one look at myself in the mirror, I decided I might as well take a quick shower, and before my hair was even wet, Paul was setting a protein shake on the counter. "Take your time," he called as he headed out.

Was it normal for women my age to feel butterflies over their lovers? *He's your husband,* I told myself. Honestly, neither term felt appropriate to me. Taking a lover was scandalous. Assigning "husband" to someone who wasn't Randall was alien.

*But here we are.* Here I am. Widowed. Remarried. In a new house. Down one uterus and some cancer cells. And totally, completely, ridiculously in love to the point of butterflies with Paul.

They still swirled as I dried off and heard the sustained buzz of a phone call. Either Sam or Maggie was late for the daily check-in. Sam usually didn't call on Saturdays. But Maggie –

"Mags!" I expected to sound as cheery as I felt, but my voice came out raspy and a little weak.

"Finally!"

"Good Lord, do you have a camera on me or something? I woke up like ten minutes ago."

"My best bro Pablo said you were emerging. How do you feel?"

I hoped she could hear the eyeroll in my voice. "I don't know yet. Other than groggy... a little lightheaded... slightly ravenous but sort of afraid to eat."

Authoritatively, Maggie said, "We should only be afraid to eat when we have a formal occasion requiring Spanx."

"Or when radiation causes us to crap seventeen times a day..."

"Ah." My sister was unphased, as usual. "There is that, I suppose. So, make sure whatever you eat is worth it."

"Paul cooked *dinner* last night!" I sounded like a schoolgirl, forgetting that Maggie had helped him with said dinner.

Her voice lost its constant amusement for a moment. "Yes. Sweetest little thing, that Paul. Look at my girl, striking gold twice in a lifetime."

I almost got caught up in the moment and said, "So did you," but it really wasn't true. She had a wonderful second husband, many years after her fairly awful first. We'd all recently made a tentative peace with her first husband, who always happened to be my only sibling, who'd fathered her daughters, who wrote everyone off for most of two decades and then came back last Christmas and told us all he was gay.

Tentative peace was hardly "gold."

"I just hope we can start our actual marriage now," I said, mostly to myself. "More of the fun stuff. Less of him taking care of me."

"I think it's been a wonderful start, actually. Save for the big C, of course. It took you right out of your comfort zone and made you learn to lean on him. And it opened him up to intimacy in a way he never had in his first marriage." Quintessential Maggie had said something only she could get away with saying and made me believe it, because she was her.

"Okay, yes. It's been fine for now, but I'm the one who roasts the chickens around here, you got me? Now let me go so I can finally taste it!" I was pulling up some jean shorts and contemplating whether I should put on some CC cream real quick.

"Jessie." Her voice got serious. I stood still to listen.

"It was cancer. And it's gone now. We believe that. We know that. We trust God and those doctors healed you completely. But calm the hell down, okay? You aren't going to take an extended post-radiation nap and be back to fighting form this afternoon, okay? *Okay?*"

I took a long sip from my green shake and nodded as though she could see me. My stomach felt more settled, but I had to admit to myself that just showering had made me tired again, and I hated thinking about how dry everything was below my belly button.

"At sixty years old, I have the chance for newlywed sex again, and I'm missing it. Hard to be calm."

"Stay newlyweds longer then, Jess," she said. "He ain't going anywhere."

I stifled a sigh. We both knew how quickly that platitude could prove false. I looked in the mirror, checking out how much my new-ish bra picked my breasts beneath my black tank top, but my face was pale, my hair dry and disheveled, and overall, I was not how I wanted to appear for a late brunch with Paul, that he had cooked. I wanted the butterflies, the magic, to show in my appearance.

"Go eat," she said. "And even if it tastes like monkey balls, or even if you're running to the john two minutes later, tell that sweet man what a good job he did."

"Of course, I will. Love you."

We hung up, and I took the requisite few minutes to spruce up a bit more until I heard Paul calling for me. I downed the shake and then my coffee and looked back into the mirror. I couldn't hide *recovering cancer patient.* I couldn't hide *no longer thirty-five.* But hopefully, I could hide *scared to death one of us is going to die before we get the chance to live.*

# CHAPTER ♡ TWELVE

## *Julie*

*ON TV, THEY ALWAYS SKIP PAST THIS PART,* JULIE THOUGHT TO HERSELF. Some brilliant, quirky, size zero heroine with an inexplicably perfect wardrobe she bought at Goodwill for eleven dollars embarks on a new career and instantly takes command of it: improves the running of the business with unconventional ideas, revitalizes the community with her charm and grit, and makes lifelong best friends and probably marries the onery owner or mayor or someone.

*That is not my story. Not this time.* No, Julie had done this before. Her natural leadership qualities – or bossiness, Katy would say – always escorted her to the top of the pecking order wherever she went. At least, that's what she thought. After a few months in the medical field, she learned quickly that the hardest worker, even the smartest worker, wasn't always the one to get promoted. No. It was often the one most willing to look where she was told to look, look away when something she didn't agree with was being swept beneath the rug, kiss the correct ass at the appropriate time. She'd excelled at it, until she got to Arizona, and that system failed her.

*You failed yourself,* Leah's voice told her.

"Thanks for the pep talk," she said aloud, as she parked in the back of the strip mall and gathered the I Work at the Running Store Essentials Starter Pack: her coffee, her obnoxiously large water bottle, her protein shake, a change of clothes and shoes (it was Running Club night), and her laptop, in case she got to actually accomplish something on her lunch break besides resentfully eating Dad and Jessie's leftovers and scrolling crap that made her sad and anxious on Instagram.

"Good morning, Julep!" Julie couldn't help smiling. Julie's first week had gone so well, with Darcy or Robin covering the bulk of the customers while Hazel trained her, that Robin had decided to hire Hazel as well. She was the official store opener five days a week, coming in for the first few hours, so Darcy would get in her long runs and Robin could, well, do whatever he did. Julie didn't want to know.

"Hey, Hazel! Be right there." She organized all her stuff into the makeshift spaces in the back of the store, lockers in the bathroom for gear, hooks to hang a few bags, and a dorm sized refrigerator to stuff all their healthy *fuel.* Julie rolled her eyes as she tried to make room for her stir fry and yogurt containers. Robin probably had a fridge this size in his house. All he ever seemed to eat were the jellybeans they sold, disguised as magic carbs for long runs, and bagel sandwiches from next door.

"Sister girl, I think we need to get the rest of this inventory in from yesterday. Robin is meeting some brand reps here today, and we don't want it looking like we sat around and drank all afternoon."

The truth was, the day before had been mind-numbingly slow, and Hazel came back after she clocked out with two bottles of champagne and a tiny, individual sized carton of orange juice... the kind you order at Dunkin Donuts. Robin had already left for the day and Darcy was off, and the two of them were one bottle down when UPS delivered seven big boxes of shoes.

Julie stacked everything neatly and kept her patience with Hazel's septuagenarian method for putting inventory into the POS system (every...shoe...took...five...minutes...!) for approximately half a box worth before she called out, in exaggerated brightness, "HAZEL! Why don't you pour another round and let me practice this?"

Hazel looked relieved. Within a half hour, there'd been no more foot traffic, all but one box was scanned and put away, and Hazel was cackling her way through more stories, from marathon hijinks ("Howie had arranged a big celebration at the house afterwards, and I was so chaffed and knackered, I put my bathing suit on and greeted them all from the bathtub!") to the decidedly not-funny but funny catastrophes of her last few years ("Then she told me she was gay, like she was dying of liver cancer. I mean, once your husband has a stroke and you get a hit by a car in the same month, what's the big deal if your granddaughter likes kissing girls?").

Julie could barely see the tablet screen through her tears of laughter. A few people came in, and the afternoon passed by in a blur of sweet drinks in plastic cups, customers leaving with colorful boxes, and Hazel's constant running commentary on all of it. She talked more than Katy, and Julie adored her. She had never in her life had a drink on a job or laughed even half that hard.

So, she picked up where she left off, with nine more pairs to follow and a little bit of dread that it wouldn't be just her and Hazel today. She still felt incredibly awkward around Robin, and if he noticed, he did absolutely nothing to help matters.

At noon, right as Hazel was leaving, an impossibly skinny man-child with a beard, a bun, and neon green shoes contrasting his black skinny jeans and black hoodie (it was still eighty million degrees outside) walked into the store with a rolling case and a grin. He introduced himself as Gus, and Julie shook his hand before she fetched Robin. She was sure he heard Gus arrive; it wasn't like the store was so big he could miss anything. Maybe he liked the formality of having an underling announce his visitors. Whatever. Julie hung out until Darcy was done with her customer and then went to heat up her lunch.

Instead of sitting at the table, instead of pretending to research opportunities on her laptop, she took her Pyrex, her water, and her phone outside the back door and sat on the curb. The sun was on full blast, but there was an actual breeze and the rays felt good on her bare legs. She had to admit, working in athletic shorts and tanks every day was fantastic, once she got over the feeling of being in her jammies on the job.

She pushed play on *The Popcast* and, in spite of herself, opened Instagram. Jenna Bush Hagar had recommended a new book. Dolly Parton had posted another decades-old picture of her husband. Her former co-worker Laura made a post about Infant Loss Awareness month. *Unfollow*. In total juxtaposition, Danielle posted her weekly bump update. Julie smiled at the picture of the sweet red pepper her sister had chosen and wished she knew the gender of the baby, although she thought it would be fun for everyone to be surprised.

And then, there was Ian, again. He didn't usually post so many pictures of himself, but this time, it was a tribute post to his mother. It was her birthday, and Ian was holding a mint green t-shirt in front of her that said, "World's Best Granny." His mother did not look like a Granny. In fact, she reminded Julie a bit of Leah: all polish, from her smooth, platinum, shoulder-length hair to her Lilly Pulitzer dress and espadrilles. Obviously, the "Granny" reference was a joke; both mother and son had their heads thrown back in rapturous laughter. Julie looked at the comments. There it was. Alice Bramer: "Thank you for making me the happiest expectant ***Gigi*** in the whole world. I love you, son!" And right beneath it, there was Fawn again. *Fawn.* "We can't wait for you to love and spoil our little deer."

Why did she do this to herself? Probably because she had the same mental illness as most single, introverted people her age had. She thought she had beaten it. She *had* a life. She *had* a blossoming career. She *had* prospects. Except now, she didn't. Now, she was living at her dad's house like a stranger, had no friends, stalking her ex-not-even-boyfriend on the socials.

*I have become what I used to call Katy. I am ridiculous.*

"Who's the May-December?"

Julie felt like she'd jumped four feet in the air. Her bowl went flying off her lap, thankfully not shattering, and her phone landed face-down on the asphalt, absolutely shattering.

"Shit!"

She stood up, hastily wiping the sauce splatters from her legs and angrily picking up the broken phone.

There were a million curses coursing through her, but she managed to remember the rumpled and definitely, maddeningly amused presence in front of her was, somehow, her boss.

"Oh shit, it's busted," he said.

"You think? Why did you–? Never mind. I'm the one that was jumpy. I didn't hear the door open." It was totally his stupid fault, but she hoped her tone or her face would not betray her.

"Here. Let me see it." Robin bent down and flipped her phone over. Tiny pieces of expensive glass fell on the ground. "Shit," he said again.

"I'll say." She definitely didn't have funds to replace a phone that wasn't even paid for yet.

"I didn't think you'd react like that." His voice almost sounded serious.

"I was just... lost in thought." She was fixated on the phone in his hand. The picture was still showing.

Like he was reading Julie's mind, Robin looked down at it, studying it more closely. "I thought they were a couple at first," he said. "You know this guy?"

What a question. "Yes. I mean, I did."

"Is this the ex in Arizona?"

She tilted her head at him. "How do you know there's an ex in Arizona?"

"There's always an ex in Arizona," he said wryly. "And Hazel, just so you know, talks a lot. Like a *lot*. No filter."

Julie sighed. She didn't like Robin. She was pissed about the phone. But he was looking at her with interest, and he was the only person around her age that she even knew anymore, besides her sisters. Well, and her *stepsisters*, whom she'd managed to ignore completely.

"He's not the ex. He's just..."

Robin raised his eyebrows. "A person of interest?"

"Yeah. I suppose."

He looked back down at the picture. "What kind of putz poses with his mama on Tiktok?"

She couldn't help but giggle. "It's Instagram."

"Okay. What kind of putz poses on anything like this with his mama?" He handed her phone to her. "What time do you get off today?"

She shook her head. He really was kind of a space cadet for a boss and proprietor. But maybe, ugh, maybe it was a little refreshing. "Four," she answered.

"I'll call the phone repair place in Market Common. Stop there after work and they'll fix you up. On me."

Inside, she exhaled in relief, but outside she said, "You don't have to do that. It wasn't your—"

He held up his hand. "Not up for debate. Unless you want to look at that putz all day through all these cracks and shards. Personally, I recommend you stop looking altogether. He looks happier than you do. Work on that instead."

With that, he kept walking through the back lot to his, for crying out loud, white El Camino with black racer stripes down the hood. Everything about him was weird or ironic, but Julie found herself less irritated by him just then.

"Nope. No. NO!" She said it out loud and headed back inside to tell Hazel about her phone screen, the glass and the picture.

*He looks happier than you do. Work on that instead.*

As much as Julie didn't want to accept anything but her paycheck from Robin, his words were replaying on a loop in her head, making her feel restless to the point of queasy. The phone repair shop was roughly a mile and a half away from the running store, so Julie had literally run there after work, engaging in an old mind game her mom had taught her... what is fact versus what is truth, because what she didn't need now was some awkward stranger telling her *her* truth.

The fact was, she had let herself fall for Ian knowing it was destructive and fruitless. The truth was, she hadn't cared. The fact was, she had gotten herself so distracted that she let everything fall apart, torn her own life apart. The truth was, she still would trade where she was now to be where she was just a few weeks ago, with a promising job and an intense affair and the veneer of happiness. The fact was, she had the resources and support to get her head on straight and fix her life. The truth was, she didn't want anyone's help, Dad's or Robin's or certainly not Jessie's.

She was sick of the dialogue and sick of herself.

After dropping off her phone, she darted over to the Common Grounds a few blocks away to meet Danielle for a last-minute iced coffee. She fixed her face, assuming the position of *fine*.

"It's nice you got yourself an afternoon away," Julie said, kissing Danielle's cheek and sitting across from her at one of the spray-painted bistro tables outside.

"It took me ten minutes to disengage Vivi from my legs," she said exhaustedly. "But here I am! Sucks about your phone." Her older sister sipped from a green tea frappe and leaned back in her seat, one hand absentmindedly on her blooming belly.

"Yikes. Who's watching them today?" Julie asked.

"Oh, Jessie came over..."

Ensue awkward pause, which Julie filed under Things She Was Sick Of. She ignored it.

"What else are you going to do with your free time?"

Moment over, Danielle launched into a list of things that sounded anything but free. She went to the children's clothing consignment to find Christian a wacky shirt, a book character shirt, and a "twin" shirt for Spirit Week at school; she went to the carwash and ordered groceries real quick while going through the automatic; she stopped at Dollar Tree to stock up on wrapping paper and a few Halloween decorations; and here she was, before she'd pick up the grocery order and go home to make dinner.

"That doesn't sound like much fun," Julie said. "I mean, except for a date with your favorite sister, of course."

"Right? I'm not used to you having any free time either, much less it syncing up with mine."

She meant it nice, of course, but Julie felt the sting of failure nonetheless. She took a sip from her grande, iced, mocha latte with cinnamon, no whip. Then she took another.

Danielle watched her a bit too carefully before she asked, "So. You like this new job? I know Daddy really likes that store. And the owner seemed... nice..."

Julie coughed. "When were you there?"

"Beg your pardon! I run sometimes, too. Anyway, we stopped there together... Christmas Eve, when he and Katy and I had our... outing."

"Ah. The outing." Why did every mention of Dad have to be so awkward?

Julie remembered all too well. Her dad and sisters had started some sort of weird, new-tradition date the day before Christmas Eve, going for a run together and then calling her from their dinner at the crepe restaurant. She didn't know what had been more bewildering: her family running together when Mama wasn't making them do some damned Turkey Trot, her dad eating crepes, or the forced merriment and awkward formality of their Facetime call with Julie afterward. Julie remembered ending that call and then, with Chad working, crying to Ian over text most of the night.

"I don't know if I would go so far as to describe him as nice. He's...not mean, I suppose. He's actually pretty strange."

"Strange? Like how?"

Julie told Danielle about all the names he called Pote, and the names he had for himself. Everything Julie found off-putting, Danielle seemed to find funny.

"Don't try too hard to figure him out," she said. "I mean, this job is just killing time for you, right?"

Was it? She had brought her laptop with her to work every day, had it flipped up on the table every night, with the sole intention of getting some telehealth work, in which she would get paid to practice her profession and likely would not have the chance to kill anyone directly. But she still hadn't applied for anything.

"Julie?"

"Sorry! I'm sorry. Just lost in thought."

Now Danielle was studying her face. *Damnit.*

"Are you okay? Really? You haven't talked about Arizona once since you got back. I still don't know why you're here when you seemed to love it so much. And you don't get lost in thought. So, what is it? And please don't tell me you're people'd out. I hate that stupid, millennial copout so much."

"You're a millennial," Julie muttered.

"Yes. But I have a threshold for stress that's actually higher than an inchworm's head. And frankly, so do you. So, what has you so rattled? You can always talk to me! You know that."

"Of course, I do," Julie said. "I just... things just didn't turn out how I planned there, and I didn't see a way to fix them and stay there. So here I am. For now..."

That seemed to appease Danielle for the moment. They sipped in silence, watching the dog-walkers and shoppers and even a few tourists on Segways passing on the sidewalk. October was always Julie's favorite month, Leah's, too. They called it "Locals' Summer," when the weather was warm but not a blazing sauna, when it was less crowded at the beaches and restaurants, when the leaves didn't change so much as the atmosphere. Things got calmer and slower as the world settled in for the Holidays.

"What are the kids going to be for Halloween?"

Danielle shifted again, swiped at her phone screen, and handed it to Julie with an expectant smirk.

"What the hell is that?"

"It's Zombie Pigman. From Minecraft. Or Roblox? I don't know. It's awful, but that's what your nephew wants to be for Halloween. But we have like four weeks. He'll change his mind seventeen times before we finalize, and then he'll probably have one for the parade at school, one for the church trunk-r-treat, one for Chick-fil-A family fun night, one for actual Halloween..."

"No wonder parenthood is exhausting!"

"Mmmm. At least the grandparents help with some of that. Matt's mom is taking him shopping this weekend. And Dad and Jessie are—"

Now Julie shifted, bracing herself, and also mad at herself for needing to brace.

"What, Danielle? Dad and Jessie are what?"

"Well, they're kind of hosting Halloween. I guess their whole street does some sort of themed thing with jack-o-lanterns in their yards and hang out in the driveways to give out candy. So, they're going to have 'walking tacos' for dinner and after we go in our neighborhood, we'll head over there. Sam and Abby's kids, too."

Julie looked away.

"What? Don't tell me that bothers you? You're going to be there to see the kids, right?"

She took a pause. *Danielle is pregnant and harried and she misses Mama, too.* Julie knew it was delicate. She didn't want to explode on her. And yet...

"I think there's a run that night from the store," she said quietly. "Maybe I'll get away to see Christian and Vivi at your house."

"A run on Halloween? Okay. And by the way, you live at Daddy and Jessie's. Would it kill you to come outside and get candy with your niece and nephew?"

"Runners are crazy, and they run all the time. And it won't just be my niece and nephew, will it?"

"So, Summer and Jacob piss you off now, too? None of these kids should have family holidays because we're a blended family and not a real one?"

"We aren't a blended family, Danielle. The Brady Bunch is a blended family. We are a social experiment, and my choice not to participate doesn't make me the bad guy."

"A social experiment? Julie, this is our dad's new marriage. They're *married*. It's not a coping mechanism. He's chosen a new chapter, and he could have done much worse, by the way."

Julie slammed down her drink. "How can you act like this is normal? I'm not judging you, Danielle, but I just don't understand how you all can get together for holidays or Thursdays or whatever it all is and act like Mama and Randall never even existed."

"Julie. You know that isn't true. Believe me, no one acts that way. Their presence is always, automatically there. For God's sake. Look at Vivi. She's Mama's spitting image, even her voice.

Nobody *doesn't* see that."

Julie rolled her eyes. "You know that's not what I mean. This big happy family vibe is just too weird for me. We weren't even that when Mama was here."

The next pause fell like a brick, striking them both. Danielle refrained from tapping her foot while she waited, but her face said it all.

"Don't. You. *Dare*," Julie seethed.

Danielle's peace no longer held. "Dare *nothing*. It's not my fault, or Daddy's, or Katy's, and certainly not Jessie's, that you want to rewrite history. They were *never* like this, and you may not be around Daddy's new life, but you know it's true. We never would have happy family gatherings *like this* if Mama and Dad were still together. And I am not going to deny it to my kids, or Daddy, or myself out of some twisted sense of loyalty. Mama is gone, Julie. Resenting them changes *nothing*!"

"I'm unbelievably sick of hearing this," Julie shot back. "As if Daddy's only shot at being happy was to fucking fall in love with the first person he saw after she died. It's textbook rebound. It's not *real*, and he's going to get hurt. And humiliated. And be more alone than ever. And I refuse to be the evil twin for not playing pretend until that happens."

"Okay. Fine. I'll say it, Julie. You're not talking about Daddy. You're talking about *you*."

*Nope. Not gonna do it.*

"That's a convenient cop out. But it's not true. I'm not a child. I might not be living my finest hour, but I know the difference between projecting and seeing reality." Julie stood, itching to get out of there and end this.

"If it weren't true, then what the hell are you doing? You just quit on repeat. You quit Chad. You quit your career. You boycott the family. And you're still not happy. Your stuff apparently wasn't real. But here Daddy and Jessie are, living through the muck and making it work and, yes Julie, they are happy. They're *happy*! What does it say about you that you resent that? Daddy is sixty-four years old. He had utter crap for a childhood. He overcame a drinking problem. His wife died. *Happy* is all we should want for him."

There was nothing she had left to say. Danielle had all the facts straight, the things Julie gave up and the things Daddy overcame. But *those* facts and *that* truth were not the same thing, so all she would do was stand still.

"Danielle, I am not resentful. I am genuinely happy for all of you to have this thing that you made. But I don't want it. It's not real for me. I want Mama back, and there is no substitute for that."

The anger was turning to softness. Danielle stood and brushed her sister's hair from her face.

"I wish she was here, Jules. I always will. But... I also wish they both could have been as happy as Daddy is now. And I'm not sorry about it."

Danielle turned and walked as gracefully away as a pregnant woman could. For once, at least, Julie wasn't the first one to leave the conversation. And that realization didn't make her feel one bit better.

"Vodka soda, please."

Robin raised an eyebrow and nodded at the bartender. Hazel was downing her second craft beer and shrugged.

"Not everyone likes IPAs, honey," she told Robin.

Julie was sitting across from both of them at corner of the bar, her leg embarrassingly propped up on the stool next to her. Her fight with Danielle had led to another impromptu run, and thanks to a crater-sized pothole she had somehow missed in one of the district's busiest intersections, she ended up with scraped knees, bruised shins, a swollen ankle, and a sizeable bump on her cheek-bone. Without her phone, there hadn't been much to do except limp to the donut shop at the corner and ask to call the store. They knew Robin, of course, as he was a monument to healthy eating.

By then, he and Hazel were closing the store, and *both* of them came to collect Julie and help her retrieve her phone. Shamefully at her mercy, she only feebly protested Hazel's suggestion that they get a few drinks and get "Julie on ice" before taking her back to her car.

"There, there," Hazel said, as the bartender set down Julie's drink. Julie removed the ice bag from her cheek and downed half of the vodka like it was oxygen after a fire. "What a shitty day you've had, my darlin'."

Julie winced in agreement, not wanting to admit it out loud. This was intimate ground with two practical strangers, and it was bad enough Robin in particular was seeing her vulnerable. He'd met her at the donut shop with a first aid kit and procured a few wet paper towels from the college students behind the counter. Then he escorted her down the street to the brewery, where he apparently knew everyone, and had asked immediately for ice packs for her. He was also very quick to open a tab and raise an eyebrow at Julie in case she wanted to protest. She just shrugged and threw him a peace sign. He won today. Her pride had been shattered by the intersection pothole and still lay bleeding in the street.

"Thank you both," Julie said. "For everything."

"You're welcome," Robin said, and tapped his glass against hers.

"For nothin'," Hazel responded. "You may have just gotten here, but we operate like family in this place. Even this guy."

Robin smiled at Hazel, and Julie turned from him. He was becoming likeable. Not in the smoldering, charming Ian kind of way, or the *this is what my life should look like* Chad brand of likeable, or even the *let's really piss everyone* off David kind of likable. He was just, after all the ridiculousness about his and Pote's names, unmysterious. Nice. And that day, he was even a bit chivalrous.

When Julie let herself look back at him, his face was in his pint glass, and he gave her a small shrug. He didn't want to talk about that aspect of his personality. She got that. She respected it.

"You ready to tell your story?" Hazel said, looking pointedly at her.

Julie exhaled. Her knees were stinging and so was her cheekbone, but she was done sitting like this. She grabbed the liquifying ice bag from her left ankle and swung her legs down.

"Whoa," Robin said. "You good there? That thing looks a bit gnarly."

"My dad has Dr. Pappas on speed dial. It's fine."

"Say no more," Robin quipped, holding up his hand. "That dude sends me a tenth of my business. So, your dad is an ankle expert, or both of you?"

"Me by proxy," she sighed. "He's a chronic issue. This is fine. Embarrassing, possibly detrimental to my long run on Saturday, but fine."

"Suit yourself. How's the old lady drink?"

"Hey!" Julie and Hazel answered in unison, then laughed together.

Robin shook his head and nodded toward the bartender, indicating another round. Julie downed the rest of her vodka a little too quickly, aware of Hazel's determined look. She intended to get "the story" out of Julie, and Julie was preparing herself for this inevitable conversation, thankful for the wording she had prepared.

"I was living with someone in Arizona. The guy I was in love with was someone I worked with, too. So, when I had to quit my job, I just sort of, quit everything."

Robin was staring at Julie, looking a bit too perceptively for Julie's comfort.

Hazel, on the other hand, nodded empathetically. "Oh honey. Every story either has a mean Daddy or a shitty boyfriend."

Julie laughed. "He wasn't *shitty*, he just..."

Robin interrupted. "You're talking about two different guys."

Hazel gave a little clap and said, "Ohhhhhh..." as Julie protested. "What? No! I mean..."

"It's too late to go back now," Hazel continued.

Julie looked at Robin. He was fondling his glass with no expression on his face. Just waiting.

"You're my boss," she said.

He shrugged. "Hazel says we're all family. Go ahead and spill if you wanna spill. I'm not gonna fire you for your previous romantic entanglements, and your day can't get much worse."

"I'll drink to that," she mumbled, starting on drink number two.

"Was the douchebag in the picture the one you lived with or the one you worked with?" Robin asked.

"I thought you said he was a putz."

"Same thing."

Julie nodded emphatically at that. "Well, anyway. I haven't... I haven't really told anybody everything that happened. My sisters... my family... is sort of in a weird place right now. And my friends from before–"

"There's always a *before*, too," Hazel said.

"I don't even know if they know I'm back..."

Honestly, all Julie would have had to do was go to her church, or make one post, and she'd have initiations to everything from brunches to Life Groups to girls' nights out. But Daddy and Jessie would be at church, so there was no way, and making a stupid, social media public statement that she was back would invite a thousand questions she didn't want to answer. Someone would find her at the store before long, and that would be that.

Anyhow, she hadn't made much of an effort to keep in touch when she left. She wanted a clean break from her life at the beach. She didn't want to talk to anyone who reminded her that her mom was no longer there. Who would even care about resuming a friendship with her now?

"Friends are overrated," Robin mumbled, munching a peanut.

"Sure as shit are," Hazel said, slamming her glass on the counter. "'cept us. Except the family kind. And honey," she pointed right at Julie, "Runner family never cares about any of the crap your other people do. They care what shoes you like and which race you signed up for and whether you want to have a beer afterwards. You can talk about whatever you want or keep it to yourself and run it out. Runners are the best people."

Julie nodded, looking at the silver-haired dynamo next to her and found herself having new goals. In every conversation they'd had so far – and Hazel carried most of them – the older woman's choices reflected confidence. She'd had failures, a failed and very short marriage in her twenties, many bad dates before she met the love of her life, one son who didn't speak to her for almost a decade, and nearly giving into depression when her husband died. That darkness, at age sixty-nine, led her not to stagnation or isolation or a series of other sad events, but to running. And she was like the unofficial mayor of the running community that made the store its home. Julie couldn't help wanting what Hazel had found.

"Yeah. Yes, you are," Julie said, raising her glass again, just drunk enough and spellbound enough by Hazel's impossible positivity to give all of her doubts, pain, and regrets voice. And then, she told Hazel and Robin all the reasons why she wasn't a nurse anymore.

Two and a half hours and three drinks later, Julie found herself wincing more, limping more, cringing more, as Robin helped her into his apparent grown-up vehicle, a big, silver, South Carolina-ordained Dodge Ram. Her left knee was bleeding through the Band-Aids, and her cheek was turning black and blue, and she was so drunk that her boss of two weeks was driving her home. To her dad's.

"Where's the El Camino?" she slurred, trying not to sound like she was making fun even though she was.

"I went home to let Pote out after you left, and I brought this back so I could haul those old shelves to the dump. Sorry you missed my sweet ride."

"Yeah. Me too." She had no place to criticize his car. She might be living in hers soon.

"Don't worry," he said. "This isn't rock bottom. Rock bottom, there's no one to drive you home and when you do get there, you're locked out. You have a key, right?"

"I have a key," she muttered. "Mr. and Mrs. Oakley have Alexa for fucking everything."

"Wow. You really hate them, huh?"

Julie stared at the window, all the blurred lights and her own miserable reflection. "No. I don't hate them. I hate... my life."

"Ouch."

"I'm thankful for the job..."

"Chill," Robin answered. "I'm not delusional or sensitive about the job. You were a nurse, and now you're selling shoes part time. I get it."

"We don't sell shoes," Julie reminded him. "We sell *solutions*." Out loud, the mantra Darcy had written on a whiteboard inside the stock room made her cackle.

"Yeah. Of course. But it's not quite the same as delivering babies or saving lives and shit."

Julie sucked in her breath. "Or killing post-partum women."

If her words shocked him, he didn't show it. He just shook his head and said very quietly, "I get why you feel guilty, but you didn't kill anyone, Julie. You have to know that. "

She didn't answer. Maybe she knew that. Maybe all scientific, physiological reasoning would point to a seemingly healthy young woman with no overt symptoms dying of a rare complication anyway, regardless of anything Julie might have done or not done. But Julie could still see her face, going completely lifeless in the span of a moment. She could still hear the baby crying, knowing that the twenty-eight years Julie had gotten with her own mother were truly a lifetime compared to what that innocent child was robbed of. She could still feel her own crushing need to feel Ian's arms around her, and the rejection and humiliation when all she could possibly get from him in that room was cold, methodical questioning.

Why did she still want him?

Robin must have taken the clue that she was too tired, intoxicated, and embarrassed to say any more. He turned off his engine as he pulled into the driveway, and before she could protest, already had his own door open.

"I'm helping you inside," he said. "And before you insist that you're coming to work tomorrow, I'm going to go ahead and agree with you. Get your ass up. Pote and I will be here to get you around 8:30. Tidal Creek does really awesome breakfast sandwiches."

By that time, they were at the door. It was taking every ounce of energy she had left just to stand upright, and she still had to make it without Dad or Jessie noticing her. Thank goodness for the back entrance.

And, frankly, thank God for Robin.

"I..."

"You don't have to," he said.

"I haven't been nice to anyone lately," she said. "And I haven't deserved anyone being nice to me. So let me just be thankful, okay?"

She could tell again that he got it, and she couldn't help but wonder what kind of rock bottom he had hit that made him so understanding of an unenthusiastic new employee who had caused so much catastrophe in one afternoon.

"Okay," he agreed, turning the doorknob. "Wow. Alexa keys are pretty awesome."

"Shut up," she giggled, prepared for him to go.

"Go on," he said. There was no escaping the chivalry, as anxious as it made her. She didn't want to notice him. She definitely didn't want to *like* him. She walked slowly inside as he held the door wide, then followed.

He set her bag down on the counter and looked around. "If you have to sponge off your insensitive dad and your evil stepmom, this isn't a bad way to do it."

"Shut up–"

"You can smell the ocean from the front yard..."

"Robin!"

"All right, then. You've had enough for one day. Ice one more time and take some kind of drugs before you go to sleep. That's gonna be a shiner by morning. Think of some great race story to tell the customers."

"Robin..."

He looked down at her.

"You and Hazel have made an awful day better," she said. And she hugged him.

If he was taken off guard, he didn't show it. His return embrace was hesitant but firm enough. It didn't last long, just long enough for her to play one more mind game with herself.

The fact was, she was going to declare today her rock bottom. She was going to get her head back on straight, and she didn't need anyone's help to do that.

The truth was, she really wanted a friend, and Robin had just become one.

# CHAPTER ♡ THIRTEEN

## *Jessie*

*"So. How's it going?"*

My entire family had been on repeat for almost four months. Now, greetings didn't just mean, "How's your cancer life?" but also, "Have you and Julie come to blows yet?" And me, ever a "words person" had resorted to a single, pat answer: "Fine. And no. Not gonna happen."

"I don't really believe you, Mama," Brittney said. "Katy said Julie was pretty rude to you, and Paul got into it with her about it."

*I am not going to cuss today*, I had already told myself when Brittney called. But "FFS" was flashing like a neon sign in my brain. I exhaled. "She wasn't exactly rude, Brit. And that was kind of... at the beginning. We've settled into a rhythm."

"Is that what you call it? You've successfully figured out how to live in the same house and completely avoid each other?"

Well, yes. That was actually accurate. "We're on different schedules," I offered.

"You're not supposed to be *on* a schedule right now," Brittney scolded.

"Okay, Brit. We're on different *kinds* of schedules. And there is a separate entrance. Better?"

"Not really. I just think this whole thing is a bad idea. Everyone does."

My sigh was deep and loud. My constant weak spot with all those kids of mine was their conspiratorial ways. It was manageable and expected that I'd be at odds with one of them at a time. It was another when they were ganging up on me. It had happened when Paul and I first moved in together. It had happened when my cancer was first diagnosed. ("Mama, these doctors are quacks! At least go to MUSC and get a second opinion!") I wondered if it was really happening again, or if Brittney was just being her dramatic self. Did she not know that I was a different person these days?

"Brit, you, your siblings, Aunt Maggie, Elon Musk, Dolly Parton... you can all think whatever you want. This is what is working for me right now. For Paul and me. And if one of you needed a place to stay, then—"

"None of the rest of us, and that includes our not-evil stepsisters, have treated you and Paul like Julie has."

"She hasn't treated me like anything," I argued. "She just ignores me."

"Mama!" I already knew it sounded ridiculous. "Who does that? You married her *father*. Her own sisters hang out with you. Christian is calling you Grammy J. You are recovering from *cancer*. What is it going to take for her to stop being such a bitch?"

"Brittney! Not helpful!" God knows we did not need the answer to that question. "Let's not up the ante on what it will take, okay? It is what it is. She's making her choices, and I can choose to match her energy, or I can choose to focus mine on other things. And just so we are clear, I'm *recovered* from cancer. It's over."

"Oh, Mother." I was choosing to ignore that. What did she know, anyway?

Brittney had called approximately two minutes after my morning chat with Sam. The two of them were my kids who had office-type jobs with normal-type hours. I was seeing Mikayla and baby Josie nearly every day, and on the days I didn't, my daughter was usually texting me while nursing her daughter to sleep. David called far less often, but sent me random memes about southern cooking, the price of gas, grammar, and whatever was happening with the cast of *Yellowstone* almost every day. I had come to accept that it was our love language.

Nonetheless, two phone calls in a row had left me a little spent. I grabbed a cup of coffee and my Kindle and headed to the front porch to enjoy a breezy morning. Paul was already out running, and as much as I wanted to walk on the beach...

Well. Just damnit. All I had done so far was brush my teeth and talk to my kids, and I was just too tired for the beach. Even if I drove the three stupid blocks there, I could already tell that I wouldn't get far beyond sitting in the car being mad at my body.

Julie had been our housemate for two weeks at that point. I was walking on eggshells, when I was upright. Trying to give her space. Trying not to argue or even talk much to Paul about it. Trying to exist peacefully in my own home without causing a volcanic eruption. Katy told me Julie had had a bad break-up and some sort of catastrophe at work. She said, after five minutes of making me promise I would not say *anything* to *anyone*, *ever*, that Julie had lost her confidence. So I actually felt sorry for her.

Her life had gone sideways. That was a fact.

But the truth was, my peace was the only thing I could control. And I was done with this. Done.

I think I'm going to talk to Paul about things, I texted to Maggie. Well, I typed it. And then I didn't send it, because I didn't want to act like a teenager who needed to talk to her bestie about it first. I needed to do better trusting Paul, and our relationship, with the hard stuff.

So instead, I sat there. I unlocked my Kindle but just scrolled through the exhaustive mass of books on the home screen. Nothing was appealing to me, a lifelong avid reader. Usually, when I had writer's block, reading a new book or two, and sometimes an old favorite, would get my creative juices flowing again. At that moment, just looking at the beautiful covers and intriguing titles – even looking at the drab covers and cringe-worthy titles – made me feel more pressure than I already did, and more drained.

I had fulfilled half of my current publishing contract. I was still set to do a new women's thirty-day devotional, through the book of Galatians, though I was given a six-month extension on the timeline due to illness. Reading would inspire me. I just couldn't make myself. I didn't know why.

"Jesus, help me." I started the prayer out loud. My thoughts had gotten in the way of my prayers over that past year and a half. After Randall died, I didn't want my broken heart to heal, so I just asked God to help my kids. And then when Paul and I let ourselves fall in love, I thought it was selfish to ask God for anything. Even now, I felt guilty asking God to help me figure things out when it seemed all my decisions had caused turmoil. Even if the blended family majority was mostly at ease, Julie was a daily reminder that everyone was hurting.

*Including you.* It was Maggie's voice in my head, but Randall's face was all I saw. The fact was, Paul was the most caring and patient caretaker I could have asked for. I hated being sick, and he knew how to *handle* me. But the cancer and the surgery and the constant feeling of weakness, more than anything since last May, made me miss Randall, the intimacy and ease of thirty-six married years. And I hadn't told *any* body that. How ungrateful could I be?

I sat with it, sharing those observations out loud with Jesus, and sipping my coffee, and setting the Kindle down on the table, because we both knew as soon as Paul got home and I talked to him for a few minutes, I was going back to bed. "And Lord, I know my energy and my drive and my mojo are going to come back, but since at least part of what I am doing is Your work, can You possibly speed up this process a bit?"

By the time he came up the driveway, adorably rumpled in his gray running shorts and soaked, neon yellow tank top, my face was red, and I was certain my eyes were puffy. I didn't try to hide it because I told Jesus I wouldn't. Even though I also knew Paul was going to panic.

"Jess! What is it? Are you okay?"

I went ahead and laughed through my tears. The Steel Magnolias would be proud of me. "I'm fine," I said. "Just talkin' to Jesus."

He smiled, not before I saw the depth of worry that crossed over his eyes like a shadow. "That sounds nice, sweetheart. But was He making you cry?"

"He usually does," I said, swiping at my eyes one more time. I went to pick up my coffee mug, but it was already in his hand.

"Be right back," he said. I smiled and sighed. In less than five minutes, he would have taken the world's quickest shower, thrown on fresh clothes and cologne, and returned with two bananas and fresh coffee for both of us, plenty of cream.

"You're the answer to so many prayers," I murmured as he kissed the side of my mouth, then the top of my head. I stared at him like something out of a dream as he settled into the chair next to me. This was a typical morning for the past few months, for most of our married life together. He ran, I rested, he came home, he took care of me. It was serene and safe and so lovely, and I was so ready for it to change.

"I would really love to take you out tonight," I said, trying to sound as dreamy at the sight of him as the smell of his Burberry Touch made me feel.

"Oh yeah?" He took a long swallow and added, contently, "Where do you want to take me?"

"Ah. Somewhere without TVs or a bunch of kids. Maybe Villa Romana? Maybe if I look super pathetic, they'll bring me endless bowls of stracciatella."

"You could never look pathetic," he said. "But you can tell me what straccio-whatta is?"

I giggled and told him about my favorite Italian soup, how much it was like what my Nonna Romano used to make. He reached over and took my hand and said he'd love to take me to dinner there. It was only then I realized that we'd never eaten together at my favorite Italian restaurant. When we went out, it was usually for seafood or Mexican or someone's new happy hour. Somehow the time we'd spent together, in dog years, had melted into the time I'd spent with Randall, a lifetime. And I didn't have to explain that.

"I just, I guess, assumed you and I had eaten there before," I said, not masking the sadness in it.

"I'm excited to eat there with you tonight," he said. "As long as you feel up to it, Jess."

I sighed as fresh tears collected in my eyes. "I might have to spend the rest of the day doing only nothing. But I'll make it happen. I really want... I really *need*... a normal-feeling, lovely dinner date with my husband."

He pressed my hand to his lips. "Jessie Rose, I know this has been so hard on you. I can't wait to make it all up to you. But in the meantime, I really love hearing you call me that."

I stood then, leaning over carefully to let my lips meet his for a lingering moment. There was so much I wanted to say, even to show him, but just then I let him know that I loved hearing it, too.

I was about to have to unbutton my pants by the time we were done. Rinaldo had made Paul and me feel so incredibly at home, had sent me two big bowls of Stracciatella and plenty of their amazing bread and bruschetta, and Paul had dived all the way into his Veal Absolute. It was the only place I could taste food like my Nonna had made. I couldn't wait to eat more of it when I felt, well, normal again.

"Thanks for taking me here," Paul said, eyes shining at me over the candlelight.

"Thanks for asking Michael to play 'Sweet Child of Mine,'" I answered, and we laughed at the new memory of a song I loved and Paul hated, brandished on the iconic Michael's accordion while we ate our cannoli.

As he sipped his coffee, I stifled a yawn. He laughed again and looked at his watch. "It's way past my wife's new bedtime," he said.

"It is *not* my new bedtime," I protested. "And if you even think about saying 'new normal,' I will throat-punch you."

He reached across the table and took my hand, stroking tenderly with his thumb. Somberly, he looked at me and then said, "Sweetheart, I would never."

We laughed again at the thought of my most abhorred phrase. "This feels so good. I miss laughing. I miss... Jesus help me. I miss the way things were. It only lasted a minute, you and me and the house and the whole idea that we're settled and together."

"It's not *over*, Jessie. Dr. Masselli says you're going to feel much more like yourself in a few weeks. And then we pick up where we left off, and get back to... you know, honeymoonin'."

That was supposed to make me laugh too, but he was leaving out one important factor. It wasn't just the two of us in the house, and it definitely didn't feel settled with Julie there.

"It's hard to feel settled when we don't... when we don't know what things will look like in a few weeks," I said, carefully.

"If it takes longer, it does," Paul answered emphatically. "I wish you wouldn't worry about those things, Jess. I'm not going anywhere and we—"

"I don't mean *that*," I said. Fact was, the radiation had left my lady parts uncomfortably dry, hardly ideal for a newlywed sexagenarian. "Maggie has oils and vitamins and all kinds of witch's brew being delivered any second now. And you know, there is also the power of love."

He didn't know the mood needed lightening, but I was working on it. I couldn't think of any way to tiptoe around the subject, and he wasn't giving any indication that he knew what I was getting at.

"Then what?"

Gosh, his face was so earnest, his eyes so attentive, I just wanted to plan a six-month cruise and avoid any potentially hurtful subject altogether. All the courage I'd gathered to say anything just melted into his generosity.

"I guess we just don't know what our normal looks like yet," I said tentatively. "And I'm excited to figure it out."

He let go of my fingers and ran his through his hair. I didn't need to say a word.

"I know, Jess. Me too. I..." He paused as our bill was presented and did all the end-of-meal things as I took a long sip of Pellegrino. "I know it's been weird. And the timing is awful. I really thought... well, I guess I'm just the stupid father of girls again. I really thought the glimpses of softness I saw in Julie would take over all the bitterness by now."

And there it was. The irritation I felt toward her was much more than that for Paul. He'd opened his heart to a small handful of people in the whole world, in his whole life. And one of them, Julie, rejecting another, me, was more than annoying to him, and he was far beyond angry. He was suffering, and I hated that.

"I just want peace," I said, so softly I wasn't sure if he would hear me. "For you, even more than for me."

He looked down at the wrinkled white tablecloth, seemingly studying a blot of red sauce, the trails of crusty breadcrumbs, before he looked back up and into the depths of me.

"I love you so much," he said.

And for that moment, it was more than enough.

# CHAPTER♡FOURTEEN

## *Julie*

"IF THIS KEEPS UP, SOMEONE WILL REPORT US TO HR," JULIE SAID WRYLY.

"Oooh. I wonder what the punishment would be," Robin said. "You want to split a flight?"

"No..." Julie answered. She was back at Tidal Creek with him for the fourth time in three days, including a quick breakfast the morning he'd picked her up, and now the second day in a row of after-work drinks. It was already becoming a potentially bad habit for her addictive personality. Splitting a flight or an appetizer or anything else was going to make it feel like an actual date.

Which it *was not.*

He was undaunted, ordering for both of them without asking her what she did want. Julie leaned back in her Adirondack chair and scratched Pote behind the ears. It was nice to hang out with someone, no emotional strings attached.

She asked him about the new Hokas that had arrived that day, why he thought those shoes were really so popular when they were so orthopedic looking, and why he hadn't just hired Hazel instead of her in the first place since it was taking Julie forever, it seemed, to learn all the shoe names. Hazel could rattle off the model name, the version, the weight, the "heel-toe offset," and four best uses and then share a race story and a recipe with every customer. They were taking their wallets out and sometimes posing for selfies before they knew what hit them.

Robin smiled into his glass. "She's great," he said. "It honestly didn't occur to me she would want a job until she volunteered to train you. Her kids live all over the place, and she runs more than all of us put together, so she's been hanging out at the store since we opened. She might as well get paid for it." He shrugged.

Julie felt an odd warmth wash over her. It wasn't the toxic draw she had felt toward Ian, thank God. It was just... she cocked her head as she listened to him... he seemed genuine. And she honestly hadn't really made a friend since she moved away, and based on her life since she came back, she probably didn't have many before that.

"How long have you had the store? Four years, is it?"

"Yep."

"And it was... a family business before that?"

"Yep."

"What kind of family business?"

"Are you writing a book?"

"Ha!" That made her think of Dad and Jessie, and she finished her drink before answering. "Definitely not. And no offense–"

"That always means someone is about to be shitty and wants a free pass for it..."

"No *offense*, really. You just... you don't seem that interested in running. Or the things we sell. I mean, we tell people to dedicate their shoes just for their runs, and you hit the streets at four o'clock most days and wear the same shoes you work in all day. You don't carry water in this hellacious humidity. You just don't seem interested in all the *stuff*."

"I'm interested in selling it," he said.

"Yes, of course, but..."

He shrugged. "Just because I don't use all the things doesn't mean they aren't good to use. They're just not for me. I don't require a bunch of gear. Or fuss. No different shoes for different days. Or race T-shirts with fresh logo designs and matching medals. When I want to run, I run. I run enough that I can eat donuts and drink whiskey as much as I want."

Julie nodded. She really did get it. But something else was knocking at the back of her mind, and suddenly, she laughed.

"What?" Robin said. Surely, he'd learned in those outings with her that drinks made her emote. She couldn't stop laughing.

"*What*?" he repeated, starting to laugh companionably.

"No fuss," she managed. "You're a... a casual fellow!" And then she nearly fell over as her laughter intensified.

He tilted his head to study her. She probably looked like a lunatic. She would have to explain, when she could catch her breath.

Robin waited patiently for that. He sipped his drink and looked at his phone. She tried once, twice, and even a third time to explain to him why it was funny. Finally, the words came out.

"Last year," she said slowly, so as not to trigger herself again, "I moved to Arizona with a *casual fellow*. That's how one of my friends from the hospital described him. He was a surfer, he wore orange Crocs – and not the hipster kind, the original hideous kind, and he barely had a B average studying logistics. He didn't have a credit card or a decent haircut. But I tried to love him, so much, I moved away with him. And he was the definition of a 'casual fellow.'" She sniffed, almost laughing again, but now also reminded of all the ways this particular memory was pathetic.

"Casual fellow. Okay. I see it," Robin said, still looking at her like something was growing out of her forehead. "I don't see why it's so funny, but it's definitely a phrase that could describe me."

"He's my stepbrother now," she said, in a much more monotone voice. She knew it wouldn't sound funny.

Robin's eyebrows shot straight up. "Wait, what?"

"That guy. Arizona guy. The one I moved away with. The casual fellow is named David, and he is the youngest son of my father's wife."

"That is a damn country song if I ever heard one."

"Yeah, well. I think I need another drink and maybe it will be funny again."

She got up and waited a moment for the stiffness to shake out of her healing knees. In the time it took to walk to the bar, get them each another, and ignore the fifth text of the week she had gotten from Chad, she was more than regretful that she'd started telling Robin this story.

"Thanks," he said, accepting the drink. "So David wasn't the one you worked with; he was the one you lived with."

*Shit.* This really made her sound like a slut. She took a sip of her vodka soda, licking the remnants off her lips as she thought of how to answer.

"I already told you," Robin said, "You're not going to get any judgment here."

"How do I really know that?" she answered, only half-teasing. "I don't know you that well. I barely know your real name. Or your dog's real name. Or if you really have a stepdaughter."

"You know," he said, much more somberly. "And I wouldn't lie about her. She's real."

"Okay." Now she *felt* quieter. "Okay..." She glanced down at her phone. Chad's text read, "Please just answer. I am coming to Myrtle Beach this weekend and I would like to talk to you first." Praying hands emoji. Orange heart emoji.

"Shit!" she said out loud.

"What now?"

"I need to make a phone call. I'll be right back."

Chad answered midway through the first ring.

"I knew that would get your attention."

"Chad, don't manipulate me. I am trying here, to move on, and you're making it so difficult." She sat on the curb, pre-exhausted from the conversation she anticipated.

"Good," he answered. "I hope it's the hardest – no, the most impossible thing you ever have to do. Don't move on, Julie. Don't just get over me."

"Chad–"

"Just listen." She could picture him, then. He was probably sitting on their amazing couch, beautiful, buttery soft and bright linen, stuffed just right, with tiny gold and sage pinstripes running through, so light they could barely be seen. He was probably in his gym clothes, getting ready to go. He probably had the TV remote in his other hand, checking scores. He probably looked wide awake and completely untousled after a long day of seeing patients.

Did she miss all that? Enough to go back with him? Enough to welcome him to her home, her beach, her complicated family life?

"I'm listening," she finally answered.

He'd really done it. He took a job at Ocean's Edge Hospital, where she used to work. He was going to be living in Market Common, less than a mile from the store, though she hadn't told him its location. He was coming in two weeks. He wanted her to live with him, even as a roommate, so they could talk through everything and figure out a future. He still wanted one with her.

"I shouldn't have expected you to make clear decisions," he said, so much regret in his voice. "You were going through so much grief, confusion, probably feeling backed into a corner. I know you saw me as a safe solution, maybe even an unadventurous one, but Julie, I want you to see more of me. I want to try again now that your head is clearer."

She listened, and she managed not to laugh at him or correct him. She was no less confounded now then the day she told him she was leaving him. How was he confident enough to change jobs and move more than halfway across the country? And how was she going to explain when she resumed the conversation with her new friend, who was still waiting to hear all the confusing parts that happened *before* this phone call added to them exponentially?

"I can't stop you from coming, Chad. But I am no more certain about myself or my feelings or decisions than I was a few weeks ago. I want to see you, of course, but you're going to have to give me space."

"Deal," he said, with too much hope in his voice.

After he shared some logistics, she dragged herself back inside. Robin had ordered some pretzels and cheese and was munching while playing Candy Crush. She couldn't believe anyone under the age of sixty was still playing that game.

"What's wrong?" she said. "Is Farmville incompatible with

your device?"

He put his phone down and looked at her, ignoring her question. "Which one was that?"

"Sigh..." She used to think people saying "sigh" were ridiculous, like people who said "LOL." But since she started feeling defeated by basically everything in life, it made sense to her.

"Which question do you want me to answer first? Because I think we were still on the whole stepbrother thing?"

He shrugged. "I think that probably sounds far more scandalous than it actually was, but go ahead and start there."

She was grateful when the next round was set before her. She only took a tiny sip, but she was grateful to have the glass to hold. She looked at Robin, his brown eyes looking back without their typical gleam of mischief and teasing. He was really going to listen. Her butterflies swirled at the memory.

"The day my mama died... well, she was in a car accident. So Jessie, the one my Dad is married to now? They worked together for years. They wrote textbooks. And they had just finished their last project, so Jessie's husband Randall and my mama were surprising them. Dad and Jessie thought they were meeting at this diner to go over their stuff, but Randall and Mama were going to be there and take them out to celebrate. But Randall had a heart attack behind the wheel, and the rest..." She looked away.

"Jesus," Robin said. "I'm sorry. That's awful."

"Yeah." Her chin was already trembling. She still wasn't used to telling it. "Anyway, our families have known each other for a while. Cousin-like, I guess. Summer holidays and stuff. And there's a lot of us. We were all at the hospital in one room before long. It was like an ER without the blood. Every human emotion. A million conversations. Paperwork. Chaos. It was so chaotic, and when I got there, my daddy was shellshocked, and then he cried in my arms. It was…" She paused. Telling him was one thing, falling apart completely was out of the question. "I guess that was the worst part. So after that, a few of us kids decided to get coffee, and I was dying to get out of there, so I volunteered to go. And David, Jessie's youngest – and when I say youngest, I mean he is the baby of the family by like, six years, and the absolute doted upon, blonde and blue-eyed golden child – said he would go with me.

"Up until then, I'd only known him as the kid brother. Jessie's daughters are around my age, and we would talk through the years about school and jobs and stuff. Nothing major. My older sister has always been pretty close friends with Mikayla, the oldest one. Anyway, it should have been awkward, driving to Dunkin and Starbucks with this… kid. He was twenty at the time. But I guess it was like a form of triage. I didn't know what to say, but he must have felt safe, because he just verbally threw up on me. He was so worried about his mom, and so certain that he had no role to fill in what was happening. He wanted to be strong for her, but his older brother – Jessie had him when she was a teenager, and they've got that 'us against the world, kid' kinda bond – always takes that on. He was so lost."

"So many characters," Robin observed. "So you helped him." He seemed way more interested in all of it than she expected him to be.

Julie shrugged and frowned. "I tried. I really did. I didn't see him again until my mama's funeral, and then just for a minute. We just started messaging over Facebook, then texting, and then hanging out. It was very unlike me. I've always… preferred the company of my peers. Same age or older. Professional. Established. David was none of those things. He was barely grounded at all."

"So you helped him." The repetition should have made her nuts, but he was proving a point, and he was doing it well.

"I gave him direction," Julie answered, thoughtfully. "He had... has, I'm sure, a lot of energy. He's bright. He's great with people. He's smart. But he never got a chance to stand up or really to see his potential. He was too busy being an adorable moppet. And as soon as he got over the shock of his dad and the adventure of moving away from home, that was his default. And—"

"And you realized your mistake?"

She nodded, silently.

The rest was relayed in as little detail as possible. Julie met Chad at church, and he was much more on her wavelength. David had second thoughts about pursuing a career in midwifery. *A twenty-one-year-old male surfer decided not to be a fricken midwife? You don't say,* Robin quipped. Julie couldn't fake it anymore and had asked him to leave. And, if she was being completely honest:

"I knew when I broke up with him and told him he had to take the apartment himself or move out... I knew that was going to cause an earthquake back here. I knew Jessie would hate me for it. And I could pretty much bet she and my dad would fight about it."

"Did they?"

Julie's third drink was empty. She had to shake her head to clear it, and she had to stop herself from manifesting the guilt she felt. "They broke up the next day. Daddy moved out. The whole thing was more like a tsunami. He moved into one of his little rentals. He had to have surgery for his ankle, NWB for four weeks. And I was nowhere to be found. I barely communicated with him that whole time. And Jessie's dog died."

"Jesus," Robin said again. "And they let you live with them

now?"

Julie looked at her hands.

"I'm not an asshole," she finally said.

"Yeah. Yeah, you kind of are. I'll be right back."

When he came back, he set a fourth drink in front of her but sat in a chair closer to her.

"I meant what I said. No judgment. I want to hear the rest of this. And then, we're drinking some coffee, and I'm taking you home, and tomorrow, we try something different."

"You're firing me?" She swallowed. If she were him, she would.

He narrowed his eyes and shook his head, taking a sip of his own drink. "I can't fire you for decisions you made in your personal life before I even knew you. I mean, I could. South Carolina has that lovely at-will employment law. But I'm not going to. I'm frankly just intrigued by how this series of romances took a seemingly discerning woman from being an ambitious nurse to being a miserable, part-time retailer. And I don't really have anyone else to talk to anyway."

"*That* sounds like a story to me."

"Later," he said, with any trace of humor gone from his voice. Geez. Julie would have never predicted she and Nick-Robin becoming a couple of down and out drinking buddies.

"So. Where were we?"

"You were interrupted by dude number two, or maybe three, when you were telling me about little David. So let's circle back to that."

"Dude number two was on the phone," she mumbled.

"Lived with or worked with?"

"Lived with."

"So not the one you were 'in love' with?" He used air quotes.

"Don't do that," she said. "Just because dude number three was no good for me doesn't mean it wasn't real."

"Yeah. We'll circle back to that, too. So what did number two want?"

Julie kept her hands clasped around the glass. She hadn't processed it yet. When she said it out loud, it would be real.

"He took a job in Murrells Inlet."

Robin threw his head back and let out what could only be described as a guffaw.

"Shut up," Julie said, feebly. It probably would be funny if it was happening to someone else.

"I really just can't wait to hear about number three."

"And why is that?"

Julie had been staring at her hands, but now she studied his face, almost never all the way serious. His hair was always a mess. His face always had stubble and not the kind that looked curated or even on purpose. But his dark brown eyes retained equal parts mischief and... was it wisdom? She couldn't tell. It was definitely... seeing. Knowing. She found herself looking forward to whatever he was going to say.

"Well, your story involves two different guys moving across America for you, but the putz is the one you're still hung up on. And by the way, putz is just a polite way of saying douchebag."

"He's not–"

"Julie." For the second time that night, Robin's tone and expression turned completely somber. "You actually don't have to tell me anything else about him. I saw the picture the other day. He's married, right? And now his wife is pregnant? I told you... no judgment. Shit happens. I could give you a textbook response about every decision you've made for the past year and a half. I've

been blindsided before, too. It can cause you to be hasty and reckless. And a real man would have turned you in the other direction.
A real man would have never let you get that close in that situation
to begin with. He's a dick. He's a putz."

She finished her drink, still wishing strongly for another. "Putz.
Maybe I'm the putz."

"Well. Maybe," he said, shoving the remains of a pretzel in his
mouth. "But he is for sure. Get off his Instagram." He stood.

"I thought you were going to tell me your story," Julie protested. "It's only nine o'clock."

"I think we've had enough story for one night. Tomorrow. But
you better drink some water. We're going to run."

# CHAPTER♡FIFTEEN

*Jessie*

I SAW HEADLIGHTS FLASH ACROSS THE PICTURE WINDOW. Paul had gone upstairs to shower, and I was lying on the couch, watching the third season of *Downton Abbey*, again, and hoping that somehow Sybil would live, *again*.

The highlights of my day had been a ten-minute walk on the beach and a phone call from David. He was coming home for Thanksgiving. We had more than a month to figure out what that would look like, but I wanted my son in my house. Since he'd moved to Arizona, and then to Tennessee to finish school, he'd only been back a few times: Christmas, our wedding, and a few weeks later when I had surgery. All of those instances were full of hustle or stress. I wanted to make him dinner and have a game night and see a movie or two. Everything about his sudden launch out into the world was fraught with sadness and complication. I wanted to hang out with my boy and get to know him again.

All Paul had said, quite stoically, in response was, "Julie can stay somewhere else for a few days." It was meant to be helpful. It was helpful. David didn't need the guest suite; we essentially had two other guest rooms and the magical bunks. But it would be, thank you kids, *hella* awkward for him and Julie to sleep under the same roof.

Paul didn't care about awkward; he just cared about respect and taking care of me. So he said *if* Julie was still *camping* with us when November rolled around, he would let her know she needed to spend that week with one of her sisters.

That is him saying 'I'll handle it' and 'Jessie, don't you try to handle it.' Maggie's response to my text had been clear, and I knew she was right. Paul was plenty chivalrous, but that wasn't all. He also knew me and wanted me to stay out of it.

I'd acquiesced. I didn't need to go from negative zero to one hundred miles per hour with Julie. I had only seen her twice since she'd been there, other than occasionally through the window when she couldn't see me. I thought maybe the grocery offering would garner at least a "Thank You" note left on the counter or something, but the slight hope had been not only fruitless but a hard reminder that we were not living in *The Brady Bunch* or *Full House* and no one writes notes to people in the same house, old lady.

Ah, well. Perhaps if we lived at Downton Abbey, we'd have space for everyone to cohabitate and avoid each other, and we would also be better able to fake good manners and mutual consideration. That was my thought when a knock on the door interrupted my internal strategy-session.

I paused at the unfortunate sight of poor Sybil bucking back in her bed, her neck swelling as she tried to breathe. I took a moment to arrow to the next screen, which was poor, soon-to-be-dead Matthew grasping the bed post and closing his eyes to shut out the nightmare. I supposed that was better.

I looked through the peep hole to see none other than Julie.

Julie was physically, completely her mother's daughter. She was long and lean, as tall as Paul and in any hint of heels, taller. But where Leah's hair was classically trimmed past her shoulders, Julie's, also a rich, bronzy-brown, hung down her back, typically in an intricately-styled ponytail or braid. Sharp cheekbones flanked her intense brown eyes. While Danielle carried softness and Katy carried sparks, Julie carried... steel? Stone? She was smart and strong for sure, and even before she hated me, it made her sort of intimidating and unapproachable. Now it just seemed terrifying.

Even then, she was standing there, very possibly at the mercy of her arch enemy to be let in the house, with her arms crossed, her hip jutting out, sporting an RBF, minus the resting.

I waited a moment, my heart beating out my chest. Chances were, she would do nothing more than nod silently or walk past me all together. *This is my house. I will protect my peace.*

I opened the door.

"Forget your key?" I asked, even though it was dumb. We had everything set up on apps, like, you know, the Jetsons.

She did look at me, likely thinking the same thing. "I saw the light in the window. I figured Dad was up."

"Oh," I said. Though it was my instinct to add "Sorry," I did not. Score.

"Is he here?" she said, making it sound like an accusation and pissing me off immediately.

*Don't match energy. Don't match energy.* "He's taking a shower, Julie."

Why is it when we use people's names, whatever we say immediately sounds hostile?

She felt it. She knew it. I returned her gaze. My heart was still thumping, and quite possibly with the excitement over David's impending visit foremost in my thoughts, I felt a strong need to mark my territory.

"Okay. I'll just text him."

I could hear Maggie's voice saying, "Girl. Let it go. Let it go or no one is sleeping peacefully tonight." I might have heard Randall somewhere in there, too. "Jessie, nothing productive happens when you and the girls are in the same bad mood." They were both right, of course. I willed them to shut up.

"Is there something I can help you with? A message I can relay?"

We both knew I was crossing the Rubicon. I was sick of ignoring the obvious, and of being ignored.

She took the bait.

"I can handle my own conversations with my father."

"Can you?" I said. "Like a real one? With a conclusion?"

"Don't." She said it very softly, but all the steel and ice were there.

"Don't speak to a person sleeping in my house?"

Julie's eyes turned from irritation to anger. *Good. Come for me, little girl. I ain't feeling meek tonight.*

"Ma'am." Southerners have a way of fully loading that word. I may not have been born there, but I lived here long enough to have command of it. "Let's not pretend. I don't wish to hear you speak to me about my father. Not tonight. Not ever."

"Not ever? Not even if he has a heart attack or a car accident or busts his ankle trimming the bushes, and I'm the only one who knows? Not ever?"

She wasn't swayed. "Not ever."

"Forever is a long time, Miss Julie."

"Not long enough."

Good Lord, this child bled bitterness. "I understand—"

"No. You really don't."

"Fair enough. I don't. I've never been where you are. I mean, at your age, I was already raising kids. Not being one."

*Shit.* Maggie and Randall's voices had been joined by Paul's, and they were all yelling at me now.

"Fine. *Mrs. Oakley.* You can go ahead and tell *your husband* that I'll be out of the house by the weekend. You tell him. You explain. Hope it goes well."

"Where are you going?" I said. The anger had drained from my voice as quickly as I let it rise up. This was a shit show, and I knew I was going to be picking up the mess for days.

*Yep*, my inner Maggie agreed. *Cancer ain't getting you out of this one, either.*

"It clearly does not matter. I simply won't be inconveniencing you any further."

"Julie..."

She held up her hand. "You're not going to get the response you want out of me. No matter what you're about to say."

"I can handle it," I said. "All I'm going to add is that... forever *is* a long time. But it gets shorter every day. You don't want me to tell you anything about your dad, so I will respect that. But I don't mind reminding you that tomorrow isn't promised to any of us. You resent the way he's found new happiness? Fine. That's your choice. But he's sixty-four years old. You won't have him forever. You won't have the chance to actually participate in his life forever."

Julie shook her head with a grunt. "He knows I'm a part of his life. And so do you. Just because I'm not participating in the *blender family* or whatever made-up term you want to use for it—"

"There's no difference," I said. "The family is his life. Our family. We are both in it. We are all in it."

"It's not all or nothing to me."

"It's not up to you. Not really. And I think you know that."

From the way her expression changed, she confirmed that she did know it. Her venom softened, but not in a way that made me feel one bit victorious. In fact, the sadness washing over her caused me to sit down.

"Are you saying I'm going to lose him if I don't accept all this? Is that really what you're saying?"

Of course, it wasn't what I was saying. It wasn't true. But how could I explain nuance to someone who insisted on things being black and white?

"You won't ever lose him. But there is a difference between being on the perimeter of someone's life and being in it. The perimeter is safe. The inside is messy. If you're on the perimeter, you can turn around and look away whenever you want. On the inside, you're going to see and smell and hear stuff you don't like. But you're in the middle of all the good stuff too. You don't miss a thing. And he doesn't want you to."

She shook her head. "Is that from one of your *devotionals*?"

She tried to make my new writing projects – encouragement for women – sound like a crime. But her steel was weakening. Maybe, like me, she was just growing tired.

*Be brave.* That was Randall. And maybe Paul, too. He was going to be mad at me, but he probably also knew that this conversation was inevitable.

"It's from my heart, Julie. You are not my enemy. And I don't want to be yours. I don't want to be delusional about what we can be. But I don't want things to stay like this."

"Julie?"

At that moment, of course, Paul appeared at the bottom of the stairs, in his boxers and a t-shirt, his hair still wet, his glasses on, his face going from confused to slightly betrayed.

"Hi, Dad." The switch between "Daddy" and "Dad" or "my father" was another no-longer-subtle Southern hint.

I watched him change his expression as clearly as if he actually donned a mask. As though he was a just being a casual fellow, observing a perfectly normal occurrence in his living room, he said, "What's up, ladies?"

If I hadn't been completely agitated, I might have laughed. Julie, just as masterfully as Paul, put on a new veneer, too.

Fake politeness was probably the last thing we needed.

"Julie was looking for you." I did not inject anything but fact into it, hoping he would see the truth for himself.

"I just wanted to talk to you for a second," Julie told him carefully. "But I think I'm all talked out for now."

I shook my head, holding in an eyeroll.

"Jess?"

"I have no idea," I said, a little sharply. "I just answered the door."

"Why didn't you use Alexa?" he asked her, and I admit, it always sounded so dumb to me, like we had Alice the housekeeper but we treat her like a *thing*.

She stared at him but said nothing. It was actually kind of impressive.

Then, the whole conversation went in a direction I was not expecting. Paul walked closer to her, I thought maybe to give her a hug. But instead, he studied her eyes and then he sniffed the air around her, and then, in a low voice that was almost a growl, he said, "You've been drinking again tonight."

Still, there wasn't a word from her.

"Is your car here?" he asked pointedly.

"No, sir." I could barely hear her.

"How did you get home?"

"Robin."

I had no idea who Robin was. Julie hadn't had any friends around since she got to town, as far as I could tell. But nothing was being explained, and I felt like I was watching some other father with his teenager rather than my husband and his twenty-nine-year-old.

"You barely know him. This is how you make an impression on your new boss? That's twice, Julie. *Twice.* It stops now. Do you understand?"

Julie's chin was trembling. She was looking down at her shoes. She nodded. And then, barely above a whisper, answered, "Yes, sir."

"I'm done with all this." His voice grew louder, and he took a step back so that he was actually addressing both of us. "No more veiled comments. No more creative avoidance. Get over yourself." That was directed to Julie. "And be yourself." That was addressed to me. "You're my wife. We didn't get caught out back after curfew. You don't have anything to apologize for."

Maggie would have been laughing at the way both my and Julie's jaws were practically on the ground. I recovered as quickly as I could, just nodding at him. Julie, however, seemed to come out of a trance.

"I'm working on a different place to live." There was no tremble in her voice. "I don't know what else you mean by me getting over myself. If you mean get over Mama, then—"

"You *know* that's not what I mean." Paul's voice was dripping with anger now. I actually wanted to leave the room.

"But that is what it boils down to," Julie seethed right back. "You think I'm being rude and selfish, and I just think that I don't have to accept this. I don't have to be a part of your second-chance-romance, your new family, your next chapter, or whatever creepy little title you all want to give it to make it more palatable. I don't want it."

"What do you want then, Julie? You want me to move back into our old house, live there by myself until I die? Wait around for you to get your shit together and get married and have babies so I can, what? Be available for babysitting and carpools? Watch everyone else have a life? Just do *nothing*?"

"No."

"No, what?"

The tension had mounted to the point of combustion. I nodded to Paul and started to walk out of the room. He stopped me with a hand on my arm and a stormy look that almost scared me.

"No, sir, that's not what I want for you." Her voice had faltered again.

"Then tell me what you do want."

"It's too late, Daddy. Just—"

"Just *what*?"

I really wished he would stop yelling. I didn't think Paul was traditionally a yeller, but I did think his daughter was carrying around a lot of trauma, and he wasn't helping.

"This is the first time since Mama died that you've asked me what I want. About anything. Any of it. Her arrangements. The house. Where you live. What you're doing…"

"Julie, I know you've been a big ol' boss at the hospital, and maybe out in Arizona, too. Maybe even with Robin at the store, but you're not the boss of me."

She let out a lengthy exhale. "That's not what I mean!"

"Paul–" I started, trying to walk away again.

"No, just stay," he said, not snapping at me, but not softening either. "I want whatever is said here to be between all three of us because I am sick of living in the middle of hostility. And hostility for *what*? No one did anything to Julie. Nothing. *Nothing*!"

I took his hand then. He was shaking a little, and Julie had started to cry.

This moment was not in any way about what I wanted, but there was no doubt just then that I didn't want this. I didn't want these two – yes, *two* – people I loved to be in such turmoil.

But I also knew that sometimes, the steps to get to a better place are covered with burning coals, and it takes courage *and* pain to get to where we want to be.

As though he read my mind, like he often did, Paul squeezed my hand and looked at me, and nodded. Then repeated his question to Julie: "What do you *want*!?"

"All I want is Mama back," she whispered. It sounded so loud in the quiet room.

Paul's own tear ran down his face. "I wish I could give you that, Jules. I do. But I have to tell you, even if she was still here, *we* would probably still be *here*, in this place. You want to control everything around you, and you do it out of love, baby. I get it. I know you love me. I do. But you can't control anything, really, except your own decisions, your own reactions. *You* are making *yourself* miserable."

The last sentence hung in the air. Jesus, help us. We had all been there. Paul had stories, from even before I met him, times when he was his own worst enemy. I certainly still struggled with that, overanalyzing and overcompensating to the point of sabotaging my own relationships, my own peace.

I didn't know in what way Julie had done or was doing this, but Paul knew. He looked at her with the distinctive, knowing love that parents have. It says two things at once: I would cut my veins and bleed for you. *And* I would like to take you by your shoulders and shake you until you have the good sense God gave a goat.

"Can I go now?" she said. I still could not believe how Paul's dressing-down had reduced her to a child right before my eyes. I had never seen an ounce of humility in her before.

Paul took a step back to her and kissed her forehead. "Do you want me to drive you to work tomorrow?"

"Yes, please," she answered. "Good night. Um, good night, Jessie."

She didn't look at me, and she walked away very swiftly, but I basically fell back on the couch, shock, awe, and exhaustion finally taking hold.

Paul sat next to me, leaning forward so we could see each other. I was no longer afraid that he'd be mad. The air was much too heavy for such simplistic reactions.

"What was that?" I asked. "What just happened?"

"That was Julie," he said, emotion still thick in his voice. "Probably the first time you've ever really met her."

I nodded. I got it. I reached over and rubbed his back. When I felt his spine relax, I scooted closer and wrapped my arms around him and leaned on him, and finally said, "She's so much like you."

# CHAPTER♡SIXTEEN

## *Julie*
### *About a Month Ago*

*THEIR* CORNER WAS NOT NEAR HER HOUSE. IT WAS NOT NEAR IAN'S HOUSE. It was at a park inside of High Street, the commercial district where the clinic was, close enough that if someone did see them, they could at least pretend they were together on business. As if the head of a birthing center and a fairly new nurse had out-of-hours, outside-the-walls *business*.

*I am so stupid,* she told herself waiting on the bench and wondering if it was going to rain.

He was there, one minute late. He was always just a little late, and she always noticed. Did he do it on purpose, to test her? To remind her that his was the upper hand? As if she needed reminding that she had no power, other than to simply cut Ian off and continue with Chad as though none of this had happened.

...as though she wasn't certain she was in love with Ian and wanted, well, what she almost assuredly couldn't have with him.

He smiled sympathetically down at her. Her heartbeat accelerated, welcoming the emotion from him, hating that it was pity.

She waited him out, not rising. He finally sat next to her, as close as possible without touching her. Would she touch him first?

She was breathing him in like incense, not just his scrubbed, masculine scent, but the aura of accessible confidence he carried.

She had never known anything like it, how he managed to make her stronger and make her melt all at once.

"I don't want you to go," he finally murmured. "I feel like if you leave the clinic, you're definitely leaving me. And probably Arizona."

Did she hear pleading in his voice? She thought so. *Score.*

"You're probably right," she answered, with a coolness she did not feel.

"Have you told... Chad?"

She stiffened. He shouldn't say Chad's name. Chad did not deserve one bit of what they, what she, was doing to him.

"Not yet." She would not elaborate.

"How can I convince you to reconsider, Julie? I am not making light of what happened. The absolute worst thing about what we do is losing lives. But it will always happen. It happens to each of us, and the first time remains among the hardest. You can't–"

"Among the hardest?" She scoffed bitterly. "You must think I am made out of much stronger stuff than I am. Because if this isn't the *hardest*, all you're doing is convincing me that I can't. I can't do this."

He sighed, out of patience with her.

"If you give it a minute, you'll get through it. Not *over* it, but through it."

"I'm sure you're right," she said.

"But?"

"But I don't want to. I'm done."

They'd been looking out in parallel, not facing each other, but now, he turned to her, and when she looked back, his face was angry.

"You're right," he said. "I did think you were tougher than this."

"So sorry to disappoint *you*."

"Don't make this about me," he shot back.

"Of course not," she said. "Nothing is about you. You just exist in your own reality, untouched by it all. *Above* it all. A woman dies, I am to blame, but you just... go about your day. Go home to your *wife*."

"There it is!" he snapped.

"There it *always* is," she said. "It doesn't go away, Ian. You are married, and I... what am I doing here with you?"

"You're the only one who can answer that." His tone was softer now, but his words still cut.

"You pompous son of a bitch." She didn't seethe it or yell it. She stated it as fact. It didn't rattle either of them.

After the beat of silence, she added, "What are you doing here with *me*?"

Now he replied with a laugh that wasn't really a laugh. She stared at him, his short and perfectly, subtly gelled brown hair, his chiseled face, clean-shaven, unmarred by wrinkles or scars of any kind. His steel blue eyes could burn with intensity or radiate inspiration. He made patients, partners, and Julie Jameson believe every word he said because he always appeared to be staring into their souls. His words dripped honey. His sure hands, which had delivered and rescued thousands of babies, restored heartbroken infertile women, given families hope, seemed to carry magic in their touch, whether they'd held on briefly mid-handshake or rested seductively on her hips the first time their flirtation had manifested into something else.

"If either of us could answer those questions, I guess everything would be different, wouldn't it? I don't know, Jule. I know that seeing you and hearing from you is the highlight of every day for me. You think I have it all, and I'd be perfect without you, but that's just not true. You've added... well, honestly, you've been like sunshine for me. And I'll miss you more than you know."

*I will miss you.* Oh, the other things he'd said had been more of the same, more of the honey. But that's how he did it. Wrapped sugar around bitterness. Wrapped his shitty leftovers in secret smiles that touched her in the same way his hands did, knowing her, reassuring her, and letting her believe in a magical reality that ultimately did not exist.

"It was never going to be real," Julie murmured.

He put a magic hand to her cheek. "It was real. How I feel is real."

She closed her eyes and inhaled him once more. And then she exhaled as deeply as she could, so that when she looked at him again, she didn't see magic.

"How you feel, Ian, is self-serving. I am not sunshine. I am not *your Jule.* I needed what I thought you were offering, and it turns out it was just..."

She held her hands out in front of her, struck by how much they looked like her mama's, struck by their emptiness. She thought learning to deliver babies would be the most natural thing for her to do with them. She thought she'd be at least engaged to someone by now. Now she had nothing to hold. Nothing.

"...vapor," she finished.

"I'm not," he said, rising. "I'm just not the answer to everything."

"I didn't ask you to be!" The panic started. *Don't go. I'm not ready.* She stood.

"Then what?" he said, taking a step toward her. It was all she wanted, and he probably knew that.

She looked down at their shoes. It was starting to drizzle. Almost unheard-of in the late summer of Arizona.

"I want how you make me feel. I want it all the time."

The rain pelted them. He put his hands to her face and pulled her to him, and the kiss lasted, and she melted into him without a single thought of what would happen after.

She was dried off and waiting at the kitchen table when Chad finally got home. She had grown used to the waiting; it was part of the lifestyle choice, part of healthcare. That they both worked in it made it easier to understand. He might come home three hours later than anticipated and not have ten seconds to text her a heads up. He might come home so drained from the day that they wouldn't talk about it at all. It was one of a list of six hundred things that meant they should have worked out together.

But she was sitting there with her mind made up. Nothing she had done since she left Surfside Beach had worked for her. Not the *three* relationship attempts. Not the way she'd treated her father. Not the colossal career fail. None of it.

"You're still dressed, babe. It's so late."

Chad had his black dress shirt unbuttoned. It was a hybrid day for him, office hours in the morning, hospital in the afternoon, and a few emergent cases kept him there late. His hair was a little disheveled and his eyes a bit shadowed, but the rest of him looked just as he had that morning when she'd tried to avoid his goodbye kiss. He was all perfect, wavy hair, long on top, short on sides, wide hazel eyes, strong chin, chiseled cheeks with the right amount of gristle, generous smile.

*He's all yours*, her mother's voice whispered. *Keep him.*

She almost told Mama to shut up. Instead, she didn't take Chad's offered hands. She rose from the chair. She took in his head tilt and his warm stare and proceeded to break his heart.

"Chad. I have to go."

"Okay. Go. Go for a walk. Take a little while. Did you eat? We have any good leftovers?"

Of course, she couldn't tell him. How could she tell an established, already award-winning pediatrician that she had basically killed a new mother the day before? How could she tell him that her arrogance led to negligence that led to a little baby boy who was now motherless?

And how could she tell him that even though he'd been the most wonderful, accommodating, supportive, and on-paper perfect boyfriend she had ever had, she'd been cheating on him almost the entire time she had worked at the Babymoon B&B, and definitely the whole time they'd lived together?

This was *ridiculous*. This was something *Katy* would do! This was not something Julie did. This was something that would disappoint her mother. It was something she could never tell her father.

This was not something she could continue.

"Chad, I appreciate the time we had. But... it's just not working for me. I don't belong here. I'm not myself here. And I have to figure out where it is I can be myself, whoever that is now. Because everything has changed."

"What has changed? You came here, into this house, with your eyes wide open. You broke up with David. You put a stake in the ground and decided to make a real home here. We bought a couch! We're church greeters, for crying out loud."

"Chad, you're in medicine. Don't you know anything about grief? I was grieving my mother. I am *still* grieving my mother. I don't know who I am without her in this world. David was a mistake, and I'm sorry but–"

"Don't say it."

"I really think this was, too."

She couldn't look him in the eye. He deserved so much better than what she was leaving him with right now. Everything about them had looked like a step toward Mr. and Mrs. Happily-Ever-After, everything except the other half of her that waited for Ian, inhaled Ian, wanted Ian.

She wanted to want Chad that way. Why couldn't she?

"I'm going to find a place to spend the night. And then I'll come tomorrow and get things together. I... I'm sorry."

"You owe me a better explanation than this, Julie. "

"You're right. I probably do. I know I do. I do. But this is all I have to give right now. I gave you everything I had to give, and you can see. It's not much."

Weeks later, in Surfside Beach, she still wasn't giving much to anyone. Julie had spent all night rehashing. David, Chad, Ian, even Robin a little, and the man who ran a thread through it all: her dad.

They would leave at 10:30 for her to get to work in time. She had slept approximately two hours, and she was out of coffee in her little guest-suite .

*I should check the mirror and make sure my tail is all the way tucked between my legs.* Her head, and her pride, were throbbing.

She practically tiptoed into the main kitchen, as though they wouldn't be up. As though she couldn't make out the din of their little sing-songy routine every morning. Nineties' country or '70s rock playing. The smell of coffee and the sound of a pan moving or a toaster popping. She wouldn't be waking them. She would just be... trying to go around them as much as possible.

But when she walked in, the coffee pot was full, and everything was quiet. The blinds in the front of the house were still closed. She checked her phone against the clock on the oven and saw it really was 10:15. She wondered if Daddy had forgotten. She wondered if she should see if Robin could pick her up after all. But she sat there completely inert, drained, lost. It was only about seven miles to the store. She could probably tell Robin she'd be late and just run there. Maybe–

"Good morning."

Paul's gravelly morning voice came out in monotone. His eyes were bloodshot, and he poured his coffee without even looking at Julie. She felt like a teenager, except he was hardly ever mad at her during that era. He was too busy being mad at Katy for coming in past curfew or having a forty-one percent average in all her academic classes during eleventh grade. Who had time to notice when Julie was up on the phone all night with Dylan Miller or that she and her friends Stacy and Shelly had spent the night at Josh Ritter's after his cast party?

*Shut up, Julie. Drink your coffee and stop remembering anything.*

"Are you ready to go?" Paul asked.

"Oh, yeah. I mean, it's early, but whenever you are."

He stood with his back to the counter, jangling his keys in one hand, tipping back his cup with the other.

"Are you... okay?" she asked.

Paul shook his head. "No one is okay. But I get to come home and go back to bed at least."

"Oh. Are you sick?"

He cocked his head at her. "Julie, we just didn't sleep well. You clearly haven't either. But I'm retired. I'm driving my grown, professional, hungover daughter to her job, and then I may sleep the rest of the day."

"That's good, then. Yeah. Okay. I'm ready."

They drove the first five minutes in silence. Julie watched the distinctive small-town views of Surfside Beach go by. This wasn't the town of her childhood, although this was where they went to the beach, sometimes the waterpark, definitely to eat at Crabby Mike's or down on the Marshwalk when people came to visit. Now, the old side of Highway 17, "17 Business," was already familiar. The pancake houses, the quaintly southern village hall, the poor old theater that was now a golf cart store, even the perfectly named "Jerribob's," the shipping store where she was getting her mail for now. Truth was, she was falling in love with the little town, with being so close to the beach, with the old trees and the charming houses. She would be sad to run elsewhere when she moved out.

Because she was going to move in with Chad. There really couldn't be a question. She couldn't stay with Dad and Jessie any longer than absolutely necessary.

"Please stop drinking like that," Paul said. He still hadn't looked at her, and that made her stomach feel much worse than the vodka. "Please. I'm not going to ask you for anything else. You do what you want with where you live and how you act. That's on you. But you drinking and being reckless, Jules, that's on me. I won't let you. I will fight for you. I will fight you."

"Daddy..." She didn't want to cry anymore. She was dehydrated. How was there anything left?

"Please? Promise me?"

They were at a red light. She wanted to stop the car, stop everything, tell him how sorry she was for everything. But this was not the time for emotion. She ignored how much of it was on his face. She just reached over to his hand and squeezed it as hard as she could. "I promise. And I'm sorry."

He squeezed back and said nothing else. She hated how tired he looked, how somber, because it reminded her how much older he was. Thank God he was still strong, and still forgiving.

She felt the blush of humiliation darken her cheeks as he pulled alongside her parked car. "The limo service stops now," he said, a little more brightly. "Make good choices today."

"I will. And Daddy?"

Now he looked. He was taking her in, her messy bun, her dry eyes, but hopefully also the natural tan and muscle tone that was washing over her from all the miles she was running. It was the only decent thing she was doing lately.

"I'm sorry. Really. I—I want you to be happy. I'm... I'm grateful you are happy."

At that point, he reached over the console of the Jeep and without out a note of awkwardness, hugged her tightly. She figured he wasn't up to any speeches or there would most assuredly be one. So, she let go and fumbled for her stuff, and when she got out of the vehicle and he rolled down his window, she looked at him and said, "You deserve to be loved."

That triggered the emotion on his face. He nodded it into submission and simply answered, "So do you."

Julie had forgotten that it was Mini Marathon weekend. Before she got in the door, there were race participants in the store, getting buy two, get one socks, picking out their gels and electrolyte tabs, combing through the novelty headbands, and talking to anyone who would listen about the forecast, their race plan, the last time they ran this route, that time back in 2019 when it got cancelled for wind (damn tropical storms), how the Hoka Clifton and doing calf stretches *all damn day* cured their plantar fasciitis, and what they were eating for dinner. And then they would take selfies with Pote.

There was probably a time that Julie would have rolled her eyes or turned her nose up at that level of enthusiasm about, well, pretty much anything. But today, standing at the register with her whole body and soul hungover, she found them inspiring.

Hazel and Darcy worked the floor in experienced rhythm. They greeted people who only came to town once a year during race weekend. They cheered for people getting ready to run their first half marathon. They remembered people's shoe sizes, favorite colors, and dogs' names. Julie had the stuff in her to get there, but until then, she hadn't been sure she wanted to.

All day, people made her FEEL like she was part of something. She hadn't considered registering for this race. She hadn't stepped foot inside this store before she bought her shoes there. But she was welcomed and high-fived, quizzed and invited. It was the best energy she'd been around in, well, maybe her entire life.

Her favorites of the day were Bill and Trish, a pair of high school sweethearts who'd been married fifty-two years, strolling in the door hand-in-hand wearing sunglasses matching their shoes. They mostly stopped by to say hello, see other runners in town, and look at possible new shirts for their 5K in the morning. Before they left, Bill told Julie about one of the thirty-eight marathons he had run, during which he turned to talk to his friend and had a tree branch pierce his eardrum. "Dropped like a rock! Only one I didn't finish!... But don't let that scare you!"

Julie kind of wanted to follow them home and ask them how they did it... all the marathons and all the years. Naturally, that's when Chad had texted her again. He sent the link to his apartment, right down the street in Market Common, where people could walk to anything from the grocery store and movie theater to bars, smoothie cafes, and doggie day spas.

After the door was finally locked, Darcy was cashing out and Julie was sweeping, Hazel let out a "Shooooooo-wee. That was a day! You happy, boss? I think every half-marathoner out there will be wearing your logo."

Robin smiled. "Of course. It was a good day. Good job, you guys."

"We should celebrate! Who wants to hit Nacho Hippo? I'm meeting Pat and the Debbies there."

Darcy laughed. "Hazel, I'm *running* the half, remember? I can't drink tonight. I need to get my legs up. And probably eat pancakes."

"How could anyone forget?" Robin said. Darcy talked them through her training daily. Julie was in awe of her forty-ish mile weeks and super-disciplined eating. She made most twenty-somethings seem like whiny toddlers in comparison. "Um, also, you said you would meet me to get the finish line up in the morning, Ms. Hazel. Six a.m."

"Silly man. I will be there. And Darcy, baby, no one forgets. I just wanted to feed you something besides a protein shake and kale."

Darcy grinned knowingly. "After the race," she said. And then she hugged Hazel. "See you in the morning! Bye Jules! Bye Robin!"

Julie found herself genuinely grinning as she finished putting stuff away. She wondered if this was what people meant about sitting with winners. The three people here were different from her and each other, quirky and vibrant, and they made her, in spite of herself, want what they had.

She was heading toward to door when Robin called her. He was sitting at his desk, humorously tiny for his frame. He had changed his shoes and was chugging water.

"What's up?"

"I thought we were going for a run?"

At that moment, she wasn't sure she was awake enough to drive home. She might have sold more shoes that day than she'd owned her entire life. She saw someone's heel blisters and another person's X-rays. She was pretty sure she agreed to train for some sort of mountainside 10K. She was done.

"Why do people who are racing buy shoes the day before? And why do people who aren't racing come here the day before when it's bonkers?"

Robin smiled. "If they aren't racing, they don't know it's going to be bonkers. They don't know there's a race."

"It was really busy."

"Yeah. You gonna change?"

"Robin, I—"

"Julie, when Hazel suggested going for drinks, you were about to say yes."

Julie looked down. Her pretty white and teal Brooks were graying from a day of haphazard retail. She'd been saving them for work. Now she might as well get them dirty.

"I can be ready in five minutes. I have to change my shorts…"

"Drink some water!" he called after her, and she could her the teasing in his voice.

They ran four miles. Julie knew he was slowing down for her, but she forced herself not to care. They didn't say much, and she hadn't brough her earbuds, so all she heard was her own panting. She wasn't sure if Robin was breathing at all. He seemed lighter than air and like he was in his own world.

Maybe they should sell donuts and whiskey at the store instead of Gu and Clif Shots.

When they got back, she stood by the outside wall and stretched. The evening breeze had been perfect, but the late fall humidity was dropping from the end of her ponytail, her forehead, down her arms and legs. Even though she'd been going at the easier end of her pace, she felt like Jell-o.

"You good?" Robin asked her, in the midst of his own perfunctory stretch.

She nodded. "Yeah. I didn't feel like I had anything to give, but this was good. I'll probably slip into a coma when I get home."

"You want Mozzarella's first?" He nodded in the direction of their pizzeria neighbors.

"No," she said regretfully. "I need to go to bed. I need to figure some stuff out. I told my dad last night that I was moving out..."

"What?"

"Yeah. We sort of... had *that* conversation last night. I mean, with Jessie, too."

"Really? Like a telenovela. Please, let me buy you a slice of pizza."

She laughed. "No. Thank you. There's not much to say. It was a bad idea, me staying with them. It wasn't fair to them; I can admit that much. And I need to be happy my dad is happy, not just say I am. She... she loves him. and he deserves that." As long as she kept that in her mind, her own insecurity seemed to stay quiet.

"So, what are you going to do? You moving in with your sister or finding a place?"

She was afraid he was going to ask that. "No, I mean, not my sister. God bless. I've been looking for a place, every day. But I might... I mean, Chad is moving right here in Market Common, so I might try..." She couldn't finish.

"Julie—"

"I know," she said, avoiding his gaze.

"I don't think you do," he said. "You... you don't need this. You don't need Chad to get you out of your situation."

"What should I do, Robin? You want a roommate?"

"Sure." He smirked. "No. Not really. But I... listen. I don't... I don't have a lot of people. My family is close, but... This store, these are my people. Hazel doesn't need anything except a place to perform. And Darcy is pretty low-key when she's not, like, training for the Olympics or whatever she's up to. So, I'm plenty fine with helping you out. You're... we're friends, now. I know this isn't your best chapter. And I don't mind helping you get to the next one."

"That's really poetic for someone who's sober," she said quietly.

"I mean it, Julie."

She looked at him, sweat glistening on his face and soaking through his shirt. He was not at all how or whom she'd expected him to be. She wasn't sure what all the pretenses had been about on the first day they met because every day since then, he'd been one of the most genuine people she currently knew. Or maybe ever knew.

"I know you do. I appreciate it so much. And I... I know if I need a little perspective... hey, maybe even wisdom!... I can ask you. Tonight I'm just tired. The run was cleansing. The store was fun today. Maybe a good night's sleep will reset me the rest of the way."

"Maybe," he echoed. "See you tomorrow. You have the key, right? I don't have a back-up app."

Julie smiled. Since he and Darcy and Hazel would be at the race, she was opening the store on her own. And just because she had helped deliver babies didn't mean she wasn't nervous as all get-out.

"Got it, boss."

"Julie?"

"Yeah?"

"Think about it some more. I know things are tough, but you haven't hit rock bottom yet."

She went to bed early, after grabbing grilled nuggets on the way home and going in through the back door. The house was still quiet, and she figured it was best to leave it that way. Robin's parting wisdom weighed heavy, but she put it out of her mind when she sat on the bed and finally answered Chad.

# CHAPTERSEVENTEEN

## *Jessie*
### *The Same Day*

WHEN I OPENED MY EYES, THE SUN WAS BATHING THE ROOM. We had black out curtains designed to hold the intense South Carolina sun at bay and ward off its intrusions (ugly, dingy-gray curtains that Maggie helped me attach to the back of beautiful ones of bohemian gold, red, and turquoise), but if they didn't absolutely get pulled all the way across the window, they were worthless. Paul wasn't next to me, which didn't surprise me. I just knew he'd gotten up before dawn, run a hundred miles, showered, and made breakfast by now.

I stretched in an attempt to wake myself. We'd been up far later than we'd been since, well, the great *before*. But to be fair, it had been months since one of our children had caused a sleep-delaying hurricane of emotions. We'd been overdue.

"I'm sorry I engaged," I had said when we were settling in our room the night before. He was already undressed and in bed, and

I was slogging through my own nighttime routine, wishing I was the kind of person who could just collapse without the shower and toner and coconut oil and decompressing. I tried, and it never worked.

Paul peered at me from above his reading glasses, the ones he had just started wearing without lament during this season of accepting our age. Shame free lenses for him. Bioidentical hormones for me. Ibuprofen after every run for him. An ergonomic keyboard and chair for me. Less salt, sugar, and caffeine (on some days) for both of us. It was a bummer, but as the adage goes, especially for two widowed people, it beat the alternative.

"Jess." He thought better of it and just took off the glasses at that point. "Sweetheart, I knew it was just a matter of time. I mean, really. I never doubted for one solitary moment that if given the chance, you would try to talk to Julie. In fact, I'm impressed it took so long. I blame the cancer."

I exhaled deeply. Paul had taken my cancer diagnosis harder than I did. His ability to make light of it in any way was a small victory.

"Well," I said carefully. "Good, I guess. I was... I hate for you to be mad at me."

"Why would you think I could ever be mad at you?"

He was serious. I looked at him and could tell he meant the words he was saying. So, I dropped my routine and walked mid-shower-prep, which meant wearing my cami and no pants, over to the bed, and I sat down next to him, on his side.

"Paul?"

"Jess."

"Paul, tonight, talking to Julie, was the angriest I have ever seen you. I have never heard you yell before. Well, okay. Maybe I did in our past life, probably when Katy ran away. But that was intense..."

"So, you want me to be intensely mad at you?" He smiled. Jerk.

"I hate how cute you are. Stop it!" Then he laughed. "Love," I continued, "I just want to be careful. We have to be able to say anything to each other, even if it is unpleasant."

Paul shook his head. He put his hand on my face. "Please don't worry about this right now, Jess. This isn't... *before*. We are in this together. I just... I wanted to keep you from having to worry about Julie. Or deal with her attitude. But I did expect at some point that you would, well, come to blows. It was actually milder than I expected. And you have to know..." He broke off, and the shadow of what took place downstairs seemed to cover him again. "That wasn't really about you."

"Paul... does Julie... are you worried she has a drinking problem?"

He ran his hands through his hair. It was a signature sign of stress. "Jess, I don't want to bother you—"

"Paul!" Now I took his hands, both of them, and even though it was way past my cancer bedtime, I squeezed them to show him I was strong. "Please! Bother me! We have spent our whole marriage so far being bothered *by* me. My stuff. I am sick of me. Tell me what that was all about."

He looked down at our hands, at the curtains as though he could see through them to the outside, then back down.

"Look at me. Please."

He did.

"She's not you," I said. "She's not an alcoholic. She is young and fiery and angry and embarrassed. Whatever the hell happened that drove her and David to Arizona, whatever happened out there, she is reeling from it. And someday, she'll tell you about it, or she'll be healed from it. But it's not the same. You are *not* your parents, and Julie is not you. She's too strong and healthy to drink her chances away. She's just having a bad moment."

"Jess." The hands went to his hair again, and I regretted that he let go of me. It was never a good sign when he broke the connection. "You haven't been there, okay? All it takes is a few bad moments, and then yes, suddenly, you are a Christian school principal driving your own daughters home drunk. I was smart, too. I was supposedly healed, too. I had my whole life put together way better than Julie does now. And I still did it. I just can't let her, even if she hates me for it. Even if she hates you. I will be relentless about that."

"You should be," I said quietly. "But you can't control her life, Paul. They don't always learn from our mistakes."

He didn't respond.

"Okay. We won't solve this tonight. I know I don't get it all. I know I don't know Julie that well. I hope that changes. I just wanted to apologize. I'm gonna shower."

I stood and walked away and found myself hoping he was watching. I had lost another twelve pounds since our wedding and was at my lowest weight since before I had Mikayla. I knew I looked good. The catch was that I felt like crap and had physically given him next to nothing since our honeymoon in Puerto Rico. Maybe my skinny arse would entice him to get up and follow me. Maybe we could take a shower together.

But he didn't. And we didn't. And by the time I finished all the post-shower tasks, he still hadn't. Maybe he'd fallen asleep, which wouldn't be the worst thing. I knew he hadn't been resting well.

I could barely see him with his form burrowed under the covers.

I turned off the light and scooted closer to kiss his temple, and at that moment I realized he was still awake. He was praying, for Julie and for me. I briefly heard the words slipping out of his mouth. I lay my head right next to his and put my hand on his shoulder. I agreed, out loud, with everything he was praying. That any addictions Julie had would be broken. That no cancer was left in me. That Paul would see clearly and lead his family well and give me everything I needed. It was one of the sweetest and most surprising prayers I had ever heard.

When he stopped saying the words, I noticed the moisture on his face. In the dark it had been hard to see, but with the talking over, I could see the remnants of his tears. I scooted closer and burrowed myself in his chest. His arms immediately encircled me, and it was my turn to cry.

"I'm here for *you*!" I exclaimed. "Please don't carry things alone. I promise you... I'm fine. And I'm strong. And it's my job now to stand by your side and help our family however and whenever we can. And it's my job to help you!"

He didn't say anything, just held me tightly.

"Paul. I mean it."

He let go. I felt the vibrations of frustration, and I sat up. So did he. I turned the lamp on. He sat up straighter.

"Jessie, right now, my job is to help you. And protect you. And your job is to heal and recover and stop trying to be superwoman for just a few weeks. Not that much longer now. You can do it. And I can handle Julie."

"I know you can handle Julie. I'm not asking to *handle* Julie. I'm talking about you! You barely talk to me about anything past what we're eating or watching on TV. I'm not going to break, Paul. You just said... not that much longer. The worst is over."

He looked away. My stomach felt like a brick.

"Paul."

He swiped at his eyes, but they kept betraying him.

"No," was all he said.

"*Paul!*"

"No!" He might have meant to snap at me, but it came out as a sob. I could feel my heart break at the sound. Of course, I knew all of this was hard on him. We had ten wonderful days in San Juan. We had a few mostly-blissful weeks of feeling our way around married life in the house we'd moved into together eight months prior. And then, I started bleeding and the big C came crashing into our lives, all in the backdrop of our individual grief and his estranged daughter and the rest of our kids getting pregnant, changing jobs, changing boyfriends, and just living. They were around a lot; they *were* a lot. That's what we wanted. But it was all *a lot.*

He never showed anything but stoic resolve to everyone else. He never showed anything but tender compassion to me. But somewhere in there, I lost my best friend's confidence and humor, his charm.

"Paul...Paul..." I knew this part of him. I had only seen it a few times in all the years I'd known him. The first time was actually the marker of when we went from friendly co-workers to friends. He'd gotten a call that his mother died. Their relationship had the complications of its own family saga. In seconds, he went from shellshocked to broken, and he cried in my arms.

It was only years later I realized that I was the only person in the world, in his life, that he had been that vulnerable with. I carried that like a fragile, newborn bird.

And I knew he didn't want me to comfort him, and I treaded

carefully because I also knew he needed to be comforted.

After a moment, with him shaking next to me, I sat myself taller and gathered him. His face against my neck, I felt his breathing start to steady. I touched whatever parts of him my hands could reach, making those indecipherable soothing sounds that nurturers speak as a second language, and saying his name, because he needed to hear it. He needed to be reminded who he was.

He lifted his head. And this was the part I struggled with. I wanted to conclude this moment. I wanted to promise "Everything will be okay." I wanted to offer platitudes and declarations, the ultimate pep talk. *No more tears, love. You're good. We're good.*

Paul's past was so different from mine. I took my childhood and its failures, those of my parents and my own, and tried to do better. My family was guarded and negative, and while my tendency was to be cynical, I fought to be hopeful and happy and instill that in my kids. Paul's family was a nightmare. His father was violent. His mother was frozen. He grew up in fear and learned to squash it. He found his way to be better too, and his fight, though it didn't involve a baby from an ill-conceived fling with a stranger, was much harder than mine. He had no support. He was all alone, until he found Leah. And then they became partners, working partners, careful partners.

I had never asked him why he never let her in the way he did me. Maybe it was age. Maybe personalities. Maybe she felt betrayed after his years of quiet alcoholism. Whatever it was, I was certain that my arms were the only ones he'd cried in throughout his adult life. It was the saddest kind of sacred. And I learned to use my human-blanketness all by itself. He showed me that words were not necessary when I was being a soothing presence. So, I waited, blinking away my own tears.

"I love you," he said softly. "I promise you I still see all your faults." We both giggled a little. "But this is my season to take care of you, not hash all the other things out with you. There is always going to be something wrong in the family. And Jess, sometimes, I'll want you to take the lead on things. But not now. I want to give you what I never gave Leah because I didn't think I was capable. I want to give you what you give me. Just a place to rest, to be assured. You really are a couple weeks away from fighting form, and I know you're gonna launch yourself back into the world like a tiger who's been caged too long. I won't stop you then. But right now, I just want to keep you safe. Because I need you around for as many years as we can milk out of this, okay?"

"Okay, Paul. I know. Thank you so much..."

"You're welcome."

"But Paul?"

"Yes, Jessie..."

"I know this particular price of love is... a little new to you. The cost of intimacy. And I want you to know that it's hard and it's scary to admit you need anyone, but I promise you, it's worth it. I promise."

At that, he began kissing my neck, right up to my ear into which he whispered, "Promise?"

"Mmm," was my answer.

"Not much longer," he whispered, kissing me more.

"No more waiting," I said. I wasn't sure if my body was ready, but the rest of me was, so pulled him closer and gave him everything I could.

# Part 2

# CHAPTER♡EIGHTEEN

## *Julie*

"Leave me alone. I like routine. This is routine."

"Sweaty runs with your hot boss and occasional drinks with your geriatric co-worker. Okay, Jules. Awesome. Yolo, y'all. God said live."

"Someday, Katy," was all she answered. But Katy got it.

"I know. My metabolism will quit. I will have a pasta and fried chicken and beer belly, and my boobs will rest on top of it. But it will be so worth it. Plus, I think I'm happier than you are."

"Touché. I gotta go. I'm here."

"Okay. Tell Hot Boss I said hey. And I am single."

"So, what else is new? Love-you-bye."

Julie parked and took a deep breath. Since her Come to Jesus with Paul, she had embraced routine, which had always been her best medicine. And part of that routine was a callback to what it used to be. She used to call her mama every day on her way to work. For a long time, she called no one, just listened to podcasts or silence. Part of her Get My Life In Order plan was alternating days, calling her sisters.

It was mostly fine. Except they had each invited her to some damn tea party with Jessie and all of her daughters and granddaughters and the entire Oakley Nation, and that was still a hard pass for her.

Danielle's new baby was due just after the holidays. She promised her she would figure out how to live in this family before then.

For now, though, there was her routine. Julie was opening the store a few days a week now, and she loved how quiet it was before anyone else was there. She put all her stuff away, double-checked all the shelves and floors to make sure everything was put up properly. She ran the vacuum or swished the toilets. She picked out music to play and then she brewed herself her first coffee of the day because her new routine meant she had water and protein before anything else. Her head felt so much clearer.

And then her favorite part came. She unlocked the door and took the American flag outside to hang. She would stand there and look up and down the little plaza, at the pizzeria and the bagel shop, the nail salon, the bike store, the wide sidewalks, and little bistro tables. Sometimes people were outside eating breakfast. Sometimes they were walking dogs or waiting on repairs. Many times, workers from the other businesses would be walking by, and they'd stop to chat for a minute. Julie just loved how connected it made her feel, the charm of a small business, the feeling of pride and ownership. Maybe she wasn't changing the world or saving lives working there, but she was helping people. And she was changing her own life. She felt confident for the first time in weeks, hopeful for the first time in months.

The morning was slow, and she spent some time trying on the new Diadoras and visiting with Trish and Bill when they stopped by. Hazel was scheduled to be there just before lunchtime when things usually picked up, but when Julie heard the back door, she looked up and saw Robin.

"I thought you were off today?" she said brightly.

"Mmmhmm. I was."

"Wait, what's wrong?"

He squared his shoulders and sat on a stool, typing something on his phone.

Silence was unlike him. He was either explaining something or snarking, and she felt impatient. "Is everything okay?"

Tap, tap, tap, and then he finally looked up at her. "Hazel's in the hospital."

"What? Why?"

"It sounds like she had a... a cardiac event?... after her run this morning. Or during. I'm a little unclear. Darcy and I went to the hospital. A couple of her kids are on their way here. We didn't even get to see her, but Darcy is still there. I wanted to make sure you were okay here."

"I mean, whatever. Is Hazel okay? What do you mean 'event'? Did she go into arrest? What's their treatment plan?"

"Julie, they wouldn't really tell us anything. Just that she was stable and awake. My guess is she will call one of us, probably you, when she can."

Julie's insides were quivering. "Why me?"

"Because," he explained, with a small smile. "You're her favorite."

Just then, Julie felt a vibration in her pocket. Normally during working hours, with Robin standing right there in front of her, she would wait to check it. This time, she yanked it out, hoping it was Hazel with any news at all.

Can you call me, Jule? It's really important.

"Is it her?" Robin asked. She detected a hint of urgency in his normally collected tone, and it made her nervous.

"No. Um, no. It is a little timely though. Do you mind if I take my lunch real quick? If I hear from Hazel, I'll come right back."

"Where you going?" he called after her. She was already halfway to the back door.

"Just outside. I–I'll bring you something."

Julie stood in line during the midday craziness at the Bagel Factory, planning her response. Of course, she wanted to call him. Of course, it was a terrible idea. All she knew to do was order two sandwiches and wait outside and mull it over some more.

I'm not sure this is the best time. Middle of the workday. Lunch break kind of short and some stuff going on here.

As soon as she sent it, she grimaced. All that pre-planning and what she ended up sending was way too much information, and completely irrelevant to him anyway. Even though it had been nine minutes since he had sent his text, her response probably sounded so enthusiastic that he assumed she was waiting around to hear from him, which, of course, she was.

Please. I will be quick. I just... need you.

Well, there was the trump card. She knew it was a lie. He didn't need her for one tiny little thing. What he needed was to see if he could still control her, and she gave him the answer. She hit the phone icon next to his name.

"Jule!" His voice sounded like a million things to her... relief, passion, sorrow, distance, release, confusion.

"Hey, Ian. What's going on?"

"I just... I didn't know who to talk to. There's no one else I can, really. I miss you, you know? You... you really are the best. My best friend."

Julie shut her eyes. Once upon a time she took a Love Language test in the back of one of her mama's books. It determined that her primary love language was "Words of Affirmation." That was obvious enough, but honestly. It could just be "Words of Affirmation from Dr. Ian Brammer" because one kind word from him turned her inside out. She forgot about work, her lunch order, Hazel, Daddy and Jessie, Chad moving, everything. All that existed was this moment, in which Ian said he *needed her.*

"You can always talk to me..." She hoped it sounded non-committal, not overly eager, but she doubted it.

"Listen, I know you, um, maybe saw on Instagram or something. Fawn... Fawn was pregnant."

*Oh my God. Was?* "I did see..."

"She—we lost the baby. Confirmed this morning."

In one instant, billions of conflicting neurons fired in Julie's brain. What had happened? Was Ian okay? Was Fawn okay? Those were irrelevant questions; no one was totally okay after a miscarriage. Had the expectant arrival of a baby brought them closer? Would the miscarriage bring them closer? Would it drive them apart? Were they staying together because of the baby? Would Ian feel like he needed to stay all the more now, or did he feel free. *My God, Julie, you are so inappropriate right now.*

She closed her eyes and let Clinical Julie rise to the top. "Ian, I am so sorry." *Don't say it.* Don't *say it*! "Is there anything I can do?"

There was a long pause. Julie's heart was thumping so wildly she thought it might have filled the silence. "I'm fine. We were, I mean, she was ten weeks along. The... the baby was measuring at six weeks. So, for all we know, there was never a..."

He didn't have to finish. From all she had seen, she knew it was very unlikely their baby's heart had ever begun beating.

"I'm so sorry," she repeated.

Ian exhaled. "I just wanted to hear your voice. And talk to someone who... understands."

Well, the fact was she had been around probably several hundred patients who had miscarried. But the truth was, she didn't understand. She knew miscarriage held an infinite number of emotions depending on the person it was happening to, and she had sympathy for each of them but could not relate at all. And he knew that.

"How is Fawn?" she said, still sounding all business.

"I can't tell yet," he answered. "The initial... news... was emotional. And then quiet. And now she went to work. She's not cramping or anything yet. She didn't want to 'sit around and lament.'"

There was a tone in that, one that she recognized quite well from every single time Ian had talked to her about his wife or his marriage. In fact, it reminded her of how her mom talked about her dad. There was a healthy respect and a very distant fondness, like he was talking about a TV character or a long-lost cousin, not his cherished wife, not the heartbroken mother of his potential child. He spoke of Fawn as just a person he sort of cared about. And it wasn't his fault that Julie behaved like a no-good home-wrecker, but he certainly didn't present his story like there was much to wreck.

"I don't know what to say, Ian," she finally said. "I hope everything goes smoothly from this point. I am very sorry, for both of you."

"Jule—"

"I have to go. I'm grabbing lunch for my boss and me and this time of day gets really busy…"

"Jule. You really care about this job? You don't belong in retail. You're so good at what you do. There are so many other options in health care."

"You aren't even listening to me, Ian. I don't want to be in health care. I don't want to talk to you about this. You should be talking to your *wife* today. Not me!"

"Um, okay. I thought you would be happy to hear from me."

"Oh, God yes. I am so *happy* you had two minutes to call me after *four* weeks, by the way, with no regard for the fact that I told you I had to go. And I should be grateful? What kind of person does that make you? And I should be happy you're calling me because your *wife* just had a *miscarriage*? What kind of person would that make me? This is why. We are toxic, Ian. Just stop—"

"Stop what, Jule? Stop calling you altogether? Just forget about you? Is that really what you want?"

*Tell him yes. Say yes, hang up, and move forward with your life.* Leah's logical voice had never made as much sense as it did at that moment, and Julie had never had to fight so hard to ignore it.

"I just can't talk right now. There's stuff going on here, too. I'm so sorry about the baby. I have to go."

"I'm sorry, Jule-bug. I love you, my girl."

*You're not his girl, and you never were.* "I love *you*. Bye."

She pressed the end button, walked briskly inside to the counter to retrieve her order, and gave herself sixty seconds to cry before she went back into the store. The store was mercifully empty, save for Robin. He offered her a generous smile, and if he noticed the tear tracks, he probably attributed them to Hazel and left her alone. He ate grilled ham and cheese and she tuna on rye, in silence. It was silence that she found more comforting than any of the noise she was hearing those days.

"Are you ready?"

Julie looked up from her phone, without dropping it. Robin's voice was far less startling than it had been, and so were text messages from Arizona. Chad was updating her on his plans, though they were pretty cut and dry. His position with the largest regional health care system was secured. His moving truck was contracted. His apartment, less than a mile away from Run This Way, was leased starting the following week. It had three bedrooms, and he'd told Julie one was hers for as long as she wanted. Everything, as it usually was with Chad, was lined up to perfection, generous, convenient.

Today has been awful, she typed back. I think I know what I'm doing, but I'll try to call you tomorrow. Thank you.

Fact was, she sounded clinical, but truth was, she always did with Chad.

Now she looked up at Robin, his face tired with a hint of expectation, and gratefulness for his friendship washed over her.

"Yeah. Let's go."

First stop was the hospital. Hazel was sitting up in bed, her long silver hair loosed from its braid, bun, or hat and flowing freely around her shoulders. Her eyes were shadowed, but her smile was genuine, and there was a surprisingly healthy color to her cheeks.

"Look at you, darlins," she said. "All this fuss. I'm fine. It's fine. Everything is fine! Just a little stent. Routine, really."

"Good God," Robin said, taking a seat beside the bed. "So much drama, Hazel May."

"I know," she replied, with fake mournfulness. "So, Julie Bean, are you ready to fill in all my gaps at the store?"

"What? Of course not. You'll be back in a few weeks."

Hazel nodded slowly at her, then looked at Robin. "She's learning a little optimism. I think my work here really is done."

Robin shook his head. "I don't think we need to solidify all those plans now. We just wanted to check on you, and we will again tomorrow. Family gets here soon, right?"

Hazel smiled. "Mary Claire and Lacey get here tonight. Jim in the morning."

"Awesome," Julie said. "I hope we get to meet them."

"You will." She reached over and patted Julie's hand. "You're my family, too."

"Get some rest, Hazel May." Robin bent and kissed her cheek. "We will talk to you tomorrow."

They had taken Robin's truck to the hospital together, both silent for the drive back to the store. Still looking at the window, only halfway there, Julie asked, "So what now?"

"She'll be fine," he answered. "I don't know if she'll come back to the store to work, but that's okay. I never expected her to stay a long time."

"But..." She paused to choose her words carefully. "You expect me to? Just curious."

Julie watched the look on his face go from casual to intent, as though he, too, was choosing his words carefully. "You really worry about what people think of you. It surprises me."

"What do you mean?"

"I mean, you took this job acting like it was beneath you. But every day you watch Hazel and Darcy and sometimes me, I guess, like we're performing magic tricks. You keep smiling at the doorway when your customers leave. And now you're basically asking if I want you to stay or if I thought you'd fail."

"That's not it," she said feebly. "I just... a friend of mine was asking me about getting back into health care today, and I... I would never want to leave the store in a bind, especially when you don't know about Hazel, and—"

"What friend?" he said, turning onto Farrow Parkway.

"What? I mean, that's not really the point, I just... they got me thinking that maybe I shouldn't rule it out completely."

"Uh-huh. Does this friend happen to live in Arizona and have a wife named after a woodland creature?"

"What difference does that make?"

He pulled into the back lot and threw his Ram into park. "Do you want me to tell you it doesn't make any difference, or do you want me to tell the truth? Because Drunk Julie has said plenty about how this dickhead makes you feel, so I really think he's the last person you want giving you career advice. Why do you even still talk to him at all? What does he have to do with your life here?"

"He doesn't have anything to do with it," she argued. "But maybe he's right. I went through all this school and I'm just gonna—"

"You're just gonna sell shoes."

"Robin, that's not what I meant, and you know it."

He got out of the truck and didn't slam the door, but it was close. She followed.

"I'm not *offended*, Julie. I know what we do here is valuable to a lot of people. In fact, because of us, fewer people have to go see douchebag doctors like Fawn's husband."

She let it be silent for a second. Between it and the darkness, she felt still and calm for the first time all day.

"Because of us, fewer people have to see reproductive specialists?"

She tried very hard not to sound like an arrogant snot when she said it. She wasn't sure if she succeeded. Tension, silence hung in the air.

Robin was laughing, a hard, silent laughter. Once she realized it, she couldn't help but join in.

"Julie, do whatever you need to do. Do whatever you want to do. I hope you'll stay here, not just because I'm about to have a mini labor crisis, but because I think you'll do great things here. But whatever you decide, I hope you don't choose based on what that asshole says to you. Now it's getting late, and I'm beat. Do you want to run a few or not?"

Julie thought through the day, all the people she'd served, the conversations she'd had, Chad, Ian, Hazel, and the slightly stifling late-fall humidity that was assaulting her senses and zapping what was left of her energy.

"Of course, I do."

He nodded and smiled, and they ran.

# CHAPTER♡NINETEEN

## *Paul*

"How about I drive you?" Paul asked, standing at the doorway of the kitchen, dripping sweat onto the red and teal braided rug.

"Um... thank you?" Jessie answered, smiling at him from above her coffee cup. Her hair was on top of her head in some sort of tousled sculpture, her laptop and a notebook were sitting on the table, both open, along with pens of half a dozen different colors. She looked so blessedly normal that it almost took his breath away. "It's just down the street, love, and you..."

"I'll take a bath first," he said, kissing her behind the ear. "You can pretend I'm your chauffeur, and one of the seventeen girls can bring you home."

"What kind of idiot would refuse an offer like that? I guess I'll get ready, too"

"Here." He reached for her coffee cup to give her a refill, just as there was a knock on the door.

"Who comes to the side door and *knocks*?"

"One of a hundred people," Paul muttered as he opened the door.

"Jules?"

He assumed she was getting ready down the hallway.

"Where were you so early?"

She looked confused for a second, and then shook her head. "I was home—er, here. I just didn't want to barge in, and there's no other place to knock."

Jessie was still at the table with her back to the door. Paul watched her, stiffly sitting there with her hands folded on the table. He tried to catch her eye and reassure her, but she was frozen.

"Come in, Jules. You want some coffee?"

"No, um. May I sit?"

"Sure…" he said, as Jessie finally glanced back at him, nodding slightly.

"Good morning," she murmured.

"Good morning," Julie answered.

"I was just about to get ready," Jessie explained, gathering all her pens in a bundle and making a pile with all her other things. Paul fully expected her to retrieve a sponge and start scrubbing the table, too. Cleaning the surface was a classic Jessie deflective move, and she was already *leftover* tense from their conversation the night before. "I'll leave you two—"

"Actually," Julie said, and Paul recognized the effort it was taking for her to sound normal. "I really wanted to speak to both of you."

"All right," he answered. He stood behind Jessie, methodically resting his hands on her shoulders and looking brightly at his daughter. "What's up?"

Julie looked at his hands, almost trancelike for a moment of time too short to measure. She shook her head and returned her gaze first to Paul's face, then Jessie's, and back again.

"I just wanted to tell you that I'm moving out next week. I'm very grateful y'all let me stay here in between... for this time. It's a great house, and a great space, and it was exactly what I needed."

Paul tilted his head and squinted to make sure he was really hearing his daughter Julie, and not some body-snatcher. "Of course, Jules."

Jessie cleared her throat, softly. "I'm glad you like it. I'm glad you got what you needed."

Paul almost laughed. He could practically hear everything Jessie was wanting to add to the end of that, as much as he could see the energy crackling around Julie as she attempted to be as polite as possible. He wished they didn't have to try so hard, even though he was grateful they were.

"Where's your new place?" he asked.

"In Market Common. Right down the street from work."

"Wow. That's a great area," Jessie said.

"That's an expensive area," Paul added. "You get bumped up to co-owner already?"

Julie cleared her throat, tightening her bravado. "I've been talking to Chad these past few weeks." She looked at Jessie. "Chad, um, was, is, the boyfriend I left in Arizona." As though Jessie didn't know. "He took a job with Atlantic Health Care, and he'll be here next week."

"So, you're back together?" Paul asked.

Julie squirmed in her seat. The movement was so small, maybe no one was supposed to notice. But Paul did.

"We're... talking. He has three bedrooms, so for now, we'll be roommates."

The silence was heavy. Paul knew at this stage that Jessie would rather walk on her own lips than say anything to destroy the first time Julie was reaching out. But he also knew his daughter.

"Does that seem like a smart idea?"

"Daddy, I have thought about it a lot. I'm not being impulsive. This is what makes sense right now."

"You don't have to be in a hurry to make a move," he said. "You can stay here."

"Yes," Jessie added, still restrained but with her Mama Voice coming through. "For as long as you need to get settled..."

"I am settled." Julie clipped her words and then caught herself. "I mean, I appreciate the offer. But this didn't just come up. Chad and I have talked on and off about it for a while. I'm not making any promises, but he's a great guy and an extraordinary room-mate. He'll be working a lot at first getting acclimated. We won't be together constantly. It's..." She paused, clearly wondering if she'd said too much. "I want to give it a shot. Nothing is perma-nent, right?"

Paul didn't like how she looked at him when she said that. He didn't agree. But she'd lost her faith that anything was meant to last.

Julie continued. "He's bringing all our furniture from Phoe-nix, so that's a plus. Even if we decide to go separate ways later, I'll have my stuff back. Anyway, it will be a week from tomorrow. I wanted to let you know, especially in case any of the other... kids... need to move in for a while."

She meant it as a joke, but no one laughed. After a beat, Jessie offered, "David is coming for a week at Thanksgiving. I know that you... well, I'm not sure what the expectations are for holidays this year. I just wanted you to know."

"I appreciate that." The ice was creeping into Julie's voice.

Paul looked at her with wearing patience. "Let me know what you need, Jules. I would like to see the place. And I'd like to meet Chad."

"Of course." She stood. "I need to get ready to go."

She gave Jessie a small, tight smile and kissed Paul's cheek on her way back out the door. The kitchen stayed silent for a few moments, save for the hum of two already care-worn brains searching for the right words.

"I wish she wouldn't," Jessie finally said.

Paul nodded, taking her hands to guide her up. "We have to get ready."

"Tea isn't for another hour and a half."

"Nah," he said, a mixture of amusement and dismay. "Ready for however that's going to blow up."

"She needs someone to tell her how ridiculous of an idea this is," Jessie said. "Does she listen to Danielle?"

"She listened to exactly one person," Paul said. And he didn't have to say another word. Julie needed her mama.

"This looks like you if you were a place," Paul murmured in Jessie's ear.

She turned and gave him her brightest smile, and he squeezed her shoulders. He'd never stepped foot in Beachside Garden Tea Room before, but as soon as he saw it, he started to understand. He felt a pang of guilt, and he saw immediately why it was a thing for her. Everything from the quilts on the walls, the mismatched china on display, and the elaborately set tables to the flickering candles, the smell of cinnamon and vanilla, and the classical remixes of '80s and '90s songs coming softly through the speakers.

"You get me," she murmured back. "Are you sure you don't want to stay?"

There was a table reserved for the female tribe of Jessie. He stopped counting at ten seats and shook his head firmly, placing a kiss on her lips.

"This is all you, sweetheart. Carter is going to meet me at Neal and Pam's for lunch. Food that is bigger than a teabag."

"Manly food," she laughed.

"Manly food." He kissed her again. "You look so beautiful."

"I feel like myself."

"I know." He couldn't help it; not normally a huge proponent of PDA, he hugged her tightly from behind. "I'm sorry about before. I love seeing you this way, Jess. Enjoy it. You can bring me back next week, okay?"

She turned and, typically an enthusiastic proponent of PDA as long as it was rated PG, put her hand to his face. "You bring out the me in me. Thank you, love. I love you."

He accepted her gesture and words like manna from Heaven. "I know any of your expansive tribe can bring you home, but we'll just be down the street if you need me."

"Mmmm. Will you also take me back there soon? I know it's the opposite of this, but it sure sounds good."

"I will take you anywhere, anytime." One more kiss. "See you later."

"Bye."

He felt embarrassingly warm as he walked out of the quaint space. Brittney was emerging from her car and stopped to give him a hug. She was the easiest of all Jessie's kids, a little like Katy in her overall exuberance, but without getting quite as fired up over everything. Jessie called her dramatic, but compared to Paul's youngest, she often seemed a bit mellow. And she also seemed to like Paul, which wasn't necessary, but was helpful and welcome.

Just as he was starting his Jeep, he heard a horn blast right next to him. When he looked up, there was Maggie.

"Paul Neuman! Get your skinny tush out here!"

He immediately stepped outside the vehicle and accepted her practically jumping into his arms. She hugged him tight, and he felt surprisingly emotional at what felt like sisterly reassurance.

"She's going to be so surprised," he told her.

"Like I would miss my girl's 'I kicked cancer's ass' party!"

"Ah. I missed the official tea party name. It's perfect."

"It is perfect!"

Paul looked over Maggie's shoulder. "Is it just you? No girls? No baby prince?"

Maggie's first grandchild had been born just weeks before to a full-on jubilee. Because of everything else happening, Jessie and Paul hadn't gotten to meet him.

She shook her head mournfully. "I had to leave that little honey lamb for this. But soon, we will get his precious little toes in the sand. Today is all about Jessie Rose."

Paul went ahead and hugged her again. He smiled at the Jessie-ness of how caught up in the moment he felt. Jessie was going to be okay, and so he felt like everything was going to be okay.

"Paul?"

Maggie's face had gone stone serious, which was a little rare, and so he straightened his shoulders, nodded, and braced for whatever she was going to say.

"You know I loved me some Randall Oakley. I watched him rescue a fairly lost girl and give her a fairy tale life. A beautiful life. But you? You met grown up Jessie Oakley and didn't ask her to be anything but who she is, and you love her so well, and I cannot imagine her life as it is without you. I love me some Paul Neuman-Jameson. I'm so happy you're here!"

"Stop it, Mags." He embarrassingly swiped at his eyes. "I don't know what I did to deserve... this..."

"Paul. Since we already having church, can I tell you one more thing?"

He laughed. "It's not like I can say no!"

"I know, from Jessie, you have spent most of your life believing you don't deserve the whole enchilada, the whole Kwan, the life, abundantly, but you do. The things you carried from your childhood were not your fault. And the mistakes you made because no one taught you any better are in the past. You are one of the finest men I have ever met, and your kids adore you, and this family... this Oakley-mash-up family? We treasure you. We are yours. Okay? *Okay?*"

He nodded, afraid to let himself speak, and he accepted one more hug.

It was nice to have a sister.

# CHAPTER♡TWENTY

## *Jessie*

"I CANNOT BELIEVE YOU'RE HERE!" I SQUEEZED MAGGIE WITH ALL MY MIGHT. It still wasn't much, but it hopefully conveyed my excitement.

"I can't believe you left baby Abram," Mikayla added.

Then my ten-year-old granddaughter Summer chimed in, "I can't believe you didn't *bring* baby Abram!"

There was a chorus of agreement with Summer, and I giggled, knowing that Maggie likely tried. But Abram was a first... her first grandchild, her daughter Nora's first child, the first male descendant of their broken-and-restored family. There was no way Little Prince was leaving his mama's sight for some time.

"We'll come visit soon. Super soon," I said, with a wide-eyed look at Abby. We had a few plans to discuss with our tribe.

"Did y'all reserve the whole place?" Maggie asked, sitting down to my right. I was at the head of our large table and took stock: my two daughters, Mikayla and Brittney, my daughter-in-law, Abby, both granddaughters, Summer practically hosting and baby Josie not knowing where she was, two of my stepdaughters,

Katy and Danielle, along with Danielle's little Vivi, Morgan and her teenaged granddaughter, Annie. In a perfect world, Maggie's daughters *and* Julie would be there, but we were enough as we were, for sure.

*There is no perfect world*, I reminded myself. The family I was looking at was created out of imperfection. Maggie had been married to my brother, my only sibling, and when they divorced, I lost him, but kept her. And of course, Danielle and Katy, though family friends for ages, would likely not have been at this particular gathering had their mama and my husband not died. Even Morgan's presence was a biproduct of something else not going how I wanted; when Maggie, my daily-ride-or-die, moved four hours away, Morgan stepped from my outer circle to my inner one without a beat.

I soaked it in for a moment. Then I answered Maggie, "We didn't specifically reserve the whole place, but Carla mentioned there wasn't much room for any more reservations at the same time as ours. Walk-ins dine at their own risk."

At that moment, Carla and a server came and started taking our tea orders. I felt the volume rising before I even heard it, and I started to feel a little flush. Abby, who was at my other side, told me to drink some water and gave me the eye.

"I'm fine," I murmured. "Maybe a little nervous."

And of course, Maggie heard me. "Nervous about what?" she said, at full volume, because she had no chill, ever.

I glared at her and shrugged. "Been a while since I was in full party mode. Like, since the wedding."

"Ah, the wedding," she said, forgetting what I'd just said. "It was perfect. Did we get a chance to really ruminate in the perfection of it? Because it was, in fact, absolute perfection."

*Four months earlier*

"Is this too much? It feels like it might be too much."

"Too much what? Glitter? Happiness? Be more specific, Jessie Rose. How about some champagne? There cannot be too much of that."

"You're absolutely right. Fill me up."

As Maggie topped off my glass, the butterflies in my stomach went from whirling around to body-slamming against each other. In fifteen minutes, I would be picked up by Sam and David and brought three blocks down the street to the beach, where all of our family – minus one of Paul's daughters and my only brother– and a few select friends, would watch Paul and me get married.

It was thirty-seven years since I had married Randall in a completely different setting. On our wedding day in Illinois, it had been early fall and a very random, though not unheard-of, thirty degrees. There'd been frost on the ground that morning. My baby Sam, who was supposed to be wearing precious little tuxedo shorts and knee socks, required a last-minute wardrobe change and his fluffy-like-a-marshmallow winter coat. In perfect '90s-kid fashion and much to my mother's horror, I nonchalantly switched out my delicate white heeled sandals for fresh new *red* Chuck Taylors, full irony intended. She was still talking about it the week she died.

June in the coastal south was a completely different story. We were getting married at 7:30 in the evening, just at the beginning of sunset. The only real worry was wind, and we all had sunglasses and low expectations of all things hair-related in preparation for that. I was, in fact, wearing red again, and I could hear my mother's voice saying: "Jessica Rose. You can't ever just do something normal." Oh, Ma. No. Not even a little bit. My dress was completely bohemian: a halter-style top that was mostly scarlet red but kind of looked like someone had splashed turquoise paint on it, and a maxi-length skirt of the same scarlet, but with dark navy, almost black, circular tie-dye prints. Maggie styled me with a completely contrasting golden crinoline slip underneath, and so of course I wore thin, metallic gold sandals to match. My hair was freshly colored with some silver left in place and hung blown-out and loose around my shoulders. Maggie gave me smoky eyes with a bit of gold glitter on my eyelids, bronzer on my cheeks, and just enough natural lip gloss to show up in the pictures.

At first, I felt like a fraud. I was a day-to-day beach bum. Basic wardrobe. Perfunctory make-up. Black flip-flops. All *messy bun, getting' stuff done.* My body confidence had risen considerably the year before, when Paul and I broke up, and my sweet lab Cash had died, and I lost about twenty-five pounds and kept at least eighteen of it off, most of the time. I always walked a lot, but Paul had me running some, and my son-in-law Altan convinced me I had to lift weights some, too, so we set up a little gym in our garage. Even so, this exotic look belonged to someone who lived up in Grand Dunes, or someone with her own cooking/entertaining show on Food Network, not me.

But I thought of Paul. I thought of the way he looked at me, first thing in the morning when he was handing me a cup of coffee, or last thing before we turned off the lights at night, when he always seemed a little surprised at how he got there. I thought of how he looked at me the first night we walked on this same beach together after we'd lost Randall and Leah, and on my old front porch, when we couldn't bear just talking on the phone anymore and he came over and walked straight into my arms. I thought of his misty-eyed smiles when he not so much proposed a marriage but that we go ahead and "pick a date to start the rest of forever," when Mikayla handed him Josie for the first time and said, "Say hello to your Poppy," when his son-in-law Matt toasted us the night before at our "Un-Rehearsed" Dinner and called Paul one of the greatest men he ever knew.

Everything about the way Paul looked at me, as a sixty-year-old, scarred, still a little fluffy, definitely not-glamourous widow and mama/Mimi of somewhere between four and a hundred kids, made me feel confident. And he made me feel myself. And the reality was, even though I'd never worn anything like this before, I looked like the me I *felt* like at age sixty. And so I smiled into the mirror, and I thanked Maggie ten more times, and I enjoyed Sam and David's surprised little gasps when we walked outside at exactly 7:20, Brittney snapping pictures every single second.

There was no pomp or circumstance at the beach. There was somebody's Bluetooth speaker playing Paul's choice, a little-known Brooks and Dunn song called "Every River" that made me cry the first time he played it for me. There was Katy and Danielle standing on Paul's left side, and our pastor Carter at his right. There was the rest of my crew, staring at me as Maggie and Sam walked the pathway before us, and David escorted me the rest of the way, to my Paul.

Paul was my next chapter, my biggest surprise, my best friend. His eyes widened as he took me in, glitter and Boho and all. I laughed as I looked him over, in his everyday uniform, just as we'd talked about. His khaki shorts were linen instead of moisture-wicking, and his shirt, instead of black and slightly wrinkled, was turquoise and pressed. He was barefoot, a private joke in itself, as the first time we'd walked that beach barefoot together, he'd tripped in a hole and ended up in the ER. But that night, he looked perfect. I felt perfect.

Carter talked loud enough to be heard over the waves. He spoke from Isaiah 43:19, that God promised to do a new thing, to make roads in the wilderness and rivers in the desert. Mikayla sniffled behind me, and I reached over to hold her hand. Katy played her acoustic guitar while Maggie's daughter Moni sang a simple version of "The Blessing." We all sniffled then. And finally, but really just a few minutes later, Carter pronounced us man and wife. Our collected six grandkids rode in a golf cart with us down the street to Neal and Pam's, where we had reserved the covered patio for a beach-breakfast-for-dinner reception. Katy gave the most over-the-top, sentimental, precious toast, and we danced to "The Sweetest Thing." I stopped at my fourth mimosa, so I wouldn't be in the bathroom all night, and we slept in our own bed, because there was no place we'd rather be.

Our wedding night was made of a thousand broken pieces, just like us, but when it was all put together and glued and polished, it was unexpectedly beautiful.

"I can probably talk forever about how perfect it was," I said, a little dreamily. "But I also kind of want a do-over because now it's a little marred by the whole having cancer."

"Screw that," Maggie said. "Don't let that effing C-word ruin that memory. You had it. It did not have you. It doesn't get to steal anything from you."

"'cept my uterus," I said, accepting my Vanilla Rose tea.

"Hallelujah to the lamb!" she said. "You didn't need it anymore anyway."

"Ah. True. It's their turn." I gestured vaguely at our table, where plenty of women sat in their prime child-bearing years.

We'd reserved high tea, which meant we didn't have to spend any more time on menu choices. We did spend time catching up in a flurry of conversation, in and out of our seats to change dialogue partners, and also to try on the fancy tea party hats in the back of the room. Summer chose a very queenly and quite large pink number for me, and she let me pick a small white one with a large bluebird *and* nest on it for her. We laughed and snapped a few selfies and when she resumed her seat at the table, next to her mama who was next to me, she stretched her arm out to keep holding my hand.

Abby smiled at the sight and then nodded at me. I nodded back. It was time.

She tapped her spoon lightly on her water glass, and everyone looked only a bit startled when I stood up and cleared my throat. I thought about taking the hat off but then, I figured it was probably apropos for the moment.

"So, hi." I laughed a little nervously, silly though it was. I was surrounded by love and strength and inspiration in that room. And so that room was the perfect place for what I was saying.

"It's so awesome to have all of you here. Almost every single woman I can think of that I would want to have here to celebrate... well, you're here!" I paused. I had so much in my heart to say, but most of it seemed a little superfluous. They knew. The faces around the table knew how I felt about them. "There is a lot about the last few months, and really, the last year and a half, that I would have written differently. I don't even have to say that anymore, not to you. But there are also amazing surprises that I couldn't have written any better. So instead of ducking my head down and taking life easy now that the stupid 'C' word is behind us, I've decided to try something new, along with Abby."

Precisely on cue, everyone looked at Abby, who blushed and smiled all at once. Summer, who'd been told our news just that morning, was jumping up and down ever so slightly in her seat. We'd made her wait long enough.

"So as of December first, Beachside Garden Tea Room will be known as 'Whitney's,' and Abby and I will be the new co-owners!"

Summer leapt from her chair and threw her arms around her mama. The chorus from the table was a mixture of "What?" and "Oooh..." and "Yay!" and I'm pretty sure a "Bloody hell" from Brittney. I knew I was going to get a little bit of protest or at least questioning. That was okay. It would not compare to the pushback I'd already encountered.

The night before, Paul and I had sat on the back patio together. There wasn't much of a view in our little non-descript yard, but he'd planted plenty of flowers and we'd restored an old swing to Pinterest-worthy charm. Coupled with our evening tea and his company, it suited me just fine.

I'd waited two days to tell him news that I'd waited a few weeks to finalize. Abby and I had definitely mulled over Carla's selling the business. We looked over her proposal and our own finances and Abby's schedule (mine was trés flexible) and made an offer. Carla accepted it as it was, and that was that. We were not going to sign anything official until the following week, but I knew I had already put off telling Paul for too long.

"So, you know," I started, sounding so much like my teenage self, "I've been feeling so much better the past few days. Feels like it's time to get back to work."

"Mmmm," he said. "Did you actually stop working? I must have missed that."

"Haha. Yes, darling. I still have five months until my first draft is due, and honestly, two-thirds of it is already written in my head. I was thinking it might be a good time to try something new."

He took a giant drink from his jar of tea. "You finally going to try lifeguarding? Because I think that's one of the only things around here you haven't dabbled in."

"Haha. No. Midwestern me still swims like I'm made of concrete."

He gave me a squeeze. "You could do it if you wanted to. But who the hell would want to?"

"Not all of us mind the tourists and the water," I teased back. "But no. I have something completely different in mind. From lifeguarding or anything else I've ever done."

"All right." He sat up a little straighter, immediately deflating some of my enthusiasm. Paul had made no qualms about wanting me to take it easy for a *while*. He'd given me a running list of things I could stop doing with no guilt, from volunteering at church (which I already did so much less often than I used to) to hosting big family meals. He knew the latter was a foolish suggestion; I would ask for help, but I would never stop. And he also had to know I wasn't ready to give up all career aspirations and start walking aimlessly and shopping on senior days.

"Abby and I have looked in to buying the tea room." Whew. I had worked hard on a simple sentence over an exhaustive lead-in.

I hope it worked.

"Buying the tea room?" His tone suggested that I had actually just spoken in Sanskrit.

"Yes. Carla, the owner, is moving back to Concord, and she asked me if I knew anyone who might be interested in taking it on. Turns out, I do. I am."

"Jessie, I don't even understand. You want to buy the tea room? You and Abby? Drinking tea is not the same as running a business."

"It's not?" I felt an unfamiliar sensation crawling rapidly up my spine. I tried not to acknowledge or embrace it. "You don't say?"

"What I mean is that you and Abby have never run a business before, and maybe this isn't the best time to—"

"When would the best time be, Paul?"

"Jessie, don't start. You're recovering from cancer."

"*Recovered.* I'm recovered from cancer."

"It doesn't work just like that. You didn't have the flu and gathering with a few of your posse and singing 4 Non Blondes doesn't change the rules."

There it was. I was pissed off. When it came to Paul, it was such an unfamiliar feeling.

"First of all, do not make fun of MY SONG or my posse. And second of all... the *rules*? Are you kidding me right now?"

"Don't you think you should at least speak to your doctor before making a decision like this? Fine, you didn't want to speak to me, but..."

"I'm speaking to you now!"

"You've already made the decision, Jessie!

"Is that what bothers you?" I said, more loudly, standing up and turning to face him fully.

He seemed to deflate some. His voice grew quieter instead of louder. "What bothers me is that I don't want you to wear yourself out. I know you are the queen of the high threshold. I know you were multi-tasking the day you gave birth to your youngest child. I know you're used to cooking for the masses..."

"Then what, Paul?" I let my voice soften too, because the anger I was feeling was too alien to be at all comfortable.

"I just don't want you to wear yourself out trying to... trying to prove you're indestructible."

"What? I don't even know what you mean."

"You have plenty to do, Jessie, and plenty to be, even without a whole new career shift."

Plenty to be. Plenty to *be*. I knew there was some veiled meaning in that, and so I became determined to drill deeper.

"Honestly. I am not searching for a purpose. I just think it will be fun."

"Running a niche business in a fickle little tourist town will be fun? You know most new businesses here fail within five years?"

"Yes, I do, thank you." Like I didn't know all the same things he did! "Abby's been a little lost since her mama died, and we both just thought... a family business would be something amazing to build. Any one of the girls – or the guys – could take it over someday. Or, we just have this little gem that is ours for a while. We can all make memories there and help other people do the same. It isn't some grand scheme. Carla isn't asking much for the business and the assets, and the lease as it stands has less than three years left on it. So, it isn't forever."

"Nothing is permanent, right?" Paul said.

I shook my head, trying to clear it. "What does that even mean, Paul?"

"You just seem to have a real blasé attitude about taking this on. It's an investment, of your money, your time, your energy. I thought we decided to take some time to relax and settle and... recover. It's fine. Do what you want."

"Paul!" I lowered myself to the ground, crouching in front of him. He looked so defeated that any anger I felt turned into worry. "I should have talked to you sooner. But you've been so... protective... I just thought you'd try to talk me out of it, and I didn't want... this."

"You didn't want a differing point of view? That's pretty unlike you, Jess."

I took that to heart and settled right on to my bottom there on the concrete. Why hadn't I told him? If I let myself be completely honest, it was because I knew he wouldn't agree, and I didn't want to fight. So, I had delayed it, and here we were, with our discussion much more complicated than it needed to be.

"I assumed you would see it this way, and I didn't want to be at odds with you," I said quietly.

"Did you think waiting would change how I felt?" He sounded softer.

"No."

"Did it change how you felt?"

I shook my head.

"Are you going to proceed with this whether I agree or not?"

What a question. I considered my wording carefully because I already knew my answer. "I don't think it's a matter of whether you agree. I believe you will support any decision I make that isn't reckless or dangerous, and even though you might think this isn't the best time, we both know it's not a terribly risky proposition. Abby is going to hold majority on the division of labor. We should have plenty of margin to keep on a part-timer or two. And if it makes you feel better, there's an escape clause for me."

He listened as carefully as I spoke. "What does Sam say?"

I tilted my head to look into his eyes. "I haven't talked to Sam. I wouldn't talk to Sam before you."

Silence.

"Paul, we shouldn't doubt us. I think that's what's happened here, don't you?"

He sighed, still avoiding my eyes. "It's complicated, Jess. I know that. Sam is kinda your go-to guy."

"Sam is my first born and my stalwart child and an amazing man... and Abby's husband. You are mine. I know it's new and yes, it's complicated, but please don't doubt your place to me. Please." I reached for his hands.

"Tell me what you're really thinking," I added.

It took a few beats, and I waited it out. Paul had grown much more comfortable sharing his feelings in our short time together, but it still wasn't easy for him. I needed to know, though, so I would wait.

"I don't want to lose you. I just got you."

"Paul!" I inched my way closer to him. Somehow, whenever I needed to reassure him, I was in a ridiculous physical position.

"Get up," he said, noticing, fixing it. He pulled me by my underarms back onto the swing, right onto his lap.

We became a tangle of limbs, burying our faces in each other. I uttered reassurances, and he murmured his acceptance of them. I wondered if we would ever truly trust in our chance together if there would always be doubts. But I was okay ignoring them for every little bit of time I could.

When everyone had settled back into their tea and scones and flurries of overlapping conversations, Maggie hit me up. "Bold move, Jessie Rose. You excited?"

"Of course, I am!"

"It's sort of the opposite of taking it easy for a while. I thought you were going to be the first bride in the history of the world to take a second honeymoon during the first year."

I rolled my eyes at her. "We're still going to. We're going to travel. We're going to come see you in Greenville before this gets started. And we're going to Tennessee for New Year's. And next year—"

"Jess, that sounds great. I believe you. I believe you *mean* to. But I also *know* you. You'll be hook, line, and sinker in and have to be talked into walking away for a few days. That's just how you roll."

Well, damn. What was it with everyone knowing me so well that they refused to let me change?

"You been talking to Paul?"

"Not about this. What did he say?"

I gave her the thirty-second summary, knowing she was going to take his side. Inexplicably, after forty-ish years of sisterhood with me, she usually did.

"So, Abby is taking the lead on everything?" she said.

"I'm going to focus on the food and a little on the atmosphere. Abby will be the day-to-day operations. It's not a complicated business. Look at the table: pretty linens, tea, and simple, tiny food. Our biggest task will be keeping reservations going. I'm not going to knock myself out here."

"And you're still going to write?"

I gestured vaguely at the room. "What better environment?"

"And you'll have plenty of flex time for your lazy coffee mornings and Taco Tuesdays with your grands, watching baby Josie, and being spontaneous with that man of yours?"

I stiffened a bit. The list form made the idea seem daunting.

"I'm not afraid to try," I finally said.

She picked up her teacup and smiled at me over it. "Of course, you're not." After a sip, she added, "You should try to get a liquor license while you're at it. A Bellini would be just the thing right now."

I took stock of the table again, the tiny plates and cups, the variety of ages of the women around me, the din of chatter against the backdrop of "November Rain" via violin. It was somehow peaceful and chaotic all at once. Maybe that's why it felt so right to me.

# CHAPTER♡TWENTY-ONE

## *Julie*

"THANKS FOR COMING WITH ME." JULIE SAID IT SO LOW THAT IT WAS ALMOST INAUDIBLE.

"You kidding?" Katy answered, her voice as loud as Julie's was soft. "I can't wait to finally meet this guy. Who you lived with. Who's moving across the country to live with you again even though you dumped his ass."

"Stop. See? This is why—!"

"I'm just messing!" Katy continued. "Come on. I'm not a buffoon. I'll be cool. But seriously, Jules. I'm supposed to be the feral twin. Your life is giving *me* whiplash these days."

"Well. What can I say? Me, too. Can you grab this bag?"

Muttering, Katy took a duffle from Julie to add to the two tote bags and the Route 44 sweet tea she was already holding

They wordlessly walked up the three, zigzagging flight of stairs to the apartment where Chad was waiting. Julie had already seen his blue MX-5 in the parking lot, and her heart was now thumping so hard she couldn't believe Katy couldn't hear it. When they reached the door of 3B, Julie stood still, her arms full.

"You need me to knock?"

"Katy..."

"Jules. Listen. I know things are not okay. If they were, you never would have asked me to come with you today. You never need me for anything."

"Katy—"

"No. *Listen.* If you don't want to do this, we can just turn around. You can come home with me and commute until you figure it out. Hell, we can even find a couch. Just don't use this as an escape. Your life isn't that bad. You—"

"Julie!"

The door had opened. And there stood any woman's dream, wearing black gym shorts and a fitted black T-shirt and black On Clouds and radiance on his chiseled face. Katy actually gasped, which made Julie laugh, which brought a moment-saving escape from the knots and nerves she was battling.

"Chad!" She cradled the stuff in her arms and awkwardly accepted his embrace. She kissed his cheek and momentarily felt an eruption of relief in the familiarity of him. They'd been together for less than a year before she'd left, but in a time when nothing had been stable, he was a reminder of what it could feel like.

*That's why you're here, isn't it?* Leah's voice asked.

"This is Katy."

"Of course. Hey, Katy!" Chad leaned in and kissed her cheek, and Katy giggled. Julie already knew she would never live down the fact that she'd left this beautiful, charming man who smelled like good news and fairy tales. If she could wave a magic wand and make everything as she wished, she'd give him and Katy to each other.

And keep Ian for herself.

*Damn. It. Julie!*

Chad began offloading their bags as he led them into the apartment. Julie had to choke back a sob when she saw her couch. It was so stupid, of all things, to get emotional about the couch, but it was the one piece she had to have, and she had loved everything about it. She had spent one solitary evening on it with Ian, watching *The Family Stone* and drinking red wine and fantasizing about a world in which she and Katy and Daddy, Danielle and Matt and the kids, were all together, and Ian was there, too. And it was free of complications and sadness.

That same night had ended before the movie was even over because Ian got an emergency call. But Julie had rested her head against the cushion where he sat for hours after he left, soaking in the memory of his arm casually draped around her shoulder and his attentive eyes on her every time she spoke. They hadn't been more intimate than that. It had been perfect to her, nonetheless.

She snapped herself right out of that memory and smiled at Chad. "I can't believe you just got here this morning. It looks like you're practically settled."

He smiled. "All the boxes, and I mean every, single one, are in the third bedroom. So here. Let me show you yours."

Katy made a grimace at Julie behind his back. She couldn't even argue with her sister. It was so awkward. How could they possibly make this work?

Chad invited Katy to stay for dinner. Julie was completely torn whether she wanted that to happen, but Katy made it simple and decided to head home. Saying goodbye down at her car, she hugged Julie in a normal-human-being sort of way and said,

"Jules. You don't have to do anything you don't want to do. Okay? *Okay?*"

Julie heard the same old zeal in her voice that was always there, but it was layered beneath maturity and compassion that she hadn't recognized before. She hugged her back tightly and simply said, "Okay."

Upstairs, she started putting her things away in the second bathroom. It was marvelous to have all the non-essential little things back that she'd left in Phoenix: her perfume, her heated hairbrush, her extra towels, her robe. Taking stock of it all, she realized how hasty she'd been in leaving, and for the first time in weeks, her heart went out to Chad. She'd really given him no warning and no explanation, and she left him with a mess that was so completely unfair. And here he was.

He was back ten minutes later, carrying a huge takeout bag from Nacho Hippo. As soon as he set it down on the table, Julie let herself melt, and she gave him a much less perfunctory hug than the one she'd greeted him with hours before.

"I don't know how to say how sorry I am, or how to thank you. I don't deserve any of this from you. Nothing."

Chad gave her a squeeze back; she felt him briefly smell her hair and kiss her head beneath it before she pulled away.

"I don't think of it that way, Julie. I care about you. I'm excited to be here. And I believe in us, even if you don't right now. Maybe if you're close, you'll be able to believe again."

He was so earnest that she felt her fight-or-flight instinct activate. *Calm down*, she told herself. *Just eat dinner. One step at a time.*

How should she proceed? How could she? She didn't want to

lead him on, but she didn't want to hurt him.

*And you don't want to be homeless.*

*And you're not in love with him.*

Had Leah been standing there, Julie would have told her to shush. Being that she was not, Julie was stuck with her mama's voice, which had gone from a cautious whisper to a warning siren, telling Julie that what she was doing was very, very wrong.

Chad had to be at his orientation at eight the next morning. Julie was grateful for a few hours alone, checking out the nooks and crannies in the space. She would need to get herself a dresser since most of her clothes now were running shorts and t-shirts or tanks. She kept them stacked in a few canvas bins in the bottom of her closet, and she chuckled to herself at the sight of the shoes she had accumulated during her month at Run This Way. She had two pairs to rotate for work, the pair Robin had sold her when she first shopped at the store, and one additional, more-cushiony pair that had come in handy as her runs had gotten longer. In fact, she should have been off on a 10K this morning, but she found herself enjoying a home in solitude for the first time in forever.

Even though it didn't feel like home. Not yet, anyway.

Robin seemed sullen when she got to work. He didn't say anything besides "Hey" and gave her a single nod and grunt when she told him she was going to walk Pote. Thankfully, Darcy was there to keep the apparent tension at bay.

Shortly after lunchtime, a middle-aged mom and her petite young daughter came in. The daughter was smiling shyly and wearing a huge brace on one of her very thin legs. The mom looked weary, and wary, as Darcy started talking to her and then to her daughter. When she walked into the storage room to start retrieving shoes, Julie met her there.

"How are you going to get that brace into a shoe?" she asked.

"Come on with me, and we'll figure it out."

The mom, Wendy, did most of the talking to Darcy. Julie focused on the daughter, Lillian. She was so small and very shy. When she asked her what school she went to, she and Wendy both giggled. "I'm twenty-seven," she said in her tiny voice.

Julie was immediately embarrassed, but they assured her it happened all the time. Julie said it will feel like a compliment when she's older, and then she methodically fit Lillian's left foot, with the very bulky brace, into a shoe that was two-and-a-half sizes bigger than the one going on her right foot.

It fit. And the shoes matched down to the color, a huge feat in a marketplace with somewhat sporadic inventory.

Julie felt like celebrating, but Darcy motioned for her to come back to the storage room.

"That was great," she said. "Now let's see if we can find an option."

"Whew," Julie said. "I feel like finding one match was a miracle."

"It was." Darcy smiled. "Now if we can give her a choice, she'll never go anywhere else for shoes. And she will leave here feeling so empowered."

She smiled back. "New Balance?"

"I was thinking the same thing."

They managed to find another pair of size six with an eight-and-a-half wide match. Julie smiled reassuringly at Lillian again as she fit both of the shoes. Darcy chatted away to Wendy. Lillian walked and smiled with confidence. It was another win.

"I guess I should ask how much they cost," Wendy finally said. "I don't care anyway. I was prepared to buy two pairs, but we will go ahead and take all four."

Julie hated this part. At the hospital or the clinic, she was never in the room for the financial questions. It seemed if patients had a nurse's attention, they only wanted to ask about extra details of their prognosis, or if they could get just a little something solid if they were on a liquid diet, or if the baby was *really* getting enough to eat when their milk hadn't come in. She could speak a few encouraging words in the face of a disheartening diagnosis, but she never had to talk about how much treatments were going to cost.

The fact was, running shoes were costly. But as Robin reminded her every few days, they were also utilitarian, and as a small, local store, they were keeping consumer dollars in town while providing a specific and mostly lost service. Still, four pairs would equal over 600 dollars, and while Julie was pretty sure they could offer a discount, she wasn't certain *she* could offer such a thing. So, she stood there awkwardly.

Darcy chimed in with her youthful ease and expert knowledge. "Oh, no. No, no. You don't have to buy all four pairs. We will sell them to you as two pairs."

"Mismatched like this?"

"Yes, ma'am. We'll work with the shoe companies on our end. You don't worry about a thing." She winked and nodded at Julie.

"And we will get you in our loyalty program and take your first discount off today, okay?" Julie added, beaming at Lillian.

The rest of the transaction was completed smoothly, and after they left, Julie was sure Darcy felt as relieved and well, excited, as she did.

And that's when Robin came out from his cave.

"That was awesome." His tone was deadpan. He might as well have been saying, *It looks like rain* or *This lunchmeat smells bad*, but he at least looked as happy as he seemed capable of looking.

"And perfect timing," Darcy added. "Good to show Julie some of those little tricks now."

"I love the tricks!" Julie said. "I'm ready."

"Good!" Darcy said just as Robin said, "You better be."

"Okay. What is up, you two?"

Darcy looked from Robin to Julie and smiled a bit more shyly. "I gave Robin my notice yesterday. I took a job with Boston Athletic Association! I'm going to be the Assistant Director of Athlete Services!"

"What? Really? That's great, Darcy!" She pulled back her enthusiasm a touch. "I mean, sucks for you, boss, but Darcy! Congratulations!"

*She's six years younger than you and on her way. You're twelve credits and a clinical short of a Master's and making thirteen dollars an hour. You idiot.*

That wasn't Mama's voice. It was hers. Well, if she was being honest, maybe it was Ian's, too.

"We'll figure it out," Robin said. "It's an awesome job for our ace, here."

"It really is. I can't wait to hear more about it."

"Give her all the details, Darcy. Pote and I have a meeting with some running club people."

"You doing the scholarship this year?"

He nodded. Darcy beamed.

Julie felt like a third wheel. Was this really her world? Did she belong anywhere at this point?

She turned to Darcy, ready to hear all the greatness, whether another guy was going to follow a girl to a new state. She hoped maybe she'd be inspired to find some greatness herself.

Chad texted Julie right before the store closed. There was a friend from his residency who was also starting at Ocean's Edge. They were going to get a drink, did Julie want to go?

Her answer was to look up from her phone and ask Robin, "Hey. Are we running tonight?"

"Didn't you run this morning?"

"No." She fiddled with her phone case. "I..."

"Slept in? Had breakfast with your *roommate*?"

"Can we not?" she snapped. "Actually, no. I was unpacking some stuff. Do you want to run or not?"

"I ran this morning. I figured your schedule was changing."

"Well, it's not." She picked up her phone and replied to Chad. I have a run scheduled. I'll just see you back at the apartment.

"You're really going to blow him off to go run?"

*He really doesn't know me, yet.* She huffed a bit. "I'm training. I take it seriously."

"Okay. All right. Pote and I are a little worn out, but..."

"I can run by myself, Robin."

"I know you can, *Julie*."

She shook her head. "Are we fighting? Because it sounds like you need me as much as I need this job right now."

Robin smirked and shook his head. "We're not fighting. Go run. Are you going home right after? You have time for a staff meeting?"

"Is that what we're going to call it?"

He shrugged. "Just playing the hands I'm dealt. Looks like

you're getting promoted."

Julie had forty-five easy minutes on her training schedule. She didn't obey. Instead, her heartbeat already thumping as she started, she played her "Run Swift" playlist and had Taylor cheering her onto the more rapid end of her pace. Before she knew it, she had completed nearly five miles. She was a red-faced, dripping mess as she found Robin outside at Tidal Creek, another signature smirk on his face as he offered her a fried pickle.

"I kind of hate you," she said, dropping into a chair and taking his water.

"Really? You look like you hate yourself," he quipped.

"I ran too fast."

"No such thing."

"Well... my training plan said–"

"Screw your plan. Did it feel good to run fast tonight? After you moved yesterday and worked all day today?"

"Well." There he went, making her rethink again. "Actually, yeah. Yes. I feel much better."

"So, it's awesome you're gonna do a half, and it's smart to follow a training plan. But unless you're Darcy and trying to break some kind of land speed record, try to remember why you like running in the first place."

She nodded.

"Why *do* you?" he pressed.

"Hmmm." Julie smiled, not sure she wanted to share the memory, but she did anyway. "When I was thirteen years old, and believe me, had no interest in anything my parents did, my mom trained for a half marathon. My mom was not athletic. She didn't like to sweat. She didn't even like to wear shorts or t-shirts, let alone athletic attire of any kind. But someone she worked with asked her, and it became kind of a dare. I think she was, well..."

She really wasn't sure she should go there with Robin. She wasn't sure she'd ever talked to anyone but Katy about this. But since he didn't press, it felt safe to say.

"I don't think Mama was really happy with her life. She worked really hard to make it nice... our home, our childhoods, our family. But, you know. You know how Hazel and Darcy sort of... sparkle? My twin sister is like that. My parents were not."

"Neither are you," he said, not missing a beat.

"That's another story." Two beers appeared in front of them. She wasn't sure whether to be offended or grateful that he'd ordered, but he simply shrugged and pointed to his water glass. She finished the rest and then lifted the pint for a slow sip. She wasn't a fan of beer, but after that run, the chill of it tasted wonderful. "Mama trained for that race like her life depended on it. She woke up way earlier than usual. She ran in the rain. She let people see her without makeup on, and seriously, that never happened in my whole life. So, the day of the race, Daddy got us girls up, we made signs, we tracked her at miles three, eight, and ten, and you better believe we were at the finish line.

"I had never been to anything like it before. I saw so many different kinds of people. Just like at the store: old, young, overweight, limping, braces on their legs, carrying flags, carrying... burdens. I just stood there in awe. And when Mama passed us on her sprint to the finish, I cried. She looked so beautiful and so alive, and I was so happy for her. And I wanted it for her... and for me."

*Wow*. She couldn't believe she had said that much, but it really was one of her favorite memories.

"After that," she continued, "She took a few weeks to recover, and then she started running smaller races. She probably did five or six 5Ks every year, and I always did the holiday ones with her, Thanksgiving and Fourth of July and sometimes silly little ones like President's Day or Labor Day. Running just became part of her life, and for my sisters and me, it was this little suspension of reality. Whenever we ran with Mama, it was like all the heavy stuff she carried just disappeared."

"She sparkled?"

Julie widened her eyes at him. "Yeah. She did."

"You sparkle when you talk about her."

"I do?"

"You do. And you look like her, too."

She tilted her head. "Have I shown you her picture?"

"Jules, I have Facebook."

*Had he ever called her Jules before? Were they Facebook friends?*

She didn't ask out loud, but he answered her.

"Look. Let's go ahead and take the kid gloves off. We're not new here, anymore. I've carried your drunk ass home a few times, so no need to be formal. We know each other's deals. So, I'm asking you to take over some management duties at the store, and I'm also saying that we're friends. Good friends. And I'm going to look out for you, and I'm going to be a little grumpy when I think you're acting like a dumbass. Fair enough?"

She picked up a pickle, considered it, and put it back down. "Fair enough. But I don't really like fried stuff, and I don't really know your deal. Also, if I am your only employee, who exactly am I managing?"

"Well, Princess," he said, reminding her of Han Solo referring to Leia. "Let's order some more edible food, and maybe I'll tell you."

♡

It felt later than it was when Julie got home. The apartment was dark, and her eyes were immediately drawn to a note, on actual paper, on the counter next to the coffee maker.

Guess you <u>ran</u> late. Ha. Hope it was fun. Proud. Sleep tight. – C : )

Even without her propensity to read between the lines, she immediately felt guilty for not being there to ask about his first day. On the flip side, he was the one who told her they were just roommates. No expectations. She was probably dumb to even consider that might work. Robin sure thought so.

They had talked shop while waiting for their food. They needed to hire someone pronto. Did Julie know anyone? He needed her to focus in on customer experience and sales and general upkeep of the store, so he could keep the reigns on inventory and community relations and hiring. Did she mind working full time for now? He would raise her pay by over thirty percent. Did she know anything about websites? Darcy had been handling that, too.

"We'll stay closed on Sundays for now." He had been planning to open up seven days once Julie was full trained. "And we might do a half day on Tuesdays. I know it doesn't give much in the way of a break, but it's so slow on Tuesdays, we might as well for now. Hopefully, just for a few weeks."

"Is this okay?" Julie said. "I mean, do you feel like the business is going to take a hit."

Robin shrugged as their meals were placed on the table, fish tacos for him, a grilled Caesar wedge for her. He wrinkled his face up at her plate, and she waved him off. His palate left room for little besides bar food.

"We're pretty strong," he said. "It's going to suck for a little bit until we can find a few more hires, but if we're both in, I think we'll be fine."

Julie concentrated on her lettuce and her beer as she mulled over the meaning behind those words. This little retail job, which had seemed such an embarrassing departure from her burgeoning career as a health care provider, a saver and bringer of lives, was turning into something else quite rapidly. Four weeks in and the proprietor was saying he needed her to keep it going. She had no doubt that buried in Robin's nonchalant demeanor was a man very capable of working his ass off if he had to do it on his own, but she was impressed with the quiet, unemotional way he was saying, "I'd rather have some help."

"Let's do it," she said, and took a bite.

They ate in silence for a few minutes. Julie finished her drink and felt her shoulders relax. She couldn't believe Robin could eat with her being so sweaty and gross, but she supposed he was used to post-run meals.

Actually, she had no idea what he was used to.

"So, tell me about you."

"What?"

"What *is* your deal? I don't actually know, other than you have a small identity crisis when it comes to your name, that this used to be a family business, which makes no sense, since you're still *in* business, and you have or had a stepdaughter, but clearly... not a wife."

"You are correct on all those fronts."

"Nick-Robin..." she scolded.

He pretended to choke on his taco. "Okay, okay. I'm not an open book like you. I admit it."

"I'm usually not either," she muttered. "You brought it out of me with your whiskey and your no judgment zone and the fact that you don't know a single other person I know."

"I know your dad."

"Him buying shoes here every other week doesn't count. Now. Your turn."

He nodded and said "okay" several more times. Julie watched in awe as he seemed to prepare himself like a toastmaster of something. He took a swig of his beer. He wiped his mouth and folded his napkin. He sat a little straighter and leaned a bit forward. And he sort-of looked into her eyes, but he gave her the feeling he was looking somewhere else, very far from there.

"The name thing is silly. It's exactly what I already told you, and I've pretty much dropped it since you called me on it." Julie flashed him the victory sign and he smiled for a second. "The family business is a really long story, and I don't want to get into all of it. I'll give you the back-of-the-book version, okay?"

"Sure."

"My dad's family were ranchers in Wyoming. Four generations. When it was my dad's turn to step up, he basically discovered that he had nothing to work with. No cash. Limited inventory, so limited income. And because of some old debts, not the best name to go on anymore. He probably could have tried to turn things around, branched out into a cowboy camp or an event venue or something. But the truth was, he didn't want it in the first place. He had two sisters, one son and two daughters, and no real plan of succession."

"Yeah. That's hard." Julie knew how feeble it sounded.

Robin just nodded. "For him, it was impossible. My sisters and I were young. My mom was great at keeping books. He had a big variety of skills that you collect when you start working at age seven. So, he sold it all. Every bit of it. He made sure my grandma and my aunts all got their share, and he moved us here, and he opened a liquor store."

Julie's eyes went wide. "A liquor store?"

He laughed sardonically. "I know. Not the logical next step. But you know, he did okay."

"Is it still open? Here?"

Robin raised his eyebrows at her. "No. I mean, I thought you knew. Its last location was where the store is now. Dad was ready to retire, and he turned it over to me. And I changed it."

"Oh. Wow. Yeah. I guess you did. I just didn't put two and two together."

He shrugged. "It's not a logical equation. My dad definitely was not happy when I flipped the whole script. He thought he'd built a family legacy of his own, and I went and changed it."

"But why?"

Shrug. "I like running more than drinking. And there wasn't another store like this within 200 miles. So, I researched while I worked *his* plan, and then I changed it when my parents were out west visiting family. My wife had just... Well. I guess that's the other part of the story."

Julie identified with the look in his eyes. It was a mixture of turmoil and shame and it hurt to look at, especially because she still felt it, and more now because he had become one of the few people she really cared about anymore.

"You don't have to tell me if you don't want to," she said.

"I said I would. It's not a secret. And it's not all that dramatic. I got married. She had a kid. I loved her, and I really loved the kid."

"What's her name?"

He smiled. "Elsa." And from the way he smiled, Julie knew he didn't mean the wife, but the kid.

"How long ago did you and her mom divorce?"

"It's been about two years."

"How long were you married?"

"Four years. We started dating when Elsa was not even one. She–" He paused, clearly wondering how much to say. He allowed himself an indulgent smile. "She stole my heart. That was probably part of the problem. Tonya was great and all, but if not for Elsa, maybe I wouldn't have married her. Or maybe not as quickly as I did."

"So, you broke up over Elsa?"

"Nah." He shrugged. "It's never that simple, right? Tonya's a little younger than I am. She was twenty-one when she had Elsa. I probably seemed like a perfect solution for her. I was all in on being a family. But she wasn't ready. Who's ready at that age?"

Julie thought of David. He was twenty when he moved to Arizona with her. Everyone thought they were idiots, and she fought tooth and nail to convince them all they were wrong. They had been so, so right.

She titled her head at Robin. "How old are you now?"

"Nice segue. I'm thirty-six. Old man."

"Please. Forty is the new twenty, or some such bullshit."

"Yeah. Good thing for us, huh?"

Julie couldn't help it. The "us" sounded nice. She felt like such a floater these days, no place that she *really* belonged. The store felt the most like home. Even with Hazel and now Darcy not being there, she felt like part of the team. She would take it.

"So. Anyway. Elsa. Do you still get to see her?"

He ran his finger alongside his glass, his guarded expression momentarily turning into regret. "It's been over a year. Tonya said I could visit with her whenever I wanted, but then she moved out near Columbia, and... you know how that goes. Two hours might as well be the other side of the moon. Anyway, she's getting remarried. And Elsa still sees her biological dad, so..." Another shrug. Julie wondered if his shoulders hurt from it.

"You seem... well, if you don't mind my saying—"

"You wouldn't shut up if I do mind."

"Well, no. I wouldn't," she laughed. "You just seem kind of lost sometimes, kind of sad. Maybe you should see Elsa. If you miss her, just go see her. Because you never know."

"She's almost nine now. She's like a different person. I don't think it will mean anything to her."

"Do you still talk to her?"

"Yeah. Tonya has her Facetime me pretty much every Sunday."

"So, she knows you."

"Yeah. I mean, I'm not saying she forgot me."

"Of course not. Kids remember who keeps them safe and who makes them feel loved. Quit overthinking it, and go to her. You still have a chance. And Robin, if you shrug one more time, I'm going to pick up something fried and throw it at you."

He smiled instead. It wasn't his tight, controlled smile, or his teasing one. It was wide, filling his face and reaching his eyes. He unlocked his phone and scrolled through for a moment, then held a photo up for Julie to see.

She took it from him and beheld a little sprite of a girl with two dirty-blonde braids hanging down well past her shoulders, big brown eyes, blushed apple cheeks, and her own wide smile that said, *I know I'm cute. Just watch me.* She was wearing a blue Buzz and Woody t-shirt and a white tutu and bright yellow galoshes.

"Is she super smart?" Julie said.

"Oh yeah."

She nodded and handed the phone back to him. "Thanks for sharing with me."

"We're even now," he said. "Now we need to get home. Running a former liquor store is going to be exhausting for a little while.

Home was such a fluid concept to her. It was just shy of 9:30 and Julie was tiptoeing around, trying not to disturb the early slumber of a man she used to sleep next to. Everything about this space felt foreign (*You've spent about eight collective hours there*, her Mama's voice whispered). Even her beloved couch looked strange in a place that held no context for her. Why was she here? What were she and Chad together?

Tomorrow, she decided, she would make dinner. He might get home before she did, so she would shop early in the morning, so she could get right to it after work. Some steaks, a little pasta, salad, a good bottle of wine. They could talk and eat and reminisce and maybe reconnect, and then maybe everything would stop feeling so damn weird.

She showered quietly and flipped her little speaker to instrumentals and burrowed under her old comforter – not the one from Arizona, but the one she'd brought out there and forgot to take back. She'd gotten it right after college, and it was getting washed out, the tiny pattern of green leaves and lavender butterflies against a light blue background almost not discernible anymore. But its weight and warmth were perfect. She started to drift.

Her phone dinged.

She reached for it with her eyes half shut, and then opening one, saw:

Ian: So did you really do it? :half frown emoji:

She was so tired. And yet, she sat up in bed like someone had kicked her, turned on her light, grabbed the phone with both hands.

It's quite a bit later on the east coast, doctor. I'm trying to sleep.

She knew that wouldn't stop him.
She knew she didn't want him to stop.

Ian: I'm just really surprised you're back together.
Julie: We aren't.
Ian: You didn't move in?
Julie: Sigh. I did. I have my own room.
Ian: ...
Julie: You're not supposed to actually type 3 dots. You should just make me wait for you to figure out what you're going to say.
Ian: I have no idea what to say. None. :red face emoji:
Julie. You can't even begin to think you're allowed to be mad.
Ian: I'm allowed to be whatever I want. If you are going to back to someone, why not me?

Was he kidding?
She walked down the hall and stopped at the door to the master bedroom. It was closed. There was silence. She opened it slightly and observed Chad's form, covered to his neck and sound asleep. Her walk back to her own room was more purposeful. She didn't know why after all these months she was in such a hurry. But she flopped on her bed and hastily tapped Ian's name. He answered

before the first ring was complete.

"I guess that got your attention."

"I guess you're still a pompous asshole."

"Why are you mad, Julie? Because I'm calling you out on your shit?"

"My shit? Mine? Where are you right now? How are you even answering the phone when it's me? Your mistress? Your *ex*-mistress?"

There was a pause. Julie assumed he was coming up with a story.

"I'm not with Fawn."

She rolled her eyes. So vague wordplay it was instead. "Okay. So, you're still at the office? Meeting people for happy hour? At the gym?"

"I moved out for a while."

She felt inexplicable. Cold. Shocked. Crazy. He moved *out*? "You left Fawn?"

There was another pause before he said, "We agreed we needed some time to be... not a couple. Look. Can I video you?"

"I guess—"

Before she answered, her screen was changing. She paused for a moment, too, but there was never really a question. She wanted to see him. She wanted to see his face, live and talking to her, so badly that her stomach flipped as she tapped the green button.

"Hi." His blue eyes looked more brilliant on the screen. Was he using a filter? Was her adrenaline just at an insane level upon seeing him for the first time in so long?

"Hi." She hated her voice. She sounded desperate. She sounded how she felt.

"I wanted to show you I meant it," he said, flipping his camera around. She looked at a standard-issue furnished apartment. Factory countertops. Non-descript ceramic floors. One bunch of bananas on the counter, lying on a paper towel. His gym duffle tossed next to the front door. No pictures, no papers, no signs of life. Perhaps he was actually telling the truth.

"I don't understand," Julie finally said. "I thought you were never going to break up. And the miscarriage..."

A shadow passed over his eyes. "The miscarriage, as we have seen before, acted as a catalyst. And a flashlight, shining on everything that was wrong with us. We aren't mad. We're disappointed. And so we decided to uncouple for a while and see where that takes us."

"Uncouple. *Uncouple.*" Where had she heard that absurd term? Oh yeah. That actress who named her kid Apple. *Intentionally uncoupled* from her husband. It sounded even more ridiculous when a non-A-lister used it.

"Well. Congratulations?"

He gave a tiny laugh. "I guess." He shrugged, and Julie found her eyes drawn to the way his gray golf shirt hugged his shoulders. She remembered what it felt like to lay her head there. "It's weird," he said. "It's a lot. And I don't know what's going to happen, but I did think, if you were here, maybe you could help me figure it out."

*Help him figure it out.* Leah's voice was more clipped and firm than ever. *Julie Anna Jameson, you are the hottest of messes you've ever thought about being. Maybe you should start figuring out your own stuff. Don't you dare get involved with his again.*

*Oh, Mama.* Julie wished many things in that moment. She wished Leah was there to actually yell at her. She wished she could talk to Katy and Danielle and maybe Hazel and Robin without being completely humiliated. She wished she could actually chuck the last few weeks and just go to Ian and live happily ever after, somehow. She wished she could turn back the number of seconds it would have taken to notice something besides a little post-partum anxiety happening with Alley Prosser and changed that family's fate. And the simplest, smallest, stupidest wish: she wished she was lying in her bed in some other home that was actually hers, not here at Chad's, where she definitely did not belong.

"I can't help you figure anything out, Ian." She looked him in his beautiful eyes, knowing the danger that was there. She knew he could turn on whatever magnetic power he'd held over her, and that after weeks of distancing himself, giving her one-word answers, ignoring her altogether, he could once again beckon her, throwing his metaphorical pixie dust around and saying all the right things. And no matter how dejected and rejected and torn apart and angry and humiliated she felt, how many times had she lapped up his leftovers like a lost and pitiful dog?

"I won't come," she said, her voice smaller than she'd ever heard it. "If you wanted to be with me, you should have said so before I moved 2000 miles away. Before I made myself homeless."

"So, I should have left Fawn when she was pregnant?"

She almost laughed at the feigned incredulousness on his face. "So, you knew she was pregnant when I moved away?"

"Well, I—"

"Ian. I think we're done."

He narrowed his eyes at her, his mouth crinkling at the corners. "You should get some sleep. I'm sorry it's so late, Jule. Can we talk tomorrow?"

Her right hand held the phone. Her left hand balled into a fist. She looked across the room to her desk, the only flat surface in the room. There were random bits piled on it, her untouched planner (she had no plans), a few books, a little dish holding earrings and bracelets, an empty coffee cup, and one frame. Her mama's picture. Well, the picture was Mama and Daddy, Daddy's arm around her, waving at Julie the day she drove off for the College of Charleston. It was one of the only pictures of them that looked fun and carefree, and her mama's hair was blowing in the wind, a sleeveless blouse showing off the strength in her thin arms, and she was happy. *In that moment, they both sparkled.*

Julie had let them down. She knew they'd let her down sometimes, too, but she wanted to write a conclusion to this particular chapter. She couldn't if Ian was still in it.

"No," she finally said.

"No?"

"No, Ian. Not tomorrow. I don't think we should talk anymore."

"Jule, you say that and then—"

"I know." She would let him win, just a little. "It's unfair to you, to let you have any hope. The truth is, I don't love you anymore. I can't love you anymore. I can barely stand myself at this point, and all you do is confuse me. Maybe if you'd figured out your life with Fawn a few months ago, this would be different. But I don't want your leftovers, and I sure as hell don't want hers. So, you figure out your own stuff. I'll figure out mine. But not together. It won't work out."

"But it's going to work out with Chad? Just like that, all of a sudden, he's the right guy for you?" His smile was gone. The softness in his eyes was gone. Likely, Julie thought, his affection for her would follow shortly.

"I doubt it," she said. "But it's not your problem. It makes no difference to you."

"Jule, can we just—"

"No." This time her voice was stronger. "We can't. I can't. I... God, Ian. I loved you so much. I turned myself inside out loving you. I gave you more than I had. I gave you what you had no right to get. And it wasn't enough for you."

"That's not fair."

*Fair?* She shook her head. "That's the best you have? You want fair? Me too, Ian. I want to be in love with the guy who wasn't married to someone else. I want to have banked on a career I was actually cut out for. And I want my mom! Nothing is fair."

"Jule, at some point you have to get over—"

"Don't! Don't say a word about it!" She was yelling. *Oh, please God, don't let me wake up Chad.* "I have to get over you. Bye Ian. Just... bye."

She tapped the phone screen and threw it across the bed. And then she threw her own self down, face buried in the pillow, hot tears and choking sobs coming out of her as she tried to push Ian's face out of her mind, one more person she'd disappointed, one more person she shouldn't have counted on, one more person she would never see again.

# CHAPTER♡TWENTY-TWO

## *Paul*

PAUL TEXTED A PAT RESPONSE TO HIS FRIEND JOHN-NY, OFFICIALLY BLOWING OFF THEIR BREAKFAST PLANS FOR THE NEXT DAY. He wanted to re-organize his office space in the second bedroom well before he had to start grading finals. He wanted to make dinner at home instead of taking Jessie somewhere convenient. He wanted to finalize some vacation plans.

He wanted to figure out what to say to her.

Lunch with Carter during Jessie's tea party – and the announcement she was going to make – had been a little helpful. Carter had known Jessie even longer than Paul had; he'd been her and Randall's pastor during some of their toughest years, when they had a stillborn son and Jessie's subsequent depression (though she never referred to it as such). But he was also Paul's pastor, and they'd grown as friends in the months Paul and Jessie had been together.

"Your fears are understandable," Carter had said. "But they're unfounded. Jessie is not like Leah. She's ambitious, and she does need stuff to do, but she also prefers to do everything in the company of her people. And you, brother, are right there at the top of her people list."

Paul knew he was right. He just couldn't shake the feeling of being left behind, or unnecessary. He'd lived most of his life feeling unnecessary. Leah was good at reminding him he was capable: he was a beloved principal; he was a hands-on-dad; he was a pillar of the dang community. But he always knew that if he ever decided to just walk away, she and the girls would be fine without him.

Back then, Carter told him that was a lie.

He had no way of disproving his theory now, but he could make sure that Jessie continued to want a life *with* him, that if she did need him, he was worthy of the call. Declaring she was almost back to SUPERSTRENGTH, she was spending most of the day with her various and sundry daughters, so after his morning run and a little time working on prep for his class, Paul spent the day curating niceties to welcome her home that evening: her favorite Carolina Gold roasted coffee beans and sourdough bread from Benjamin's, fresh vegetables and her favorite Jupiter pie from the farmer's market, and a silly painted wall hanging with a gnome on it, eating pumpkin pie and drinking coffee. She would love it.

By the time she got home, he had a vegetable quiche and cinnamon toast in the oven, the coffee ground and brewed, and some crazy playlist playing in the background that included The Eagles *and* Adele. He knew he was in her favorite state: clean and dressed in black. Maybe it went with her Johnny Cash love. Regardless, he just wanted her to smile.

She walked in the kitchen and set her ginormous bag on the chair. Her eyes were tired but bright at the same time. She inhaled the air and exhaled deeply, taking him in, and then walking to him for a full, long embrace.

"Nothing like the smell of freshly showered husband," she sighed. He smiled into her neck.

"You cooked?"

"I did."

"Darling man." She walked over and peeked into the stove. "And you shopped. We were out of everything."

"Well, we still are. I just shopped at the farmer's market, so..."

"Paul Jameson. *The farmer's market*? You are a light unto my world."

"What can I say?" he shrugged, and she kissed him.

"I'm going to freshen up real quick. Be right down."

He watched her walk up the stairs, from the curve of her bottom to the muscles in her calves. She'd thinned out a little too much while she was having treatments, but he would never tell her. She was under that deceitful spell most women seemed to be, that being skinnier was better. He liked it when she looked stronger. She would again. They were going to start walking and maybe running together soon.

*If she still has time*, he thought.

This frame of mind would not do. Paul started setting out all the dinner accoutrements and pep-talking himself. Jessie could have done anything with her life after Randall died. She could have stayed on her own. She chose to be here. She chose him.

Self-affirmation seemed like something more fitting for his daughters than him. But Carter had encouraged him to try it. So, Paul, only mildly convinced no one would hear him, poured two cups of coffee and said out loud, "God made you everything you are, and you are enough."

"Yes. Yes, you are."

*Dang it.*

Jessie was filling the doorway. She'd changed from her denim shorts and black tank top to cozy little green gym shorts and a different black tank top. She was smiling at him, but one tear had escaped and was rolling down his face.

"What's wrong, baby?" she said.

She had only called him that a few times. He felt his face get hot when he heard it again. It seemed such an odd turn of phrase for a kind-of old man. But so help him, he *liked* it. Because *she* was saying it.

"Nothing," he said softly, crossing the room to her. He didn't offer an explanation for the moment of transparency she witnessed. He trusted she probably knew exactly where he was coming from. So, he just gathered her and held her, waiting for her to hold him back.

It was their magic.

"I hope nothing I ever do makes you feel like you're not enough," she said, without breaking away.

"It's nothing that you do." He stepped back because he wanted to see her face. "You are so splendid at being *you*. I know all the people and all the energy is just how you roll through life. I just want to be one of them."

"Paul..." He knew what she was going to say. And his instinct was to tell her she didn't need to. But he thought of Carter's words, and he let her say it anyway.

Jessie took his hands as she launched into her Jessie-logue. "Your wife is a li'l crazy. *Crazy*. And I do get restless for the work, the creativity, the projects. But that is just me. It has nothing to do with how I feel about this part of me. Our life is *my* life. I love doing this life with you. I don't even feel like we've really started yet. You? You are the best surprise in the worst time. But not just that. For me, for now and the rest of my life, you are more than enough for all my days. And if you ever doubt it..." She released his hands and took hold of his face instead. "All you have to do is come here. Right here. And I promise to remind you."

Paul looked away. Her tornadic intensity would gather him up and spin him around, and he loved it, but he –

"I feel... Jess, it's almost *embarrassing* how much I need you. I crave you. I love you."

"Why is that embarrassing?"

He shrugged. "I just didn't know this was what it could be like."

"Can I tell you something? This, in my opinion, is what it is supposed to be like. Remember that time you called me a quilt with arms? And a snow globe?"

He laughed. "That's not exactly what I said..."

She shrugged. "Semantics. Anyway, if you can't lavish love on your mate, on your family, then what's the point?"

His response was a shrug.

"Paul, I know that's not what it was like for you as a kid. Me either. And I know you and Leah didn't operate that way. But I'm here to tell you: it's okay here. You can love me big all you want. And you can be confident that as big as I am loving everyone else, I am loving you. I love starting my days with you, and I love our good nights. And as much time in-between that we are together, I love that, too. And I hope you come have tea in our tea room because it's mine, so that means it's yours, too."

He shook his head, still feeling a little too needy. "Jess, that isn't what I meant for you... I don't have to be part of the tea room. I just worry—"

Jessie grabbed the hand he had been gesturing with. "That's what I am telling you. I know you're worried. I know you don't want to ask me for anything. *You don't have to.* You are a part of everything I do. That's why we're married."

His manfulness always got alarmed when she disarmed him like this. But the rest of him knew it was just *nice*, part of the gift of her, of his second chance, of their second chance. When the tears burned in his eyes, he tried not to curse them or swipe them away. He just nodded wordlessly and let his quilt with arms cover him again.

# CHAPTER♡TWENTY-THREE

## *Julie*

"I CAN'T WAIT TO SEE THE STORE!"

It was Saturday. Julie had worked every Saturday since she'd been hired. It was her "turn" to be off, and Darcy's last weekend as an employee. So there Julie was, free as a bird to enjoy Chad's first weekend in Myrtle Beach. The possibilities were endless. There were festivals everywhere in the fall. They could shop for some of the things he still needed for the apartment. The beach was still perfect in mid-October. But he wanted to visit Run This Way first.

Julie dreaded it.

First, they walked to the crepe place and had a late breakfast. Julie had already run eight miles that morning, and now she was scrubbed and polished and ravenous. She remained busy with mimosas and coffee and a big platter while Chad told her all about his week of orientation and how excited he was to swerve from a clinical practice to being a hospitalist.

"You'll never be looking for patients," Julie observed. "So many people are moving here, and it's not just retirees or enthusiastic snowbirds anymore. Kids everywhere. I can't believe my sister is having her third."

"That's right! When is she due again?"

"January."

"Wow. Exciting." Chad paused to sign the credit slip, then smiled a little shyly at her. "My parents would love to have one grandkid right now, much less three."

*Oh Chad.* "Yeah, well, my dad sure loves hanging with Christian. He's going on six now. Vivi is still a bit much for him, but she's a toddler. They're a lot for most of us."

She tried not to be sad as she passed him her phone to show a current photo, Vivi on a swing in Danielle's backyard and Christian pushing her. Danielle and Matt would not be finding out the gender of baby number three, stating that since they "had all the stuff," they might as well be surprised. Julie felt like a third baby in six years was enough of a surprise, but what did she know, really?

"Do I get to meet them?" Chad asked. "You guys hanging for Halloween or something?"

Halloween was in four days. Julie still had not committed to the gathering at Dad and Jessie's house. The group run was going to be the night before, so she no longer had that as an excuse. She would probably still be at work when her niece and nephew trick-or-treated in their own neighborhood.

She looked at Chad's expectant and kind face and willed herself to soften. "I just can't decide," she said honestly. "They're doing a whole thing at Daddy's house... my dad and Jessie's."

"Aw, Jules." He wouldn't say anymore. One of their only real fights was the one time he encouraged her to "try Jessie." It had been just after the anniversary of her mama's death, one of her darkest weeks in Arizona. Ian had been completely unavailable; he wasn't even at work that day, and he was all Julie had wanted to console herself with. When Chad mentioned Julie going for a visit and making peace with her dad's new life, she had ranted and yelled and even threw a plate, which was not her typical M.O.

Well, what was typical for her anymore?

She shrugged. "I do really want to see them..."

Tentatively, Chad reached across the table and took her hand. Julie did not feel anything electric. In fact, he reminded her a little of Hazel, patting her hand during her particular brand of pep-talking. "If you decide to go, and that's entirely up to you, I would love to go with you. I work the next three days, and then I'm off for Halloween."

She didn't move her hand, and she smiled at him. "But you'll miss all the stomach pumping and Jack-o-lantern burns."

"It's okay," he said. "I can deal with the post-traumatic allergic reactions, minor car accidents, and drunk moms tripping on sewer grates."

"Yeah. Good times."

It struck her then how much she *didn't* miss medicine. The night before Halloween, she would be running in a pirate costume with potpourri of good-natured athletes, and the day after, she'd be sharing mini Reese's cups with whomever happened to walk in the door for new gear. It sounded so lovely and mostly uncomplicated to her. And running in a costume sounded like something her mama would have loved.

Gratefulness for Chad and his optimism washed over her. She stood up. "Let's go. You'll love the store."

"I love whatever you love," he murmured behind her. His words made her stomach swirl, but she didn't know why.

"Brought you a fitting!" Julie called. She and Chad entered the store from the back, which she was coming to think of the family door. It was only delivery drivers, employees, and regulars who came in that way. She couldn't help herself; she loved the uncomplicated family feeling there.

"Hey Jules!" Darcy was standing with her back to the counter, her ponytail piled high on her head and sporting a Boston Marathon finisher shirt. Julie gave her a hug. Darcy was extra elated now that her boyfriend had decided to go ahead and make the move with her, and Julie was so excited for her.

"You must be Chad." She shook his hand and gestured to the store. "Welcome to our second home. It's about to be Julie's domain. She's right at home here."

Chad beamed at Julie, then at Darcy. "Thanks for taking such good care of her. I hear congratulations are in order for you."

And with that, the two extroverts in the room started a full chat. Julie listened half to them and half to Robin, who was getting the process started with a thirty-ish, maybe forty-ish woman who looked somewhat plus-sized and like she'd rather be anywhere in the world.

"I know I don't look like a runner," she said.

Julie winced. Whenever someone started that way, they were typically ashamed of something. Julie thought just walking into a store branded for runners was a pretty brave first step.

Robin didn't miss a beat. "A runner looks like someone who runs," he said. "We all had to start somewhere."

"I'm pretty sure a tall drink of water like you didn't start walking three minutes for every thirty seconds you jog. Call me Michelle."

Julie turned toward Darcy so they could both giggle quietly. When Julie turned back around, the tips of Robin's ears were red.

"I didn't start that way, Michelle, but these days, I'm walking a lot, too. Moving forward is the most important thing."

When she started her gait assessment, Robin briefly turned and gave Julie a pointed look that sent her stomach knots to *vibrate* again. He didn't have to say a word.

She was running thirty miles a week and hadn't moved her life forward more than an inch.

By the time Robin finished with Michelle, she had a new pair of Hokas, three pairs of socks, four kitschy headbands, and a huge smile on her face. Julie wanted to high five him. She felt so victorious on Michelle's behalf.

Robin, however, stoically put all Michelle's rejected shoeboxes away and piddled with something in the storage room. Darcy and Chad were still talking endlessly, and no one else had come in. Was he really going to avoid them altogether?

Then the Liu family walked in. Julie felt that warming feeling all over again; she adored them. The parents, Wes and Daisy, were both practicing physicians right there in Market Common, and they were runners, *and* they homeschooled their six *beautiful* children who were softball players and dancers and karate masters and overall geniuses. Their buzz filled the whole store. Darcy eventually started bringing shoes out for He-Doctor, as they called Wes, and their teenage son. The rest of them pranced around the store, visiting, trying out massage guns, picking out snacks. Even off the clock, they made Julie want to stay.

Amid all the noise, Robin finally re-emerged. Julie and Chad were at the counter taking to Daisy, and after taking it all in, Robin joined them. Julie was inwardly cringing before a word was even uttered.

"You must be Robin," Chad said, offering his hand.

Robin shook it firmly. "Nice to meet you."

RUN THIS WAY | 256

"Chad," Chad finished.

*For crying out loud. You know his name, Robin!* Julie kept her game face on. She'd rather be over with Darcy playing with the shoes.

"Yeah, yeah. Welcome to town. Julie's so excited to have you here. I'm gonna help Darcy, but enjoy the store. Julie can help you out if you need anything. I'll make sure she's compensated for her time."

"Extra fifty cents, 'eh?" Chad quipped.

Julie visibly cringed at his comment. It was uncharacteristically snotty of Chad, and Julie sensed, perhaps, there was a bit of jealousy behind it.

Robin stopped and feigned thoughtfulness for a second. She steeled herself for whatever he was going to say.

"I understand Julie left a promising medical career, so as a seasoned entrepreneur, I ensure she feels valued on a daily basis for the work she does here and what she brings to the overall table. So, to answer your question, Chad, a dollar. At least."

He turned, signaling his doneness. Daisy raised her eyebrows as Chad frowned at Julie and asked if she was ready to go.

Julie nodded, saying hurried goodbyes to the Lius and to Darcy. She didn't bother with Robin, because he couldn't have made his feelings known more if he was wearing a t-shirt that said I AM IGNORING YOU.

"What the hell was that?" Chad asked as they walked toward home.

Best to be honest, she told herself. "Well, I mean, the fifty-cents comment was kind of insulting, don't you think?"

"What? Why? I was kidding."

"You were insinuating that he doesn't pay me decently."

Chad stopped walking. "No. I was insinuating that helping me wasn't worth your time."

"It didn't sound that way, Chad. It sounded like you were looking down on the store."

He started walking. "It *sounds* like your new boss is overly sensitive. And it *sounds* like maybe you are, too."

Was she? Maybe. She had looked down on the store when she started. She saw it as a step backwards. And now...

She caught up to Chad. "You know. Maybe you're right. It's a big change for me, and I am touchy about it. And I am also growing to love it. And Robin... he is defensive because he built the business in the face of some adversity. He really prides himself on training experts and paying them well. You just hit the wrong button this morning..."

He took her hand. She couldn't tell whether she found it comforting or presumptive. "I get it, Jules. I'm glad you like it so much."

*Yeah. That's what I said.* He didn't get it. Had she not explained it well? Maybe anyone she knew in the medical field wouldn't understand her choice, ever. Who gave up life-saving potential for... anything?

Wait. She thought of Hazel and her magic, of Darcy and her big dreams, of Lillian and her mismatched, perfect fit, of Michelle's smile on her way out the door. Certainly, her conversations with the He and She Drs. Lius had been affirming. What they did at Run This Way was life-*giving.*

*I'm not going to downplay it anymore. This is what I do now.*

She was twenty-nine years old, and nothing had to be forever. Nothing was forever.

♡

The rest of the day passed in pleasant enough peace. Julie was all unpacked and worked on making her room slightly more than functional. She and Chad drove to Old Time Pottery and picked out some new throw pillows and kitchen towels. They ducked into the Gretel's Candy House, so she could buy a few treats for the kids and make up Halloween bags. She was still unsure when and where she would see them, but she wanted to be a part of whatever they would be doing, somehow.

It was the kind of day she used to have *before*. On her Saturdays off *before* the first of her worlds came crashing down, she would work out in the mornings, sometimes take a run or maybe a yoga class, sometimes go to the gym. She would run her errands and usually meet up with Danielle or Katy or both at Mama and Daddy's to swim or hang out. Every so often, it would turn into a whole night, and Daddy would grill something, or they'd order in. Mama would make sangria, maybe they'd watch a movie. Sometimes, they would get cleaned up and go somewhere for seafood. Sometimes Julie had a boyfriend with her, but they were never around long. They weren't what she remembered so fondly of those happy, faraway times.

She sighed. She no longer had Mama and Daddy's home to visit. It didn't exist anymore. Maybe she could go to Danielle's? However, they'd been a little tense with each other since their coffee date.

*You're not going to get what you want if you keep doing the same things.* That was definitely Mama. And Julie obeyed.

"Hey. You want to stop by my sister's house? Meet the kids?"

Chad looked at her with a little surprise and immediately said,

"That sounds great. Tell me where to go."

Danielle and Matt lived inland a bit more, in an area called Carolina Forest, which Paul joked was a half-day trip from Surfside Beach. There was always so much traffic. Julie punched in a message to make sure they were home and told Chad to get on 544. They rode pleasantly toward the beginning of sunset for a few minutes when her phone rang.

No one but Katy, Danielle, and, whenever he had decided she was available, Ian called her. But when she looked down, her screen read "Nick-Robin."

"Weird. It's my boss," she said. The phrase sounded strange to her.

"What's up?" she answered.

"Hey. I'm sorry to bother you."

"It's fine. What's going on?"

There was a pause, and she heard bustle in the background. She couldn't really make it out, but it *felt* familiar.

"Robin, where are you?"

"I'm at the hospital. Up at Grand Strand."

"Oh my God! Are you okay?" They were at a stoplight, and Chad turned to her and started mouthing questions. She waved them away with her hand.

"Yeah, yeah. Um. It's just weird. I actually came here with my dad. He's going to be okay, I think, but crazy thing... Hazel is here, too."

"What?" She actually shouted. Chad echoed her. "Jules! What?"

She put her hand over the mouthpiece. "Hazel. My co-worker. One second."

"Okay. Robin is anyone with Hazel?"

"No. I talked to one of her daughters. They went back to Raleigh for the weekend. They're on their way now, but..."

"I'll be there as soon as I can. ER?"

"Yeah. Oh shit. Jules, I gotta go—"

He hung up.

"Oh my *God*."

Chad pulled over into the Chick-fil-A parking lot. "Julie. What?"

"Robin is at Grand Strand – the hospital on the north end – with his dad. I don't know what's wrong. But my other co-worker, Hazel, is there, too. She had a heart attack a few weeks ago, and he can't tell yet what happened, but she's there alone."

"So, we need to go there?"

"Oh, Chad." She turned to him with grateful admiration. "If you maybe don't mind dropping me off there, I can figure out how to get home. You don't have to stay..."

"Let's worry about that later. Just tell me where to go."

Julie gave him directions as she texted Danielle to apologize and explain why they weren't stopping by after all. And she felt so bad she added:

Please tell Christian and Vivi I will see them for trick-or-treating.

Danielle's three dots stayed on the screen for a while. Then it just said, I thought you had a work thing.

Sighing, Julie returned: Well, things are a little up in the air, but the latest I'll be done is 6.

She knew it was coming:

We'll be at Daddy's...

She looked straight ahead into the heavy Saturday traffic. She looked at Chad as he concentrated on the road. She looked at her own reflection in the windshield.

*You don't have any enemies here,* Mama's voice said. *Except sometimes, yourself.*

Julie opened the mirror and methodically put her hair into a topknot. She smiled back at Chad when he looked over to her. She put a cinnamon Altoid in her mouth. And then she typed her response.

I'll be there.

Good God. She didn't know what she was doing, but it couldn't keep going on like it had been.

They arrived.

"Chad, you really don't have to stay."

"Jules." He reached over and squeezed her hand. "Go see about your friend. I'll park and come find you, okay? Do we have friends on staff here? Anyone you want me to call?"

"We'll see. Thanks, Chad!" She jumped from the car and race-walked to the lobby.

She still had her badge from Ocean's Edge in her bag. She had taken it out and was just holding it in her hand as a small flex as she gave Hazel's name. For the inevitable, "Are you family?" question, she lied in simple words. "Yes. I'm her daughter."

She would likely never truthfully say "I'm her daughter" again, and she was not prepared for how much saying the words felt like a knife in her heart. The added distress, over and above her distress over Hazel, must have helped her plea a bit because the security guard gave her a little smile as he handed her the visitor sticker. She rushed past him looking for room number three.

But before she found it, she found Robin. He was slumped in one of the chairs outside the patient rooms, talking into his phone, his eyes red.

"Hey!" He looked up at her and immediately away, but he patted the seat next to him. She waited through his "Uh-huh" and "Okay" and "All right!" and then his goodbye. He set his phone in his lap and mussed his own hair.

"Hey..." she tried again.

"They brought Hazel to the cath lab already," he said. "Hi."

"Robin, what's—"

"My dad is in surgery. They rushed him. I don't know... it seemed pretty critical..."

"Oh Robin." She put her hand on his shoulder. "What happened?"

"He wrecked. I don't know all the details of the accident yet. He called me afterwards. Said he didn't want to worry Mom. And then he must have passed out. He was conscious when I got here, but then he coded, and they took him away. That was my mom on the phone. I don't even know what to tell her."

"Oh, Robin." She felt helpless. It certainly didn't sound good, but there was a long list of things that could be wrong, and though most of them were serious, not all of them were life-threatening. "We'll see what we can find out, okay? Is there anyone else we need to call? Your sisters? Does your mom need a ride here?"

"No. My older sister will bring her up here in a while. It will be a mess. And hopefully Lacey and Mary Claire will get here before Hazel comes back. You might not have to even stay."

"Robin!" He looked at her wearily. "I'm not leaving, okay? Do you want some coffee or water or anything?"

He shook his head. "No. No, I'm good."

They sat there wordlessly for what seemed like an endless time. When Chad walked in, Julie met him at the lobby entrance and gave him the heads up. He looked over at Robin, now on the phone again, and back at her.

"If you don't need me here, why don't I leave you the car and take an Uber home? You're going to be a while."

"Chad. You don't have to do that."

"I know." He took her hands and smiled down at her. "Jules, these are your people. You... you have a tribe here. It's good. I mean, what's happening isn't good, but you have the opportunity to be here making things better. I don't need to get in the way, and I don't want you not to have a car, so... here."

He put the keys in her hand and kissed her cheek. "Call me and let me know when there's news."

Without giving her much of a chance to protest or respond, he turned and left. She looked at the keys in her hand and shook her head as if to clear her vision. It didn't work.

She walked back to Robin and resumed the waiting game. He was a flurry of texts and calls. She started, too, texting Darcy, Katy, Danielle, and Daddy, letting them all know the little she knew. She tried not to fidget or ask Robin any questions. There was nothing to do, at all.

Over an hour later, a nurse appeared and called, "Murray." Robin jumped to his feet and headed over. Julie wanted to follow, if nothing else, to help him interpret, but he seemed to have forgotten she was even there. In the midst of the events, he had put her in touch with Hazel's daughters, and Mary Claire was texting her while Lacey drove. They were still an hour away. Her phone was dinging non-stop.

*You need anything, honey?*

She smiled at her dad's words. She did. She needed a lot of things, clarity being the top of her list. She just sent back three red hearts and looked expectedly up at Robin as he returned.

"He's stable," he said, his voice taking on a weird higher tone. "He has broken ribs, and one of his lungs was punctured. He was having trouble breathing, and that caused... that's why he passed out on the phone. And he went into full respiratory arrest when they got him here. They said it's all common. Common. They did a minor procedure, and he'll be fine. I can see him in a little while."

"Nothing feels common in the ER," Julie said. Robin gave her a withered smile. He sat back down next to her, and when she squeezed his hand, he held on.

It was something like twenty minutes and forever when another nurse appeared and called Hazel's name. At last check, her daughters were still almost an hour away, so Julie jumped up and played the role.

"What can you tell me?" she said. She flashed her old employee badge.

The nurse side-eyed the badge and didn't miss a beat. "Miss Hazel had another heart attack. It was very soon after the last one, and the on-call doctor consulted with her cardiologist. They performed an emergency angioplasty, but they're considering a valve replacement. We will need some consent forms signed if they go that path. We'll know when Doctor..." She glanced at the file in her hand, "...Brass gets here."

"Okay. Her oldest, I mean, my older sister will be here soon.

She's the one with the POA."

"Yes, of course. Well. As soon as Hazel is in a room, we'll let you know."

Julie wandered back toward Robin. He was now talking in person to two women, one gray-haired, tan, and sinewy, the other shorter with perfect golden highlights and full curves. She wasn't sure if she should return to him, but without looking her way, he stuck his arm out and waved her over.

It was such a familiar gesture, she felt oddly safe and warm walking to his side.

"Julie, this is my mom, Caroline, and my sister, Gretchen."

Caroline immediately took Julie's hand in both of hers and looked her in the eye. "Thank you for being here with Robin, dear. We've heard a lot about you."

That was a surprise. Gretchen nodded at her and smiled, distractedly. She murmured something about going to find a bathroom and said she would meet them in the room. Caroline looked at Robin with anticipation. He spoke to Julie.

"We can go see my dad now. But is Hazel..."

Julie tried to sound more confident than she felt. "It was another heart attack. They did a routine procedure and stabilized her, and when her own cardiologist gets here, they're deciding on next steps."

He nodded. Julie was shaken to see *him* so shaken. She was glad his family had arrived, even though watching them made her feel alone.

"Okay. If I don't see you, we'll talk later."

"Don't worry about the store Monday, okay? I got it."

He looked down at her with shining eyes. "I know you do. Thank you."

Taking his mom's arm, he walked her down the hall and disappeared. Julie sat, not taking her phone out, just watching. The ER waiting room wasn't too busy for a Saturday evening. There were a few miserable people holding ice packs or bandages in various places, some squirmy kids, a crying baby. No one looked too traumatized, which was a big plus. She didn't like being there; in fact, she had never liked working in the emergency department. So much of it was dealing with people on their worst days, and one of the reasons she was drawn to OB was knowing that many of her patients would be having their best days. Oh, she knew there would be challenges and upheaval and even tragedy.

But nothing could have prepared her for her first birthing loss.

Working at the Babymoon B&B (Birth & Breathe) had been like a dream job. She was still an L & D nurse, but because she was working toward Midwifery, she got so much extra insight. Ian, as well the midwives who worked there, took time to instruct her, to explain, to involve her. She loved every minute of it. When she had started her first set of clinical hours, she got to help "catch" two babies in the first week.

And then the Prosser family had come along. Troy and Alley, who had been college sweethearts, entered real estate, got wildly busy and successful, and then tried to have babies. They needed help, and that was Ian's specialty. As a reproductive endocrinologist, he had helped hundreds of couples start their families. Alley had two miscarriages before her dream came to fruition. She had planned to give birth at Babymoon, and she did. No complications had been foreseen. She was monitored but allowed to labor according to her preferences. She gave birth to a healthy, seven-pound, five-ounce baby boy. She held him and named him Carson and took pictures with Troy. She'd mentioned to Julie she felt so disoriented, and she was sure it was just pure euphoria. Fifty minutes after, she'd gone into cardiac arrest and was dead.

Julie knew with all her intellect that Alley's death was not her fault. It was no one's fault, really. The post-mortem analysis showed that Alley had suffered an Amniotic Fluid Embolism, which was incredibly rare. There was a small chance that if her agitation had been mentioned to the doctor, he'd have caught it in time to intervene, but based on statistics, it still would have been too late to really help her.

And so watching Troy, stone-faced and in complete shock, holding his newborn son, who was perfectly healthy and wailing, became the tragedy by which Julie would measure everything, even her own unexpected loss of her mother. It was the worst thing she had ever seen, and no matter what Ian or any of the other staff at Babymoon told her, showed her in studies, offered her as encouragement, she never wanted to be part of a situation like that again.

She'd prefer never to be in an emergency room again, where she might witness something akin to that nightmare, but thinking of her new friends and how they'd helped her find some purpose again affirmed her. They thought she was worth it, so she would take a risk for them.

Lost in thought, she felt someone stand next to her. Thinking it might be Hazel's daughters, whom she'd only met once, she looked up to see Robin. From the expression on his face, she expected the worst.

"Hey! Hey... how is everything? How's he doing?"

Robin gave his signature shrug and just stood there. Julie rose to her feet.

"He's stable, right? Breathing okay?"

He nodded. "Tube in his chest for a little bit."

"Okay," Julie said, nodding as well. "That's pretty standard, I think. Your mom okay?"

He was silent at first, looking off to the side. Julie still felt like she didn't know him very well, but she'd been around enough of her patients' husbands and boyfriends to read some signs. So, she took a risk again.

"It's okay to be shaken up, Robin. This was a lot, and interventions for a collapsed lung are scary. Seeing... seeing your daddy weak is scary." She paused to contain her own emotions. "Can I do anything for you?"

There was no answer, not a mumble or a nod or even a shrug. He looked stony and fragile all at once. "Robin?"

That garnered a headshake and a little sound escaping him, so she put aside her own fear of looking stupid or being rejected and hugged him. She hugged him like she might have a patient's family or a discouraged colleague or a distant cousin. But he held her back with the fervency of panicked kid and the strength of an intimate friend. She took it, not realizing until that moment his arms pressed her against his solid chest that she needed it, too; she needed a friend, she needed comfort, she needed to trust someone, and she needed to be needed.

That was all. He returned to his dad's side. Mary Claire and Lacey arrived and took over Hazel-watch. So Julie weighed her options. It wasn't that late. She could still go see Danielle, but... no. Maybe she and Chad could go for a late dinner and talk. But he would have eaten already, and she didn't know what to say just yet.

She could fall off the wagon and call Ian. Or....

She knew what she decided in that moment didn't matter nearly as much as what she would decide over the next few days. So, allowing herself a moment of hope, she tapped out a message, Meet me at the beach? In between the piers, and she headed for the car.

# CHAPTER♡TWENTY-FOUR

## *Jessie*

THE TABLES WERE SET. I LOOKED IN THE MIRROR AND FUSSED WITH MY HAIR ONE MORE TIME. Abby was in the kitchen. Travis, her oldest child and my oldest grandchild, was helping Summer fill the water glasses. It was just a dry run on a Monday, a day the tea room was typically closed. It was just a few friends and family coming along with a few hand-picked members of the local business community. Still, I was striving for excellence and preferred perfection.

There were concealer-proof bags under my eyes. It would just have to be. Paul had been out until the wee hours of Sunday morning, dealing with Julie. He was still sleeping when I'd woken to start prepping for this event, and by the time I got home, exhausted, he not only shared my fatigue but didn't seem to want to talk.

I hoped everything was okay for Julie. I had to believe it was okay with us because he *said* it was, and I didn't have time to walk on eggshells or second guess at the moment. Maggie had just walked in, her husband Don on one arm and our local celebrity meteorologist Ed Piotrowski on the other.

She had done it. Maggie had been Ed's banker for years, and when I told her I wanted to get at least one buzz-worthy person in the room for this, crazy-nervous though that made me, she insisted she could get Ed there. She was magical, and so was he.

Abby stepped out of the kitchen to check in with me at just that moment. My Audrey Hepburn black dress and red apron firmly in place, I began to work the room. Maggie sparkled, and I couldn't help myself; I kissed her cheek, then Don's, then, what the heck, Ed's, too, since he was throwing in an endearing a bit of sparkle himself.

"It's so wonderful that you came," I said. "Our whole family feels like we know you. You're always the center of our pre-hurricane dinner parties."

Ed gave a little cough and smiled good-naturedly. I was certain he heard things equally as cheesy all the time. "This looks like a great place," he said. "I'll be sure to bring Cindy here after it opens."

I tried to be cool. I don't know if I succeeded. But I made small talk for a few more moments until Maggie nodded that I should speak to the others coming in. I smiled grandly and promised they could order their favorite tea soon.

We'd only invited thirty people, but it seemed that most of them were coming: Brittney and a few of her co-workers from the Myrtle Beach Chamber of Commerce, Mikayla and Danielle, each bringing a friend, Janice and Melissa from Broadway at the Beach, the Neeves women, who owned and operated the dance studio where Summer attended, Morgan and a few ladies from the church, Debbie and Vickie from the Surfside Beach town offices, Cathy and Megan from the library. My stomach was on red alert, and as I ducked into the kitchen to grab a water carafe (my only job for the day was hostessing and refilling water glasses, Scout's honor to Paul and everyone else), I took a long swallow of my stashed ginger ale and took a deep breath. Was Paul right? Was this the dumbest leap ever?

"This is a great turnout, Miss Jessie!" I smiled at Savannah, one of the sweet servers who would be staying on with us. I don't know if she was just being nice or it really was a good turnout, but the room was abuzz with chatter, and Savannah and Bella were already bringing out teapots. Travis and Summer were following with cream, honey, and lemon. Abby was shadowing the cook, Sarah, but she was going to help serve the main course, so she could greet everyone, too.

We had developed a prix fixe menu for our "High-light" Tea Preview. Everyone would get their choice from six teas, cranberry orange and cinnamon blueberry mini scones, either asparagus and white cheddar or bacon and Swiss quiche atop a bed of "kilt" spinach, and a sampler of berries and cream, salted dark chocolate mini brownies, and lemon cheesecake bites for dessert. Abby and I had been consulting with Abby's friend in Georgia; her mom owned a tea room there and shared some of her best practices and even a few favorite recipes from across the years. We had made all the sweets the day before, and even though we were using all of Carla's china and linens, we felt like the menu was really introducing our signature "classy country" style.

After the quiche was served and an instrumental version of Pearl Jam's "Alive" was softly playing, Abby and I stood off to the side admiring the view. The tables were full. The chatter was endless. The cups and plates were being emptied. Maybe we were really going to pull this off.

It was then that Brittney came to stand beside us and motioned to Maggie, who clinked her spoon ever-so-not-delicately against her water glass. The room shushed itself as my youngest daughter put on her Chamber of Commerce voice and welcomed them all.

"It matters *so much* that this is the vision of my own mama, Jessie Oakley Jameson, and my sister-in-*love* Abby Oakley. They are wonderful at everything they touch, turning everyday occasions into celebrations that charm and sparkle and comfort and are memorable for everyone there. But it matters just as much that they are keeping a wonderful local business, created by Ms. Carla Cowell, *local*, and it's truly a lovely gem in this great town that deserves to be around for many years to come! So, if you enjoy yourself today, please, please, please tell your friends. *Bring* your friends. And from now as we countdown to December first, post about it. Schedule a day for your next staff meeting or Bible study or a Christmas brunch with your friends. Men–"

As if on cue, and it likely was, Paul and Sam sauntered in the door and stood awkwardly just inside.

Brittney smiled and gestured grandly at them. "...such as my big brother and my stepdad here..." Oh, how that term muddled together pain and gratefulness in my overflowing heart. "... bring your sweethearts for a different kind of date. Bring your daughters and granddaughters and your mamas for a unique treat."

There were sweet little nods and murmurs in the room. Brittney had done a great job conveying what we were hoping for, but it appeared she wasn't done. "Perhaps you don't know this, but my mama has endured quite a challenging, crazy, complicated last year and a half." She cleared her throat. I really wasn't sure what she was going to say, and I was feeling pretty sure of what I *didn't* want her to share. "It was all capped recently when she was diagnosed with cancer less than a month after she got remarried. A *month*! But here she is today... cancer-free, radiation finished, and excited to start something new at the ripe age of... just kidding, Mama. I would never share that!" We smiled at each other.

"And then there is my sister, here. While raising three amazing children – two of them are helping to serve you today!" She paused and led the room in applause for Travis and Summer, one whom looked like he wanted to be swallowed by the very earth and one who curtsied. "She worked at one of the biggest marketing firms at the beach. And this past year..." Brittney paused again like a pro, but also like the giant, loving heart I knew her to be, and put her arm around Abby's shoulders, "She lost her own mother after a lifelong battle with respiratory disease." The room took its own respectful moment of silence. "On December first, the Beachside Garden TeaRoom will be rechristened 'Whitney's Tea Room' in honor of Abby's mother." There was applause, and Abby beamed.

Brittney raised her voice to finish. "I have watched these two women grow through their grief and embrace life's array of curveballs and opportunities with grace and passion. And so, in their honor, I encourage you to try something different, whether it's a unique and charming little place to have a cozy and classy light meal or a chance that may never come your way again. Now in honor of Jessie and Abby, and in memory of Whitney, let's raise a teacup." The room followed suit as Brittney finished with, "God said live, y'all."

*God said live.* My eyes were full as I embraced her and then Abby, too, tightly. Mikayla and Danielle had come up to join us. Katy was working, and Julie, of course, was not there, but they were all my girls. I could only hope Julie would free herself to join our ranks before long because I believed we were becoming a pretty formidable tribe.

♡

Paul and Sam were still sitting at a table for two with about six little dishes of pastries between them when the rest of the room had cleared out. Sam also had a twenty-ounce bottle of Coke Zero in front of him. I brought him a glass with ice, passing it over as I sat in the chair I had dragged between them.

"You're messing with the ambiance, Sam," I said.

"Sorry, Mama." He poured what was left with a smile on his face. "The brownies are my favorite."

"Of course, they are," I said. "We made them with you in mind."

My sweet boy, which was how I always thought of him, might have blushed a bit as he shoved another in his mouth.

"Maybe when David gets to town, we can score some Snicker-doodles," Paul chided.

I leaned over and kissed Paul's cheek. It had taken me until now to be mostly comfortable showing him that level of affection in front of my kids. Sam didn't look, but at least he didn't flinch.

"Deal," I said. "So...?"

Sam shook his head. "Mama, you can do anything." It was my turn to blush.

"Ha! This time, my smartest move was hitching my wagon to your amazing wife," I said.

"She is amazing," Sam said, and Paul raised his own glass of iced tea to toast her. My men were such non-conformists.

"I'm gonna find her," he added. He kissed my cheek as he left the table, and when I looked back to Paul after watching Sam walk away, he was smiling more fully at me than he had in weeks. *Weeks*.

I returned it to him. And I asked again, "So?"

Paul took my hand in both of his. He kissed it, and put it back on the table, and sighed. "I can't say it better than Sam does, sweetheart. You can do anything."

"Well, I mean. We *knew* that..." I said, only half kidding. I was feeling pretty damn invincible at the moment.

"Can it just be okay if sometimes I don't want you to do *everything*?"

The smile was gone from his mouth, but it was still in his eyes. He looked as tired as I did. I supposed that two ambitious people like we were, with a pretty big family that was some blended together and some not so much, were never going to be fully satisfied with everything the other was doing, or not doing.

And I supposed at sixty-ish, we both needed to have peace with that.

"Yes," I said, nodding for emphasis. "As long as you tell me when you're not okay, so we can talk through it together. Don't go stormy on me if you can help it."

Paul nodded thoughtfully. "I can try. This leopard is changing a lot of spots these days."

I caressed his hand. "I know you are. I'm extremely proud of you."

He looked at our hands, nodding. "Yeah. I never thought I'd still be growing up at my age. But at least I'm setting a good example."

I didn't flinch. I would no longer avoid hard subjects when I had just asked him not to. "How is Julie?"

Shadows eclipsed the joy in his eyes. My stomach sank, wondering what fresh drama was happening.

"She called me and asked, if she brought Oreos, would I meet her at the beach."

I couldn't help but smile at that. It seemed like such a sweet and normal thing when the two of them together had been anything but. "Wow. That late? What the heck was going on?"

"It was fine. She was taking care of her work friends." He smiled a bit at that. "She wanted to talk, finally. Honestly."

"Really?"

He launched into a bit of a long story, mostly about Julie's time in Arizona and what shape she was really in when she came back.

"Oh, Paul." My heart ached for her. But it was also fluttering with nerves. "Am I supposed to know any of this?"

He actually laughed at that. "I really can't wait for you two to be friends because you honestly know each other pretty well. She told me that I should share the basics with you, so that I wouldn't feel like I was keeping anything from you, and so that you would know she wasn't just being ridiculous or bitchy sponging off our apartment. And she also said for me to make sure you knew that I had permission to tell you whatever I told you."

"Holy shit," I murmured.

"Indeed. Oh, and she's coming over for Halloween."

"*What*?!" There was no chill to be had for me.

He shrugged. "She wanted to see Christian and Vivi, and Danielle told her what we were doing, and she said she can't miss it. So, gird up your loins. Get extra wine. Whatever you need to do. It's gotta be a start, right?"

"Pau-aul!" I reserved my two-syllable declaration of his name for the most momentous occasions. A fresh beginning with Julie sure felt like one. Before it even happened, I could feel a weight on us and between us lift. I looked around the remnants of chaos in our soon-to-be tea room, Travis and Sam standing by Abby throwing brownie bites for the other to catch, Summer sipping tea next to Maggie, looking like she'd just run a marathon or single-handedly hosted the Queen's Platinum Jubilee, and felt all the ambient warmth that had been confined to the corners of my life wash fully over me. This was *us*. We had new chapters starting, and my littlest team, the one that consisted of Paul and me, was a pretty formidable one, too.

# CHAPTER♡TWENTY-FIVE

## *Julie*

MONDAY WAS THE LONGEST, FULLEST DAY JULIE HAD HAD SINCE LEAVING HER MEDICAL CAREER, SAVE FOR THE LONG DRIVE FROM PHOENIX TO SURFSIDE BEACH. She woke up at 5:30 to complete her run. She had coffee with Chad, keeping conversation fairly informational and perfunctory. Then she got to the store at nine, where she met with Mary Claire to talk through Hazel's next steps before she opened up the store to tackle her first day alone. Darcy might be able to spare a few hours, but she had already worked her notice and was packing to leave for Boston by the end of the week.

The store had, in fact, been steady all day. There'd also been inventory to check in and a few online orders to pack and ship.

"Mom is going to come live with me." That's how Mary Claire had stoically opened her conversation with Julie. Hazel had gotten the valve replacement and would spend a few weeks in rehab. Mary Claire had a husband who traveled and an empty nest, and she was in the best position to let Hazel *room* with her. The only thing was, Hazel's six-year-old corgi, Dolly, could not come. Mary Claire had allergies; they had no fence; and yada yada yada. Julie couldn't imagine how Hazel was dealing with that news, and without giving much thought, she *assured* Mary Claire she would find Dolly a suitable home herself.

It gave her a project, if nothing else. She certainly couldn't keep a dog when she wasn't even sure where she'd be living in a month.

She was still pondering as she prepared to lock up at 6:02. Chad was going to meet her for a quick dinner at Gordon Biersch at 6:30. She checked herself in the mirror and prepared to leave, but Robin was standing in the back doorway.

"Oh. Hey. I wasn't expecting to see you today."

There was the shrug. "Sorry to disappoint you."

"Stop." She studied his face in the dim light. "You look tired."

"Yeah. I'm gonna sleep at home tonight," he said. "Dad is doing better. He'll probably come home on Wednesday. Mom is going to stay tonight even though he insists it's stupid."

"Dads are the most stubborn humans on the face of the earth," she said.

He nodded and smiled wryly. "How did it go here? Thank you for stepping up. I know we have a lot to talk about..."

"It's fine." Julie waved her hand. "I'm fine. You're fine. Everything is fine." She laughed nervously.

"You convincing me or yourself?"

"Both!"

He laughed a little, too. "I don't think it's working."

They were still standing in the hallway, both of them now leaning against a wall, facing each other. Julie could hear a little theme song playing in her head; she couldn't name the tune. She wasn't sure if it was real. But she knew it ushered in the strange and welcome warmth she was starting to feel whenever Robin was around.

She told him about Hazel's moving and about Dolly. He

frowned and appeared to think it through.

"Did you ask Darcy? She loves Dolly... might be perfect timing."

Julie shook her head. "She rented a place that doesn't allow pets."

"Stupid places," he said. "I would take her, but Pote isn't even getting enough attention right now. I was actually thinking he could spend the daytime tomorrow with you."

"Um, yes, please," she said.

"So, Chad's place doesn't allow dogs either?"

Julie sighed. Once she said it out loud, it would be real.

"I don't know, honestly, but I'm not going to stay there."

"What? Why?"

"You don't have time for this right now," she protested.

He let himself fall gracefully into a heap against the wall. He glanced at his watch and said, "Sit down. I need to let Pote out in the next hour. And I'm starving as usual. But I have time for the highlights."

"Ha! What a choice of words." She went ahead and sat against her wall. They both stretched out their legs beside the other. It wasn't wide enough for him. His knees were bent, and his own size eleven blue Kinvaras had seen better days.

"Chad is probably the nicest person I have ever met," she said. "If I could make myself love someone, I would marry him this weekend. He's that perfect. Which is exactly why I can't stay there. I'm using him, as I'm sure you know because you thought it was absurd from the get-go. The problem is, I need a minute to find a place. So, Wednesday, I am going to my dad and Jessie's for Halloween. I will fall on my sword. I will eat the chili and drink the punch."

"Wait. There's punch?"

"Oh my gosh, yes!" she assured him. "Not like the cult Kool Aid, necessarily, but there will be punch. Probably a themed punch in a themed bowl with floating eyeball ice cubes or something. Anyway. I'm going to try... just to... relax, I guess? I don't know what else to do. I've made all these assumptions about what things must be like when they're all together, but the truth is, I haven't been around all of them in over a year, since Dad married Jessie, since all the... raw... has scabbed over a little. Maybe it's fine. And maybe even if it isn't, I can be fine."

Robin was nodding consistently as she ticked off her points. "You're solving most of the problems, Julie. So, I have two more solutions to offer."

"Nah." She shook her head vehemently. "You've done enough for me."

"You really underestimate how much you're going to be working your ass off for me in the next month or two, so just listen." She sat up straighter.

"Let me loan you the security deposit. I know there are places available right here. You should be able to get at least a studio for starters. Live by yourself. It does wonders for your clarity." He shrugged. "And if you can't find a place that takes dogs..."

"Yeah?" she said, not sure whether to anticipate wisdom or smartass-ery.

"Give Dolly to your stepmom."

She looked at him, then past him, then in her mind's eye, directly into the cozy house on Sparrow Drive. Jessie, *her stepmom*, had had a beloved yellow Labrador when Julie moved away to Arizona. Cash was a beach-loving, frisbee catching, bucket of golden fluff that everyone loved. Even she had been sad when she heard through a long and winding grapevine that he had died. She remembered it happened right after she and David broke up; Dad and Jessie had broken up just a few days later, basically fighting over them and their ridiculous decisions. Had she not been completely distracted, trying to move in with Chad, dump her apartment, and carry on like an idiot with Ian, she would have felt terrible about Jessie's losing her dog. It was a lot for a person to handle at the same time.

*And you, my dear, are an empathetic person. That's why you were a good nurse. And that's why you're so great at what you're doing now.*

"Thanks, Mama." She didn't realize she'd said it out loud until Robin looked quizzically at her, nudging her hand with his foot.

"So, you think it's a good idea?"

"I think," Julie started, "that if I can navigate us through the next few weeks and keep our sales on target, you should think of giving me a bonus instead of a loan. And let's make tomorrow the first Tuesday we close early, so I can actually go secure a place as soon as possible. And Robin?"

"I didn't just stop listening," he said with a giggle.

She nudged his ribs with her foot. "I think giving Dolly to Dad and... and Jessie... is a great idea."

His eyes smiled at her even while he shrugged again. "I know it is, Jules. I know."

"*Julie.*"

Frustration was overflowing in Chad's voice. It was not the desperation or pleading tone he'd used when she broke up with him. It was incredulousness. Even anger.

"I told you," he said, "No expectations. I got a third bedroom to help you. I have given you space. I haven't asked for anything. You're really moving out? Already, Julie?"

When he put it like this, it did sound shitty.

"What do you want me to do?" she said. "Is there an amount I can pay you to settle the difference between a two bedroom and a three?"

He glared at her, pushing away his barely-untouched dinner. "I don't need the money. That's not the point."

"It's a little bit the point," she muttered.

"Julie, honest to God, I think you've lost your mind a little. You can't commit to anything. Jobs, states, places to live, relationships. Do you even have any idea what you want?"

*Don't shoot the messenger.*

*Shut* up, *Mama.*

Julie pushed aside her own dish and tried to keep her anger out of her voice. "That is the *whole* point, Chad. No. I don't. I thought I did. I always think I do. But this has been different. Everything since I met you. Everything since right before."

"Well, thanks for dragging me into it."

For the first time, Julie saw something in Chad she didn't think was perfect. "Chad. I don't blame you for being mad. Or hurt. But don't judge me. Your parents are *alive*."

He was quiet for a moment. She already knew what he was going to say.

"You can't–"

Julie held up her hand. "No. I can't. Not forever. And not from this point forward. But it's taken me a lot of failures and bad decisions over the last year and a half to get to this point, where I can see clearly. Everything – everything during that time – was done from a place of grief that I hid from, and I hid it from you, but it was so hard and so *always there*, I can never describe it to you."

They both stayed silent for a few minutes. The server came and read the mood and left. Julie drank her peach tea like it was a lifeline. Chad checked his messages. And finally, she added, "My mama was my anchor. And I was trying to replace her."

He was still looking down. They went silent again.

"I'm sorry, Chad." It was all that was left.

When he looked at her again, his expression was less stony. "Me, too. I wish I could have known you when you weren't... "

"Lost," she finished for him.

"So, what are you going to do now?"

Julie laughed sardonically. "Isn't that a great question? Well, tomorrow I'm going to look for a place. And Wednesday I'm going to trick-or-treat with my niece and nephew. You're welcome to come, by the way. I remember what it's like to be new in town."

"Yeah, so you remember that, not to brag, but being a single, decently attractive practitioner of medicine makes one quite eligible in a new place."

"Ha! Touché."

"I will probably pass on Halloween," he said. "But I would like to meet your family at some point. Because again, I meant what I said. I didn't move out here convinced we'd end up together. I hoped, Jules. I really did. But if in the long run, we're friends, I'm glad."

She shook her head. "It's so funny you say that. I haven't even talked to any of my friends from here since I moved back. I don't know why, exactly. But I'll take a friend, especially a friend who gets that I'm a little crazy right now. That would be excellent."

"You're not crazy, Jules."

She raised her eyebrows.

"Well. Not too crazy, anyway."

She felt crazy. Standing in her borrowed bedroom, mere days after she moved in, late at night and tired to the bone, packing duffle bags again.

Mama and Daddy's picture was staring at her. She knew she and Daddy would be okay, probably.

She hoped her next steps would not be ones of such abject failure.

Ian had texted her every single day since she had hung up on him. The messages ranged from playful song lyrics ("Why you gotta be so mean?" "My life would suck without you...") to heartfelt pleas: Fawn isn't coming back. I wish you would. Please? She didn't answer any of them, but she couldn't bring herself to block his number. And now, she wanted so badly to reach out to him and say it was over with Chad for good. She was making peace. She was moving forward. She had nothing for herself that was tying her here.

Except that the last part wasn't true.

So, she did type out a message, exhaling. She wrote a few lines about how scary but how freeing it felt to have three apartment listings saved, most of her stuff packed, and an actual ounce of optimism about where her life might be headed. And then, she sent it to the only person she could think of who maybe wasn't sick of her or had whiplash over her life decisions of late.

Robin responded right away.

*Part 3*

# C H A P T E R  T W E N T Y - S I X

## *Paul*

"Jess, what in the actual hell is staring at me right now?"

"What? Oh, it's my Halloween bark. Your sweet tooth will love it."

Paul shook his head and picked up a piece of hard white... something... that was covered in pieces of crushed pretzel, chocolate sandwich cookies, orange and purple sprinkles, some kind or kinds of candy bar, and candied googly eyes. He popped it in his mouth.

It was delicious.

"I should have known, Jess. This is madness, sweetheart."

She left the sink to walk over and kiss him. "This is like five things. It's fine."

"I thought Halloween was a *candy* holiday."

"It's an eating holiday. Everyone will be here at dinnertime, so we need to have things to eat that aren't candy."

"Like this healthy cheese dip?" He took a sniff from one of her full slow cookers, filled with a shiny orange substance dotted with peppers and tomatoes.

"Precisely."

"Jess..."

"Nope. Don't say it."

He sighed and ran his hands through his hair. She was going way overboard, and she knew he thought so. So, he didn't say it.

"I'm gonna go for a run."

"Mmm. You sure?"

He'd been dressed for one for hours but kept finding things to do around the house. Jessie had been spending long days at Abby's trying recipes and evenings with her laptop working on the menu design. But that day, she'd been bustling all around the house making treats and putting various colored pumpkins on every available surface, and he just wanted to be close to her.

And now, she walked up to him and put her hands in the pockets of his running shorts, not the '70s-era shorties but shorter than anything else he ever wore.

"But I'm done making the food. All I have to do now is get a quick shower. Or not quick..." She nuzzled into his neck, kissing him there.

"Oh. Hmmm..." He wrapped his arms around her back. "I guess running can wait. I was gonna get all the calories gone in advance."

She kissed the other side of his neck. "In advance of what?"

"Eating all the bark." He took hold of her face and kissed her mouth.

"Here." She grabbed a piece and fed it to him. "You're about to taste so good."

After cutting his run short and quickly showering, Paul observed his wife fluttering in double time to "stage" everything on the kitchen counter before they took it all either outside for the

Halloween block party or to some other surface in the house for just the family. It clearly made sense in *her* mind, and only she could direct it into reality. But first, he stood between her and the refrigerator door and took her by the shoulders with feigned somberness.

"I'm sorry I messed up your schedule."

Jessie scrunched her face up for just a moment, considering, and then she dissolved in laughter. "No, you're not!" She kissed him quickly, looking glowy. "Go get the tables set up."

"Yes, ma'am." He glanced at the clock. "What time did you tell everyone?"

"Seven. The kids all wanted to trick-or-treat at home first."

"Yep, yep. You know, if Julie is truly coming out of the dark, she's probably going to get here early."

Jessie stared at him again before simply asking, "You serious? Wait. I know you are. Dang it, Paul. Get outside and get it together!"

He actually giggled as he jogged to the driveway. That thing bubbling up inside him could only be described as cautious hope with a side of joy.

# CHAPTER♡TWENTY-SEVEN

## *Julie*

HERE WE GO.

The store had been blessedly, mercifully quiet that day. Halloween being on a Wednesday seemed to throw off everyone's rhythm a little, so Julie just enjoyed it. She worked on scheduling some social media posts; she listed a job opening everywhere she could think of; and she straightened up everything that had been neglected the past few days while she held down the fort.

And here she was, sitting in her car down the street from Dad's house, dressed in shorts and tie-dyed softball socks *and* the softball jersey she had saved from high school for God-only-knew what reason. She had painted visors under her eyes and borrowed a mitt from Chad.

He really was like, the best roommate ever, she thought a bit mournfully.

She checked herself in the mirror and turned up the radio. Pink was playing. She could see Danielle's mini-van parked in the driveway and what she was pretty sure was Abby and Sam's Wagoneer on the street.

*Maybe I'm not ready,* she told herself.

*You're way past ready,* Mama's voice said.

*Don't be such a baby.* Hm. That sounded like Robin.

"*Tryna stand up on my own two feet, this conversation ain't comin' easily...*" Definitely Pink.

Then there was a knock on her window, and she nearly jumped out of her skin.

"Christian! Does your mom know you're out here?"

She opened her door and before she was all the way out, her nephew jumped for her with a big hug. He was dressed not as a zombie pigman but as... Lego Batman? Yep. She was pretty sure she was being attacked by the world's cutest Lego Batman. And she didn't care. His lanky arms were choking her, and it felt wonderful.

"Daddy's right behind me!" he said. "Do you want to trick-or-treat with us?"

Giving him another squeeze, she laughed. "Yes! Let me see your face!" He wore a Batman mask over his big brown eyes and a goofy grin with one front tooth missing. He looked just like Danielle's husband, Matt, who had even darker eyes and hair, and a serious face until he deemed something worth his huge smile. Apparently, Julie was worth it that day.

"Hey sister," he said, giving his own hug. It caught her by surprise. She hadn't realized how much she missed–

*It won't be the same*, she told herself.

*Calm. Down!* Mama again.

*Maybe give it a chance for two seconds before you decide how it's going to go.* Yep. Robin had definitely become a voice in her head.

Bless it. She was going to do this.

"Where's Princess Vivi?" she said, smiling back at Matt.

"Danielle is giving her the finishing touches inside the house. The same ones she gave her two hours ago." He shrugged. They reached the end of the driveway.

"Come on, Aunt Julie! Come see the punch with the eyeballs in it."

She couldn't help laughing at that, and Matt looked at her like she was crazy. "It's fine," she told him. "Everything is fine."

"You sure? I can... tell Danielle you're here."

"Matt." She looked him in the eye as she took Christian's hand. "I'm fine. This is fine. It's time for... it to be fine."

Matt nodded and patted her back as they walked up the driveway to the front door. He opened it for them, and she and Christian glided on through.

Julie took in the immediate scene. Danielle, her baby bump putting her in a very awkward posture, had Vivi sitting on a kitchen counter. Vivi was crying, holding a red lollipop, and having bright pink blush applied to her already reddened, Little Bo Peep cheeks. Summer was dressed as Wonder Woman, and her little brother Jacob was dressed as Hawkeye, and they were using his bow and arrow as separate swords to swing at each other. Sam was scolding them. Abby was deep in conversation with Jessie, in front of the open refrigerator door, and Daddy was talking to Travis and some teenage girl Julie didn't know. Was this everyone? It was loud. Christian left her and sprinted over to Paul.

"Poppy! Aunt Julie's here! And she did not bring any of her boyfriends!"

*Sweeeeet Jesus.* Julie swallowed the lump in her throat and smiled wanly at her dad. He kissed her cheek and introduced her to Cali, apparently Travis' girlfriend. They said polite hellos and sauntered off. She couldn't blame them. The awkwardness and her own embarrassment seemed to permeate the air.

"Thanks, Christian," Paul said, making a *kids will be kids* face at Julie. "Go find your bucket. We're going to leave soon."

As he galloped off, Julie asked, "So, was there a pool? Who will Julie bring to Halloween? Good payout, I hope."

He rolled his eyes. "Of course not. He heard me tell your sister that Chad wouldn't be coming, and *she* asked me if maybe you were bringing Nick. Er, Robin."

Sighing in defeat, she said, "You can call him Nick, Daddy. He answers to both. It's a whole thing."

"Okay. Whatever. You're more my concern. You have everything set?"

"I can get the keys tomorrow." His face brightened, and it matched what she felt. "Robin is going to work the store on Friday, so I'll rent a U-Haul and get my furniture and stuff while Chad is at work."

"Clandestine?"

She couldn't blame him for that, either. "No, no. If I did it while he was there, he would want to help me, and he's done enough. I hope we'll be able to be friends, especially since he's new in town, but I don't want to lean on him for anything. I don't want to lean on anybody."

Paul studied her in his go-to Dad way. "So, you gonna grab the couch and everything by yourself?"

She frowned. She hadn't figured that part out yet. "Daddy, I know you can help me, I just thought with your ankle—"

"It's fine. Been fine for a long time. Just ask me, Jules."

"Okay. But also, I saw Danielle share a post about the tea room. I figure you're pretty busy with that."

"That's Jessie and Abby's deal, honey. It doesn't keep me from helping you move a couch."

"And a bed. And a desk, nightstand, and kitchen table, to be exact."

Paul's eyes bugged out a little. "He's letting you take all of that?"

"Most of it was *mine*. And I helped buy the couch and table, and they're not really his taste. I'm not stealing it...!"

He shook his head. "That's not what I meant. But okay. Let me see if I can get one more guy, so we have some reinforcements, okay? It won't take long. Just let me know what time you can get the U-Haul. I'll go with you to pick it up."

Her face reddened again. She didn't feel like she deserved any of it, Chad's forgiveness, Daddy's help, even Christian's welcome. And now, she looked past her dad's shoulder back into the kitchen, where the sweetest little buffet of comfort snacks and themed treats had been assembled. The house smelled like cider. There were lit pumpkins literally everywhere, and she couldn't help wanting to sink onto the couch and cover herself with one of the plaid blankets piled there, inviting her. Everything was warm in here, and it was overtaking her.

"Thank you, Daddy." She kissed his cheek and walked past him into the kitchen. Vivi had exchanged her sucker for a tiny bag of M&Ms and was all smiles. Danielle looked completely done. Julie walked to the already-famous punch bowl and ladled some out for her sister. And then she wondered if that was a good idea.

"Um, excuse me, Jessie?"

Jessie and Abby both snapped to attention like Julie was a drill sergeant. Not quite the effect she wanted, but it might be humorous later. "I mean, hi. Happy Halloween," she said weakly. "I was just wondering if the punch was safe for Danielle." She gave them a small smile. It was no secret this family liked their wine.

"Oh, yes, yes. There's a pitcher of...um.. adult cider in the fridge, though. Would you like some?"

In the moment, all Julie wanted was to do something nice for her sister, but she realized, Jessie probably just wanted to do something nice for her. So, she said, "How about after trick-or-treating?" And before Jessie could answer, she crossed back over to Danielle, handing her the cup and trying not to let her see the tears forming in her eyes.

After all of that lead-in, trick-or-treating, for Christian and Vivi anyway, lasted somewhere around thirty-five minutes and two blocks. Julie, Matt, and Dad had taken them along with Sam and his kids. The older Oakley children were faring much better. Julie found herself sliding into some conversations with Sam and also with the precocious Summer.

*It's good not to be angry all the time.*

*Yes, Mama. I know...*

Once they got back, Julie decided that Vivi's discarded peanut M&Ms were not going to be a worthy supper. With Vivi on her hip, she walked to the kitchen and beheld the spread. Her memory went back to last Fourth of July, less than four months from the time Mama had died. Daddy was moving in with Jessie, and everyone had gathered at her beach house to "celebrate." She and David had just made their plans to move west. Katy and Danielle had decided to put on brave faces for Daddy's sake, and the best Julie could do was shut up until Jessie questioned her.

It had been God-awful. *God-awful.*

This night would not be *that*. With one hand, Julie filled a pumpkin-printed melamine plate with tortilla chips, dollops of chili, some irresistible fake cheese sauce, and slices of avocado. Vivi had lain her head on Julie's shoulder, and she lugged the toddler and the plate to a seat at the dining room table, where she had never sat before. Danielle and Abby were already seated there.

"Vivi. Are you hungry?"

"That!" she replied, pointing to her mom's plate.

Danielle rolled her tired eyes. "She wants chips with just cheese. Here, baby."

"No, no," Julie said. "I'll get her her own. Vivi, sit here for a second."

"No!" Goodness, her little voice could suddenly add volume. "With you!"

"Okay, okay!" She lifted her back up to repeat the whole process, very much feeling the fatigue of the last few weeks and its chaos, but also enjoying the moldable heft of a petite toddler in her arm. By the time she added olives and grapes and more M&Ms to Vivi's plate, both her arms were about numb, and Vivi seemed to have her second wind.

"Juice?" she said as Julie sat down with her. She let out an exasperated sigh and the others around the table laughed.

"I'll get it." Mikayla, Jessie's oldest daughter, had appeared and was now jumping out of her chair and heading toward the kitchen. Julie didn't know where she'd been earlier, but she was now set up in the seat across from her, looking almost as tired as Danielle. Abby was holding her baby, Josie, who was nearly asleep in her rumpled Minnie Mouse dress.

Damn *it*. There was the warm feeling again. And she hadn't even had the cider yet.

"How were the tricks and treats?" Abby asked.

"Did you have fun, Vivi-lu?" Danielle added.

Vivi nodded with her mouth full of tortilla chip as she reached for a grape. Julie swallowed her own bite and answered. "We didn't get too far, but we did get to 'full-size candy bar lane.' The big kids were very excited. Vivi gave me her Reese's cups. Do not tell her what a grave mistake she has made."

"Oh, child," Danielle said, "I have so much yet to teach you."

"Josie is really at the perfect age," Mikayla said, and then she looked at Julie. "We went out a little earlier than y'all. She kept her Minnie ears on like a boss, so a few of those houses rewarded this person with one tooth two full size candy bars. And all she wanted was a blow pop, which will last two minutes. And Altan and I get the rest! Chocolate for dinner the next three nights."

"I don't think so." Mikayla's handsome Turkish husband appeared like a Hallmark-movie hero behind her. Clad in a Mickey Mouse t-shirt, he bent to kiss her cheek and then popped a square of the crazy-looking Halloween bark in his mouth. "Want me to take the baby?" he asked Abby.

Julie was staring. She sat up straighter and focused on her niece. Were their gatherings always like this... food and people everywhere, passing back and forth kids and cups and quips? She felt like she was in a movie.

And she could admit to herself she was falling for it a little, but every time she caught a glimpse of Vivi, her coloring so, so, so like Leah's, she felt many other things, mostly, overwhelming.

*It's okay to want this*, Mama said.

*No, it's not*, Julie answered.

The chatter continued. Abby was talking about a friend of hers coming to visit, someone she'd met at camp a million years ago in Wisconsin. Now she lived in the Blue Ridge Mountains where her parents owned a tea room, and she and her mom were coming to visit. Maybe they'd stay here since Abby had no guest space that wasn't a couch.

"Do people ever consider getting hotels?" Mikayla asked the table. Julie sat like a deer in headlights as she turned to her, being inclusive, clearly awaiting a response.

"They're practically family," Abby said. "Vanessa has had a really hard time of it. Single mom for the second time. And they're doing us a favor coming here to help us get squared away. We'll figure something out."

*Practically family.* They should post that above the door. She wasn't sure this Oakley-Jameson mashup knew how to just be friends with people or have acquaintances. Everyone was part of the clan and automatically included in everything.

Around the time Julie's plate was cleared and her stomach thankful, Vivi had had enough. She called out to Danielle with fervor and almost launched herself across the table. Wide-eyed and giggling, Julie delivered Vivi into her mother's lap. Danielle looked at her sister somberly and murmured, "*Thank you*, Auntie Jules."

"My pleasure," she said back. "I'm going to go find Daddy."

She paused in the hallway to tap a message to Robin. There is absolutely eyeball punch here. I hope you at least get some candy. Or beer. Or a run. Kinda miss you. Two seconds later, he tapped the "heart" response, so she put her phone in her pocket with a smile.

Paul was sitting on the front porch with Matt, what looked like a one-liter sized jar of tea, and Jessie. He and Jessie were on the swing, and there was another chair next to Matt. Julie just stood there frozen, staring at a blue Jack-o-lantern bucket on the ground that was overflowing with candy. She bent down to pick up two mini Twix, a Twizzler, and several of those unknown substances that always came wrapped in all black or orange and were never eaten by anyone. She didn't know what to do next.

"Jules, sit," Matt said. He kicked the chair a little closer to her. She sat.

"You can have those," he added, gesturing to the shrink-wrapped nuggets of whatever still in her hand.

"Can I trade them for a Twix?" she asked, still looking at the pile of candy.

"Nope." He snatched one. "You won't eat them anyway. Dad said you're on a runner's meal plan these days. Half marathon coming up?"

"Not until March," she said, opening the good candy. "And all a runner's diet means is I want to eat everything, all the time. So, if I only eat some of the candy I want to eat, I'm coming out ahead."

"Don't bother arguing with her," Paul called.

And she was frozen again. The likelihood of a conversation about candy going much farther or deeper was slim. Should she try to perpetuate it? Should she just be quiet? What were they talking about before she made her awkward appearance?

"Does Danielle have Vivi?" Matt asked.

"Yes. I think she might finally be crashing."

"Ugh. I'll go help her. Halloween should always be on a Saturday..."

He unceremoniously walked inside the house. *Thanks a lot.*

"You get some food, Jules?" Paul asked.

"Yep. The chili was really good. Thank you."

"It's not as good as the Twix, though." It was Jessie that time. Maybe they really could talk about food for the rest of the night, or for all of eternity.

"Twix... are... the best," Julie said. She picked up the Jack-o-lantern and rifled through the top layer. Twix were everywhere. With an inward shrug, she tossed one to Jessie.

"Thanks," Jessie murmured as Paul asked, "Whose bucket is that?"

"No idea," Julie answered as Jessie said, "Who cares?"

All three of them laughed at the same time. And then they stopped quickly, shocked.

Paul smiled at Julie, and she smiled somewhat shyly in the general direction of the swing. Maybe it wouldn't actually kill her to be nice. Maybe she could –

"Mimi. Miiiiiimiiiii! Josie threw up and Auntie Kayla doesn't know where the throw up rags are!" Summer appeared in the doorway, so frantic looking that Julie almost laughed some more.

"We have throw up rags?" Paul asked. Jessie gave him a murderous glance as she mumbled "FFS" and hurried inside with Summer in tow.

"Sounds like you need to be brought up to speed on the types of rags available in your house," Julie said.

"And their location." He patted the now-empty seat next to him. "Come sit."

"But Jessie–"

"She won't be back out for hours," Paul said. "It will be throw up rags, and then she'll see something that needs to be refilled. Then she'll look at the clock and decide she should make coffee. She'll then start asking who wants coffee, while she is making it. And then she'll probably condense a few of the serving platters, maybe throw a few dishes in the dishwasher. And then Jacob will ask her for something ridiculously grandkid-ish like chocolate milk or a grilled PB and J, and she will start to accommodate him, and then Abby and Sam will scold both of them on how ridiculous they are being. Oh, and Summer probably will, too."

"Wow. That's a lot."

He shrugged. "Just how it goes. She slowed down for a few months. Now she'll be making up for lost time."

They were swinging, both of their feet pushing off the ground at the same time. Paul let his dangle. Julie's legs were a bit longer, and she held them up in front of her, stretching her calves.

"Nice shoes," Paul said.

"You like these? I don't run in them; I just use them for work. They're awesome."

"What brand?"

"Diadora. They're Italian."

"Ah. Do they come with a matching handbag?" She moaned at his Dad-joke. "Nice calves, too. You're really building some muscle with all those miles."

"Yeah. I was up to about twenty-five a week, but that will take a hit this week." She patted her flat belly. "Although, an extra workout to burn off the Twix might be in order."

"I think you're fine, Julies."

The sentiment hung in the air, along with the din of family chaos just beyond the door, and the candlelight from a dozen Jack-o-lanterns lining the walkway, the memories of Halloweens past, when a harried but all-in Daddy would take three little girls around the neighborhood while their mama answered the door and had pizza waiting for them, and the way he had just described the inner-workings of his new home and his new family.

"I think I will be," she said, barely audible.

Paul let the silence sit. Julie was grateful for his ability to do that because she knew their next words were going to be very purposeful. They kept swinging for a few minutes, a silly little playlist coming from a Bluetooth speaker by the door ticking off "Monster Mash" and "Thriller." When Vincent Price's laughter stopped, Paul was ready.

"I'm really very happy you came tonight," he started "Did you have an okay time?"

She stretched her neck, looking upward, as though God or Leah would write the perfect words for her in the stars. She could still feel the heft of Vivi in her lap, smell the chocolate mingled with baby-sweetness in her hair, and hear the inclusive tones of that dining room table.

"Bewildering," she said. "I had a bewildering time."

Paul nodded. "Honestly, I understand."

"They're a lot, Daddy." Thankfully, it came out how she meant it, as a fact and not a criticism.

"I thought so, too," he said. "But I guess now I just think of it as, we're a lot. I bring some crazy into this merger, too. People. Baggage. Expectations. We all do. But the end result, I think, is pretty remarkable. Everyone seems to find a place. No one is ever lonely, that's for sure."

"Dear God, surely not! *Anything* but that!" The mix of fake-and-real laughter came out again.

After a beat, she finally asked the question she'd been so afraid of.

"Is it for real, Daddy?"

He wasn't phased though. "What, exactly?"

"This family dynamic? All the reflection and affection and pro-cessing and gathering? Is it like this all the time? Because it really is a lot."

He nodded slowly, then leaned forward so he could look at her.

"We've known them for a long time, Jules. I know this is a much different capacity, but they're not insincere. They've always been this way."

Julie nodded. "I don't know, Daddy. They were fun to have BBQs and stuff with, but this is way different. I'm surprised you're not exhausted by it."

"Because Mama and I weren't that way?"

Julie's nods became more emphatic. "Are you kidding? Not at all. Your whole thing was to, pardon me, get shit done. Power through. Move on. Not sit and talk about it over two carafes of coffee followed by two bottles of wine."

"True. And how do you think that worked for us?"

Julie sighed. She thought of her framed picture of them, of Paul and Leah looking how this family seemed to feel all the time. "I know. I know you were just... making it work. Not... sparkly."

"Sparkly..."

He hadn't asked a question, but Julie answered anyway. "Like Katy is most of the time. Like Danielle is when the kids aren't driving her crazy. Energetic. Passionate. Exuberant... And not afraid to show it."

"We're not like that," Paul affirmed.

"No. I'm not zany or playful or sparkly. I overanalyze. I over-criticize. I don't hug enough. But you... when you're around Jessie, you seem..."

He waited.

"Peaceful. But also? Happy. So happy. *Almost* sparkly."

He nodded.

"You almost never seemed that way... before..."

"Aw, Jules." Paul exhaled, sitting back in the swing and copying her look to the heavens for help. "Your mama and I just didn't quite know how. We tried so hard. She tried to give me things I never had before... like the simple feeling of being valuable. And capable. And I gave her her dream family. It was hard for us. I didn't come with a model to follow. I just knew what she wanted and worked to give it to her. And when I started falling apart under the pressure, she rose up like... a superhero, really, and was strong when I wasn't. And gave me an ultimatum that saved my life. Your mama *saved my life*, Jules."

They let that sit for a moment, Julie's tears freely falling in her lap.

"I wish I had made her happier. I wish I had been happier. And as long as we had each other, there was always the hope we could do better. We could be better. When Danielle had Christian, it gave us a new outlook. A fresh start. The last few years were lighter. I promise you. Mama didn't die unhappy. And I wasn't waiting for my chance to try again. *It just happened.*"

Julie tried to muffle the sounds, but she was sobbing.

Paul put his arm around her and said almost into her ear. "Don't let *goodness* repel you, baby."

"It's not just that..." She took a deep breath. "They're always collecting people. Everyone is family. You said it yourself. Everyone has a place at the table. That's all fine and good, but I don't want you to be just another stray they pick up."

"Julie..." Paul tried not to laugh, but she could see it in his eyes. "I promise you, I *promise* you, I'm not someone's pet. Not anyone's. Jessie is for real. Maybe I should have cut through some of this tension and resentment a long time ago just to look you in the eyes and tell you. Because I know it's hard to hear. But Jessie and I are for real. All of it. You don't have to protect me, or yourself. This is life *now*, and it is meant for us to enjoy."

Julie surprised herself by not feeling resentful or angry or even sad at his words. She wasn't thinking of Jessie in that moment.

"Can I ask you one more question?"

"Of course."

"When it all started for you, when you realized it was love, even if it wasn't the right time or circumstance or maybe person... Did you constantly feel like you were going to explode? I mean... *love*. I mean like, when you see someone or hear their voice... you just shake inside? Like all defenses are gone. Like, you want to be with that person all the time."

Paul nodded slowly. "I'd probably use different words, Jules, but yes. It's big feelings a lot of the time. But also, it's a steady feeling. Not just fireworks. And not just work. But a constant, respectful, generous partnership." He paused. "And butterflies. Lots of butterflies."

She let herself smile. "I don't think I ever had that before. I thought I did. Several times. I tried to force it with Chad. But..."

"Are you feeling that way now about someone else?"

Julie shut her lips tight, like she was trying to keep the words in. Finally, she answered. "Maybe. But I'm afraid. Because I might be wrong. And I'm so, so sick of making a fool of myself."

Paul kissed her temple and stood up.

"My daughter. You have not ever, once in your life, looked like a fool. You've looked overly ambitious, isolated, proud, critical of everyone and yourself. But not foolish. Not once."

"If you say so."

"I do."

"Okay... well, I don't want to be *wrong*. Is that better?"

"Yep." He picked up the blue Jack-o-lantern. There was yet another Twix on top, and he handed it to her. "You will be wrong a million more times before it's over. So, the only question you have to ask yourself is whether it's worth the risk. And only you know."

She unwrapped the gold cellophane without thinking and popped the chocolate-caramel cookie into her mouth. There was a picture becoming clearer in her head. If she ran toward it, quite honestly, she didn't have anything to lose.

She stood and hugged her father, tightly.

"This was a good night, Daddy. I'm gonna go say goodbye."

His smile was wide. He opened the door, holding it for her, and followed her inside the house, where Halloween was still in full swing.

# CHAPTER TWENTY-EIGHT

*Jessie*

"Are they gone? All of them?"

I turned from the sink to my husband and gave him my sweetest smile. "Kayla and Altan are changing Josie before they leave."

He gave me his fakest smile and proceeded to take out the trash. I dried my hands and wiped my brow and sighed deeply. And I pasted my smile back in place as the three remaining kids appeared in the kitchen. They looked how I felt.

"Don't worry, Anne," Altan said, using his native term for *Mama*. "We're as wrung out as you are."

"Look at our Minnie," I said, caressing the sweet head that lay on Mikayla's shoulder. "She had a pretty great first trick-or-treat."

"Almost perfect, Mimi." My daughter's face said everything. *I love tonight. I love this child. I love my life. I love everyone. I miss Daddy. How can he not be here?*

"He sees," I murmured in her ear, hugging her and Josie together. "And we are so blessed."

"Yes, we are," Altan added. "Let's go, my treasures. Everyone is ready for sleep."

Paul walked in in time to kiss Josie's head and pat Mikayla's back. Altan, however, gave him a hearty man-hug and said, "See you Friday."

"Love you, Mama," Mikayla called. The door closed.

I felt kind of glowy, and also kind of like falling down.

"Sit," Paul said, reading my mind like he always did and possibly also reading my face. "No more tonight. What do you want to drink? Water or water?"

"Not even cider?" I whined, already on the couch.

"Nooooo! Definitely not cider."

"I mean just the regular stuff," I protested, but he was already on his way to me with a glass of ice water and a mini Twix bar.

"Are these things reproducing?" I laughed, tearing it open.

He sat next to me and stretched. "I bought a whole bag for the trick-or-treaters. But somehow, it was still in the pantry behind some stuff."

"That's amazing," I said, as seriously as I could.

"An absolute miracle." He popped one in his own mouth.

"So, what are you and Altan doing Friday?" I asked.

"What? Oh. He's gonna help me move some stuff for Julie. She's moving in that day."

"What?" I sat up straight and narrowly avoided jumping. "She got a place? Where?"

"Right in Market Common."

"Wow. That's just perfect." I leaned back again, then forward again, just to see his face. "And *Altan* is helping? *My* son-in-law?""

Paul shook his head. "I know this is asking the impossible, but try to calm down just a little bit. She came tonight. She's... open to things. Baby steps, sweetheart. One at a time."

"You're right. You're right. I know you're right."

"Stop quoting movies."

He'd tried to sound harsh, but he was smiling from ear to ear.

"You had a good talk outside then? While I was fetching puke towels?"

"I thought they were throw up rags?"

Now I shook my head. "The chaos is never-ending. Mikayla wasn't even holding Josie. Cali had her. *She's* the culprit who didn't know where the appropriate cleaning instruments were."

"She should be banned from the next three family gatherings," Paul said somberly.

"I would never do that to *anyone*," I said.

"Mmm-hmm. Speaking of which..."

I felt like I knew what was coming.

"We don't have to decide tonight, but tomorrow, there needs to be a discussion about Thanksgiving, Jess. And how you will not be hosting it. Not this year."

"Oh, Paul." I had to at least try to protest.

"Nope. Not a month outside of treatment and a week before you open a damn restaurant. Come on!"

"But—"

"Nope."

"Well Abby—"

"It doesn't have to be Abby either."

"It can't be Danielle."

"Likely not."

"But David's—"

"David would happily eat a sack of Big Macs, Jess. Nope. Can't use David."

"It has to be *here*," I said, not quite convincing even myself.

"Jess, I'm pretty tired, so I might be missing something. But if it's here, doesn't that imply that you, and therefore we, are hosting?"

"Well," I said again. "-ish."

"Jesus, help me."

I lay my head on his shoulder. This wasn't a fight. I felt confident that it possibly could become one, but this was play. He knew good and darn well we were having Thanksgiving here. But I would compromise.

"Maggie is probably coming, so she can help."

He sighed so deeply I felt the breath leave his soul. "If Maggie is coming, on the first Thanksgiving of the very prince of Earth Himself, I can guarantee that at least one of her children, and that kid's 'partner,' and that kid's precious baby, and probably a few of the others are going to come, too. And then instead of having two dozen people here, now we have close to three."

"Uh-huh, uh-huh." I nodded like he was enlightening me to some amazing fact. "I mean, that would probably be happening under any circumstance anyway. If I had one arm cut off, she'd be coming to be my other arm. If I suddenly employed an entire kitchen staff, she'd be coming to help me boss them around..."

"So, I've been had, then? Is that what you're saying?"

I kissed him. It was my favorite trick, like the moms on Instagram who squirt whipped cream in the mouths of their tantrum-throwing toddlers. I lingered a little until he melted a little, opening his mouth to welcome me. Twix was even better than Halloween bark.

"You don't fight fair," he said, when I eventually pulled away.

"This isn't a fight," I said. "I'll tell you what. I will find out who's coming. In fact, no. I will put Mikayla in charge of that. And then we will ask everyone to bring *one* thing, and we will order turkey, and whatever we end up having, it is what it is."

"So, we're hosting Thanksgiving?"

"Well..." I kissed him again, a little less intensely. "Yes. We are. But we won't project manage it, okay? That's probably what you meant."

"Oh, Jess." He put his arm around me and pulled me in. I rested my head on his chest, fantasizing about the sleeping, and per our agreement, the sleeping in, we were about to do. "You are the darlin'-est girl I've ever met."

"I'm really happy Julie was here," I murmured into his heartbeat.

"Me, too," he said, with a little squeeze.

"You think she'll come for Thanksgiving?" I asked. This time, I raised my head to look at him.

His face was thoughtful and solemn and a little something else. It was more than the absence of tension. It was, I believed, his well-deserved peace.

"I think she might," he said. "And thank you, for not pushing it. I know you want to love her. I want her to love you. Just keep being patient. You're getting so good at it."

"That's a straight-up lie," I said with a laugh.

"You're getting better," he said. "It's getting better all the time."

I was pretty sure he just quoted a song to me, and I felt deeply satisfied at my influence on him. I kept my head right where it was. I knew eventually we'd have to go upstairs and handle ourselves and all our night rituals, but for that one frozen moment, an aftermath of the loud blender that was our family, it was the two of us, a reminder that every ripple that came out of the stone in the water that was us, was worth it.

# CHAPTER♡TWENTY-NINE

## *Julie*

"I PROMISE, I WILL EAT DINNER. I DON'T SKIP MEALS, DADDY. THAT WAS COLLEGE ME. NOT RUNNER ME. THIS GIRL IS RAVENOUS MOST OF THE TIME."

"You are living in the center of excellent take-out," Paul acquiesced.

"Exactly. See? I got this." She gestured to a very messy, tiny living room that was littered with boxes and sacks and also held... her couch.

He nodded, jingling his keys in his hand. "You do. Good work, Jules."

She stepped forward to hug him. "And you had me. Thank you, Daddy."

There wasn't any more that needed to be said. She felt confident that they were back where they used to be, understanding each other.

"And Dad?" He paused at the door.

"Tell Jessie thank you for the granola bars. And the mandarin iced tea. She's really good at the culinary offerings."

"She will love hearing that. And Jules? Maybe before too long, you can tell her yourself."

The pause was only brief and not *too* heavy.

"I will. I'm... almost there."

He kissed her head and left.

Julie turned around and took in the room. It was a living/dining room with a small kitchen, big enough to cook a meal, small enough to make it a challenge. But it fit her couch and a small, refurbished trunk from Daddy's storage that would double as a coffee table. Her kitchen table fit perfectly on one end. The bedroom was almost the same size as that room, so she didn't have enough to fill it. Her bed and desk were all she had, but they were enough for now. She'd look for a chair or something, maybe a bookcase. Maybe she would relax. She had time.

Even though she had to clear a path to the couch, she sat on it, holding her phone and a paper cup of Jessie's amazing tea. It had only taken Dad and Altan a little over an hour to move the furniture over. Altan had stayed for a few minutes and showed Julie pictures of Josie at the beach, pictures of Josie with their cat, pictures of Josie trying to eat Mikayla's ice cream cone. She was a cutie, and she admired how he knew to use the universal language of cute baby pictures to bridge a gap and cut through awkwardness. He even gave her a hug when he left and wished her "beautiful times" in her new home.

Sigh. They were a *lot*. Today, it made her smile.

Dad had stayed for a few hours and helped her hang some shelves, unpack her hanging clothes, set up the TV and the internet. They talked about everything, not just the safe stuff. He mentioned his worries over the tea room and Jessie's health. Julie proposed to him that Jessie having a big project would likely help her long-term recovery by warding off depression. Daddy called her a smarty pants. And then they talked about running and the store while he changed out the toilet seat in the sole bathroom.

"There have been exactly three applicants, and two of them suck," Julie said. "Robin's sister is taking over some of the caretaker duties for their dad next week, but it's still a lot. And I can be at the shop basically all the time since I have no life, but with holiday shopping season coming, I'm not enough."

"What kind of hours are you hiring for? You know, Brittney works for the Chamber. She probably knows some people."

"Well, just part-time. If we can find two people right away, I'd say less than twenty hours each. Nothing major."

"Huh." It wasn't a question, and Julie knew the look in his eye.

"Who you thinking, Daddy?" *Please don't let it be someone horrible. Or one of my new step-siblings.*

"I mean... is nepotism an issue?"

"Daddy, who in the brood needs a job? Everyone is employed or pregnant or opening tea rooms."

He started spinning the wrench he was holding. "I'm none of those things."

"What? You?"

He shrugged. What was with the men in her life and the incessant shrugging?

*The men in my life?*

"Are you serious? Daddy, you don't want to work at a *store*. You're a professor and an author, for goodness' sake."

"What does that have to do with anything?" he said. "I teach one class a semester. I don't want to work all day every day. I already like being there. I can learn things quickly, you know, as a *professor and all*. And you're there. Sounds very much like a win-win to me."

She felt a little shell-shocked, but not so much she didn't step forward and pluck the wrench out of his hand.

"You're making me crazy with that."

"Well, I guess there's our answer," Paul said. "I make you crazy."

"Daddy, hush. I think it could be good, but... I have to talk to Robin. And *you'd* have to talk to Robin."

"Of course, Jules." He grabbed the wrench back and returned to toilet seat duty, with Julie staring at the back of him, musing again how completely life had changed in the last year and a half.

The caffeine that was surely present in Jessie's magical tea had definitely not taken hold. It was almost dinnertime, but sitting in the middle of her mess, she could have skipped it all and gone to bed. Tomorrow would be another day alone at the store, and she had to admit, she was done craving solitude. She was craving company.

She looked down at the screen again and saw that the red number next to her message icon had gone up again. There had been no alert, which meant that a muted conversation had been updated again.

Ian.

*Why don't you just block him? He will never be an answer to your loneliness, or anything else.*

*I know, Mama.*

Clearheaded, she opened the thread. He had sent three messages that day. She had let him know she was moving. *Just to keep that door open*, Mama's voice had warned her. Of course, she was right. And of course, he took the bait. And his new messages showed no chill whatsoever –

I hope you have a big bed.

There is nothing stopping me from coming to see you. If you want, it can be just the two of us for a few days.

Imagine...

She didn't even finish reading that one. She deleted the whole thread. All of it.

Her mother's guidance. Her father's faith. That warmth she felt at the shop and on Halloween. That was what she wanted. So, then she typed:

I wanted you to know that I landed okay. That I will be okay. In spite of where we ended, you did teach me. And my time in Arizona ultimately helped me. But that chapter is over. Please, please don't be in touch. I wish you nothing but good.

She did not add "you toxic, self-serving asshole" at the end. Felt like a victory.

And then she blocked his number and rose to clear more rubble. She wanted all the cardboard out of her sight, though it seemed impossible. By 6:30, she was starting to notice her hunger and considered running down to one of the restaurants to stretch her legs and eat something little. That's when there was a tentative, kind of magical, knock on the door.

"Heeeey! Oh my gosh! Is this Dolly?"

Robin was standing there with cutest, squattiest, buttery-gold corgi on a neon pink leash.

He nodded and thrust Dolly right into her arms. "Go get her, girl."

"Come in," she said. "Wait. Why do you have her? I thought I was getting her from Hazel next week—"

Robin walked over to her table and set the bag she hadn't noticed on it. He sat in one of the chairs and exhaled.

*Oh no.*

"Jules—"

"No!" she said.

"Wait. No. It's not—She's fine. Hazel is fine. But her daughter had to get back, and there were a thousand moving pieces, and so I told them to drop this girl off at the store today and we would take care of everything."

"So, Hazel's gone?" Julie's heart was thumping, and she felt a telltale sign of storms behind her eyes.

"Just to Raleigh. She'll be back. She—"

Julie sat on the floor, and something about it kept him from finishing. She focused on Dolly, removing her leash, calling her, patting her, but her sobs came anyway.

How many times was she going to cry in front of this poor man? Why was she crying again? She barely knew Hazel. She wasn't dead. Robin was using the magical "we" again. *Everything was fine.*

He was next to her on the floor then, kneeling awkwardly. Why did movies always make it look so smooth and romantic? There was nothing sexy about her. She smelled like sweat and Mrs. Meyers lavender surface cleaner. Her ponytail was limp, her face was soggy, and she was gasping a little with the force of her emotions. He finally stopped trying to fold himself around her and lifted her off the ground.

And without asking a single question, he held her.

"I thought she died," she finally managed.

"I know." He caressed her hair and sent shockwaves down her back. "I would never have told you like that."

"I never got to say goodbye."

"Jules. You can call her. And it's only a few hours away."

"Not..." She couldn't finish. "I know I should be over it, but when my mom—"

"Oh, honey." He somehow pulled her tighter, and she knew she didn't have to explain anymore. The relief washed over her. She felt like she was melting, like maybe she didn't want to stand anymore. And Robin took that moment to notice his surroundings and whisper, "This couch, though." Julie's next sound was a teary laugh.

They sat there next to each other, slumped, legs stretched out, not a word between them. Julie heard Robin's stomach growl and felt the hunger in her own. She also felt the shared exhaustion, maddeningly partnered with restlessness. She could smell orange and spices from the kitchen, a promise of decent Chinese food for dinner.

"We need to eat," she said. "Soon. I have to be at work soon."

"In like fifteen hours, Julie."

"It will be a lot fewer by the time I get all this done and go to bed. And I need to deliver this puppy tonight, too."

"What?" Robin picked Dolly up and placed her across their laps. "I thought you could have a pet here. You can't keep her for a few nights?"

"I *can*," she said, wondering if a pet deposit would be necessary for a short stint. "But if she stays that long, I'll end up keeping her. Look at this face!"

Robin scratched Dolly's belly, which she had generously faced upward for them to admire. "Would that be the worst thing?"

"No," she said. "But we already decided who should have her. And with the chaos of my life the last few months, I'd rather settle myself before I invite someone else all the way in, you know?

Dolly had turned over, and Julie's hand was resting on her back. Robin put his hand over hers, and she wasn't sure, but there might have been another shockwave.

"I do know," he said quietly. His words carried other weights, but she wasn't sure she could bear them.

"How's your dad?" she asked.

"He's getting better, but he's so pissed off. Terrible patient. So, Mom is irritated with him, and they're all around agitated and not resting, which is the whole point, right? Then my sisters argue with her about it. I'm just... taking out trash and helping him with his breathing exercises. It was a *pleasure* to be at the store today. I'm gonna try to come help you for a few hours tomorrow."

Julie had been quietly dreading handling a Saturday by herself, and she was relieved. "We got a new applicant today. Maybe I'll tell you about him then."

"Julie—"

She didn't want to look at him, or be quiet, or talk about anything meaningful. She'd seen his face like this a few times, and she didn't know what to expect, and it unnerved her.

"It's my dad, and I know it might be weird at first, but he's certainly capable and loves the—"

"Julie!"

"What?" *Brace yourself.* "What is it?"

"Thank you," he said quietly. "I don't know... I mean, I know you just got here, but you made these past few weeks so much easier and better for me."

She raised her shoulders, trying to shrug off the racing of her heart. "I'm just trying to do a good job for a change."

He squeezed her hand. *Shockwaves.* "You do a good job. You are good at everything you try to do. But that's not all it is. You've been good to me... a good friend... and I didn't even want one."

Julie looked down at their hands. It perplexed her how comfortable she had grown with him after everything started so weird, not even knowing his real name, her total embarrassment over her *career change*. She avoided all her old hospital friends and school friends because she felt like no one would understand, or even want to know, who she was becoming. But he did. He didn't seem to mind any of it.

"I didn't either," she answered. "And here you are."

"Here we are," he said softly. Then he took his hand from her lap to her face, cupping her cheek, looking more deeply into her eyes. She closed them, too scared to look ahead. But damn. She was sick of looking back, too.

Before she could open them, his lips were pressed to hers. It didn't surprise her. She pressed back, breathing him in, lifting her hands to his face, trying to relax into him, trying to keep herself steady, but being overcome by the feeling of melting. She could melt into him. He felt so safe, and so...

*Ugh. I can't.* Her voice.

*Slow your roll. This is different.* Mama's voice.

*You better lose yourself in the music, the moment, you own it, you better never let it go.* Hmm. Eminem, being wise.

Even so, she pulled away.

"I can't, Robin. Having you for a friend is everything right now. You look out for me. I love my job. I can't risk that."

"I know. I knew you would say that." He was looking so intently at her, brushing a lose strand of sweaty hair off her face. "Maybe don't think of it as risking anything so much as... expanding your role."

She shook her head. "You already gave me a promotion this

month. I'm manager. Of precisely no one, unless you hire my dad."

He smiled. "I would hire five of him. We'll work out those details. But Julie... what I'm saying to you right now is that..."

He'd seemed so sure when he started, and his voice faltered just as swiftly.

"See?" she said. "This is scary. And big."

Robin nodded. "Because it's real. Not an escape. Not out of convenience. It's because I get you. And you get me. And I *like* you. Like, I genuinely enjoy being around you and talking about stuff."

Julie couldn't help laughing. "That does seem to be outside your wheelhouse."

He nodded. "See? You get me."

"I agree." She was fighting not to let go of his hand. She really wanted to be in his lap, but Dolly was already there, and Julie was way too scared. "And you get me, so you know... this is terrifying. I have screwed up *every single decision* I made from the day my mother died to the day you hired me, and several big ones after that. This is the most stable and hopeful my life has been since then. And I don't want to make a mess out of it."

Robin responded by leaning forward and kissing her again, more lightly and less lingering, but reassuring. When he broke away, she pulled him back, welcoming him with her lips parted. Dolly got the hint and jumped onto the floor, lying right in front of them. "Me either," he murmured. Their arms went around each other, and before a few seconds had passed, she almost was in his lap, her heartbeat bordering on panic and her mouth desperate to stay connected to his.

And then Dolly barked, and Julie's nervous laughter put an end to the moment. She slid a little bit away from Robin, blushing.

"You think she needs to go out?" she asked, putting the dog back in her lap.

"I think she doesn't like not being the center of attention," he answered, his fingers still entwined in her hair.

"Hmmm." She reached her hand up to touch his. "I was kind of enjoying it, too."

"I want..." He paused and looked away. She felt the heaviness between them, a thousand things that had been shared in the last month, countless more that were unspoken still. And her fear was there, too. She couldn't help it.

So, she didn't ask him to finish. She stroked Dolly's cushiony fur and waited.

"I want to give you attention. I want to give you everything you want, but I also want to give you what you need, which is time. A little space. More than one day off next week..."

Nodding and smiling, she added, "A trip to the dumpster with some of these boxes. Dinner..."

"Yes." He smiled back, and she noticed the tiny dimple on the left corner of his mouth and the way his skin crinkled around his piercing brown eyes. "Okay. We eat. We do thirty minutes of power unpacking. A dumpster trip. And then, you take Dolly to your dad's, okay?"

"Okay..."

"What's wrong? Disappointment ten minutes into a budding relationship is not very promising."

"It's not that! I... I just know it's about to be complicated, and I want it to be simple. And I simply want to sit here and eat and talk to you and go for runs and talk to you some more. Simple."

He threw an arm back around her shoulder. "Me, too. We'll get all of it. You're moved. My Dad's getting better. We'll get some help at the store. And then we'll have more fun."

"It's been a long time."

"Yeah. It has."

"Are you…" She paused, studying Dolly, wishing she didn't feel so afraid. "Are you scared? Of this? Of trying? My track record sucks. You know all about it."

"I know all about it, and I'm here anyway. I'm not. I mean, I'm not scared. There are just so many summers."

She scrunched up her face at him. "It's not summer."

"I'm quoting an old song, youngin'. *I know you're afraid of rushing in, but there're just so many summers and just so many springs.*"

Julie didn't recognize the lyrics, but they struck her anyway.

"I've already wasted so much time."

"Hey." He pulled her closer to him again. "It's not really wasted if you learned. And it all brought you here. Right here. You're not in a bad place, Julie."

She looked at the dog in her lap, the man next to her, the home surrounding her, even the couch cushion beneath her, and knew he was right.

"This is actually a pretty good place," she said.

"Then let's just start there."

Julie could smell him on her t-shirt as she drove her and Dolly the seven miles to her dad and Jessie's. Dolly fussed for most of it, and then Julie had a thought and turned on "Jolene." And that doggie stopped her whining. It was so very *Hazel* that she laughed and cried. Life was bonkers, in every way, but for the first time in forever, she felt like she was living one, not just waiting for something else bad to happen.

It was almost nine by the time she pulled in the driveway. The house appeared to be lit up like the height of noon, which wasn't surprising. They probably had clan members coming and going at all hours anyway.

"Now listen, Dolly," she said as she gathered all the effects that came with the tiny creature, "You are still *Hazel's* dog. Okay? But you're going to be a little bit theirs, too. Just... try to have enough room in your heart for... all three of them. Okay?"

*Damnit.* Her tears were falling on the poor, confused animal. She felt like Simba seeing his royal father in the constellations. Mama's voice wasn't even necessary in the moment. She felt like God Himself had just pulled the exact words out of her mouth that she needed to declare.

*Go. Show them you have room.*

She walked to the front door, knocked once for good measure, and then went ahead and turned that knob. It was open, so like one of the kids would do, she walked in. Daddy and Jessie were seated on the couch, Jessie's laptop closed under arm and Daddy's stockinged feet in her lap. Some courtroom show was on the TV. About nine candles were lit. And their jaws hit the ground when she set Dolly down.

"Go on, girl. Go see."

"Jules!" Daddy called. "What's up? Who's this?"

"This is Dolly!" she said, admiring how Dolly wagged her tail while trying to jump for Jessie's coffee mug. She picked her up and, closer to Jessie than she'd been since *before*, put her on Jessie's lap. "She belongs to a friend of mine who couldn't take her when she moved away, so if y'all want her... she's yours."

"Oh!" Jessie's exclamation came out in words, a shocked and somewhat leery facial expression, widened eyes, hands flying to cradle Dolly. "She's... *beautiful*. Oh!" Jessie picked up Dolly and cradled her, almost making Julie cringe with her exuberance. Instead, Julie recognized that Jessie was acting exactly how Julie felt inside. That sweet pup made her feel almost no chill whatsoever. "Really?" Jessie asked, incredulously.

"I don't understand, Jules. Hazel's right? Why can't she keep her?"

Julie gave them the brief explanation, all while stroking Dolly's head. Her hand came perilously close to Jessie's. And then Jessie...

Held on to it.

"Thank you, Julie. If you are sure, we would love to keep her. She's..." Jessie paused and took her hand away. She focused on Dolly and Julie could see what was happening, and she had to look away. She felt like the Grinch when the Whos started singing on Christmas morning. All she had done was take things away. She didn't deserve this.

"Dolly is really special, and we will love her. I will love her. I will love her well."

Julie nodded, her eyes filling. She looked back down at Dolly, and saw Jessie out of her peripheral vision, her eyes filling. And then she looked at Daddy, and he was smiling, his eyes clear.

He nodded at Julie. They'd learned how to speak to each other again, and she knew right now, he didn't need to say a word. Only she did.

She inhaled, one more nod to assure herself. "If you love her like you love my Daddy, she will be so happy."

A few hours later, from the amazing, luxurious comfort of her own bed, in her own room, under her own blanket, Julie typed one long text message to Katy and Danielle. She ended it with –

My life sucked for all this time, and now I've taken 800 leaps forward in one night. Or at least three hops. Thank you for being (mostly) patient with me.

She smiled at their sisterly responses, and then she reread several text messages she'd received since she got home.

Hazel: I'm glad my daughter's folly was used for good and not evil. You tell Dolly to live it up, but it wasn't my fault. And send pictures... of her and of you! :sunglasses emoji" :kissy face emoji:

Jessie: Picture of Dolly peeing on the front stoop. Picture of Dolly playing with a felt pumpkin. And the words This is everything. Thank you. :yellow heart emoji:

Robin: Do not unpack another box. Go to sleep. Run 2 instead of 4 tomorrow. Drink your coffee strong. Know that I'm thinking of you, even while I listen to Dad tell Mom that if he can't even take the garbage out, he might as well be dead. Tomorrow, I'm out of here. He's fine. So are you. My work here is done.

She smiled and tapped back, "Good. Now the fun can start." And she slept.

# CHAPTER♡THIRTY

## Three Weeks Later

### Paul

PAUL WALKED INTO THE HOUSE SWEATY, ELATED, AND DEEPLY INHALING THE SMELL OF ANYTHING OTHER THAN HIMSELF. He was greeted with the aroma of pie in the oven.

So, then. Jessie had picked her one thing to make for Thanksgiving.

"Jess? What kind is it?" he called, not having any idea where she was.

And then she appeared, from the direction of the laundry room.

"French apple. So, lots of cinnamon, to make up for the lack of Snickerdoodles."

"Mmm. Almost as good."

She smiled and raised her brows. "I'm just following your rule. Just make one thing. And I can't believe I picked dessert. We are probably going to run out of sides. Everyone picks dessert. Dessert is eas—"

Paul shut her up the best way he knew. But when they came up for air after the kiss, she continued.

"Brittney and Katy are probably going to bring hard lemonade or something."

He laughed. "Aw Jess..." And then he wrapped his sweaty arms around her. "I promise it will be fine."

"It would be better with mashed potatoes," she muttered, half teasing.

Paul swayed with her just a little, a kitchen slow dance to music that was only in his head. *All* the kids would be there for dinner. It would be unprecedented in their time together. He knew Jessie was a little nervous – probably a lot, but she wouldn't admit that. He, on the other hand, was excited. Especially since, unbeknownst to Jessie, one final piece would hopefully fall into place that night.

"Let me make you a deal," he said, pulling away to look at her – and relieve her.

She nodded, eyes twinkling at him.

"You and me and David eat this pie tonight, and I will make mashed potatoes in the morning."

He might as well have said *Let's scrap this whole idea and order Domino's.* Jessie shook her head emphatically.

"First of all, darling man, there are two pies in that oven. I am not new here."

Paul gave a little whoop. His wife was a genius.

"Second of all, you're running a turkey trot in the morning. I will not have you coming home to make mash potatoes. That's my job."

"But you made the rule…"

Touché. Jessie was considering.

"Okay, new deal. Pie is taken care of, for tonight and tomorrow. You can do the potatoes *if* you promise not to count the fresh cranberry sauce or…"

"You're such a cheater, Jess…"

"Well, perhaps. But I made this last week and froze it so, technically..."

She pulled a bag from the freezer and held it up proudly to him. SNICKERDOODLE DOUGH.

Paul could not resist. He hugged her tight and picked her up off the ground a little.

"Gotta get ready for work." He kissed her again and nearly found himself skipping to the stairs, breathing in the smell of apple pies and home.

The store was in a welcome lull by four that afternoon. Julie was taking care of "manager stuff" in the back room, and Paul was studying the Hoka rack, still trying to memorize names like Clifton and Gaviota and know what the differences were. He was wearing a pair called Arahi because Julie said they'd be good for him and also, her shoe addiction was frighteningly contagious.

He looked at his watch. Julie was actually getting off at four, and he and Robin were working the last bit together. Paul had never before seen her more comfortable or sweet or *herself* with a guy. And he'd never worked a job before that felt less like a job.

When the front door chimed, Paul was surprised to see exactly who he was expecting arriving exactly on time.

"Hey Paul."

"Hey David." He clapped a hand on the boy's back... well, on the young man's back. Paul could scarcely remember being twenty-two years old, but he knew he'd been a different kind of twenty-two than his stepson, the youngest of their combined brood. When Paul was twenty-two, he'd been on his own for the better part of six years, couchsurfing before it was a word until he could get himself to a college and live on campus and set up his life.

David had lost his father and, temporarily, his way, but he retained the optimism of a kid, and more specifically, as the baby of Jessie's family.

"Hey!" David still didn't know what to call Paul, not that Paul expected anything other than his name, and so he avoided calling him anything.

"This is a cool place," David said, walking to the wall and picking up random, brightly colored shoes. "I ran cross country in high school, but you know, Mama just had me order stuff online."

"Ssssh," Paul said, half-joking. No one else was in there, but ordering online was the general enemy of any small local business. David was too young to get it. "If you decide to start running again, we'll make sure you get shoes here."

David grinned. "Not likely any time soon. Although with nowhere to surf in Knoxville, I should probably find some other sport." He patted his non-existent belly, which was covered by a bright orange Vols shirt. After his brief stint in Arizona and the time it took to regroup, he now had two semesters left to finish his own degree in nursing.

His time with Julie, it seemed, had not been a total, utter, complete waste.

"Look around. I'll be right back," Paul said. David nodded, and Paul headed to the back to inform Julie who was there. He was thankful no customers had entered because God only knew how she'd react.

She was facing the computer screen, so he spoke to her back. *Coward*, he mused to himself.

Julie turned immediately as soon as he got the words out.

"David is *here*? Right now?"

Paul shrugged. "It needs to happen, Jules. Preferably before there is a big turkey in the middle of it."

She sighed and glared at him as she stood up from the desk. "Daddy. You have to trust me a little. It would have been fine. It's going to be fine now, but it would have been fine tomorrow."

He exhaled. He could handle glares and admonishments much better than emotional outbursts.

"I do trust you," he said, and meant it. "But there is a lot of atmosphere to a holiday and a big gathering, and I just want... everyone, including you... and yes, including me, to have a peaceful day."

Julie looked at him without speaking. He studied his daughter's features, the late-autumn tan that had never been there before, the hair that was longer than ever and always braided down her back, the brightness of her eyes and ease of her smile.

Jessie had most recently written a little book called *Redeem the Time*. He got it. Every time he looked at his daughters, his grandkids, he saw something in them that reminded him of Leah or himself, but better. Freer. Happier. As parents, that was all they ever wanted, to see the struggles they'd had redeemed for better days, better lives.

"I'm on board with that," Julie finally said. "Why don't you send him back here? We can go for a walk before I have to leave. As long as you have the store?"

"Think I can handle it," he said. And he did as he was instructed, trying not to let her see his fatherly pride.

*Julie*

All they said was "hello," and then Julie wordlessly led David out the back door. It was almost dark already, and they wouldn't need to go far, but they walked to the well-lit sidewalk and kept walking, awkward and silent.

Finally, she asked the most cliché adult question she could think of to the first man she'd ever lived with. "How's school?"

David, with the unironic enthusiasm she had immediately admired in him launched into a monologue about his classes, the mountains, and how much better he liked it than boring old logistics, his first major.

"That's great," she said. "I am really glad you found a place you like so much."

"Yeah. Me too."

"David... I am... really sorry. That doesn't feel like enough, but I don't know what else to say. I was a mess, and –"

He stopped walking. When Julie looked at him, bathed in the streetlight, she saw the change in him, and she hoped his recovery from their folly had meant growth without tarnishing what was pleasant and easy and hopeful about him.

*A unicorn.* Sheesh. That might have been Jessie's voice, which she had heard much more from in the past few weeks.

"We were both a mess," he said, shrugging, the male universal sign for "It's all good, don't fuss" apparently.

"Yes, but I should have—"

He cut her off again. "Yes. You're older, and you knew better. Maybe you even knew it was never going to work or that it wasn't really... love. But so did I. Just because they all think I'm a baby—"

"No, they don't, David. You're just... *their* baby."

"But not grown."

She saw flickers of the same disappointment and yearning on his face that she saw the day his dad and her mom had died. And she wondered if they could redeem this relationship, if maybe it would not be impossible to love him like a brother.

"Not grown. You're right. But very much a young man who was fresh away from home and had lost his *father*. And believe me, David, I know the emptiness it leaves. Things are better now, but I'll never not want my mom. I will always want to know what she thinks and what she would say. I will always want to share my life with her, and that never stops hurting. And you are your family's... baby. And no one wants to see a baby suffer. Katy is the baby by three minutes and drives us all bananas, and we would all cut someone for her."

David smiled. "Katy would just do it herself."

Julie couldn't argue. "And so would you. But nonetheless."

They started walking again, and David asked, "So. Anyway. We're okay?"

She laughed so hard she nearly snorted. "David, if you say we are, we are. As long as you forgive me, we can work toward existing as..."

"Don't say it!" he said.

"Step-siblings!"

"Oh, my God." He shook his head. "I'm sure someday it won't be weird, but for now, let's not tell the story at any gatherings. Especially if we have dates there."

"Oops," she said.

"Wait, what?"

"Someone will be with me tomorrow. But he already knows..."

David shook his head in disbelief. "And he hasn't run away?"

"It's crazy, right?" she said. "We'll see how he does tomorrow."

"I know they all think you and I making peace was the last big holdout, but with all these people, I think *that's* crazy. I mean, did you hear about Christmas Eve?"

"No one really shares details with me yet. They probably still worry I might rev up and explode again. But you know... if you want to share..."

"Well," David began, "There were a few surprise guests, including my cousin's secret baby daddy, and my mom's long-lost and not-missed brother."

"Oh geez," Julie said. "Yeah. They probably won't have time to worry about us for long. Now... tell me more."

*Jessie*

I probably wouldn't admit this to many people, but I love Thanksgiving Eve about as much as Thanksgiving Day. It's quieter, and the house smells good. I play music and prep and *usually* welcome just a kid or two, and we have a drink and take care of some tasks together.

Last year was a one-off. Paul and I had just gotten back together, just moved into this house together. It was the first for everything, so we let the grandkids choose a brunch menu, and we worked at the community kitchen that afternoon. And that night, Paul and I were each solemn, each craving more isolated grief. I sat on the porch and talked to Randall. I slept on the couch instead of next to Paul, just holding sorrow like a shroud around me. It was sacred and sad, and I didn't want to repeat anything about it.

I honestly don't know what the hell happened this year. By 7:00 p.m. on Thanksgiving Eve, our house was full. *Full.*

"Jess, what the hell is going on?" Paul had come home from the shop, showered, and gone to pick up dinner at Bojangles. By the time he came back, an impromptu happy hour was taking place, with everyone standing around in the kitchen passing my mandarin iced tea and Julie's sangria, snacking while trying to decide if they should "order food," both David's and Katy's seemingly favorite pastime.

"Well, hey Daddy!" Katy exclaimed. "It's good to see you, too."

Paul accepted her kiss as he said, "I did just see you on Sunday, but hello, baby. I simply thought Thanksgiving was tomorrow."

"Me, too," I murmured as he kissed me. "Sorry..."

"No, you're not." In a whisper, he added, "We are not sharing the extra pie." Then he stole my tea and walked to the table. "And I'm not sharing my chicken."

I watched him sit down and spread out his meal. David followed, making me smile. Of all my kids, he was the most comfortable with Paul. Maybe because he wasn't around all the time being reminded that Randall was gone, or maybe just because he was still so young and needed a dad, but whatever it was, he seemed to have a new best buddy.

Slowly, some of the kitchen crowd followed to the dining room. Julie sat on Paul's other side, and Robin stood behind her, his hands on her shoulders. His calming effect on her was a thing of wonder. Sam and Travis trailed behind; Sam would never be far from the snickerdoodles that David had carried with him, and Travis was never far from David when he had a chance.

Jacob and Summer stayed at the counter with me, Katy, Brittney, and the cheese dip (fit for any occasion). Katy and Britt were getting a little silly with the sangria, already, but since they were both spending the night, I didn't worry. Abby was home working, and Mikayla and Danielle were home with their babies. I didn't think anyone else would show up, at least not for another sixteen hours or so.

"Mimi, we should watch a movie," Jacob said.

"Hmm. I don't know, bud. It's getting kind of late, isn't it? We have a big day tomorrow!"

"What's big about it? I'm gonna eat Mama's pancakes while I watch the parade, and then come over here and eat turkey!"

"Jacob, you're so dumb," Summer told him, not looking up from her chips-and-cheese sculpture. "Mimi, do you have any of that green salsa?"

Seven-year-old ease versus ten-year-old pragmatism made for great conversation over appetizers.

"Summer, we ate dinner!" Sam called from the dining room. I don't know why they all had radar hearing when it came to me spoiling their kids. I opened the fridge and promptly fetched some salsa verde for Summer.

"Oh, look!" Summer said then, but she no longer cared about the salsa. Dolly had just waddled into the room. Summer crouched on the ground and started petting her. Dolly immediately turned on her back, so Summer could scratch her belly. All my girls, canine included, knew just what they wanted, apparently.

Julie walked back into the room, filling her sangria cup with water. "We're gonna take off soon," she said. "Have to be at the Turkey Trot before dawn."

"God bless y'all," I said. "Are you running it or working it?" Paul was helping check people in at 6:00 a.m. and running the 5K at 7:00 a.m. We'd very much switched places as far as who wanted to embrace lazy mornings.

"Both." She smiled widely, seeming very much like a different person from the one who knocked on our front door seething at me not so many weeks ago. Then she reached down to help Summer pet Dolly.

"How is Ms. Hazel?" I asked.

"Oh, she's good. She going to come visit before Christmas. I think she might even stay with me, if I can convince her to take my bed."

"Will you go sleep in Robin's bed?" Jacob asked. *Oh Lord...*

"Jacob!" Summer yelled. "So *dumb*! Aunt Julie, he's only seven. He doesn't know anything. Just ignore him. It's no one's business when you sleep in Robin's bed."

I had to turn my head. I was shaking with laughter. Both of my grandkids needed a few tips on what was appropriate conversation, for sure, but that was Sam's problem. And I didn't know what was making Julie blush more, the mention of sleeping arrangements or the "Aunt Julie."

"I'm sure we'll figure it out," Julie stammered, but there was a gleam of amusement in her eyes. "You want to help me take Dolly for a little walk before I go?"

She took the two kids and the dog outside into the crisp night. I made my move into the dining room, starting to feel a little tired and happy that I had, thanks to Paul, literally nothing to do after they all left. And most certainly, Paul was going to kick them out soon.

"So, you want to start off around 9:05, and then you're just shaving about five seconds off each mile. Or just plan for a consistent nine-minute pace. You can do that." Robin said, showing Paul something on his phone, and everyone at the table seemed intrigued. I was thinking of which parts of my husband's body were going to require ice the next night.

"That's pretty fast," David said. "I wonder if I could keep up with you."

"Ha!" Sam said. "Maybe if you were running after a taco truck."

"Can't argue with that," David answered. "But maybe I'll try. Is it too late to sign up? Mama, would you mind if I went with Paul in the morning?"

I shook my head, wide-eyed. "We can get you in," Robin said, and he looked around the table, taking stock of the unspoken thing that was happening. My heart leapt that David was planning an activity with his stepdad, even while it grieved for him losing his daddy. *Randall*, I offered up silently, *I hope you don't mind this. I just want our boy to be happy.*

Deep down, I knew he didn't mind. But I also knew, I would always worry about it just a little, even if I only admitted it to Maggie. She would be absolutely dying over this entire exchange.

"All right David," Paul said, clearing his place and rising – which I knew was an indicator that people needed to start thinking about getting the heck out of our house. "Drink some water tonight. Your ride leaves at 5:30 in the morning."

"And don't wear Crocs," Sam added.

"Right. No Crocs!" Paul looked at Sam. "You and Travis want to join in?"

"*No!*" they said in unison. Travis followed it up with a belch and a "Please pass the cookies."

*My boys.*

Robin got up next and then, no sooner than I'd sat down, so did I. If I waited any longer, we'd have another scene from *The Brady Brunch – A Very Brady Christmas*, to be exact, and there'd be no pie or anything else left for the next day.

Julie returned with Dolly and the kids, and she and Robin stood by the counter with their arms sweetly around each other. Paul stood by me and took my hand. I almost needed to pinch myself.

"Running really, really agrees with you," I told Julie. "I hope y'all have blast in the morning."

"Aw, you're not coming?" Robin asked. This was only the second time I'd met him. The first time, we four had dinner over at the pizza place next to the shop, and he and I had a long discussion about Romano versus Parmesan cheese that made Julie and Paul roll their eyes. Tonight, he had brought a bag of treats for Dolly and a bag of mini-Twix bars for me. He was winning.

"I will come to the next one, maybe even run it," I said, meaning it. "The only trotting I'll be doing tomorrow is around this kitchen, getting everything ready."

"Mama would not believe it if she saw all of us doing these races without her," Julie said softly. "Most of us never wanted to, and even I only did them because of her."

It was a poignant reminder we'd carefully avoided, that we'd all been a form of family before this, that we'd all loved Leah. My heart leapt and wanted to reach out to Julie. Instead, I reined myself in and repeated, "Running looks good on you. Whatever changed it for you, I'm glad."

Julie nodded at me as Paul said what I wanted to but couldn't. Not yet. "I know she's proud of you. And happy for you. We sure are."

"Falling in love with running has changed my life," Julie said, with a small shrug and a tiny squeeze of the man next to her, who was just a bit taller than she was. He seemed the perfect fit, not towering over her, not made smaller by her, but at her side, looking out for her. "It was what I needed to help me change my life."

*We all needed something*, I thought, with our new little tea room and a thousand little dreams and plans running through my head.

We started saying our goodnights. Jacob and Summer were arguing over who was going to give Dolly a treat, and Travis and Sam, who'd come in separate cars from separate places, were arguing over who was going to drive Summer and Jacob home. "Separate them!" I called. Brit and Katy were close to knackered, sitting on the couch with *White Christmas* on the TV. They should have turned on *It's a Wonderful Life*. Was I ever feeling it.

Paul was right behind me as I opened the door to let everyone out. He saw it before I did. "What the hell, Jess?" and I laughed at his attempt to be Grinch-like, when I knew he was going to be just as happy about this one as I was.

Headlights turned off in the driveway. A tall, dark, and handsome man emerged slowly from the driver side, but not in time to catch the blur of black curls with gold tips and a scarlet red pashmina that came tearing up to the front door and straight into my waiting arms.

"Don't say a word, Paul Newman," Maggie said. She opened up our hug to let him in. "Especially not to Jessie. Don't tell her I'm as excited to see you as I am to see her."

We all giggled, me, my husband, and my sister, with her newish husband, and I simply told them, "Happy Thanksgiving."

*Julie*

"I'll see you in a few hours," Robin said, pulling up in front of the sidewalk of Julie's building.

She felt the tiny pang of sweet sadness at the thought of saying goodbye to him. They'd spent two nights together since the day she moved in, and everything changed. She wanted to see him all the time, but she knew taking it slow was important, especially for her.

*You're still healing*, Mama said, about ten times a day.

Julie had since written to her manager Rhonda in Arizona, apologizing for her lack of professional decorum in leaving so abruptly, and leaving Ian out of it altogether. She also included a note that could hopefully be forwarded to Troy Prosser. She was not allowed to say anything of substance, but she told him that the moments she witnessed his wife with their baby were absolutely beautiful, that she had been a warrior, and that she prayed for him and his son daily.

She closed the chapter, knowing it was all she could do.

Julie put her hand to her best friend's face. His schedule was back to normal, but a night at Dad and Jessie's before an early morning was enough to make anyone tired. "Get some sleep," she said. "We have miles to go this weekend, the race, your parents' house, my family dinner, the sales, the..."

He took her hand and kissed it. "We'll make it, Jules."

Sometimes, he reminded her of her dad with his patient logic. Sometimes he reminded her of her mama and her subtle sarcasm that helped her shift her perspective. But mostly, he was like no one she'd ever met before, constantly using his words, his strength, and his adoring looks, less reserved every day, to calm her, motivate her, and reassure her.

"I know," she said. "One mile at a time."

For the first time in a long time, she was moving forward.

More SURFSIDE BEACH series is on the way!

In the meantime, catch up:

**The Tentative Knock**

**Another at the Table (Christmas Novella)**
**The Second Date (e-short story)**

ALSO BY KELLY:

**Swerve: When Life Throws Curves,**
**But God Said Live**
21 Stories of Messy Lives & Amazing Grace

# ACKNOWLEDGMENTS

*Because honestly, the thank yous are my favorite part to write.*

To Shannon Marie, my ride or die. Every crazy mental roller coaster starts to make sense when I'm sitting next to you. Thank you for the journey and for my beautiful nieces and nephews.

Diane, my baby sister, thank you for letting me borrow your shoes for the front cover. Literally, that's all. Nobody cares, anyway.

Whitney, my early reader and big sister... we are just getting started!

To the daughters and sisters and gathered ones who make my life so full and fulfilling, especially my Kaity, Miranda, Paige, Kirsten, & Nora. Thank you to my Black Dog Running family for constant encouragement in all the things, my church family for the prayers and the cheers, and all those words and hugs from my circle that come at the right time. I am so blessed.

Mom & Dad, thanks for moving to South Carolina!

Wayne & Wanda, thank you for being along for the ride—and all the rides you give, too!

Mike Hopkins, who would have thought back in 2004 that I would ask you to get out your red pen and rip me to shreds? You're the best (and funniest) editor and a wonderful friend. Carla, what would he do without you? Thank you for your friendship and for joining the team!

To the Good Men... starting with my own sons, Jack and Josh, and extending to the brothers who have chosen me. The world needs you, and I am grateful for you.

To all the book clubs I've had the joy to be part of, and especially to Darcy and Rosie who became friends.

Thank you, Caleb Wygal, for sharing your experiences and advice with me. You're an inspiration.

Alicia Ortman, Goal Sister, thank you for escorting me out of my comfort zone and helping me attain a vision.

So much appreciation to the bookstores, booksellers, and librarians who have shown me such support... Back Again Bookshop, Barnes & Noble, and The Bookworm in Myrtle Beach, and Book Bound Bookstore in the second home of our hearts, Blairsville, Georgia.

Our Southern Comfort family, for pure joy in the form of music. I will always bring the cupcakes and be your number one fan!

To the senior runners, Bill, George, Tucker, Slim Jim, Nancy, Harvey, & Linda. You're a light to the rest of us. I am proud to call you my friends.

Through the magic of the real-life running store where I work, and the generosity of an owner who thinks books should sell right next to shoes, I have met so many readers... so many widowed, so many finding love, again. I carry your stories with me. I am eternally grateful that you have shared them with me. Run This Way the store is inspired by

Black Dog Running Company, which originated in Myrtle Beach and has now branched out to Conway. Come visit when you're in coastal South Carolina!

Other real places in this story include Benjamin's Bakery, Tidal Creek Brewhouse, Neal and Pam's, Mozzarella's Pizzeria, Bagel Factory, Villa Romana, and though it is no longer with us, Whitney's Tea Room, which I loved so much I had to resurrect it in fiction. Thanks to all of these for being fabulous places to eat, drink, be merry, and solve the world.

Two special people passed away while I was writing this story. One was my friend, Pastor Mike McGirt. Mike spoke amazing things over my life and my family. He was a strong believer and great comedian. I miss him daily, and send much love to his wife, Tonya.

I also honor the memory of my cousin Johnny Novelli, who became more like a big brother to me in later years. Thank you for the photos and cards, the CDs, the times you were there and the little things you remembered. I hope you know how much I treasured you as my family.

Rod: Every romantic hero I have imagined is rooted in you. How you support me, how you love our kids, how you encourage your friends, how you share your song with the world, is the key to my happily-ever-after. Let's keep on pushin'...

# NOTE
*from the author*

Thank you for reading this far! It's an uphill climb for independent authors to get their books into your hands, so however you found this one, I am grateful.

If you enjoyed the story, you can help me more than I can express to you by leaving a review of this book on Goodreads, Amazon, and/or wherever you purchased it.

And if you belong to a book club, get in touch with me! I love joining in your discussion, and sometimes, I even bring my own Maggie!

kcb@kellofastory
Instagram @kellofastory
Facebook @kellofastory

# ABOUT THE
## *Author*

A native of South Chicago Heights, Illinois, Kelly Capriotti Burton is a professional running enthusiast, a licensed minister, and a marathoner, who resides in Surfside Beach, South Carolina. She does life with her husband Rod, their five kids, granddaughter, parents, two dogs, a Harley, a rock band, and lots of gathered family. It is the perfect setting to explore for her writing mantra: happily ever-afters for complicated relationships. She is the author of the Surfside Beach series and the inspirational collection, *Swerve: When Life Throws Curves, But God Said Live*, an Amazon #1 New Release.

STAY IN TOUCH:
KELLOFASTORY.COM